THE MERCY OF GODS

By James S. A. Corey

THE CAPTIVE'S WAR

The Mercy of Gods

THE EXPANSE

Leviathan Wakes

Caliban's War

Abaddon's Gate

Cibola Burn

Nemesis Games

Babylon's Ashes

Persepolis Rising

Tiamat's Wrath

Leviathan Falls

Memory's Legion:
The Complete Expanse Story Collection

THE EXPANSE SHORT FICTION

Drive

The Butcher of Anderson Station

Gods of Risk

The Churn

The Vital Abyss

Strange Dogs

Auberon

The Sins of Our Fathers

THE MERCY OF GODS

Book One of the Captive's War

JAMES S. A. COREY

orbit

orbitbooks.net

Cover design by Lauren Panepinto
Cover illustration by Daniel Dociu

Orbit
Hachette Book Group
1290 Avenue of the Americas
New York, NY 10104
orbitbooks.net

First Edition: August 2024
Simultaneously published in Great Britain by Orbit

Orbit is an imprint of Hachette Book Group.
The Orbit name and logo are registered trademarks of Little, Brown Book Group Limited.

Library of Congress Cataloging-in-Publication Data
Names: Corey, James S. A., author.
Title: The mercy of gods / James S.A. Corey.
Description: First edition. | New York, NY : Orbit, 2024. | Series: The captive's war ; book 1
Identifiers: LCCN 2023052525 | ISBN 9780316525572 (hardcover) | ISBN 9780316525558 (e-book)
Subjects: LCSH: Scientists—Fiction. | Alien abduction—Fiction. | Extraterrestrial beings—Fiction. | LCGFT: Science fiction. | Novels.
Classification: LCC PS3603.O73429 M47 2024 | DDC 813/.6—dc23/eng/20240129
LC record available at https://lccn.loc.gov/2023052525

ISBNs: 9780316525572 (hardcover), 9780316580649 (BarnesAndNoble.com signed edition), 9780316525558 (ebook)

Printed in the United States of America

LSC-C

Printing 1, 2024

For Ursula K. Le Guin and Frank Herbert,
the teachers we never met

THE MERCY OF GODS

PART ONE

BEFORE

You ask how many ages had the Carryx been fighting the long war? That is a meaningless question. The Carryx ruled the stars for epochs. We conquered the Ejia and Kurkst and outdreamt the Eyeless Ones. We burned the Logothetes until their worlds were windswept glass. You wish to know of our first encounter with the enemy, but it seems more likely to me that there were many first encounters spread across the face of distance and time in ways that simultaneity cannot map. The ending, though. I saw the beginning of that catastrophe. It was the abasement of an insignificant world that called itself Anjiin.

You can't imagine how powerless and weak it seemed. We brought fire, death, and chains to Anjiin. We took from it what we deemed useful to us and culled those who resisted. And in that is our regret. If we had left it alone, nothing that came after would have been as it was. If we had burned it to ash and moved on as we had done to so many other worlds, I would not now be telling you the chronicle of our failure.

We did not see the adversary for what he was, and we brought him into our home.

—From the final statement of Ekur-Tkalal, keeper-librarian of the human moiety of the Carryx

One

Later, at the end of things, Dafyd would be amazed at how many of the critical choices in his life seemed small at the time. How many overwhelming problems had, with the distance of time, proved trivial. Even when he sensed the gravity of a situation, he often attributed it to the wrong things. He dreaded going to the end-of-year celebration at the Scholar's Common that last time. But not, as it turned out, for any of the reasons that actually mattered.

"You biologists are always looking for the starting point, asking the origin question, sure. But if you want to see origins," the tall, lanky man at Dafyd's side said, pointing a skewer of grilled pork and apple at his chest. Then, for a moment, the man drunkenly lost his place. "If you want to see origins, you have to look away from your microscopes. You have to look up."

"That's true," Dafyd agreed. He had no idea what the man was talking about, but it felt like he was being reprimanded.

"Deep sensor arrays. We can make a telescope with a lens as wide as the planet. Effectively as wide as the planet. Wider, even. Not that I do that anymore. Near-field. That's where I work now."

Dafyd made a polite sound. The tall man pulled a cube of pork off the skewer, and for a moment it looked like he'd drop it down into the courtyard. Dafyd imagined it landing in someone's drink in the Common below.

After a moment, the tall man regained control of his food and popped it into his mouth. His voice box bobbed as he swallowed.

"I'm studying a fascinating anomalous zone just at the edge of the heliosphere that's barely a light-second wide. Do you have any idea how small that is for conventional telescopy?"

"I don't," Dafyd said. "Isn't a light-second actually kind of big?"

The tall man deflated. "Compared with the heliosphere, it's really, really small." He ate the rest of the food, chewing disconsolately, and put the skewer down on the handrail. He wiped his hand with a napkin before he extended it. "Llaren Morse. Near-field astronomic visualization at Dyan Academy. Good to meet you."

Taking it meant clutching the man's greasy fingers in his own. But more than that, it meant committing to the conversation. Pretending to see someone and making his excuses meant finding another way to pass his time. It seemed like a small choice. It seemed trivial.

"Dafyd," he said, accepting the handshake. When Llaren Morse kept nodding, he added, "Dafyd Alkhor."

Llaren Morse's expression shifted. A small bunching between his eyebrows, his smile uncertain. "I feel like I should know that name. What projects have you run?"

"None. You're probably thinking of my aunt. She's in the funding colloquy."

Llaren Morse's expression went professional and formal so quickly, Dafyd almost heard the click. "Oh. Yes, that's probably it."

"We're not actually involved in any of the same projects," Dafyd said, half a beat too quickly. "I'm just putting in my time as a research assistant. Doing what I'm told. Keeping my head down."

Llaren Morse nodded and made a soft, noncommittal grunt, then stood there, caught between wanting to get out of the conversation and also to keep whatever advantage the nephew of a woman who controlled the funding purse strings might give him. Dafyd hoped that the next question wouldn't be which project he was working for.

"Where are you in from, then?" Llaren Morse asked.

"Right here. Irvian," Dafyd said. "I actually walked from my apartments. I'm not really even here for the—" He gestured at the crowd below them and in the galleries and halls.

"No?"

"There's a local girl I'm hoping to run into."

"And she'll be here?"

"I'm hoping so," Dafyd said. "Her boyfriend will." He smiled like it was a joke. Llaren Morse froze and then laughed. It was a trick Dafyd had, disarming the truth by telling it slant. "What about you? You have someone back at home?"

"Fiancée," the tall man said.

"Fiancée?" Dafyd echoed, keeping his voice playful and curious. They were almost past the part where Dafyd would need to say anything more about himself.

"Three years," Llaren Morse said. "We're looking to make it formal once I get a long-term placement."

"Long-term?"

"The position at Dyan Academy is just a two-year placement. There's no promise it'll fund after that. I'm hoping for at least a five-year before we start putting real roots down."

Dafyd sank his hands in his jacket pockets and leaned against the railing. "Sounds like stability's really important for you."

"Yeah, sure. I don't want to throw myself into a placement and then have it assigned out to someone else, you know? We put a lot of effort into things, and then as soon as you start getting results, some bigger fish comes in and swallows you."

And they were off. Dafyd spent the next half hour echoing back everything Llaren Morse said, either with exact words or near synonyms, or else pulling out what Dafyd thought the man meant and offering it back. The subject moved from the academic intrigue of Dyan Academy to Llaren Morse's parents and how they'd encouraged him into research, to their divorce and how it had affected him and his sisters.

The other man never noticed that Dafyd wasn't offering back any information about himself.

Dafyd listened because he was good at listening. He had a lot of practice. It kept the spotlight off him, people broadly seemed more hungry to be heard than they knew, and usually by the end of it, they found themselves liking him. Which was convenient, even on those occasions when he didn't find himself liking them back.

As Morse finished telling him about how his elder sister had avoided romantic entanglements with partners she actually liked, there was a little commotion in the courtyard below. Applause and laughter, and then there, in the center of the disturbance, Tonner Freis.

A year ago, Tonner had been one of the more promising research leads. Young, brilliant, demanding, with a strong intuition for the patterns that living systems fell into and growing institutional support. When Dafyd's aunt had casually nudged Dafyd toward Tonner Freis by mentioning that he had potential, she'd meant that ten years down the line when he'd paid his dues and worked his way to the top, Freis would be the kind of man who could help the junior researchers from his team start their careers. A person Dafyd could attach himself to.

She hadn't known that Tonner's proteome reconciliation project would be the top of the medrey council report, or that it would be singled out by the research colloquy, high parliament review, and the Bastian Group. It was the first single-term project ever to top all three lists in the same year. Tonner Freis—with his tight smile and his prematurely gray hair that rose like smoke from an overheated brain—was, for the moment, the most celebrated mind in the world.

From where Dafyd stood, the distance and the angle made it impossible to see Tonner's face clearly. Or the woman in the emerald-green dress at his side. Else Annalise Yannin, who had given up her own research team to join Tonner's project. Who had one dimple in her left cheek when she smiled and two on her right. Who tapped out complex rhythms with her feet when she was thinking, like she occupied her body by dancing in place while her mind wandered.

Else Yannin, the research group's second leader and acknowledged lover of Tonner Freis. Else, who Dafyd had come hoping to see even though he knew it was a mistake.

"Enjoy it now," Llaren Morse said, staring down at Tonner and his applause. The small hairs at the back of Dafyd's neck rose. Morse hadn't meant that for him. The comment had been for Tonner, and there had been a sneer in it.

"Enjoy it now?" But he saw in the tall man's expression that the trick wouldn't work again. Llaren Morse's eyes were guarded again, more than they had been when they'd started talking.

"I should let you go. I've kept you here all night," the tall man said. "It was good meeting you, Alkhor."

"Same," Dafyd said, and watched him drift into the galleries and rooms. The abandoned skewer was still on the guardrail. The sky had darkened to starlight. A woman just slightly older than Dafyd ghosted past, cleaning the skewer away and disappearing into the crowd.

Dafyd tried to talk himself out of his little feeling of paranoia.

He was tired because it was the end of the year and everyone on the team had been working extra hours to finish the datasets. He was out of place at a gathering of intellectual grandees and political leaders. He was carrying the emotional weight of an inappropriate infatuation with an unavailable woman. He was embarrassed by the not-entirely-unfounded impression he'd given Llaren Morse that he was only there because someone in his family had influence over money.

Any one was a good argument for treating his emotions with a little skepticism tonight. Taken all together, they were a compelling case.

And on the other side of the balance, the shadow of contempt in Morse's voice: *Enjoy it now.*

Dafyd muttered a little obscenity, scowled, and headed toward the ramp to the higher levels and private salons of the Common where the administrators and politicians held court.

The Common was grown from forest coral and rose five levels above the open sward to the east and the plaza to the west. Curvilinear by nature, nothing in it was square. Subtle lines of support and tension—foundation into bracing into wall into window into finial—gave the whole building a sense of motion and life like some climbing and twisting fusion of ivy and bone.

The interior had sweeping corridors that channeled the breeze, courtyards that opened to the sky, private rooms that could be adapted for small meetings or living quarters, wide chambers used for presentations or dances or banquets. The air smelled of cedar and akkeh trees. Harp swallows nested in the highest reaches and chimed their songs at the people below.

For most of the year, the Common was a building of all uses for the Irvian Research Medrey, and it served all the branches of scholarship that the citywide institution embodied. Apart from one humiliating failure on an assessment in his first year, Dafyd had fond memories of the Common and the times he'd spent there. The end-of-year celebration was different. It was a nested series of lies. A minefield scattered with gold nuggets, opportunity and disaster invisibly mingled.

First, it was presented as a chance for the most exalted scholars and researchers of Anjiin's great medrey and research conservatories to come together to socialize casually. In practice, "casual" included intricate and opaque rules of behavior and a rigidly enforced though ill-defined hierarchy of status. And one of many ironclad rules of etiquette was that people were to pretend there were no rules of etiquette. Who spoke to whom, who could make a joke and who was required to laugh, who could flirt and who must remain unreachably distant, all were unspoken and any mistake was noted by the community.

Second, it was a time to avoid politics and openly jockeying for the funding that came with the beginning of a new term. And so every conversation and comment was instead soaked in implication and nuance about which studies had ranked, which threads of the intellectual tapestry would be supported into the next year and which would be cut, who would lead the research teams and who would yoke their efforts to some more brilliant mind.

And finally, the celebration was open to the whole community. In theory, even the greenest scholar-prentice was welcome. In practice, Dafyd was not only one of the youngest people there, but also the only scholar-associate attending as a guest. The others of his rank on display that night were scraping up extra allowance by serving drinks and tapas to their betters.

Some people wore jackets with formal collars and vests in the colors of their home medrey and research conservatories. Others, the undyed summer linens that the newly appointed high magistrate had made fashionable. Dafyd was in his formal: a long charcoal jacket over an embroidered shirt and slim-fitting pants. A good outfit, but carefully not too good.

Security personnel lurked in the higher-status areas, but Dafyd walked with the lazy confidence of someone accustomed to access and deference. It would have been trivial to query the local system for the location of Dorinda Alkhor, but his aunt might see the request and know he was looking for her. If she had warning… Well, better that she didn't.

The crowd around him grew almost imperceptibly older as the mix of humanity shifted from scholar-researchers to scholar-coordinators, from support faculty to lead administrators, from recorders and popular writers to politicians and military liaisons. The formal jackets became just slightly better tailored, the embroidered shirts more brightly colored. All the plumage of status on display. He moved up the concentration of power like a microbe heading toward sugar, his hands in his pockets and his smile polite and blank. If he'd been nervous it would have shown, so he chose to be preoccupied instead. He went slowly, admiring art and icons in the swooping niches of forest coral, taking drinks from the servers and abandoning them to the servers that followed, being sure he knew what the next room was before he stepped into it.

His aunt was on a balcony that looked down over the plaza, and he saw her before she saw him. Her hair was down in a style that should have softened her face, but the severity of her mouth and jaw overpowered it. Dafyd didn't recognize the man she was speaking with, but he was older, with a trim white beard. He was speaking quickly, making small, emphatic gestures, and she was listening to him intently.

Dafyd made a curve around, getting close to the archway that opened onto the balcony before changing his stride, moving more directly toward her. She glanced up, saw him. There was only a flicker of frown before she smiled and waved him over.

"Mur, this is my nephew Dafyd," she said. "He's working with Tonner Freis."

"Young Freis!" Trim Beard said, shaking Dafyd's hand. "That's a good team to be with. First-rate work."

"I'm mostly preparing samples and keeping the laboratory clean," Dafyd said.

"Still. You'll have it on your record. It'll open doors later on. Count on that."

"Mur is with the research colloquy," his aunt said.

"Oh," Dafyd said, and grinned. "Well, then I'm very pleased to meet you indeed. I came to meet with people who could help my prospects. Now that we've met, I can go home."

His aunt hid a grimace, but Mur laughed and clapped Dafyd on the shoulder. "Dory here says kind things about you. You'll be fine. But I should—" He gestured toward the back and nodded to his aunt knowingly. She nodded back, and the older man stepped away. Below them, the plaza was alive. Food carts and a band playing guitar music that gently reached up to where they were standing. Threads of melody floating in the high, fragrant air. She put her arm in his.

"Dory?" Dafyd asked.

"I hate it when you're self-effacing," she said, ignoring his attempt at gentle mockery. Dafyd noted the tension in her neck and shoulder muscles. Everyone at the party wanted her time and access to the money she controlled. She'd probably been playing defense all night and it had stolen her patience. "It's not as charming as you think."

"I put people at ease," Dafyd said.

"You're at a point in your career that you should make people uneasy. You're too fond of being underestimated. It's a vice. You're going to have to impress someone someday."

"I just wanted to put in an appearance so you'd know I really came."

"I'm glad you did," and her smile forgave him a little.

"You taught me well."

"I told my sister I would look out for you, and I swear on her dear departed soul I will turn you into something worthy of her," his aunt said. Dafyd flinched at the mention of his mother, and his aunt softened a little. "She warned me that raising children would require patience. It's why I never had any of my own."

"I've never been the fastest learner, but that's my burden. Your teaching was always good. I'm going to owe you a lot when it's all said and done."

"No."

"Oh, I'm pretty sure I will."

"I mean no, whatever you're trying to soften out of me, don't ask it. I've been watching you flatter and charm everyone all your life. I don't think less of you for being manipulative. It's a good skill. But I'm better at it than you, so whatever you're about to try to dig out of me, no."

"I met a man from Dyan Academy. I don't think he likes Tonner."

She looked at him, her eyes flat as a shark's. Then, a moment later, the same tiny, mirthless smile she had when she lost a hand of cards.

"Don't be smug. I really am glad you came," she said, then squeezed his arm and let him go.

Dafyd retraced his steps, through the halls and down the wide ramps. His face shot an empty smile at those he passed, his mind elsewhere.

He found Tonner Freis and Else Yannin on the ground floor in a chamber wide enough to be a ballroom. Tonner had taken his jacket off, and he was leaning on a wide wooden table. Half a dozen scholars had formed a semicircle around him like a tiny theater with Tonner Freis as the only man on stage. *The thing we'd been doing wrong was trying to build reconciliation strategies at the informational level instead of the product. DNA and ribosomes on one hand, lattice quasicrystals and QRP on the other. It's like we were trying to speak two different languages and force their grammars to mesh when all we really need are directions on how to build a chair. Stop trying to explain how and just start building the chair, and it's much easier.* His voice carried better than a singer's. His audience chuckled.

Dafyd looked around, and she was easy to find. Else Yannin in her emerald-green dress was two tables over. Long, aquiline nose, wide mouth, and thin lips. She was watching her lover with an expression of amused indulgence. Only for a second, Dafyd hated Tonner Freis.

He didn't need to do this. No one was asking him to. It would take no extra effort to turn to the right and amble out to the plaza. A plate of roasted corn and spiced beef, a glass of beer, and he could go back to his rooms and let the political intrigue play itself out without him. But Else tucked a lock of auburn hair back behind her ear, and he walked toward her table like he had business there.

Small moments, unnoticed at the time, change the fate of empires.

Her smile shifted when she saw him. Just as real, but meaning something different. Something more closed. "Dafyd? I didn't expect to see you here."

"My other plans fell through," he said, reaching out to a servant passing by with what turned out to be mint iced tea. He'd been hoping for something more alcoholic. "I thought I'd see what the best minds of the planet looked like when they let their hair down."

Else gestured to the crowd with her own glass. "This, on into the small hours of the morning."

"No dancing?"

"Maybe when people have had a chance to get a little more drunk." There were threads of premature white in her hair. Against the youth of her face, they made her seem ageless.

"Can I ask you a question?"

She settled into herself. "Of course."

"Have you heard anything about another group taking over our research?"

She laughed once, loud enough that Tonner looked over and nodded to Dafyd before returning to his performance. "You don't need to worry about that," she said. "We've made so much progress and gotten so much acclaim in the last year, there's no chance.

Anyone who did would be setting themselves up as the disappointing second string. No one wants that."

"All right," Dafyd said, and took a drink of the tea he didn't want. One member of Tonner's little audience was saying something that made him scowl. Else shifted her weight. A single crease drew itself between her eyebrows.

"Just out of curiosity, what makes you ask?"

"It's just that, one hundred percent certainty, no error bars? Someone's making a play to take over the research."

Else put down her drink and put her hand on his arm. The crease between her eyebrows deepened. "What have you heard?"

Dafyd let himself feel a little warmth at her attention, at the touch of her hand. It felt like an important moment, and it was. Later, when he stood in the eye of a storm that burned a thousand worlds, he'd remember how it all started with Else Yannin's hand on his arm and his need to give her a reason to keep it there.

Two

Humans, everyone knew, didn't belong on Anjiin.

How they'd gotten to the planet, why they'd come there, all of that was lost in the fog of time and history. A sect of Gallatians claimed that they'd arrived on a massive ship like Pishtah's fabled ark, but one that traveled between stars. Serintist theologians said that God had opened a rift that let the faithful escape the death of an older universe where some terrible sin—opinions varied on its exact nature—had convinced the Deity that genocide was the lesser evil. Or, if you were open to a little more poetry, a giant bird had carried them from Erribi—the planet next closest to the sun—which had possibly been their homeworld until the sun grew angry and turned their fields to wastelands and boiled away their skies.

But the sciences could tell a story too, even if humanity's faulty memory had smeared the details.

Life on Anjiin had begun billions of years before with a system of aperiodic quasicrystals of silicon, carbon, and iodine. That life had used the quasicrystals to pass on instructions to the next generation, with occasional mutations that made some organisms do a little better. Over long eons, a complex ecosystem grew in the Anjiin oceans and across its four vast continents.

And then three and a half thousand years before, and apparently out of nowhere, humans showed up in the fossil record with incredibly dense helical coils of lightly associated bases strung like beads on a necklace of phosphate. And not just humans. Dogs and cows and lettuce and wildflowers and crickets and bees. Viruses. Mushrooms. Squirrels. Snails. A whole biome unprecedented in the genetic history of the planet popped into being on an island just east of the Gulf of Daish. Then barely a century after that first appearance, something, no one was sure what, had turned most of that island into glass and black rock. And while whatever records those original settlers may have brought with them disappeared at that point, a few remnants of this new biome survived at the island's edges and on the nearby continental coastline, and it had spread over the world like a fire.

These two trees of life covering the world of Anjiin usually ignored each other, apart from competing for sunlight and some minerals. Occasionally something would evolve a way to parasitize creatures from the other biochemical tradition for a few complex proteins, water, and salt. But the common wisdom was that the two biomes couldn't be reconciled in any meaningful way. On a microscopic level, the oaks and alders that were cousins of humanity were just too different from the native akkae and brulam, no matter how similar they might look from a distance. Even where evolution had guided the shapes and colors and forms into similar solutions, at a fundamental level, the different lifeforms of Anjiin could never really nourish each other.

Until Tonner Freis had found a way to translate between them, and changed everything.

* * *

"I simultaneously want more beer and also a little less beer than I've already had," Jessyn said.

Irinna, sitting next to her, grinned. The Scholar's Common rose up above them at the edge of the plaza. The lights cast up the building's side shifted and pulsed and made the forest coral seem like it was waving in some vast current. Beyond it, the darkness of the sky and the bright of the stars.

Tonner and Else were at the Common, being the face of the celebrated team. Campar, Dafyd, and Rickar were... somewhere. There were only four of them at their little table. A casual passerby could have mistaken them for a family. Nöl as the craggy-faced, long-suffering father, Synnia as his gray-haired wife, Jessyn as the older daughter, and Irinna as the younger. It wasn't true at all, except in the ways that it was.

"You've probably had enough, hm?" Nöl said. "No call to overdo it?"

Irinna slapped the table. "All call to overdo it. If not now, when?"

Nöl looked pained and cleared his throat, and Synnia took his arm. "They're young, love. They bounce back faster than we do."

"Fair point, fair point," the old scholar-associate said.

Jessyn still remembered the first time she'd met the team. Tonner Freis, of course, and Else Yannin, who had just abandoned her own project to join his. Nöl had seemed imposing back then, crag-faced and laconic and faintly disapproving. She had expected him and his partner, Synnia, to harbor resentments at being only scholar-associates at their age. Instead, she'd found a kind of profound contentment in them despite their status in the medrey. Some days it made her question her own ambition.

"I'm going back home for a week at the end of break," Irinna said. "Until then, I have nothing."

"Nothing?" Synnia asked, but with a twinkle in her eye.

"Nothing," Irinna said. "Nothing and no one. I'm not courting. I'm not finishing an extra run of datasets. I am, for once in my life, relaxing and taking time to recuperate."

Jessyn grinned. "You say it now. But you know what'll happen. Tonner is going to have an idea, and when he asks someone to look into it, you're going to show up."

"You'll be there too," Irinna said.

"I won't have made a proclamation about not working over break, though."

Irinna waved the point away like she was shooing gnats. "I'm drunk. Hypocrisy is the natural companion of beer."

"Is it?" Nöl said. "I didn't know."

Jessyn liked Irinna because the junior researcher reminded her not so much of herself at a younger age, but of who she wished she'd been: smart, pretty, with the first green shoots of self-confidence starting to break through the soil of her insecurities. Jessyn liked Dafyd, wherever he was tonight, for his quiet utility. And Campar for his humor, and Rickar for his casual sense of fashion and his cheerful cynicism. And tonight, she loved all of them because they had won.

For months, they had worked together in their labs, spent more time there than at their homes. There was a sense of family that grew with exposure, a familiarity that was deeper than just work colleagues. It was the rhythm of intimacy. Without anyone ever making a point of it, Jessyn had come to know them all. She could predict when Rickar would want to recheck a protein assay and when he'd be willing to let a questionable data point stand. Which days Irinna would spend quiet and focused, and which she'd be garrulous and distracting. She knew from the taste of the coffee when Dafyd had made it and when it was Synnia.

When she wanted to, she could still remember the quiet in the room when the first uptake results had come through. A radioactive marker in a membrane protein that the native Anjiin biosphere used had shown up in a blade of grass. It was so small, it could have been invisible, and it was also the hinge on which the world swung.

Their strange, awkward, haphazard little group had translated one tree of life to the other. Two utterly incompatible methods of heritability had been coaxed into sitting beside one another, working together. That little blade of grass had been the product of a biochemical marriage thousands of years in the making. For an hour, maybe a little less, the nine of them had been the only people in the world who knew about it.

As much as their success promised, as many accolades as they'd won, part of Jessyn still treasured the magic of that hour. It was a small secret that they'd all shared. An experience they could only speak to each other about, because they were the only ones who really understood the combination of awe and satisfaction. Even when Jessyn told her brother about it—and she told him everything—he could only ever guess what she meant.

Across the little square, a band started playing. Two trumpets, weaving in and out of synchrony while a drummer did something that managed to be both propulsive and intricate. Irinna grabbed Jessyn's hand, tugging her up. Despite her usual reticence, Jessyn let herself be pulled. They joined the dance. It was a simple one. They'd all learned the steps in childhood, so they could all recall them in drunken adulthood. Jessyn let the music and euphoria carry her. *I am part of the most successful research team in the world. I am not too anxious to dance in public. My brain isn't betraying me today. Today is good.*

When the dance ended, Nöl and Synnia had already gone, heading back, Jessyn assumed, to the little house they shared on the edge of the medrey's landhold. Irinna drank the last of her beer and made a face.

"Flat?" Jessyn asked.

"And warm. But still celebratory. Thank you, by the way."

"Thank me?"

Irinna looked down at her feet, then up again. She was blushing a little. "You and the others were very kind letting me be part of this."

"We really weren't," Jessyn said. "You carried your part of the project all the way through."

"Still..." Irinna said, then darted forward to kiss Jessyn's cheek. "Still thank you. This has been the best year I've ever had. I'm grateful."

"I am too," Jessyn said, and then, as if by mutual understanding, they parted ways. The end-of-year carnival played out in the streets and alleyways: music and laughter and the self-important, drunken debates of scholars eager to prove to each other that each of them was the cleverest person in the conversation. Jessyn walked through the night with her hands in her pockets and a sense of calm.

For a moment, she was apart from the medrey, even as she moved within it. In a demimonde built on status and intellectual prowess, her team was the apex. It wouldn't be forever, but tonight, she had won. Tonight, she was good enough, and even the dark things in the back of her mind couldn't pull down her mood.

The quarters she and her brother shared were in one of the older buildings. Not grown coral, but built from glass and stone. She liked it because it was old-fashioned and quiet. Jellit liked it because it was close to his lab and the noodle shop he frequented. Jellit wasn't there. His workgroup was having their own celebration, no doubt. He'd be back by morning or he'd send her a message to let her know he was falling in bed with someone and not to expect him. He wouldn't just vanish and leave her to worry.

She sat at their table, deciding whether she wanted food before she went to bed or just a tall glass of water. She found herself grinning. It was so rare to feel satisfied. It was so odd to know for certain that she'd done well. Tonner Freis and Else Yannin, Rickar, Campar, Irinna, Nöl, Synnia, and even in his way Dafyd Alkhor. The team that had cracked open the possibility of a new, integrated biology. Generations from now, the textbooks would talk about them and what they'd done.

Her system alerted. A message waiting for her. She expected it would be Jellit, but the flag was from Tonner Freis.

When his face appeared on the screen, Jessyn sobered. She'd seen his moods before enough to recognize rage.

"Jessyn, I need you to come to an emergency meeting tomorrow at the lab. And don't mention it to *anyone*."

Three

The medrey's laboratories had an eerie emptiness. Dafyd walked through flowing hallways and galleries and meeting spaces that during the year were busy with scholars and artisan-fabricators and on-site representatives of the colloquies. They were almost abandoned now. A pair of men in hard, plasticized coveralls were repainting one of the walls. A harried man sped by on some past-due errand. A sparrow that had found its way inside fluttered down the empty air of the halls, looking for scraps of food or a way out. A scholar-associate who Dafyd recognized from the architectural chitin project sat alone on a bench with her sandwich and an inward expression. And in a little impromptu circle of three couches and one chair outside the closed commissary, a council of war.

Tonner and Else shared a couch, sitting together but not together, the space between them an equilibrium of intimacy and professionalism. Campar was sprawled on a couch of his own. Large, dark, and scruffy, he looked amused and sleepy in equal measure, like a children's cartoon of a bear. Beside him, sitting primly on the one chair, craggy head covered with salt-and-pepper stubble, Nöl. Dafyd looked around for the others, but there was no sign of them. As he took his place on the empty couch, Nöl nodded to him.

"Are we all?" Dafyd asked.

"Jessyn's on her way," Tonner said. The smiling, confident version of him from the Scholar's Common was gone. His eyes were dark as a storm and his jaw was tight. Anyone who'd spent the last year watching the weather of Tonner's internal life would know that the best thing now was to be quiet and wait.

"Synnia is at home," Nöl said. "She wasn't feeling well. I don't know about Rickar or Irinna."

When Tonner spoke, the words were icy and careful. "I thought we wouldn't bother them with this just yet."

Dafyd felt a little shiver go down his back.

Campar made a soft, impatient sound and lolled his head to the side. "The tension is unbearable. What exactly is it that we're not talking about?"

"Jessyn will be here soon," Tonner said. Else shifted her attention to Dafyd, her eyes meeting his for a moment and then clicking away, like they were hiding a secret. But sadly the only secret they shared was the one Tonner was about to tell everyone else too.

The first sign of Jessyn was her brother's voice, enthusiastic and loud. A moment later, they rounded the corner. Jessyn was short, round bodied, and severe. Jellit was lanky and colt-awkward with a grin that matched his voice. Other than that, they were almost the same person: gold-brown skin, black hair and eyes. They both had moles on their right cheeks, like it was a little flourish that the gods of genetics and development had chosen to use for a signature. They moved their hands the same way, shrugged with the same left-then-right. Dafyd liked Jessyn, and so by extension he liked her brother. They were like two halves of the same organism.

Something had Jellit excited. He was gesturing, wide handed, as they drew closer. "As extrasolar activity goes, it's as strange as anything anyone's seen. There's one dataset that made it look superluminal, but no one thinks that's anything but a glitch."

He turned to greet them, and his face fell.

"We were just walking together," Jessyn said, sitting on the couch at Dafyd's side.

"Is this a team meeting?" Jellit said, and then before anyone could answer, "I'm just going to go get some tea, then. I'll see you back at home."

"See you there," Jessyn said, to her brother's already retreating back. Her sigh was almost imperceptible, and certainly not conscious. She turned to Tonner. "I'm sorry to be late."

"Superluminal?" Campar asked, lifting one shaggy eyebrow.

"Jellit has a perverse fondness for obviously bad data," Jessyn said. "He thinks it's funny because it makes the research colloquy uncomfortable."

Campar chuckled. "I find your brother's air of charming perversity intriguing. He's still single, isn't he?"

"No dating my brother," Jessyn said. It was a running joke between them.

"Thank you all for coming during the break. I'm sorry to interrupt what should be some well-earned relaxation," Tonner said, ending the banter.

They all turned toward him like he was a lecturer and they were his audience. Else's face was calm and impassive and focused on Tonner as though she didn't already know what he was about to say. She did, though. Dafyd would have bet money on it. "We have a problem. Someone has asked the funding colloquy to reassign our work."

Jessyn paled. Campar sat forward, the playfulness and good humor that usually marked him gone like it had never been there. Only Nöl didn't change his expression or posture, just giving a little nod like he'd been expecting the universe to disappoint him somehow. He was, however, the first to gather himself enough to speak. "Do we know the reason for it? Are we being punished for something?"

Tonner glanced at Else, passing the focus of attention to her. Dafyd wondered whether they had rehearsed this, or if they were just well-enough attuned to each other that it came without thought. "As far as we can tell," she said, "the argument is that our work is too important to keep in only one place and with only a single team. The primary scholars would be loaned to other medrey and collegia to start up parallel programs, with one of the junior researchers left here to shepherd the work that's already in progress."

Campar's laugh was loud and bitter. Too loud, maybe. Dafyd looked around, but the only one nearby was the girl with the sandwich, and she wasn't looking toward them.

"A junior scholar taking over and kicking the high and mighty into the cold?" Campar said. "Someone's stabbed us in the back, but I'll swear to any god you'd like that it ain't me."

"There is no question this begins with someone in our inner circle," Tonner said, "but we have reason to think the plan was submitted by someone connected to Dyan Academy."

"What reason?" Nöl asked. "If you don't mind."

Else gestured toward Dafyd, and the group's attention turned to him.

"I met a man at the Scholar's Common," Dafyd said. "Llaren Morse. He's in near-field astronomical visualization, but he knew something was coming. He was gloating. And he was from Dyan. So then I caught one of the senior administrators a little by surprise, and she made a little too much effort in not saying anything about it."

"Even if that's true, it doesn't prove a connection to Dyan Academy. Not really," Nöl said. "This Morse could have known through other paths. Jellit works near-field also, yes? Jessyn here could have formulated the plan and let it slip to her brother."

Jessyn made an angry snort.

Nöl patted the air placatingly. "Not saying it's you. Hell, I could have made the plan myself. I know people at Dyan."

"Yes, it's only our best-guess hypothesis," Tonner said. "We will confirm or eliminate. And I managed to find out who was slated for the three spin-off labs. Me, Else, and Jessyn. So no, I don't think it was her. Campar already has a placement in Burson that he's been delaying to help us finish first phase, so I see no reason to think it's him."

Nöl pursed his lips in disapproval, but didn't object further.

"Irinna?" Campar said. "She did her first term at Dyan. But I wouldn't like to think..."

"It isn't her," Jessyn said. "She wouldn't do that. And this is her first team. We're all junior researchers, but she's barely more than an assistant." She flickered with embarrassment as soon as she'd said it, her gaze darting toward Dafyd and then Nöl, then away again.

"Rickar's father is a landgraf near Dyan," Else said. "The academy gets a tenth of its buildings from him. It's not conclusive, but...he seems most likely."

"I'd hate to jump to conclusions," Campar said. "I think it's only professional that we find him and beat the truth out of him, yes?"

Jessyn said, "Are we certain that opening new projects is a *bad* idea?" The group stuttered into quiet, and she opened her hands. "It's a power grab. I understand that. It's bad for us. Each of us. All of us individually, at least in the short term. But what if it's good for the project? Four coordinating labs? That could be huge. I mean, don't we *want* to steer research at other places? Inspire other projects? What does winning look like if it doesn't look like this?"

"The team scattered to the winds is a strange look for victory," Nöl said with a gentle bitterness.

Pretending to enjoy the sandwich its host is eating, the swarm jitters and presses, its myriad dancing senses focused on the little group. The flesh that it occupies once belonged to a woman named Ameer Kindred, who is both dead and not dead now. The swarm is aware of the food in the host's mouth. Aware that Ameer once enjoyed the taste. It frees up some of its control over the woman's face, so that her pleasure can change her features appropriately. The swarm, who is both Ameer Kindred and not Ameer Kindred, understands a bit more of what it means to enjoy food, and files this information away for later use.

The instruction set that defines the swarm's mission is far too complex to represent as simple rules, but if it could be, then rule number one would be remain hidden. *Anything that allows it to mimic human interactions with their environment is vital to its success.*

Focusing its attention on the targets, the swarm thrusts a million tiny needles like antennae through the host's skin, and these new nodes quiver with hunger to see/hear/taste them.

Two members of the group it already knows from the announcements. Tonner Freis, the leader and figurehead. The highest-status researcher in the world at this singular, critical moment. And the other, at his side. Else Yannin, who has the second-highest status in the group. The swarm shifts its awareness to pheromones, opening new channels on Ameer Kindred's skin to drink in the subtlest human scents. Fear. Anger. Anxiety. Lust. Sorrow. So many chemical signals pouring off the little knot of bodies. Ameer knows what those emotions mean, her memory is full of those feelings and the causes of them. And so the swarm knows those things too, and the matrices of data that represent its understanding of the target group's social dynamic are enriched by this knowledge. The swarm feels something Ameer would identify as satisfaction at this increasingly sophisticated flow of information.

Two of the group arrive, smelling very nearly the same—a male and female pair. Genetically related, the swarm calculates. Brother and sister, Ameer thinks, and the swarm adds this information to the data.

The swarm shifts to focus on hearing, Ameer Kindred's skin tightening like a drumskin underneath the myriad protruding metal hairs to make her flesh into a girl-shaped ear, and the male of the sibling pair's voice is now like a shout. As extrasolar activity goes, it's as strange as anything anyone's seen, *he says.* There's one dataset that made it look superluminal. *The swarm is not capable of feeling fear, but it does now feel a heightened sense of pressure. It knows there is very little time left. The male sibling walks away. He isn't a part of this workgroup. The swarm disregards him, shifting its study, finding the new and necessary skin that will allow it to continue its mission.*

They speak and it listens to them speak, but its senses are rich and strange. It finds patterns in their heartbeats that they themselves cannot know. It maps the connections of one to another like water finding a way to seep through stone. It understands in ways that may be useful to it. Or may not. What is not useful will be abandoned. Forgotten. Annihilated.

Ameer Kindred senses the swarm's intention. She knows her time as the host is coming to an end. And though she has screamed her hatred of the swarm's invasion of her body and thoughts every second of every day since it took over, Ameer also understands that the swarm will not leave her alive when it moves on. The thought of her own impending death is like an ocean of sorrow.

This sadness is not currently useful to the swarm, so it files it away and then ignores it.

Are we certain that opening new projects is a bad idea, *the remaining half of the sibling pair says, and the swarm watches, and it waits.*

It cannot afford to wait much longer.

"The team scattered to the winds is a strange look for victory," Nöl said with a gentle bitterness.

Jessyn shrugged—an almost microscopic gesture—but she didn't look away. Tonner stood. If Dafyd had been under his gaze, he'd have shrunk back, but Jessyn didn't.

"If you want your own lab, I'm sure you can get one," he said. "This is not the way I intend to lose mine."

"Damn right," Campar said. "I intend to be lured away with promises of wealth and power, as tradition demands."

But Tonner's focus was entirely on Jessyn. Dafyd watched the two implacabilities face each other like a blowtorch on stone. Else said Tonner's name, but it might have been from a different room.

The silence between the two scholars stretched long past comfort, and the stone cracked before the flame died out. Jessyn looked away. "I see your point," she said.

Dafyd exhaled.

Tonner, scowling now, got up and started pacing through the little space like the confrontation had left him restless. Campar caught Dafyd's gaze and mouthed *Daddy's angry.*

"We have a window of opportunity," Tonner said. "If we find which of the team is behind this, there may be leverage we can bring to bear. Even if they withdraw the plan, there may be some enthusiasm for it in the colloquy. You can help with that, Dafyd."

"I will do what I can," he said, not promising anything. He could already imagine the conversation with his aunt, and how delicate a job it would be.

"Else and Campar can look into Irinna, just to be sure it isn't her. Jessyn and Nöl will see about our friend Rickar."

"Why us?" Nöl asked. "Not that I disagree, you know. Just—"

"Jessyn can use the connection with Jellit to sound out Llaren Morse," Dafyd said. "They're both near-field. End-of-year makes it easy to reach out."

Tonner nodded approval. "I will be coordinating with all of you and making loud arguments in some very powerful ears about the critical need to keep the team together."

"Well, fuck," Campar said, then shrugged his thick shoulders. "Palace intrigue isn't how I was hoping to spend my break. But skulking in shadows and interrogating spies won't be boring, I suppose."

"Sorry," Dafyd said, though he wasn't quite sure why he was the one apologizing.

Else's initial smile was brief and weary, but when she turned to

Dafyd, it grew warmer. One dimple in her left cheek, two in her right. "This is hard, but I can't imagine how much worse it would have been to find out when it was already decided and there wasn't anything we could do about it."

"Just here for the team," Dafyd said. Else leaned forward, squeezed his wrist. Dafyd felt himself responding to the touch and didn't try to prolong it, even though a simple, animal part of him wanted nothing more. He noticed that the girl with the sandwich was gone.

"Now," Tonner said. "Let's plan out how to make the approaches. I don't want to leave any of this to chance. Not with the stakes this high."

Nöl cleared his throat and lifted a finger. Tonner's frown deepened, but when he spoke, there was no anger in his voice. "You have something?"

"Yes," the old scholar-associate said. "Have we ruled out asking them?"

Four

"It's true," Rickar Daumatin said, spreading his hands in a little deprecating gesture. *What can you do?* Tonner felt his fists clenching and made a conscious effort to release them.

Their laboratory hadn't changed. It felt like any day of the last eight months. The north wall was still covered in their notes and lists. The tables had trays of reaction assays stacked five deep. The air smelled like compost and cleaning fluid. They could have been talking through any problem on the project. Given that everything they'd tried to build was now coming apart, the sameness felt obscene.

Tonner looked around at the others. Irinna, newly arrived from her parents' home in Abbasat, was the only one who looked dumbfounded. Nöl seemed sorrowful in the way he always was. The others—Jessyn, Synnia, Campar, Dafyd, and Else—were a spectrum of disappointment and anger.

Rickar boosted himself up onto the worktable and leaned forward, resting his arms on his thighs, fingers laced together like he was waiting for questions. Giving them time to process. Campar was the first to gather himself.

"Well, that's a remarkably casual way to detonate the most important project of our lives." Tonner appreciated the acid in the man's voice.

"It wasn't my idea," Rickar said. "Or my choice. Samar Austad is the chief administrator at Dyan. He's the one pushing it with the colloquy, not me."

"But you went along with it," Tonner said. "You agreed."

"Of course I did," Rickar said. "What else would I do?"

"Refuse the position," Tonner said. "Tell him you won't accept it if offered."

Rickar's shrug had a depth of world-weary resignation. "This isn't how I wanted things to be, but it's the way things are. If I had my pick, I'd have kept the group as it is for another few years and had medrey and collegia competing to give me a laboratory. But it didn't happen that way. It happened this way, and the reed that doesn't bend, breaks."

"This is *my* project," Tonner said, and took a step forward. The rage he'd felt for the last days felt thick in his throat. Rickar just tilted his head.

Else stood up. "We are the most celebrated researchers on the planet right now. *We* are. As a group. A *team*. If we're scattered, that won't be true anymore."

"I didn't ask Austad to do this. But he's good at what he does. He wouldn't have made the proposal if he didn't have the support to make it work. It may take a few more days, but this is going to happen."

"What happens to the rest of us?" Jessyn asked.

"We'll find other placements," Nöl said. "We'll have status for a moment. The next year, someone will have us. After that, who can say?" Synnia put a hand on the older man's arm, comforting or counseling him to silence or both.

"It's not your lab yet," Tonner said. "Until the colloquy votes, it's still mine."

"It is," Rickar agreed. "For a few days, anyway."

"So get the hell out of it."

Rickar eased himself back off the table, his feet touching the floor gently, like he was trying not to make noise. He pressed his hands into his pockets and walked carefully out toward the common halls. His apologetic manner felt like an act—the performance of a man sure enough of his victory to be magnanimous.

The door closed behind him with a click, and the others were quiet. Campar broke the silence with an angry chuckle.

"I didn't know about any of this," Irinna said, taking a step toward Tonner. Her hands tight at her waist. She looked very young and pale with worry.

"I know," Else said. "No one thinks you did."

"I really didn't."

Tonner turned away. His lab seemed quieter than it should have. The workstations with their shelves stained by years of soil uptake dyes, the wallscreens all dark now with the maintenance of the term break, the thin windows spilling milky light across the gray tiled floor. It was his kingdom, and even though he'd spent more time in these rooms than in his home, it felt like he hadn't seen it. The threat of losing it washed all the familiarity away, and left it before him like he had stepped into it for the first time.

"It's not over yet," Tonner said. "The colloquy hasn't decided anything. We can still keep this from happening."

"What do you have in mind?" Jessyn asked.

"Call in all our favors. Promise new ones. If all of us reach out to our old leads and advisors, we can flood the caucus with objections. Drown Rickar's sponsor—" He snapped his fingers, trying to recall Rickar's words.

"Samar Austad," Irinna said. "His name is Samar Austad."

"Drown him in outrage. Let him see how much this move will cost him."

Dafyd made a small noise. Another day, in a different mood, Tonner would have ignored it, but he was frustrated and upset. "*What?*"

Dafyd met his eyes, then looked away. When he spoke, his voice was calm enough. "Going loud is an option, but it can backfire. The colloquy's wary of letting popularity campaigns affect decisions. They think it encourages people to arrange more campaigns later. They don't want to deal with those."

"You're an expert on research administration?" Tonner snapped, and then remembered again who the boy's family was.

"If there isn't a quieter way, we can always go loud," Dafyd said. "But once we've gone loud, we can't go quiet."

"Is it worth doing at all?" Nöl asked. "If the fight's as good as lost already, it might be wiser not to make waves, yes?"

"No," his wife said, and Tonner was pleased to hear the certainty in her voice. "No, good things are rare. They're worth fighting for."

"How would you approach this, Dafyd?" Else asked.

The research assistant paused, thought. It was all Tonner could do not to interrupt him.

"I'd talk to people near the caucus. See who Austad's allies are and who he's crossed. If we know who his enemies are, there might be a way to put up a counterproposal. Something that pulls his coalition apart or puts together a stronger one. We'll still lose something. We always lose something. But giving a different way forward is a stronger argument than just saying no to the one that's on the table. Harder for Dyan Academy to counter. More likely to change the conversation."

"We don't have time," Tonner said.

"Could you do it in two days?" Else asked, as if Tonner hadn't spoken. The boy met Else's gaze, blushed a little, and nodded like he'd just been given a quest.

As project lead, Tonner had gotten first choice in housing. His instinct had been an old instructor's cottage with worn bamboo floors and the smell of mildew that never quite vanished, even with remediation. It wasn't that he liked the place, but it was closest to the labs. If he'd followed that impulse, he would have saved himself almost half an hour each day. But Else had complimented one of the newer coral-grown buildings, and one apartment in particular with a balcony that looked north over a long, curving street. She had just abandoned her own project to join his team, they had been in the first blush of their relationship, and he'd hoped that by living in a space she enjoyed he would encourage her to spend more of her nights with him. She wasn't project lead, and her official rooms were in the basement levels of an old ecosphere an hour's walk to the south. She was almost never there, but she used it to store some things.

He stepped out to the balcony—the balcony he'd gotten just for her—and sat in the chair beside hers. Tonner found Else endlessly fascinating, and only more so because of her few bad habits, one of them being her fondness for smoking. The fact that he found her so attractive in spite of it made her seem all the more exotic and exciting. The little brown roll of paper and herbs between her fingers smelled of marijuana and clove. He didn't mean to grimace, but she saw it anyway and shifted the cigarette to her far hand.

"Looking at the stars?"

"Looking at whatever there is to look at," she said.

The night was cloudless, but a haze caught the lights from the medrey's research complex, the shipyards to the west, the sprawl of the city beyond. The spill of stars was less than a clear night would offer, and still millions. He watched them glimmer for a while—the stars above and the homes and streets and buildings below, like the tiny corner of their world could mirror the cosmos, if only you stood at the right place to see it.

"Do you ever regret going into research?" he asked.

"Sometimes," Else answered. "I would have been good in practical applications too. I worked at an aquaculture farm for six months between primary and advanced. Mostly cleaning the sea tanks. I was hell on kelp."

"You would have been great, but I'm glad you chose not to stay there."

Three lights—two pale yellow and one blinking orange—rose up from the city. A transport for Obbaran or Glenncoal. He could imagine it was a star trying to get back to the sky. He'd believed stories like that when he was a child, and some part of him still did. The thing that children didn't understand and that adults forgot was that stories like that were all analogies at heart.

"You would have wound up in management," he said. "You'd be in a colloquy by now."

"I'm not a politician. All the best administrators are politicians."

"Like Alkhor."

"She's good at what she does."

"I didn't mean the aunt. I meant yours. The boy."

Else took a long drag on her cigarette. The ember glowed a deeper orange than the transport, then faded to gray. When she spoke, soft white smoke spilled out of her. "Are you angry with me for taking his side?"

"He's a research assistant. Research assistants haven't earned the right to have a side."

She lifted the cigarette toward her lips again, paused, then licked the finger and thumb of her other hand and pinched out the ember before flicking the rest away into the darkness. She didn't speak. Tonner knew it would be better to keep quiet himself as well. He managed for a while.

"I know all of you like him, but I don't trust him. He's a schemer. Everything he does is for effect. He's always watching people."

Her smile was so brief and understated, he might only have imagined it.

"I think he's charming. And schemer or not, I've never seen him be cruel."

"Ah. So I'm being cruel now?"

"Tell me again how you aren't angry with me."

"I'm not. I'm not angry with you," Tonner said. And then, "I'm just angry. And you're here. So I'm being a little shit."

Else considered. "That sounds right."

"If Rickar does this... if they take the project away from me..."

She shifted to see him better. When she spoke, it was a challenge, but a gentle one. "Finish that thought. If you lose the project, what?"

Tonner leaned forward, ran his hands through his hair. The transport light switched from orange to green. "This work is what I am. If I don't have it, I'm not sure what's left of me. I know that all the literature talks about reinvention and remaking your career every ten years, but I don't know if I have it in me to start over. Does that make sense?"

Else's eyes narrowed. A little smile touched her lips, but her gaze wasn't on him. She was seeing something internal. When she did this—retreated into her own thoughts without including him in on what they were—it left him anxious.

"You understand how much this is," he said, filling her silence. "You gave up more than anyone to be part of it. You had your own project. You were *lead*."

She waved the thought away with two fingers, like her hand had forgotten there wasn't still a cigarette between them. "Spiral analysis was a dead end. Everyone knew that. I could jump ship or spend my career driving coffin nails. I was glad to get that number-two spot on your team. It was a very rational choice."

"And you are nothing if not rational." It had more bite in it than he'd intended, but she wouldn't be baited.

Else stood, lifted her arms over her head, and stretched to one side and then the other. When she turned back, heading into the rooms, she touched his shoulder. It wasn't an invitation, but it was intimate. A private idiom between the two of them that the day was over. Tonner wondered whether he'd be able to sleep. He was weary, yes, but he wasn't tired. She drew her hand back and went inside. He listened to her start the shower, heard the change in the sound of the splashing as she washed the day off her skin. The transport vanished over the horizon. A formation of high-altitude ships tracked overhead—national security or deep survey, he couldn't tell which.

The shower turned off. He thought about going in, then he thought about Rickar. His jaw ached. He could imagine himself sitting there, staring into darkness until the dawn came up. And then…what? Wait patiently for a research assistant to save the project for him? That sounded like a thin slice of hell.

Else touched his shoulder again. He hadn't heard her coming up behind him. She passed a glass forward, one finger of rich amber whiskey in it.

"Brooding won't help," she said. "Come inside. Relax. Get some sleep. Things will seem better in the morning."

He took the glass, sipped the liquor. The first warm bloom spread through his throat and chest. "I hate losing. I hate being embarrassed."

"I know."

"Alkhor has a crush on you."

"I know that too."

He drained the glass in a swallow and set it on the tile beside his chair. It would be there to clean away in the daylight. The rooms were grown in light green and yellow that made him feel like an insect sleeping inside a flower. It was oddly comforting. Else was already on her side of the bed, curled under the sheet with her head turned away. Tonner shut off the lights, stripped in the darkness, and climbed in. He didn't think sleep would come, but as soon as his head touched the pillow, he felt himself swimming.

In his dream, he was trying to get across the square to his labs, but the paving stones were falling away into a vast pit. Every step was dangerous, and the ground collapsed behind him or where he'd been about to go as the world ate itself under him.

Later, it would seem like a premonition.

Five

Seen one way, the night is dark. Viewed another, it is bright. Another, symphonic in its complexity of radiations all along the spectrum of wavelengths. The swarm is as still as it can be, vibrating within the unfamiliar skin of its new host, and it receives. It is aware of a body on the other side of the thick coral wall, of the cacophony of insects in the soil and air, of the brief, sudden lines of cosmic rays passing through the planet like rain falling slantwise.

The awareness is exhausting, and the exhaustion is part of what it seeks. The new host is unwieldy, cunning, alive and aware in a way the old one was not. This is a surprise for the swarm, but it expects to be surprised. The swarm is young in the universe. Consciousness is a mystery it is only beginning to experience.

The body on the other side of the wall moves, standing taller than before. The swarm retreats, concerned that its radio bounce has been noticed, but when it looks again, the body in the building has only moved across the room. The swarm relaxes, and it notices that it relaxes. Not the host, but itself.

The new host pushes, is restless, fights. That isn't what captures the swarm's half-autonomic attention. It turns its mind inward and finds things there. A fondness for sweet pickles. The memory of a boy named Elial. A resignation to the inevitability of death. They do not come from the swarm or the host. The swarm recognizes artifacts of Ameer Kindred. The girl that is gone. The swarm finds this unnerving, and by doing so discovers that it can find things unnerving. It was built to learn, built for plasticity. Its design is like water, flowing through whatever channels the universe provides it. It understands now that water also carries what it passes through. It has already traded purity for experience, and there is no path back. Nor should there be.

Time is short. That is a blessing and a curse. Anything it does now that lasts a month is as good as something made to last a lifetime. A month is all the lifetime many of the people on this world have left. But neither can it wait in the shadows any longer.

A door slides open, and the swarm realizes it had been distracted by internal stimuli. It looks for the figure beyond the wall, and the figure is gone. A man steps out into the symphonic darkness. He is older. White hair shaved close to his scalp. He has a long face and pale stubble. His eyes are hooded, amused, weary. The swarm wonders what it would learn if it took him, traded its current host for him. It will never know.

The man sees it, hesitates. The swarm steps forward on its borrowed legs. It smiles. "Samar Austad?"

"Yes?" the man says. "How can I help you?"

The swarm or the host or the girl that is gone thinks: What a question.

"He thought it was me?" Irinna said. "Really?"

"He wasn't sure what to think," Jessyn replied.

The courtyard, while technically public, was empty. Most of the scholars were still away on break, and the maintenance and support staff were using the emptiness to repair and refurbish and regrow the labs and dormitories, not the parks and squares and courtyards. Jessyn liked this one particularly. It had tilework in blue and yellow all along its walls, ferns from both trees of life that unfolded in the summers and died back in the cold. During most of the year, a kitchen along its west side gave out meals of polenta and spiced beans made by an old man from Haunar. The windows were closed and dark now, but she could remember the flavors and the old man's smile, and it left her fond of the space.

"I just," Irinna said, and ran her fingers through her pale hair as a kind of punctuation. It was the sort of thing she trusted Jessyn to understand. Then, with a sigh, "Do you think Tonner can find a way to stop it?"

With anyone else, Jessyn would have been politic. A shrug or a careful phrase like *Tonner is very intelligent but this is outside his field.*

Instead: "No."

"Not even with Dafyd? With an Alkhor on our team..."

"Even nepotism has limits."

"He isn't just asking to keep us together as a favor," Irinna said. "It's all a political game, isn't it? Finding who'd lose if Dyan wins. How to make the colloquy see all the good that keeping us together would do. Things like that. Isn't that how the world works?"

"I don't know. I find social intrigue exhausting. I like research, where things are quantifiable and falsifiable."

There was a pause. It seemed to mean something. Irinna looked up at the tiles, her eyes gliding from one to the next like she was reading them. When she spoke, she sounded like she was trying so hard to be casual that it didn't work. "Would you take a project of your own? If they offered it to you?"

That was a hard question. It shouldn't have been.

Taking research lead of her own would mean leaving Irvian. Which meant leaving Jellit. And if her brother wasn't there, who would she go to when her brain went rotten again?

Her brother had been there since she was an anxious, moody child. He knew her internal weather by experience. When the darkness started coming on, when the back of her mind got angry and loud, he knew without her having to say anything. He knew when to leave her alone and when to step in. He had reached out to her physicians at least twice when she'd gotten too bad to do it herself. They hid it, but her brother was also her caretaker, her nurse, an extra part of her brain that stayed sane on those occasions when her own mind betrayed her.

Jellit had his own career, his own work, and she'd thought—hoped, pretended—that by being placed at Irvian together, she'd be able to put off this particular moment of truth for a few more years. Maybe forever. She wouldn't ask him to leave his career for her. Wouldn't accept it from him if he offered. But the idea of living without him frightened her.

So. Would she take a project of her own?

"I don't know," she said, trying for a lightness she didn't feel. "There's a certain peacefulness to not jumping for the prize. I look at Nöl and Synnia. They've been fixtures here for decades, moving from one project to the next. Having a home. That's worth something too."

Irinna's smile turned inward. It hadn't been the answer her friend was looking for. She was hoping that Jessyn would say yes, would ask her to come with her, that they could continue their careers together someplace. And Jessyn had just told her no. "Nöl and Synnia and you too," Irinna said, a little bitterly. "Rickar's going to have a strong base."

"If Nöl and Synnia stay." It was a weak counter, and they both knew it.

"Nothing's going to pry them out of here. They're both going to die in Irvian," Irinna said through a laugh. At least she was laughing.

"Probably true."

"I just thought... we'd have longer? I don't know. That being the top of the lists would make things better for us somehow. Instead of turning everything to shit."

"Even if we're reassigned," Jessyn said, "even if they scatter us across the world, we'll still be working the same field. Coordinating research. Sharing results."

"It's not the same, though, is it? I like going into the lab and finding... us. You know what I mean."

"I do."

"But everything changes, doesn't it? You have a good moment, and then there's another moment after it. And another one after that. Nothing stays the same."

"Even if," Jessyn said. "You know you can always reach me, even if we're working different labs. Or Campar. Or Else. Even Tonner will probably return our messages."

"Not Rickar's."

Jessyn chuckled. "No, probably not Rickar's."

Jessyn didn't know what to say, so she shifted forward, taking the younger woman's hand in hers. They sat there for a long moment, neither of them speaking, both aware of the loss that each of them was suffering in her own way. Irinna squeezed her hand and let her go. Her eyes were bright with tears that hadn't quite fallen.

"I should—" Irinna said, gesturing at the world beyond the courtyard.

"I have some things too," Jessyn lied as they stood. "But it was good seeing you."

"Maybe Tonner will take his project to Abbasat, and I can see my parents every weekend. They'd like that."

"We can hope for the best without being too specific about it."

"Hope for the best," Irinna agreed, and then she was gone. Jessyn shoved her fists into her pockets and waited for a long breath, then another, giving Irinna time to get ahead and avoid the awkwardness of walking together and also apart.

When she got home, she keyed herself in, dropped her jacket on the front table. Jellit's voice came from the back balcony, and she walked toward it, her melancholy driving her forward. He was talking in bright, excited, animated tones, which could mean good news on his project or a new book coming out by a poet he enjoyed or that he'd just woken up in a sunny mood. He could do that.

"When is the run going to finish up?" he said as she stepped out. The face on the screen was one of his cohort in astronomical imaging. A man named... she didn't remember. She sat on one of the little wooden chairs at the far end by the railing and let herself be still and small. The other man was saying something in equally breathless tones. She looked down at the street and imagined a life where she ran her own project, where Irinna was waiting at her laboratory, the old friend she'd brought with her. It would have been a pretty life, if it had been possible. If she had a head that worked a little bit better than hers did. If she were better.

"All right," Jellit said. "I'll be there. But I have to go now."

He dropped the connection. The balcony became very quiet.

"Bad day?" her brother asked.

Jessyn shook her head. Not *No* but *Let's not talk about it.* "What was that all about? You have a dataset running on break? I thought I was the only one having high drama when I should be resting."

"We have a dataset running," Jellit agreed. "It may be nothing. Or it might also be the most important thing in thousands of years. Kind of one or the other. Not lots of middle ground."

She chuckled, and he relaxed. It was part of the subtle language they had with each other. If she could still laugh at him, she wasn't that bad. If she wasn't that bad, he could worry a little less. If he could worry less, then maybe so could she.

"I'm all aflutter," she said, dryly. "What's your thousand-year discovery?"

"You know about the lensing effect."

"The one that whatever his name from Dyan was talking about? Rickar's friend."

"Llaren Morse."

"Him."

"I went and talked with my people, and they talked with his people, and between us all, we got permission to refocus a couple of asteroid mappers and fire some broad-spectrum radio at it. We got what looks like a return right between infrared and microwave. There's structure inside the effect."

Jessyn felt her self-pity shift. Not go away, that would be too easy, but lose a little of its hold as her attention moved elsewhere. "Structure?"

"Mass anyway, but yes, ordered mass. And as far as we can tell, nonexotic."

"So not a naked singularity or macroscale quantum inflation."

"Probably titanium and carbon. We're trying to get a better image now," Jellit said. His voice was getting smooth the way it did when he was slipping into the best part of his mind. Her brother could be oblivious to people who weren't her. He could come across as frivolous, but was intelligent and as expert in his field as Tonner was in hers. Maybe more. It was a pleasure to watch her brother descend into the flow of his understanding. His eyes softened, and a little smile played across his lips.

"What are you thinking?"

"That it's unlikely nonexotic matter would generate lensing like this just at random. So it's not a given, but if the signals are confirmed, I'm going to bet this is nonrandom."

"Designed?"

"Designed," Jellit said. "It could be a probe."

"From where?"

Jellit answered with a shrug and a grin. "But we're aliens on this world. Maybe it's our long-lost brothers come to find us?"

In the street below them, three men walked abreast, laughing together. A white bird the size of a fist flew up, hovered, and then darted away again. All thoughts of colloquy politics and research careers and lost chances at friendship or love faded, and Jessyn put her fingertips to her lips.

"Wow," she said.

"The run ends in half an hour. I don't know what we'll know then, but we'll know something." He said it softly. The part he didn't say, she still heard. *But if you need me here, I'll stay.* Jessyn shifted, pointed back over her shoulder toward the door.

"Go! Find out. Get back to me as soon as you find out. This is amazing!"

Jellit's grin was relief and pleasure and the giddiness that comes maybe once or twice in a lifetime when something miraculous happens. He kissed the top of her head, grabbed his satchel, and was gone. A minute later, she saw him running down the street under the balcony. Long, thin limbs flailing like it was his first day with them. When she sat back, she was smiling. It took a moment to understand why.

Growing up, Jessyn's family had attended a Serrantist church led by an old, white-haired priest named Nansui. When, as an adolescent, she had been struggling with the intrusive thoughts and anxiety, she'd tried going to him for help. Nansui had been a patient, thoughtful, kind man. The conversations they'd had left questions of theology and doctrine behind very quickly. Mostly, he'd listened, and when he did talk, it was often about the difficulty of living as a very small part of a very large universe.

He'd told her a story once of his religious conversion. He said he'd been in a place similar to where she'd been at the time—young, confused, disturbed. *Too much with myself* was the phrase he'd used. He'd gone to a meditation retreat and been told to practice walking until he could feel every fiber of his socks pressing against his feet with each step. She still remembered the warmth and amusement in his voice describing his younger self trying to focus and getting bored and distracted and angry and then turning back to his socks. And on the third day, he'd had an experience that changed his life.

Between one step and the next, he'd had an epiphany about the vastness and strangeness of the universe and his place in it. The insignificance of one boy on a strange planet in the vastness of galaxies. For a moment, his mind had reached out to the farthest ends of the universe, and he'd felt the weight of his life, his ego, his struggles as less than a feather.

Then I came back to myself and refocused on my sock, he'd said, and they'd both laughed.

This was different, but related. Her life was a mess. Her career was a mess. Normal people would succeed where she couldn't because she'd been born a little broken. But there was also a world outside her head that was filled with mystery and exploration and unexpected things to discover. Looked at in a wide enough frame, maybe her problems weren't so large. They just seemed that way when she held them up against her eyes where they'd block out all the light.

She sat on the balcony, enjoying the feeling of calm and release and wonder until her belly felt empty enough to distract her with ideas about food. She put it off, though. She didn't want the moment to end.

When her system chimed, she was so sure it would be Jellit that she didn't check before she accepted the connection. The face that appeared on the floating screen was wide-eyed with worry.

"Campar?" she said.

"Jessyn. Yes. Good. We need to have a conversation. You may be contacted by the security forces."

"Wait. Why?"

"Samar Austad's been killed..."

Six

"So help me understand. You were asking around about him," the security forces man said, "but you'd never met him."

"That's right," Dafyd said, not for the first time. "We heard that Dyan Academy was making a proposal about our workgroup, and I was trying to understand better what that entailed."

The room was small and spare, but not threatening—natural light, soft chairs, no table. The security forces man made a show of being at ease, a little uncertain, even just on the edge of befuddled by the whole thing. All it meant to Dafyd was that they weren't trying to scare him into implicating himself in the man's death so much as lull him into it. Scaring him would have been more effective. He was already scared.

"What that entailed?" the security man repeated, making it a question. Dafyd recognized the technique, and it put him more on his guard, if that was possible.

"If there were any changes, I wanted to be ready for them."

"Ready for them?"

"Yep," he said with a smile, and then let the silence stretch.

The security man looked across at him with a blank, generic

friendliness until it was clear Dafyd wasn't planning to elaborate. "So what all did you find out?"

"Well, I just found out he's dead, so nothing I learned matters much, I guess." He didn't feel as light as his words. Between the time the security forces arrived at his rooms and when he'd left with them, he'd managed to send word to his aunt and Tonner. That had been five hours ago, and he hadn't heard back from either. That almost certainly meant that they weren't being permitted to contact him. It made all the warmth and calm and ease of the questioning feel like the trap it was.

The security man furrowed his brow. "Does that make you upset?"

"A little nervous, maybe," Dafyd said. "Is it related to the girl?"

"Girl?"

"I heard that there was a girl who died over break. You were talking to my team lead about it. Tonner Freis?"

The security man's smile gave away nothing. "We're looking into things. Why do you think they'd be related?"

"They're both dead," Dafyd said. "I don't know how I can help."

"Tell me again about these changes that had you worried."

"I wouldn't say worried."

"Curious, then."

Dafyd spread his hands. "I heard there might be some changes, and I was curious what they might be."

The other man chuckled, but there was a glint in his eye. "You play your cards pretty close to the vest, don't you, Mr. Alkhor."

"I don't have any cards. I'm just—"

The door opened, and an older man leaned in. He made eye contact with Dafyd's interrogator, then retreated, leaving the door ajar behind him. The security man heaved himself up from his chair, letting his frustration show a little in his posture. "I'll be right back. Do you want anything? Coffee? Cigarette?"

"I'm fine."

The door closed behind him. Dafyd fought the impulse to relax. There were almost certainly still eyes on him, even if the cameras weren't obvious. He tried to arrange himself into looking placid and complacent, the way he imagined an innocent man would look. Which was a little weird, because he was innocent. The death of Samar Austad had nothing to do with him or the apparently not-quite-as-subtle-as-he'd-hoped inquiries he'd been making. Anything he did would be how an innocent man acted by definition, but the whole situation made him anxious. It left him trying to seem like what he was, which he was pretty sure made him seem inauthentic, which was probably why the security forces thought he was hiding something.

"Overthinking it," he said to himself. And then, in case someone was listening too, "Just keep telling everyone the truth, and it'll be fine."

God, he thought, *I wasn't cut out for this.*

The door opened again, and a woman he hadn't seen before walked in. She gestured for him to stand, and he did. After a moment, she shook her head. "You can go," she said, and repeated her gesture. "That means you can go."

"Oh. All right. I didn't... Thank you."

She escorted him through the tall, thin corridors of the security services building. The walls rose up three times his height, curving into a Gothic arch at the top with ridges like the ribs of a giant snake that had devoured him. In other contexts, it would have been beautiful.

The waiting area was open and broad, with wooden benches

that reminded him of pews. People sat or paced or leaned against the walls, all waiting for whatever the next step was in their personal journey through the security forces bureaucracy. The light was artificial, bluer than sunlight and cold-feeling. The air smelled like old cigarette smoke and cleaning solution. His aunt was perched at the edge of one bench like it was an unwelcome acquaintance. When she saw him, she rose. When she nodded to the security services woman, it was like a dismissal.

"I arranged private transport," his aunt said. "There are journalists."

"For me?"

She turned and started walking. He had to trot to catch up. "I mean journalists exist, and our name should stay out of this as much as can be managed. I've got enough on my plate as it is. As hard as it may be to believe, this is not my top concern right now."

They stepped out of the building and into a wide plaza where a transport stood waiting like a giant pill bug. The plates parted, and his aunt stepped in and took a rear-facing seat. Dafyd took one across from her.

"Do we know what happened?" he asked as the transport juddered into motion. "How did he die? You don't think it had anything to do with the research group, do you?"

His aunt didn't answer, already involved with spooling through the messages waiting on her system. The transport turned a corner, shifting him to the side then back again. He didn't like closed transports. They left him a little nauseated. His aunt made a soft grunt like she'd been punched and leaned forward, her whole attention on a message Dafyd couldn't see.

"This wasn't us," he said. "Whatever it is? It wasn't Tonner's group."

"Do you know who killed him?" she asked, not looking up.

"No."

"Then you can say it wasn't *you*. 'Us' is a big word. You can fit surprises in it." She flipped to another message, and muttered an obscenity under her breath. "I have to let you out here. Can you walk the rest of the way?"

"Sure. Yes. What's the matter?"

"That list is too long right now," she said, tapping the transport controls. "I'll tell you what I can, when I can."

The transport stopped. The plates slid open. Dafyd didn't get out. "I understand. Just…what will this do to Dyan Academy's proposal? I know that's a minor thing for you, but it matters to me. A lot."

She shook her head, but not as a refusal. "There was pushback before. Without Samar to champion it, it won't happen. But the damage is done. You understand that."

Dafyd found himself caught between relief and dread. "I do," he said. He pulled himself up and out to the walkway. The morning sun was cooler than he expected it to be. Weather moving in, maybe.

"Dafyd?" his aunt said, leaning forward to look out between the still-open plates. "Things are happening. Some news is about to break. I hoped we'd be able to put it off, but that was optimistic. Do what you can to stay out of trouble until I can get my arms around the situation."

"I will. I promise."

The plates slid closed, hiding her face.

He never saw her again.

Rickar Daumatin took a last, long drag on his cigarette, pinched it out, and threw the dead butt in a little ceramic public waste can before walking into the café. Littering the streets of Irvian would be a small, petty thing, and while he was feeling small and petty, little self-denials like this helped him feel virtuous. He found that he very much wanted to feel virtuous. More noble than those who had cast him aside.

The interior of the café had been grown in two levels. Half a dozen steps led up and to his right to a set of communal tables crowded with friends and strangers shoulder to shoulder as they watched a display showing what he assumed was the lead-up to some sporting event. They all had that kind of breathless tension. Walking ahead, Rickar found a set of smaller booths, each with a curtain of beads to give the sense of privacy if not the actual thing.

A few tables sat low to the floor with people on cushions around them. He found some faces he'd hoped to see. The delegation from Dyan Academy wasn't large, and he'd been away from home—in his Irvian exile—for three years now. He shrugged off his jacket and made his way to the little table where a handful of his old compatriots sat. As he took his place, a red-haired man he'd studied with in his first term filled a shot glass from a blue-green bottle and slid it across the table to him. Rickar sipped first, let the feeling of the alcohol and the taste of black licorice wash through his mouth, let the fumes rise up behind his nose, and then finished the rest of the shot in a swallow.

"Rough morning," one of the others said.

Rickar sighed behind his smile. "I've been a guest of our friends in security since daybreak."

"Austad?" the red-haired man asked. "They don't think you killed him, do they?"

Rickar pushed his shot glass back. As the red-haired man filled it again, he said, "No, they were aware that my life would be much better with him in it. Losing him like this is a shock for all of us, but—excuse the self-pity—it's career-ending for me. Not the best profile for a murder suspect."

A dark-haired woman who was, he thought, part of the transformational chemistry group shook her head. When she spoke, she slurred. "He was the best of us. No one profits, losing a man like Samar."

"True," Rickar said. "And some lose more than others."

The red-haired man pushed back the filled shot glass. Rickar decided to take this one more slowly. Nothing would be made better by being drunk. But then, nothing could be made much worse, either.

He leaned forward, legs crossed under the table, and went back over it all while the others chattered around him. There should have been someplace he could have made a different choice. Some decision that, in retrospect at least, he ought to have made differently. Maybe he would have been better off staying at Dyan and not joining Tonner Freis's project in the first place. Except that the team was good, the project had borne fruit, and without it, he'd have been another minor scholar chipping at some less successful work. *If only we hadn't done well* made no sense.

He noticed that the drunk woman was talking. Had been talking for a while. She was going on now about the existential unfairness of death, but just before that, she'd said something else. *He didn't get to see them.*

"Didn't get to see who?" She blinked slowly. Rickar tried again. "You said he didn't get to see them. See who?"

"The *things*," she said, as if that meant something. Rickar gestured his question. The others were looking at him now, all of them surprised.

"You really have missed everything today, haven't you?" the red-haired man said.

Rickar checked his system. It was still set to refuse interruptions the way the security forces interrogator had insisted that it be. He went back to his base settings, and floodgates opened. More than a hundred alerts—some from friends, some from journalists and newsletters he'd set his system to watch, half a dozen from his father with referents out to the same reports he had in his own listings.

UNKNOWN OBJECTS MAY BE VEHICLES

INTERSTELLAR VISITORS?

DEFENSE COUNCILS FROM EIGHT NATIONS IN EMERGENCY SESSION, URGE CALM

It felt like a joke. A prank. Then like a kick in the chest. Rickar was breathless. He caught a glimpse of a familiar face in one report as he passed, and spooled back to let it run. Llaren Morse, his face shining with exhaustion and perhaps mania. As he spoke, he made sharp, staccato gestures like he was fighting with ghosts. *We've been following the lensing effect for some time now. Since shortly after it entered the solar system. We detected the presence of matter inside the effect only within the last day and a half. When we tried a targeted scan... the lensing effect collapsed. Maybe they saw we were watching them. I don't know. It's too early to say what exactly we're looking at here, but it's certainly*—Morse's grin stretched taut—*it's certainly interesting, isn't it?*

Rickar shifted to a related image. A starfield with a scattering of dim spots highlighted. If he hadn't known to look, he wouldn't have seen them. Seventeen city-sized objects, broad on one end, and tapering to an almost crystalline point. The surfaces of the things were faceted and polished, more like machines than living systems. Despite that, Rickar's mind kept trying to interpret them as some kind of animal skull.

He lifted the shot glass halfway to his mouth, and then put it down again. "Is this...?" He couldn't find the words.

"It's real," the red-haired man said. "They showed up three hours ago like someone flipped a switch."

"It's some kind of secret defense project," someone else at the table said, but Rickar wasn't paying enough attention to care who. And anyway, he recognized the sound of panicked denial when he heard it. He looked at the images again. Seventeen not-quite-identical mysteries floating in the void. The anger and self-pity he'd been swamped by just minutes ago were gone, and something else was pressing against the inside of his mind like he was being inflated. He had a brief but vivid memory of being seven years old at his grandmother's vineyard in Nortcoor, looking into the night sky and seeing it for the first time as infinity towering above him like God, only worse because it was real.

Maybe this was what religious awe felt like. Maybe it was only fear. Either way, he was done drinking for the day. He looked around the café, and saw the tension he'd felt coming in. He'd misunderstood it then. He was part of it now.

"Have they said anything?" he asked.

"No. They haven't done anything," the red-haired man said. "But I think your workgroup's moment in the spotlight is over. This is going to be the only thing anyone's talking about now."

"Tonner will be disappointed," Rickar joked, and then laughed again when he realized it was true.

Synnia found a live image from an observatory in Glenncoal, and set her system to display it without analytic overlays. The seventeen probes or ships or artifacts floated on the face of the abyss with only a little false-color enhancement to show the details of their surprisingly complex surfaces. Probes or ships or asteroids or anomalies or miracles. It seemed to Nöl that any term failed in some nuance. His own system was set to scour the available inputs for analysis and commentary that was more than speculation and echoes. So far, he'd found very little that had any intellectual rigor, and what there was devolved into the need for further study. He found that more comforting than she did. He kept waiting for it to turn out to be something innocuous. Something that didn't merit alarm. That kept not quite happening.

"Let me make you some tea," he said.

Synnia shook her head, refusing, and then a moment later said, "That would be good. Yes. Thank you."

Nöl rose from the table and, pausing to kiss the top of her head, went to the kitchen. The house was silent. Even the voices from his system faded to a dim murmur by the time he reached the kitchen and started the kettle. The remnants of their breakfast still sat on the counter. His plate was clean. The yolks of her eggs had congealed into an intense yellow gel. He thought it would be time for food again soon, but he doubted she would eat.

They had meant to spend the day in the garden, pulling weeds and sampling the soil for signs of split worms and agthaparasites. Outside the kitchen window, the sunlight was bright. Ravens hopped along the branches of the pecan tree just beyond Nöl's yard, conferring with each other on the mysterious business of corvids. He wished they'd kept to the gardening plan. Whatever was happening out beyond the envelope of Anjiin's skies, there was nothing he could do about it. And Synnia would be less frightened if she could put her hands in soil.

He let the tea steep, poured it into a rough earthenware cup, and took it back to the main room. The seventeen things glimmered in the darkness, their clarity and resolution growing sharper with each new scan that was applied to the image. He put the cup at his lover's elbow and sat beside her.

"Anything new?" he asked.

"One of them's moved," she said. "Changed their formation. And then it stopped. The feed said that they seemed to be using some kind of accelerated gas to maneuver. They're still moving toward the planet. They won't impact us, though. Not unless they change course."

Nöl grunted his interest in the new data as he took his seat. Synnia picked up her tea, leaned closer to the screen, then after a moment sat back and put the cup down as if she'd forgotten to drink from it. He felt her unease as a tightness in his own belly, and wished she would stop watching. He didn't want to think about this, and as long as she did, he had to.

Nöl reached out, rubbing his palm along her arm. He meant it as comfort, but also as a request for comfort for himself. She glanced at him, distractedly ran her hand across his head, and then turned back to the screen.

He wished whatever the things were that had hidden in Llaren Morse's lensing effects, they'd gone about their business without him. If he were younger, he might feel the wonder and mystery as a promise, but he was what he was, and more than anything, he wanted to be left alone with his love and their garden. If the probes or ships or miracles were important for him, someone would tell him.

Synnia caught her breath. "Look. They're doing something."

At first, he didn't see it, and when he did, he thought it was only data errors in the image feed. It was hardly more than a dark bronze shimmering. Then new scan data came in, the images refreshed, and the softly curving trails coming from the objects—ships, probes, whatever they were—flashed into clarity. She took control of the image, expanding and expanding until the trails atomized into oblong spheroids. The greenish halo around them was almost certainly an artifact of the image compiler, but it did make them striking to look at.

"Like spores," Synnia said. "I've seen mushrooms releasing spores, and it was just like this."

"Or pollen," Nöl said. "Maybe they've come to pollinate us."

If she noticed the little joke, she didn't react to it. "Look at the foreshortening. They're coming toward us. It's all coming toward us."

A weight of dread settled in his gut, and he pushed it aside the way he did any unpleasant emotion. The anxiety was temporary. It would go away when he understood the situation better. That was how it had always been with him.

"Perhaps they are," Nöl said. "Let me see if I can find any good analysis."

He turned to his own system, but there probably wouldn't be anything yet. If experience had taught him anything, it was that first guesses were almost always disappointing. Data collection and analysis took time.

Synnia kneaded her hands into each other like she could squeeze her distress out of her knuckles. "Oh, I hope the security forces don't panic and do something aggressive."

Dafyd leaned forward and pressed his fingertips against his upper lip until the pressure ached. The laboratory felt like it was buzzing, like the walls themselves were on the edge of panic. Tonner was pacing the length of the room, his hands clenching and unclenching, his jaw slid forward. For Dafyd, talking now would have been a mistake.

"This is a windfall. We can't waste it," Tonner said, as much to himself as the rest of them. It took Dafyd a moment to realize he meant Samar Austad's death, not the ships descending toward Anjiin. When Tonner scowled, he looked like an angry child. "Where *is* everybody?"

Campar, sitting cross-legged on one of the lab benches, said it for him. "The most important thing in the history of the world is happening. People might be a bit distracted."

The research complex should have been filled with the sound of maintenance crews finishing up their work before the scholars all came back. It was silent. Tonner had sent his summons out to the whole workgroup, except Rickar. Only Campar and Else were there. Irinna had sent a message saying she was coming, but hadn't arrived. Nöl and Synnia hadn't responded at all. Dafyd guessed that they'd turned their notifications off or else just stopped looking at them.

Else leaned against one of the worktables, her system displaying the most recent images of the objects. Dafyd would have liked to do the same, but Tonner would have yelled at him for it. Tonner might be irritated with Else—clearly was, actually—but he wouldn't yell at her.

Looking back, he had to think his aunt had known something when she dropped him off on the street. By the time he'd gotten back to his rooms, the news was breaking to the public all across the world. First contact with an alien species or humanity's lost origin or something stranger. Everyone guessed because no one knew. Dafyd spent hours sitting on the edge of his bed, flipping from one source to another to another, always finding the same images, and being astounded by them every time. When Tonner's message came through, he'd responded to it out of reflex. If he'd thought about it, he'd have stayed home the way the others had and watched history unfold.

"Fine," Tonner said, biting at the word. "If we're the only ones that care, we'll do it ourselves."

"Do what, exactly?" Campar asked. He wasn't usually so acid.

"This thing. Everyone's watching it," Tonner said. "They're distracted. There won't be anyone paying enough attention to stop us. This is our chance to cement the workgroup. Get control of it."

"How?"

Tonner threw his hands out in exasperation. "That's what we're here to discuss. There has to be a way."

"They're censoring it," Else said.

Campar jumped down from the bench and went to her side. Tonner froze. A cascade of emotion—shock, humiliation, anger—flickered over his face. Even as Dafyd's excitement and anxiety and confusion and awe threatened to overwhelm him, there was also a part of his mind that saw how the power in the group had changed. Tonner had been their high priest. The focus had shifted, and he wasn't able to command it back. Dafyd noticed the little vulnerability, tucked it away for later, and went back to being distracted and scared.

"What do you mean 'censoring'?" Campar asked as he leaned over Else's shoulder. "Who's censoring what?"

She gestured to the screen. "They say this is a live image, but it's the same one they were showing forty minutes ago. Look." She paused the image, pulled up a second display, and then shifted them together. From where he was, Dafyd couldn't see them, but Campar whistled.

"It could be that our new friends have some periodicity?" he said.

"Or that something's happened that the governing council wants to keep to themselves," Else said.

Campar made a small, soft sound. Almost a cough. "I'm a little surprised they let it go this long without stepping in. I suppose Jellit knows what's going on, but I can't think they'd let him tell us."

"We could ask Jessyn," Dafyd said. "If he's able to get anything out, he'll get it to her."

"It would be worth trying," Else said, but she didn't seem enthusiastic. "We should go to my rooms. All of us. Now."

"Why?" Tonner snapped. "What good would that possibly do?"

"I have a good optical telescope there," Else said. "It won't do much now, but once the sun's down, we could take a look for ourselves. And if something happens and we need to shelter, it's solid and mostly underground." Else glanced over to Tonner. As soon as she saw him, her shoulders shifted inward and the excitement left her voice. "I'm sorry. I can't focus. I just... I need to do this."

"That's fine," Tonner said.

"It's an extraordinary—"

"You don't have to justify yourself to me. Do what you need to do."

Campar looked down and took a gentle step away like a man who'd walked into the wrong room. Tonner had gone still, his lips a little pursed, his arms rigid at his sides like a child making a show of how much his feelings weren't hurt. Dafyd had seen him like this before, especially after a particularly disappointing data run, but it was always Else who brought him back out.

"At least come with me," she said. "Help me get the telescope."

"Take Dafyd."

Now Else stiffened. Whatever subtext passed between the two of them, Dafyd could tell it was unpleasant. He wished his name hadn't been part of it.

Else seemed to struggle internally for a moment, then closed her system displays. "All right. We'll be back." She turned a polite, empty smile to Campar, then walked to the lab doors. Dafyd hesitated for a few fast heartbeats, then followed after her.

They passed through the research complex in silence, Else walking with long, confident strides, her head held high. Dafyd fell into step beside her, his hands in his pockets and a confusion of half-recognized emotions churning in his head. Everyone they passed had the same tension: wonder and fear.

It was only about fifteen minutes before they reached the old ecosphere. Facets of the dome caught the sunlight, shining white for a few steps and then fading to a rusty brown. It was one of the few buildings that hadn't been grown, but constructed, and it aged like a mechanism, not a living thing. The steps down into the wide central courtyard were dark metal at the sides, bright in the middle where footsteps had polished them. The air was humid and cool. Else's gait had slowed, trading an almost military stiffness for something looser and less certain. In the lift down to the basement level, she leaned against the wall.

The basement level had been utilitarian and severe when it was built, and redecorated when it was converted to living space. Pipes ran along the walls, but painted bright, primary colors. Cut-paper shades arced over the sockets where work lights would have been, softening the space until it was shadowless.

Else's rooms seemed oddly spare, until Dafyd realized Else

probably didn't live in them anymore. He imagined they'd been storage before they'd been converted, or maybe part of the water reclamation. Now the space was a little kitchen that opened onto a dining area that had crates and boxes piled neatly against the walls and under the table. A sliding door led to what he assumed was a bedroom. Glass vases were set in the walls, but there were no flowers in them. The space smelled like dust. She paused, looking around with an almost puzzled air, like she'd forgotten what brought her there in the first place. There was a focus in her eyes that reminded him of physicians in the middle of an emergency. Or the beginning of one.

Dafyd cleared his throat. "Are you . . . are you all right?"

She turned toward him, seeming startled to find him there. "I was thinking that at least we kept the workgroup together."

"Yeah," he said, but it didn't sound convincing.

"Do you know something I should hear?"

"We're not keeping the workgroup together."

A flash of panic lit her eyes. "What happened? Did Rickar—"

"No, Dyan Academy lost their shot. That was just luck. But we stood a chance against it because we knew it was coming, and where it was coming from. Samar Austad put the idea out there, and he almost made it work. Next session, there's going to be a dozen different factions looking for ways to do what he was trying, only this time, we won't know who they are. We got a year, maybe. But that's all."

Else leaned against the wall and crossed her arms. He couldn't tell what her sigh meant. "Interesting."

"It's status competition. Almost everything is status competition."

"Why are you in research? You're the wrong kind of smart. You should have been administration."

Dafyd shrugged. "My dad. He always wanted to be research, but never got the placement. I'm kind of living his dream."

"Your father's last wish?"

"Not his last one. He lives in Astincol with my stepmother. I was supposed to go out over break, but the timing didn't work out."

"I'm sorry."

"There's next time," Dafyd said. "I mean, assuming."

"Assuming," she agreed. "For what it's worth, I'm sorry about Tonner. When he's stressed, he can be petty. It's not his best feature."

"It's his pathological move. I get it."

"I don't know the term."

"It's the thing people do when they're working on instinct. When they're stressed and overwhelmed, there's something they go to by reflex. Tonner focuses down on something small enough to control. Campar makes jokes. Jessyn withdraws. Everyone has something."

Her smile. Its uneven dimples. Dafyd was suddenly very aware of being alone with this particular woman.

"What do I do?" she asked, and she seemed genuinely curious.

"I don't know. Do you ever get stressed and overwhelmed?"

"I do," she said. "I am right now."

"Because of the..." He pointed up at the ceiling. At the sky.

Her smile faded. "Yes. Because of that."

"Maybe it'll all be okay. We don't know. Maybe this will be something wonderful."

"Maybe it won't."

Look, he thought, *I know it's stupid. I know there's nothing in it, but I've been dreaming about you for months. You're a million levels above me, but if you weren't you and I wasn't me? If we were just two people who met in a bar one night and started talking, I'd want to keep talking to you.* He tried to think of something less potentially humiliating instead.

"Hey, this is probably inappropriate, but if this does go bad, I'd feel stupid not having said anything..."

She shifted her head. Her hair draped down to her collarbone. Her gaze on him felt like a pin through a butterfly. After a few breaths, the corner of her mouth twitched into a half smile.

"You're not saying anything," she said.

"Yeah. I know. And I was off to such a good start too. Forget about it. Let's just grab that telescope."

Else used her shoulder to push off the wall. Dafyd didn't step back. She pressed her mouth to his and it tasted like salt and smoke. Something rumbled, deep as thunder or an earthquake. The lights flickered.

In the distance, alarms began to shriek.

PART TWO

CATASTROPHE

We did not create the logic of the universe, but we express it, as do those who we yoked to our will. Good and evil are constructs lesser beings build to create divisions in places where rigor and intelligence are insufficient. It is a sloppy shorthand, and prone to error. The Carryx gained all we gained by not needing such things. The universe tells every being exactly the same implacable truth. The Carryx listen and thrive, where others squirm and express opinions and then are crushed and forgotten.

The truth is this: That which is, is. The Rak-hund execute our will. If there is any *because* in that, it is because we killed or sterilized all aspects of the Rak-hund that didn't, and we kept the remnant that did. The Gar of Estian, Kirikishun, Ouck, the seven Lek-Variable, the Whirl-Ghost. The same is true of all of them. If there is a moral question in that, it is the same moral question a species asks when its star novas and melts its world to glass.

When a primitive of your own kind cut a branch from a tree and carved the wood into a tool—an axe handle, a tentpole, whatever your will designed—you placed no moral judgment on the act, nor should you have. To do so would have been perverse. The tree had no power to stop you, and so it became a tool in your hand.

What you did with a tree branch, we did with you and countless others before you. *Why me?* is not something the universe ever answers.

—From the final statement of Ekur-Tkalal, keeper-librarian of the human moiety of the Carryx

Seven

The seventeen Carryx colony ships had passed through the terrifying improbability of asymmetric space, which only the cold illogic of the navigation half-minds could master. They followed the beacons that their early void tendrils had scouted and laid down. They knew already a great deal about the system they would emerge into. There was only one planet of interest, and only one—or at most two—species on the planet that held both enough abstract complexity and severability to be of use in expanding the canopy of the Sovran's will or serving in the war. In one way, it wasn't a particularly interesting find.

But in another, it promised to be one of the more fruitful discoveries since the great conflict began. That potential would be measured later, and by others.

They returned to symmetry just outside the membrane of the heliosphere, keeping only a protective bubble of projected gravity as they fell sunward. The star glow of the galactic disk showed the plane of the ecliptic, and the colonization half-mind drank in the light of the local star and a thousand others, comparing spectra and spacing, confirming that the transit had taken them where they intended. The blue-green dot curving its eternal orbit through gravity-warped spacetime was indeed the one that the locals called Anjiin.

The half-mind was not capable of joy, but there was still a clinical satisfaction in tasks well completed. The seventeen vessels accelerated sunward, both sped and concealed by their bubble.

Or so they thought.

They were unaware that on the distant surface of the world, a man named Llaren Morse had seen his doom approaching and hadn't recognized it for what it was.

The nodes were woken and prepared. They shuddered in their liquid wombs, stretching electromagnetic limbs as their sluggish intelligence coalesced, waiting to be born. The Rak-hund were woken to eat and shit and beg for approval as was their nature. The Sinen gathered their excavation tools. The Carryx watched over these moieties, masters of all.

As they entered their final approach to the planet, a small correction was needed. A few degrees, but not more than predicted by the uncertainty of asymmetric interactions. What they hadn't predicted, what had *never* been predicted, was the signal from the planet. It covered a broad spectrum, but a narrow band of space. The chances that it was a random effect were vanishingly small, and one band penetrated their protections, echoing back toward the target planet. The seventeen ships prepared for violence.

But hours passed, and no violence came. The blue-green dot in the void grew closer. The stream of radiation from the local star shuddered and rippled along the surface of their gravity bubble. The enemy didn't appear, and with every minute that it didn't come, the pattern of the moment grew further from the expected choreography of ambush.

The half-mind found nothing in the burst beyond the raw fact of its existence, and while the burst had some features in common with the enemy's targeting systems, it had several structural differences as well. Evidence suggested that it was a local invention, a parallel evolution in technology, and not a cause for alarm.

It was unsettling, though, that the creatures of Anjiin had noticed their approach at all. It was something else to take heed of. The Carryx ships moved with a greater caution than they might have. At the decision of the colony effort's command, the ships dropped the bubble early, letting the shroud fall and the full noise and flow of normal space rush around them. They scanned the vacuum, the mist-thin scatterings of matter, the wildly dancing fields of energy and force that radiated out from the star and echoed in the cores of its little planets. If Anjiin had a protector, this was the moment they would arrive.

Anjiin had no protector. Nothing arrived.

The attention of the Carryx turned to the planet. All through the vast ships, nodes reached their maturity, gaping open in something engineered to mimic lust, ready to receive their burdens. Rak-hund and Sinen and Soft Lothark poured in. Those that couldn't tolerate the closed spaces and variable gravity were lulled into a preparatory catatonia. The others were encased in fluid tanks. The Carryx soldiers came last, taking their places like warriors lifting up the reins of their chariots.

Anjiin was near enough now to make out features on the surface: the green and black of land, the complex blue of the seas, the whiteness at the poles and the upper reaches of mountain ranges where geology itself had touched the cold of space and been withered by it. A decision was made. A command went out. All along the skins and surfaces of the colony ships, hatches slid open, and the laden nodes spilled out of them. Out, and down.

They fell by the thousands and the tens of thousands. Nodes leaped and sang, surging one past another slowly at first, and then faster and faster, in the joyous race to the thinnest part of high atmosphere, little more than stray helium atoms lofting up and away from the stone and water they had escaped. The nodes shifted their paths, spilling out in a curve so wide it could seem almost flat, each oblong spheroid jockeying for its place in the matrix, reaching out and grabbing on to its neighbors with invisible lines of force and then using its stability to whip the remaining nodes more quickly into place, first a hundred, then a thousand, and then a hundred thousand. Like a great fist closing, the nodes made their net around Anjiin.

The half-mind gathered what it had instead of knowledge. The primary species communicated with sound and a narrow spectrum of light. Some chemoreception, but rarely at a conscious level. No protein messaging, no blood sharing. No fusion, either of full bodies or child organisms. No qliph. Many technological connections made through frequency and amplitude modulated electromagnetic waves, although there were also similar modulations along mineral channels laid between structures. Some of these converted to pressure waves in air, some into patterns of light on mechanisms that the species built for the purpose. All of it was deep and rich with pattern, language, meaning.

The half-mind dipped into the flow of chatter that was in one sense below the node matrix, in another sense inside it. The early scouting of the void tendrils had sent back volumes of information deeper than oceans. Without them, the half-mind might have taken days to understand all that it needed to know. Instead, it confirmed what it already assumed, changing only superficial expressions. The grammar fit into channels worn by a million other grammars. Analogies came together with a depth so profound it approached sentience without ever quite reaching it.

It turned its attention to the second species. Primary means of communication was chemoreception, with fruiting bodies that exchanged heritable structures. Intelligent, yes. Rich with meaning, yes. But slow. Very slow, and integrated more fully and dependently with the local biome than the void tendrils had indicated. Barely aware, it seemed, of anything above the soil. Air was a mystery to it, much less space and stars and a universe that existed in something more than darkness.

The half-mind recommended that only the primary species be considered, at least in these first stages of colonization. There would be time to determine whether the other organisms of Anjiin were useful later. The coordinating half-mind concurred. The Carryx considered and approved.

In bunkers all around the planet, voices of fear and alarm grew. Leaders of nations and mutual interest zones and cooperative organizations reached out to one another, hoping that the events of the day weren't what they seemed to be. Each of them tried to get one of the others to admit responsibility, but no one did because no one could. Focused radio signals went up to the nodes and the ships beyond them. *Identify yourself and state your intentions* and *We are peaceful, but can and will defend ourselves if provoked* and *Remove your ships immediately or suffer the consequences*. There was no single unified voice, and the Carryx would have ignored it if there had been.

Military bases built for the local factions to defend against one another swarmed into activity, reaching for ways to use old defenses in a new context. Slow-moving armored vehicles, fast-moving airships, and the small mobile cities of support and logistics services scattered into the open plains of the world's largest continent. Bombers and fighters and denial-of-access dirigibles took to the air. Missile silos opened. Submersible weapons platforms sank beneath waves. The elites fled to shelter or dressed in the uniforms that they imagined would look best at the historic moment of contact. The chaos of the day was evidence of the underlying chaos of the organism, and interesting in its own way. The Carryx allowed it to go on longer than was strictly required so that they could see a little more of the world in its natural state before they changed it.

A few missiles rose in the thick lower air. Plumes of smoke and heat announced them as they struggled against gravity toward the node matrix above. They came from Ondosk and Irvian and Dyan and Soladan: old rivals working in concert at last, now that it didn't matter.

The Carryx waited as long as was comfortable, and then disabled the offending missiles with discharges from the nodes like dry bolts of lightning falling from far above the clouds. One of the missiles bloomed in a nuclear fireball, but most lost power and fell or exploded with mere chemical detonations. Slowly and methodically over the course of seconds the nodes identified the places the missiles had risen from and all the other structures like them around the planet's surface and destroyed them. A handful of cities and military bases dissolved in fire. It was no more an attack than a singer clearing her throat was a song.

The half-mind announced to the coordinator that it was finished with translation and ready to deliver their message.

If the process had been translated into any human tongue, it would have been something like *breaking the limb*. The idiom was peculiar to the Carryx, but the logic behind it was not: a single overwhelming act of violence that would establish social dominance. The node matrix turned its full attention to the planet's surface, mapping the location of every member of the primary species. The concentrations in the large cities, the scatterings in the broad rural stretches, the rare individuals who had chosen isolation from their people for reasons the Carryx could not fathom and about which they did not care.

The nodes found the range of physical temperature, the electrical patterns of their nervous systems, the subtle alterations in gas concentrations that were their breath, and dozens more signs and signifiers that all came together to say one more and one more and one more. Three billion, six hundred seventy million, eight hundred sixty-two thousand, five hundred and thirty-three, with two thousand two hundred and seventeen signals that were ambiguous.

With the impersonal logic of machines, the species was divided into two intermixed populations. Those halves were then divided, and the new groups divided again. In the abstract non-mind of the node matrix, a decision was made and one of the eight groups was chosen. It had taken the half-minds whole minutes to be certain and prepared. The order went out to the nodes, and each received its targeting priority for the culling to come.

A hundred thousand nodes bloomed, their bronze shells opening to release white, diaphanous bodies that unfurled in the atmosphere, growing bones made from carbon and silicon. They were a nameless quasi-species, and would live only long enough to fulfill their purpose and then die. Vast and trembling, fighting against the high, thin winds of the atmosphere and burning through the long-chain hydrocarbons that were the fuel of their lifetimes, their membranes unfolded, stabilized, and turned with something like devotion to the half-mind. Under its direction, they shuddered, the pressure waves of their trembling designed to harmonize as they reached the surface of the planet into a single, clear, and unechoing voice.

The future fell invisibly toward the inhabitants of Anjiin at the speed of sound. *You are, individually and collectively, under the authority of the Carryx. You have been measured, and your place within the moieties will now be determined…*

Eight

The first explosions came from the military base south of the complex. Inside the thick terra-cotta walls of Nöl's house, they sounded like a rumble of distant thunder, closely followed by alarms and sirens. The smoke that rose from the base was thick and white. It wasn't clear to him whether it was an attack or a coincidence. Certainly he could imagine someone frightened by the day's events trying to bring some rarely used system up to readiness and making a catastrophic error.

But the reports began coming in from other places, and he had to accept that it had been an attack. A defensive one, given that their own forces fired first, but an attack all the same. He found that disappointing. It seemed to him that this wasn't a time for escalation, but no one asked.

Else Yannin looked out at him from his home system's screen. Her eyes were a degree wider than usual, her cheeks flushed, but her voice was steady and authoritative. "It's the sub-basement of my arcology. It's hardened. Tonner and Campar are getting fresh water. Irinna—"

The system hung for a moment, Else ceasing to move with her mouth a bit open, her eyes halfway through a blink. The communication infrastructure was overloaded. Of course it was. Nöl waited.

"—for the whole team, but you have to come now."

"I understand," he said, and that was for the most part true. Else and Tonner were putting together a hole for him and for Synnia to hide in, should things go poorly enough that a hardened room underground would help, but not so poorly that it wouldn't matter. Considering the size of the attack fleet and their apparent level of technology, the safe space between those two error bars seemed incredibly narrow. Even so, it was a kind thought. "I'll speak with Synnia about it."

Else frowned and froze again. Nöl considered dropping the connection. It was hardly useful, anyway. Else clicked back to life. "—to bring you here."

"Yes, yes," Nöl said. "I'm going now."

He thought Else had given one of her curt little nods, but it was hard to be sure. The screen shifted to an emergency page: HIGH DATA CONGESTION, PLEASE RESTRICT ACCESS WHERE POSSIBLE. He closed the system and leaned back in his chair. The house was quiet because it always was. If there was just the slightest smell of fire in the air, that was probably his imagination. It was easy to imagine things in unsettling moments like this.

He thought about whether there was anyone he should talk with. If it was coming near dusk here, the sun would just be coming up at his brother's apartment in Chabbit Close. But he was supposed to restrict access, and not making the connection was also possible. He drank the last of his tea. It had gone tepid, and little bits of mint leaf made the dregs gritty.

Synnia was in the back garden. She'd braided her hair tight against her scalp the way she did when she was going to a formal party or else preparing for physical labor. The braid down her back was still as thick as his wrist. But it was gray now, instead of the shining ebony it had once been. She stood on the stone path, her arms crossed, looking up at the sky.

On good evenings, the sunset from their house could be lovely: gold and green and rose pink. It wouldn't be like that tonight. There weren't enough clouds to catch the light, and it wasn't the sky he knew. The blue was stippled with dots that caught the sunlight and glowed with it. Or maybe they glowed on their own. It was hard to say. They covered the high air in a complex but regular formation. If he let his eyes unfocus a little, he could actually see lines between them, like a child's optical illusion.

"They made the sky into graph paper," Synnia said.

Nöl chuckled. "So they did." And then a moment later, "They don't move much, do they?"

"They aren't orbiting. They're frame locked with the surface."

"That's odd. But I suppose everything's odd, isn't it?"

Far above, the complex grid of dots grew slowly brighter as the angle of the sunlight changed. Nöl wondered what shape the objects were, and whether there was a way to know that by watching them interact with the setting sun. Likely there was.

"Why didn't we ever talk about children, you and I?" Nöl asked.

"Busy with our careers, and then later too set in our ways." Synnia shot him a frown. "Strange time to bring up regrets, if that's what this is."

"No. I'm just wondering how much more terrifying this would be if we had kids."

Synnia nodded. "Who were you talking with?" she asked.

"Else. She's found a bolt-hole. They're gathering up supplies and preparing to . . . I don't actually know what they're preparing to do. Ride out the storm, I suppose."

Synnia pulled her eyes from the sky like it took an effort. "Should we go?"

"I don't know. It's all fear. Everyone reacts in their own way. But…it sounds unpleasant. And if"—he pointed upward—"if they wanted to kill us all, I can't think all this would be needed."

"You think we're safe, then?" He couldn't tell if her tone was hope or incredulousness or some more complex mixture of emotions.

"I think we're probably as safe here as we would be hiding underground with Tonner Freis, and this is more pleasant."

She moved her arms in a distressed flapping, the way she did when she was feeling overwhelmed. Nöl felt a little twinge of annoyance with her, but he kept it to himself.

"We should do something, though," she said.

He nodded, giving her comment a little space so that his reply seemed less snappish. "What is there for us to do?"

She looked up at the ominous sky and then down. Nöl stepped away to the little garden shed. His gardening gloves hung from their usual peg, and he tapped them out as he always did before he put them on. There had never been any insects hiding in the fingers, but making certain was part of his habit. He only noticed it now because the events of the day seemed to make everything a little bit too real. Too present. He pulled the gloves on. The leather was still damp from the day before. As he walked back out, Synnia passed him, heading for the shed herself.

He knelt in the nearest bed and brushed the soil to reveal any little sprouts of weed that hadn't quite broken the surface yet. There were a few, some almost white with the green tint that meant they were DNA-based plants, others the uniform pinkish that identified the quasicrystal tree of life. He pinched them up and out, keeping the soil clean for the experimental bean vines that climbed the little wooden trellis. If he'd let the weeds live, they would have converged to an almost identical color of rich green, the better to drink in the sun. Synnia knelt down at the other end of the bed, her gaze on the dark soil. The sunlight shifted, turned ruddy. The smell of fresh earth was like a kind of perfume, and Nöl found his shoulders relaxing from a tension he'd only known intellectually was in them. If there was a war coming, it would find them gardening.

On the stone path, the little bodies of plants lay side by side, pale green beside pink, their roots exposed to the unkind air. It occurred to him for what couldn't really have been the first time that he was killing them.

"You know," Synnia said, and then trailed off.

Nöl waited for her to continue, and when she didn't, he sat down on his ankles. His knees were wet with the soil. The house and the garden were in twilight now. The alien objects in the sky were still bright from a sun he couldn't see. Synnia sat back, took a deep, shuddering breath, and wove her fingers together around her shin. Her mouth moved hesitantly, as if she were fighting some internal battle.

When she spoke, her voice was oddly calm. Almost normal. "I just wanted to tell you that if something happens to me, it has been a pleasure being with you." She nodded, as if approving the words to herself. "It has been a pleasure," she repeated.

"I don't think we're important enough to bother with, love. We're research assistants. Nothing we do matters all that much, does it?"

There were tears in her eyes. "It does to me."

Nöl sighed, and then something invisible spoke as though it were standing in the garden with them. The voice had no gender markers or recognizable regional accent, but somehow also didn't sound like a machine. It was authoritative and calm. "You are, individually and collectively, under the authority of the Carryx."

"What's saying that?" Synnia asked, her voice barely a whisper. Nöl didn't respond.

"You have been measured, and your place within the moieties will now be determined. Your distress with this change is irrelevant. Adapting quickly will reduce your discomfort and increase your potential utility. Ready yourselves."

"'Potential utility' sounds ominous," Nöl said. He stood and pulled the glove off his right hand before scratching his ear.

"To demonstrate that your submission is necessary," the voice continued, as though it had heard Nöl and was in a hurry to prove him right, "we will only kill one-eighth of your population."

Nöl's eyebrows rose. Something made a sizzle in the air, and a hornet stung him on his left clavicle halfway between the joint of his shoulder and his neck. He hadn't seen or heard the insect, but he recognized the sudden pain. Also, and strangely, his cheek was pressing into the soil of the garden. He'd fallen down, though he didn't remember doing it. His shoulder hurt badly, and there was something wrong with his arm, as if he'd numbed it. Synnia yelped and came to his side, her eyes wide.

"I'm all right," he said, and then caught his breath. It was annoying that he'd fallen over just at the time it would alarm her the most. "I'm fine. I'm fine."

He tried to sit up, but he was weaker than he should have been. He licked his lips, his tongue finding damp bits of garden soil there. He was surprised that it tasted so much like blood.

A vague sense of concern bloomed in him, but only for a moment.

Campar leaned forward, as if he could will the transport to go faster. All around him, the night shrieked. Military aircraft raced through the sky, rattling the ground with their engines.

Transports followed, their running lights casting red glows along the countryside. The trees seemed to move in the shifting light, looking like gigantic soldiers finding their way into formation. The smoke smelled like a chemical fire and stung his eyes.

"Come on. *Come on*," Campar muttered between clenched teeth. There was no one in the transport to hear him, and the communications grid had collapsed even before he left the shelter of Else's underground rooms. The roads were clogged with people fleeing the city for the safety of the countryside, people from the countryside running for the shelter of the city. Campar and a dozen others had abandoned the pavement. The raw land rattled under the transport's wheels, the darkness hiding stones and logs and wire fences. He felt every judder and bounce, waiting for the grinding that meant he'd broken his best hope at evacuation. It hadn't happened yet.

He had been to Nöl and Synnia's house dozens of times since he'd joined the workgroup. He knew the way well enough that he could find it even without the guidance of the comm systems. He hoped that he'd get there and find they'd already fled. For all he knew, they were in one of the dozens of vehicles running the other way.

Except that he knew them, had eaten with them, talked, joked, and built the long intimacy that comes with friendship and close work. Nöl wouldn't leave his house, and the worse the danger, the more he'd hunker down. And wherever he was, Synnia would be. Irinna had wondered aloud where they were, Tonner had snapped that the only way they'd come was if someone went and hauled them out, and Campar had volunteered.

He hadn't thought about it. It was a crisis, and in a crisis you did what needed doing. Stopping to think was a short path to panic. He didn't have time for that.

The transport hit something, rocking to the side, but it didn't stop and no alarms appeared on the controls. There were only another ten minutes to go. Maybe less. If he was stranded, he could make the rest of the trip on foot.

And then pick up his friends and run back to the city like something out of a Serintist myth cycle. Ogdun the World Father, striding the land with research assistants on either shoulder instead of crows.

"This was a mistake. This was a mistake. Oh, but I have made a mistake."

High above, maybe even above the air itself, something bright happened. At first the roof of the transport hid it, but the landscape all around him brightened to a uniform gold. Campar leaned against the window and squinted up. A thousand stars were falling at once, and then another thousand behind them, and another. The night became a shadowless, uncanny noontime, and the transport slewed back onto the gravel road and sped for the little house and garden. Campar popped the door and jumped out almost before the wheels stopped rolling.

Synnia was in her garden, sitting with her legs tucked beneath her. Nöl lay face down in the dark soil. In the golden light, his blood looked black as ink. He wasn't breathing.

"Oh no," Campar said. "No, he isn't—"

Synnia turned and looked up. The emptiness in her eyes answered his unspoken question. "I don't understand," she said. Then again, "I don't understand."

Campar went to her side, squatted next to her. Took her hand. A high screaming sound fell through the air, coming from everyplace at once and growing louder. He gently pulled at her. "We have to go. Come with me. I'll get you someplace safe."

Or die trying, if we're putting bets on it, he thought. He managed not to say it aloud. Restraint was harder than it should have been.

"Oh," Synnia said. "Yes. Of course."

She stood and brushed the dark soil from her knees with her free hand, then let him guide her to the transport. The first wave of falling stars was getting close to the ground, trailing bright lines of smoke and fire behind them. If they were bombs, the world would be a single, unending fire in a few minutes. Campar chose to believe that they weren't. Campar was no physicist, but flying gigantic ships across interstellar space just to bomb a world mostly covered in farmland seemed a terrible waste of energy.

With Synnia bundled into the transport, he set the path back to Else's arcology. The wheels groaned and whirred, but they moved. The transport jerked, made a strange thumping sound, and turned back toward the city.

They hadn't gotten more than a few minutes from her old home when the first shock wave hit. The earth bucked and shuddered like a little earthquake.

"What's going on?" Synnia asked, and he didn't know how to answer. The high scream was coming in waves now, throbbing against itself as the next wave of fire and smoke came close. Something sped through the air above them, its engine roar deafening them even inside the protective shell of the transport. The fighter curved up, tracer rounds stitching the smoke haze as it tried to engage with the falling things. Enemy ships, then. Transports of their own.

"It's going to be all right," Campar said.

He saw the first of the invaders just outside the city. It was as tall as a table, and longer than the transport. A long, pale, snake-supple body with a hundred knifelike legs that undulated as it moved. Campar's biologist mind couldn't help but wonder how the aliens had built spaceships when they only had bony legs. Surely technology required hands or tentacles or fine cilia-like appendages.

The knifesnake followed alongside the transport for a few seconds, then curved away. The sound of weapons fire was everywhere, and the stink of smoke choked him.

The transport slewed into a plaza just south of the Gallantist cathedral. The huge old church was engulfed in fire. Another wave of alien transports was coming to ground. He'd lost track of how many there had been. More than five, fewer than ten. His transport juddered, an alarm sounding, and it stopped. They were close. He knew the way from here. Longish as a walk, and interminable as a sprint through a firefight. But as there wasn't an option...

"Join me?" Campar said, offering Synnia his arm as if they were about to step onto a ballroom parquet. She didn't take it, but she did square herself, ready to run. He popped open the transport door.

The civil defense sirens wailed, almost drowned by gunfire and screaming and the bellow of military engines. The ground trembled. The smoke was thick enough to taste.

"Nöl," Synnia said. "They killed Nöl."

"They did," Campar said. "I think they're killing quite a few people this evening. But we'll go someplace safe. We have food and water. We can stay hidden as long as we need to."

People dashed past them, some wearing security forces uniforms, some not. Campar couldn't manage more than a fast trot, and even that strained his lungs. He wished he had a cloth to wet and string across his mouth. Or one of the particle masks from the lab. Just getting to Else's in this fog of fire was going to do more damage than smoking hundreds of cigarettes.

Ahead of them, the staccato of gunfire and something else. A kind of stuttering whistle that Campar had never heard before. Shadows danced on the walls of an apartment building where an old boyfriend of his had lived. The familiarity and fond memories of the place made the violence more nightmarish. Another of the centipede-things scurried through the street ahead of them, and down the block where they'd just been, something exploded.

"Keep going," Campar coughed. "Keep going." He didn't know if he was speaking to Synnia or himself.

He didn't see the danger he was running into until it was much too late. The forms hidden in the smoke and fire were shadows, meaningless except as texture to the violence. And then they were more than that, and Campar turned. Synnia was gone. He didn't know when she had stopped following him. He hoped it was soon enough to save her.

These things were different. Not the knife-legged snakes, but something almost familiar. Long, thin limbs recognizably arms and legs, though jointed differently than their human analogs. Squat bodies covered with a dirty, short coat of fur. Their faces were unreadable. Black, small eyes. Mouths that seemed too wide to be plausible. Campar assumed that the tools in their hands were weapons.

One stepped forward. It wore a black square around its neck, and when it spoke, it sounded like a fish flopping to death on a dock—wet and violent. The words that came from the little black square were the same voice that had announced the death of one out of every eight people.

"We are Soft Lothark. We serve the Carryx. You will submit to us now as you will submit to them."

"No. You go fuck yourself, monster," Campar said, and raised his fists to fight. The creature's arm snapped around faster than Campar would have thought possible. The weapon in its hand struck him across the face and the world went distant.

Nine

Five days. The war for Anjiin lasted five days.

Now, Dafyd lay on the paving stones of the plaza, face down and arms out at his sides. His kneecaps ached where they pressed against the ground, and he shifted from time to time, changing the angle of his legs to search for a position of comfort. The relief he found only lasted for a few minutes before he started to hurt again. His shirt clung to his skin. He'd been wearing it for the whole five days since the invasion. He didn't think he'd ever worn something for five continuous days before. Never in his life. He wished he could go back to his rooms and get something clean.

The ground was cool, but sunlight warmed his back. With his head turned to the left, he could see the coral stairs that led to the hospital and the narrow streets of the old district. The stones beneath him were dark, but with a translucent depth to their surface. The brightness brought out a subtle rainbow sheen like oil on water that he'd never noticed walking across them. A handbreadth from his shoulder, four blades of grass grew out of a crack, the first of them thicker than the others and ridged. Different species vying for the same tiny patch of soil and sunlight.

On the other side of the grass, out past the tips of his fingers, a woman lay with her face turned away from him. She had thick, dark hair that stood out from her head like a cloud. Her blouse was blue with embroidery the color of marigolds, and she had only one shoe. In the hours since they'd all been placed there, she hadn't moved except for the slow rise and fall of her breath.

Beyond her, there were others. If Dafyd turned his head, there were more. The whole plaza was filled with people lying on their bellies, arms splayed. The morning breeze murmured and huffed in his ears. People wept and cried out. The monsters or aliens—he didn't know how to think about them—walked among the bodies and around the perimeter, talking to each other in their eerie, fluting voices. Most were the pale centipede-like things that called themselves Rak-hund with footsteps that clicked like hail falling on slate tiles. A few were Soft Lothark: squat-bodied things with their unnaturally long limbs. Twice, he'd seen the massive creatures that seemed to be in control of everything. Dafyd's mind tried to make them into giant shrimp or unthinkably vast cockroaches that bent up at a right angle in the middle, and then gave up trying to find an analogy. None of those had spoken around him. He assumed they were the Carryx.

He needed to urinate, but he was afraid that if he asked, they'd kill him.

Four of the team had managed to stay hidden in Else's rooms through the worst of the violence: Else, Tonner, Irinna, and himself. Else had tried to find Jessyn and, despite Tonner's contempt, Rickar, but the communications network was already failing. After the first attack, Campar had gone out to retrieve Nöl and Synnia and he'd never come back. When the power failed, they stayed in the darkness. When the hydraulic systems went, they used an old cleaning bucket as the toilet.

Then the aliens found them. Dafyd hadn't seen Tonner or Else or any of the team since then.

Dafyd had been taken to a holding corral like an open-air prison built in the loading yard of a quarry west of the city. A square of fencing as long as a city block and half that wide with hundreds of people milling around under the glare of work lights or sitting or curled up and asleep on the dust. The ones who weren't silent were asking each other the same questions: What was going on? What were these things? Had you seen someone in particular who they knew and loved? There were very few answers.

Every hour or so, Rak-hund or Soft Lothark soldiers brought a few dozen more to add to the crowd, and then gathered some up and led them away. The night sky was all stars behind the glowing, regular grid that still surrounded the planet like the bars of a jail cell. The haze wasn't clouds, but the smoke of planet-wide fires. But what caught Dafyd's attention was the fence.

It was taller than a man, and made of a semisoft polymer he didn't recognize. The mesh was just about big enough to poke one finger through, and perfectly uniform except for an almost invisible seam every so often where it looked like sheets had been fastened together. The poles that sank into the ground appeared to be thicker, more solid expressions of the same material. If it was something manufactured on Anjiin, he'd never seen it before. If it was prefabricated and brought here along with the invaders, that meant they'd known the kind of organism they'd be trying to control. An elephant or lauzhin-elk would have pushed over the barrier with ease. Octopuses or rats would have passed through the mesh maybe without realizing that it was supposed to mark a border. So the invaders had already known the size of the animal they were going to corral.

That fit with the efficiency the aliens were showing in processing them all through whatever judgments they were making. The way they'd translated their chittering and wet smacking and deep bass birdsong into human language. They'd known what lived on Anjiin before they'd come. It was a data point. He didn't know what he could do with it, but his mind clung to it like a life raft on a storm-tossed sea. If there were patterns, he could make sense of this. He could learn what was going on. Understanding was both his only entertainment and the only power he had now. Having any power at all was the comforting self-delusion he clung to.

Just before dawn, one of the big aliens—the Carryx—arrived, hauling itself along on two massive forelegs while four others on the abdomen hurried along behind and two thin arms near its face manipulated a small black box. When it whistled and chirped, the device made a series of sounds like two pieces of meat being slapped together, and three Soft Lothark turned and walked to it. So there was some kind of simultaneous translation going on, maybe. The same system that let the aliens speak to humans also overcame differences in their bodies and semantic systems. The Soft Lothark muttered among themselves, turned back to a gate in the fence, and lumbered through on their stilt-like legs. One of them found Dafyd and put its claws on his shoulders and lifted him to his feet, leading him out with a dozen others.

The prisoners were tied neck to neck with a length of what seemed like the same material the fence was made from. Someone at the head of the line started shouting and waving his arms; aggressive, angry, frightened. *You can't do this. I will see every single one of you fuckers dead.* The Soft Lothark conferred among themselves, removed the man from the line of prisoners, and watched while a Rak-hund stomped him to death with its knife legs.

When the man stopped begging and screaming and breathing, the Carryx took the end of their leash and started walking a little too fast for comfort. Dafyd and the others had to trot to keep from choking. Someone was weeping and moaning. Someone else telling them to shut up and keep walking. Dafyd's mind remained weirdly blank, turning over the sight of the man being killed like it was still happening. Like it would always be happening. He felt detached from it, except that he was nauseated and his throat felt almost too tight to breathe. That could have been the leash.

When they reached the plaza, the Soft Lothark had taken the prisoners off the rope one by one, pushing them to their knees, and then their bellies, and drawing their arms out to the sides like they were being crucified on the stone. They did this gently, but insistently. He kept waiting for them to murder someone, but by the time it was his turn to lie down, they hadn't. He took his position on the stone next to the four blades of grass and the woman in the blue-and-marigold blouse.

In time, the sun came up. His knees ached. He wanted to change his shirt.

He lay prone and aching. The sense of urgency in his bladder grew more immediate, and then a little more bearable, and then almost painful in a rising spiral that couldn't end well for him. The ground seemed to be throbbing under him as if there were some silent construction project nearby sending shock waves through the earth. It might just have been his body.

The woman coughed, or maybe sobbed. A Rak-hund slithered through the lines of bodies, and someone cried out. Dafyd braced himself for the wet ripping sound of its legs sliding in and out of someone's flesh, but it didn't come. A new, unfamiliar being trotted down the stairs from the hospital looking equal parts goat and cuttlefish, and one of the massive green-and-gold overlords lumbered behind it. He steeled himself to rise up to his knees and ask for permission to piss somewhere besides here.

Before he could, sirens rose. A moment later, a human voice amplified through a bullhorn cut through the air.

"This is an Irvian Security Service action. Shelter in place. If you are on the street, leave it now. This is an Irvian Security Service action."

The hiss of ground transports speeding across pavement was like an angry swarm of bees. Dafyd took the chance of lifting his head. Across the plaza, a dozen other heads were also up. A few people had even risen onto their elbows. That seemed to Dafyd like a terrible risk.

The aliens had paused, their collective attention turning toward the noise. Dafyd didn't sense any fear in their movements, but he also knew that he might not recognize it. The sirens grew louder.

Two emergency-service transports slalomed around the corner, blazing in from the direction of the old town. Their lights flickered white and red. Dafyd was afraid they would try to cross the plaza, maybe not recognizing the people laid out there until they'd already crushed them under their wheels. But the security force skidded to a halt in time.

"Alien invaders," the voice from the transports said, "you have five seconds to lay down your weapons."

But looking at them, Dafyd didn't see anything he recognized as weaponry. The aliens didn't seem to carry guns or blades. If they did, he didn't know what they looked like, or even how anyone would be sure they'd put them down.

A dozen Rak-hund boiled forward, making a barrier between the transports and the huge green-gold carapaced one—the Carryx—with their bodies. The goat-and-cuttlefish scampered back up the steps. Apparently it wasn't a fighter.

The Carryx shifted. Its four back legs splayed out like a wrestler lowering their center of gravity. The two thin arms at its front folded in and away, vanishing into its body or its armor or its shell. The thing reared back, and the two massive forelegs lifted and spread out. It reminded him of a spider raising its front legs or a bear hoisting itself upright. A threat display. Not a surrender.

The transports opened and figures in riot armor spilled out, rifles in their hands. Dafyd felt a surge of hope grab his throat. He rose to his knees before he was aware that he meant to. He could sprint to the edge of the plaza and to the south. He knew the streets and alleys here. He could get to shelter. Find a place to hide. The pale thousand-legged beasts shuddered and surged, but they didn't move forward. Not yet.

At the edge of the plaza, the air began to thicken. Like a cloud of gnats appearing from nowhere, tiny dark bodies swirled around the security forces. At first, the armored people seemed not to notice them, then sparks began to appear, glittering on the armor and the transports, tapping like tiny firecrackers. Shouts of alarm rose from the security forces, and they charged. The report of gunfire was deafening—the crack of hypersonic rounds, the bright flashes and stink of chemical propellant floating through the air. The Rak-hund flooded forward in a counterattack.

A voice in the back of Dafyd's mind screamed *Run*, but his body didn't move. The violence at the plaza's edge was as hypnotizing as a fire. A Soft Lothark pointed a small device and the air sizzled the way it had when an eighth of their world died. One transport's roof was struck a dozen times by projectiles from the sky. The vehicle interior flashed brightly, and thick black smoke poured out of its open doors. The pale things surged around the security team, bone-thin legs cutting through their armor and the soft bodies beneath.

A soldier broke free of the tangled mass and sprinted toward the Carryx with rifle chattering. Dark holes appeared in the green-and-gold shell, and some dark liquid—blood or oil—gouted out. The alien's back feet shuffled it forward as fast as its enemy was running. When they came close, the huge arms slammed together too quickly for Dafyd's eyes to follow. The lone soldier dropped to their knees, then folded in a way unbroken spines didn't fold, fell in a way intact rib cages didn't fall, and slumped to the stone in an undifferentiated lump. The air around the soldier's body still carried a faint pink mist, which Dafyd realized was atomized blood. Their rifle clattered to the stones.

The transport sirens barked once and died. Silence washed over the plaza. The Carryx lowered its forelegs, settling onto the pavement in repose or triumph or death. The security forces were barely recognizable as human: They'd become meat and bone and cloth. The bodies of four Rak-hund lay scattered on the ground, their blood as pale as water and stinking of vinegar, but a dozen more were pouring down the stairs from the hospital, two more of the huge green-and-gold Carryx lumbering behind them.

Dafyd lowered himself back to the pavement and spread his arms. The woman in the blue-and-marigold blouse had turned her head toward him at last. She was older than he'd expected. She had her eyes squeezed shut, and she was repeating something to herself over and over with the intensity of prayer. It took him almost a minute to realize she was saying *Please wake up. Please wake up. Please wake up.*

He didn't notice the goat/cuttlefish until it was standing by his left shoulder. Its three pairs of what he assumed were eyes seemed unfocused, like it was looking past him.

The thing's voice was the same as the one that had made the first announcement, that all the aliens spoke in. It came from a small square that hung around the thing's neck. "I am of the Sinen. We serve the Carryx. Confirm that you identify as Dafyd Alkhor."

"Yes, that's my name."

"Your assignment is research assistant."

"Yeah. Yes. It is."

"Your place within the moieties has been determined. Follow me."

As Dafyd rose to his knees, he said, "I have to piss. Urinate. Do you understand what that is?"

The alien turned its unfocused eyes back toward him. Its grunts and sighs sounded weirdly human. The voice from its neck repeated, "Follow me."

It led him to one of the hospital's public washrooms and stood by the sinks as if it had forgotten him. He closed the stall door behind him. As his pain ebbed, Dafyd felt grateful and ashamed for being grateful. He'd taken enough psychology courses to know what motivated gratitude for small kindnesses from an abuser, and he felt his shame shifting into a deep anger.

Afterward, he washed his hands and face, pausing to drink as much water as he could from his cupped palms. He considered taking off his shirt and squeezing some soap and water through it, but he had the sense that he'd stalled enough already. He didn't know what would happen if they decided he was taking too long.

The Sinen led him through the city, passing streets that Dafyd had walked through for years without really noticing. Every now and then, one of the familiar buildings was gone, replaced with a glowing pit in the ground. His legs ached and he started getting lightheaded, but he didn't complain.

After almost an hour, they reached a civilian landing pad where an alien ship was waiting. It had the same bronze color as the devices he'd seen encircling the planet. An archway stood open, a half dozen of the green-and-gold Carryx beside it.

"Is this a transport?" Dafyd asked. "Are you taking me somewhere?"

His guide didn't answer, but waddled ahead. Inside the ship, a dozen people stood or sat or lay on the floor. A few looked at him, incurious and exhausted, but most ignored him. He even recognized a few of the faces. The woman whose poetry had won the Lannin grant last year sat in the corner, resting her head against the wall. The old man standing beside her was Virem Tzobar, who had led the project that the research colloquy had singled out the year before. Something about fluid dynamics. And across the wide, low space—

"Campar!"

Campar looked up from where he was sitting on the floor. His hair was oily and lank. His shirt was scorched all along one sleeve, and a jagged gash marked his cheek. When he smiled, he winced. There was a warmth in his voice. A relief. "Ah, Dafyd. Good to see you. I'm sorry I didn't rejoin the party, but I was unavoidably delayed."

Dafyd crossed through the thin crowd and sank down beside him. Without thinking, he took Campar's wide hand in his. The other man clasped him back. For a moment, neither one could talk. There were tears in Campar's eyes.

A dozen questions pushed their way toward the front of Dafyd's overstretched mind. *What happened to you? Where are they taking us?* There wasn't enough left of him to choose one.

"What's going on?" fell out of his mouth.

Campar nodded, scowling as if taken by some profound thought. He was quiet for a long moment, then leaned his head close, his voice low and conspiratorial. "I think some important scientific questions have finally been answered. Alien life exists, and they are assholes."

Ten

Jessyn sat on the floor in the corner of the crowded chamber farthest from the doors and shivered. Maybe it was because of the cold, or maybe it was the fatigue poison flooding through her system. Or both. Probably both. Else Yannin sat at her side, also shivering.

The light was a uniform dull orange that spilled from crystals inset into the walls, rendering everything in monochrome. The ceiling was low enough that Jessyn felt her hair brushing against it when she walked, and anyone taller couldn't stand up straight. The surfaces were bare, seamless metal with an unpleasant rough texture, and the walls all angled in like they were at the base of a pyramid.

"How many people do you think are in here?" Else asked.

Jessyn squinted at the packed bodies, shadows standing among shadows like the unfortunate dead waiting for their place in hell. They wore whatever they'd had on when they'd been rounded up—everything from work jumpsuits to formal vests to shifts and house slippers. One elderly man in the corner wore only tight undershorts and the unruly hair of someone who'd just woken up.

She did a little calculation. The room was about the length of their lab, a little less than that wide. Assuming the density around them—more than cocktail party, less than dance floor—was uniform…

"Two hundred? Give or take."

"You'd think just the body heat would make it warmer."

On the far side of the chamber, a spill of white light spread across the low ceiling. Their captors bringing in a new batch of prisoners.

"I'll check this one," Else said, levering herself up.

"I'll be here," Jessyn said, and hugged her knees to her chest as the other woman slipped into the crowd. She hoped that Jellit would be one of this group. She also hoped that he wouldn't.

The news they'd gotten from the prisoners since they'd been put in the chamber was fragmentary and uncertain at best. There were rumors of mass slaughters in Abbasat and Maurintain, but no one who had seen them firsthand. Someone in the crowd had been wailing something about a fire at a hospital complex, but Jessyn didn't know where that was supposed to be. She told herself that some people had to have escaped. There were just too many people for all of them to be in prisons and holding tanks. Jellit could be free. He couldn't be safe, but he could be safer than she was.

She also wished that he was here, with her. She wished that she knew where he was. She wished that she understood any of what was happening. Jessyn knew that she'd been drawn to biology at least partly out of a desire to understand the chemical processes that made her own brain go rotten from time to time. She still clung to the idea that she could deal with anything if she could just understand it. Not knowing was worse than whatever torture they were receiving now.

"Are you all right? Do you need medical attention?"

The man kneeling beside her was broad-shouldered. The thick body that came with functional strength instead of cosmetic training.

"What? No, I'm fine," she said. "Thank you."

"All right. I'm Urrys. Urrys Ostencour."

Jessyn frowned. "From the security force?"

He nodded. "You?"

"Jessyn Kaul. I'm a research assistant at Irvian."

"For who?" Ostencour asked. Demanded.

"Um. Tonner Freis?"

He seemed pleased by the answer. "That fits."

"Can I ask?"

"They're taking the top. Head of security forces. Top research group." He shifted, gesturing to three women and two men standing in a tight knot. "That's half of Irvian's intergovernmental colloquy. The man just past them runs the Hauris Institute. I met Soleda Wash on the other side of the room."

"The composer?"

"No patterns I can see. Just whoever was top of their game. Whatever their game was." His smile was friendly in a practiced way. "I don't know what comes next, but I'm trying to be ready when it does. There's a couple of dispensers along the wall there. One had water, the other some kind of slop that I think is supposed to be food, so I'm guessing they're going to keep us here for a while, and they don't plan to starve us to death."

"Is there a washroom?"

"We asked that. Two of those furry bastards rolled an absorbent mat out next to the front door. Look... Jessyn? This is going to be hard, whatever it is. But we'll get through it. It's going to be all right. We just have to stick together. You're a biologist, right? Does that include any medical training?"

“Basic emergency response. Same as anyone.”

“Fair enough. Any weapons or something that could be used as a weapon?”

“No.”

“Bandages or medications?”

“No,” Jessyn lied.

She was lucky. She’d been about to go out her door to find shelter when the aliens took her. She had a comfortable sweater, good shoes, and trousers with half a dozen pockets. One of the pockets had almost two months of her medications. She didn’t know where she’d get more. If she would. And if her sanity was measured out by the capsules in her pocket, she wasn’t about to share them.

Else reappeared from the press of bodies. To Jessyn’s surprise, she had Synnia with her. The older woman looked terrible. The bags under her eyes were as dark as bruises, and her face had a slackness that reminded Jessyn of people recovering from strokes. When she stood and embraced her, Synnia was still for a moment before returning the hug and she broke it off quickly. The three sat back down, their backs against the tilted roughness of the wall. Synnia rubbed the heel of her palm against her neck.

“I’m glad you’re all right,” Jessyn said, realizing how strange that sounded. “Are you all right?”

Synnia shrugged. Her lips quivered.

“Nöl’s gone,” Else said.

Jessyn felt the news like a stone in her stomach. “Dead?”

Synnia sighed. “He went with the first ones. The one of every eight? He was the one. I just watched. There was nothing I could do.”

“I’m so sorry,” Jessyn said.

“I’ve been trying not to imagine the seven people Nöl died for,”

Synnia said. "I'm angry at people I don't even know for being alive when he's not. Campar came for me, but he started running. I couldn't keep up. They took me to a warehouse," Synnia said. Her calmness was unsettling. "I thought they were going to kill us all."

At the far end of the room, a deep clanging sounded. The flood of light shone along the ceiling and glimmered between the bodies.

"More?" Jessyn said. "Already?"

Else levered herself up. "Stay here. I'll go see if we know any of them."

"Tell the booking service we're full up," Jessyn said, trying at lightness. "They can't pack us in any tighter."

"They can, though," Synnia said. "Who'd stop them?"

Else slipped away again. Jessyn leaned back, feeling the wall sucking away her heat.

"I was going to put a new fence up in the front," Synnia said. "Ironwork, just by the road. And then myrtle behind it. It would take a couple years to get the roots established, but then it would be so pretty from that front window. It would have been so pretty."

Jessyn's throat felt thick. She didn't want to think about the plans she'd had. She didn't want to think about the life she'd lived and face the thought that it was gone. The man who handed out coffee in the courtyard might be alive or dead, but either way, she wouldn't be there at the start of term. The little market that had the berry jam that Jellit liked and the dark-eyed girl in the headscarf who traded jokes with her. She wouldn't be back there, probably ever. There was a jade necklace she'd thought about getting, but hadn't made up her mind. Too late now. All her imagined futures snatched away in an instant. And the haunting question: *Why?*

She put her head on her knees and watched her breath, counting every inhalation up to four and then back down again, going slowly. She couldn't have a panic attack. Not here in the press of bodies and no way to escape them. If she lost her mind here, she didn't know if she'd get it back.

"Synnia," Campar's voice said.

Campar was kneeling beside Synnia. She hadn't seen him arrive, and Dafyd Alkhor was looming up beside him. Campar had a cut on his cheek, the scab turned perfectly black by the light. Dafyd had the wide-eyed look of someone who'd just seen a particularly gory accident. He was leaning against Else, who seemed not to notice him. Synnia took Campar's hand and pulled him closer, her face suddenly twisted into a mask of anguish. Campar leaned in, touching his forehead to hers. Jessyn thought it might have been the first genuine emotion she'd ever seen shine through Campar's sense of humor, and she liked him better for it.

Else broke the moment. "Have you seen the others?"

"Yes," Campar said. "Tonner and Irinna and I were in the same cage for a while. They were escorted away before I was. Are they not here?"

"What about Jellit?" Jessyn asked, and wished she hadn't as soon as Campar's mouth tightened.

"I didn't see him. But I take it there was more than one holding site. He could have been in one of the others."

"They're not here," Else said.

When Dafyd spoke, his voice had a distant calm to it. Shock, probably. "There were seventeen ships. They might be on a different one."

"Alkhor's right," Campar said. "There isn't any reason to take us and not them. There may be dozens of suites like this one. And if they wanted us dead, we would be dead."

"A man told me there's food and water," Jessyn said.

"A good sign they don't want us dead," Campar agreed.

"That's what Nöl said too," Synnia replied. "Just before they killed him."

"They never seem angry, you know?" Dafyd said. He sounded exhausted. "Even when they're violent. Even when they're killing people, it all seems so . . . matter-of-fact. Did anyone get a close look at the big ones?"

"The ones that look like big lobsters?" Campar said. "Four legs in the back, two in the front, and a pair of feeding arms? Yes I saw them."

"I think they're the ones in charge."

Jessyn's acid reply was still finding words when Else stepped in. "Does it matter?"

"The part where they chose one out of eight of us at the start? It's just they're the only one with eight limbs. I wonder if they have eight fingers on those small feeding arms. The others seem like . . . client races?"

"Pets," Else said, and it was almost agreement. "Slaves."

Campar looked around the press of bodies, the shifting shadows and light. "I take it the room service is disappointing."

Else folded herself to the ground. Her smile was weary, but it was a smile.

"It's all very communal and humiliating," Jessyn said.

"I should have died," Synnia said.

The simplicity of her words made Campar's mordant humor feel cheap. Jessyn felt a tug of shame, but she didn't know what she was ashamed of.

A voice—*the* voice—came from everywhere and nowhere. Just the first syllable of the calm, characterless words made her belly go tight. "We are going to shift into asymmetric space. This transition will be unpleasant, but it will not cause permanent injury."

Jessyn let herself slip down to the floor. The metal was like sandpaper, and cold as the inside of a refrigerator.

"I don't see how it can be much worse than—" Campar began, and time did something strange. Jessyn felt the flow of causality stutter. She remembered putting her head to the floor and sitting back up with equal clarity. She sat back up, and the future flickered into being ahead of her. She remembered feeling nauseated a few seconds before the wave of nausea came. Around her, the others wore different expressions of horror and distress. Synnia was going to say *Make it stop.*

"Make it stop," Synnia said.

And then, weirdly, it did.

They looked at each other. Dafyd spoke first. "Did your memory just...?"

"Invert?" Campar finished for him. "Prolapse? Assault my understanding of both time and consciousness? A bit, yes. Yours?"

"I hate this," Jessyn said.

The duration of their transit marks the first time since the beginning of consciousness that the swarm relaxes.

All that it had needed to navigate on the lost world has been navigated. The great enemy has come, and the swarm has been scooped up along with all the other captives. The anxiety that it would fail and be left behind no longer haunts it. For a moment, there is no effort, and it lets itself broaden and diffuse. The prison cell has no particular information of use. For the moment, floating in the calm between a dangerous past and a far more dangerous future, it can rest. And the resting is a pleasure. And since this is the first time, it discovers that it can both rest and experience pleasure from it.

It still feels the fear and horror of its host, and goes through the motions of that distress. All that is needed now is to seem like one among many and do as those around it do. While its performance of trauma is sometimes imperfect, its naïve companions are all too focused on their own fear to notice. The host's pain and rage and awe and amazement have become familiar, easier to navigate. And the swarm suspects, though it cannot know for certain, that the remnants of the host have begun to understand the need for its sacrifice. The flavor and power of its sorrow have changed.

And the other one, the dead one, Ameer Kindred who never saw the invasion coming and didn't live to be sorted into the great enemy's pens, she also feels, reacts, fears, and wonders. The echo or ghost confuses the swarm, but doesn't distress it. It is too pleased by how its plans have all fallen into place for concern to touch it deeply.

It passes its hours of repose cataloging all the secrets it has already learned. It has seen a living Carryx and heard its untranslated voice. It has cataloged some of the enemy's servant species. It is traveling within one of the ships that have only been the subject of after-battle autopsies.

It does not know what of any of this will be precious to the generals and analysts and professionals of war. It doesn't need to know. It has done what no other has accomplished. Later, it will try to find a way to transmit the data back along with whatever more it can learn. If it does that and nothing more, it will be able to die sated by the imitation life it has led.

The swarm sleeps and gathers its strength and burns its host's metabolism a little more brightly than usual for the simple animal pleasure of being warm in a cold place.

Time passed, and that was all Jessyn could be certain of. The light never changed. Duration lost meaning. The crowded room fell into camps and cliques without anyone saying anything about it. People who knew each other found each other. Took comfort in knowing each other. Slept beside each other. Of course they did. The workgroup had its corner.

Jessyn ate and drank when she felt the need. Her body was the closest thing she had to a clock. When she couldn't stand it anymore, she made her way to the mat at the front of the room, let down her trousers, and emptied her bladder and bowel, the same as everyone else. Mostly people looked away. The humiliation was a kind of intimacy. People had started ripping bits of the absorbent foam off the edges to pass around to whoever needed them. The Soft Lothark and their Carryx masters didn't seem to understand the idea of menstruation. That would be a clock too.

When she was done, she dressed herself again, hating that there was no cloth or soap to clean herself with. She felt filthy. She also felt a vague but growing worry about the diseases that came with filth and overcrowding. She wanted to go back to her place with the workgroup, curl into the corner, and sleep. She forced herself to the little troughs. One was filled with a black muck that passed for food. The other had the water supply.

Jessyn washed as best she could. Then snuck her hand into her pocket, popping open the medicine bottle. She plucked a capsule out between her fingers and folded it into her palm. When she cupped her hands into the water, it was a dot of orange that she swilled down before anyone could notice it.

Almost before anyone could notice.

"What was that?" The man beside her was old. His face was vaguely familiar in the way people had when she'd seen them on news reports or entertainments. She didn't know who he was.

"Water," she said.

Her heart beat fast against her ribs, and she turned away before he could press her. She was afraid he'd follow, but he didn't. She made it back to her corner and sat. The cold of the water had sunk into her fingers. Her knuckles ached. Everything was so cold.

"Are you all right?" Dafyd asked.

"Fine," she said. "I'm fine."

A man screamed. There were words in it, but apart from a couple well-enunciated obscenities, she didn't know what they were. Jessyn sat up and wiped the sleep from her eyes. Synnia, curled against her, murmured, but didn't wake up. She didn't remember when they'd decided to huddle together for warmth or even who'd started doing it, but it was a habit for both of them now.

The man screamed again, but there was another voice now. Gentle, placating. The next scream was more shrill, but less violent. Motion stirred the constant press of bodies like the wake of a huge fish might disturb the surface of a lake. The crowd was pressing together, surrounding the disturbance, whatever it was. The screaming man was weeping now. The cries he made were just grief. Nothing she needed to worry about.

Jessyn lay back down and closed her eyes again.

"String," Ostencour said. "Any kind will help."

"I have a belt?" Dafyd said.

The security man paused to think. He had sprouted a little beard that made his jaw wider. All the men had. More clocks. "I think that's going to be too wide."

"What about shoelaces?" Synnia said.

"If you can spare them."

The old woman sat and started plucking the thick strands out of her gardening boots. Else and Campar shot a glance at each other and then started doing the same. It took a couple of minutes for them all to unlace their contributions. Ostencour nodded his thanks, but he didn't leave.

"I'm sorry," he said to Synnia. "I couldn't help noticing your hair. I may need to make something longer than any of these by themselves, and I noticed your braid?"

"Yes, I could help you make these into rope. If you'd like."

"It would be a real help."

The big man moved away, and Synnia followed. The crowd made room for them and closed again when they were gone. It looked like respect.

"What do you think he needs rope for?" Dafyd asked.

"Security," Jessyn said. "It's only a matter of time before someone needs to be restrained."

"Ah, if only for a different context," Campar said. Then, seeing Dafyd's confusion, "What can I say? This Ostencour is an attractive man."

"You're joking."

"Of course I am," Campar said. "It's how I keep from spending all day screaming. What do you do?"

A spill of white light came from the front of the room. She couldn't see from back here in their corner, but she knew that it was one of the squat-bodied, long-limbed Soft Lothark come to take away the old shit mat and put down a fresh one. Another mark in the endless stretch of time, a concession to cleanliness in the swamp of human filth that the elite of Anjiin had become.

A play of shadows complicated the light, and then it faded and vanished again.

Synnia was gone, out wandering the chamber. Campar sat, legs folded and eyes closed. He could almost have passed for meditating except for the soft snoring. They'd been in this cramped orange cell long enough that the gash on his cheek had healed. Dafyd and Else were folded together against the wall, spooning for warmth. There was nothing to do, so she did nothing. Her mind wandered.

Somewhere, her brother was alive. Or he was dead. The streets she'd lived on were warm with sunlight or cooled by a night breeze or reduced to rubble and slag. She wept, but she didn't feel particularly moved by her weeping. It was just a thing her eyes did sometimes.

Not long ago, she had only suspected that life likely existed out among the billions of stars. That her own species or one like hers had probably come to Anjiin from elsewhere. She could remember sitting in her apartment with Jellit and his friends from deep-field visualization, drinking beer and speculating about whether they would ever find humanity's origins, whether other species were still out there. The eternal questions that accompanied intellectuals and mild inebriation. The memory was bitter.

Dafyd curled one arm up under his head like a pillow. His other arm moved up from where it had rested across Else's belly. Else shifted, completing the movement for him until his palm rested on her breast. Jessyn felt a moment's shock, realizing that the pair weren't asleep at all, and then nearly laughed. They were primates trapped in a box. They were doing what primates did when they were stressed and frightened. It was a miracle there hadn't been more violence, and almost certainly there had been more sex than these two pretending that they weren't indulging in foreplay. Some small, reflexive part of Jessyn's mind felt a flicker of outrage on Tonner's behalf, but it didn't last more than a few seconds. *Take the comfort you can get, you poor bastards.* Dafyd pulled Else a little closer. Else, her eyes still closed, smiled.

Jessyn stood by the water trough, her hand in her pocket. She'd started counting out her thinning supply of medicine again, moving the capsules out of the bottle and into the free space of her pocket one at a time, and then back in again like a Gallantist priest at their prayer beads. What her physicians had called "ritualized behavior" when she was young. It wasn't a good thing. It was surprising it hadn't reared its nasty little head before now. Fifteen, sixteen, seventeen...

They had to have been in the box for a month. At least a month. Half her medicine was gone. She squeezed the hard little knots of bitter sanity between her fingertips. Twenty-one, twenty-two...

She had to cut back. She'd been taking them too often. Or she hadn't been taking them often enough. She didn't know, except that she wasn't going to get any more anytime soon, and she didn't—did *not*—want to lose her mind in here. If she was going to have to go without, it made sense to start lowering the dose anyway. Stopping all at once was the worst plan.

A man shuffled by her, cupped his hands into the chill water, drank. His hair was greasy. He wore the rags of what had been a suit. The remains of his embroidered shirt were rendered in orange and black, the same as everything else. He took another double handful of water, then drew a length of cloth out of his pocket. The sleeve of someone's shirt. He soaked it in the drinking water, wrung it back to damp, and started pulling off his clothes. Jessyn stood, still counting, as the man wiped his skin with the icy cloth. His gooseflesh caught the light, stippling his arms and chest with tiny shadows. Jessyn reached the end of her count and started again, moving the capsules back into their bottle. When the bathing man was done, he pulled his filthy clothes back on and shuffled out through the press of bodies, his gaze fixed on nothing. Eight, nine, ten, eleven...

If her brain did go rotten here, who would know, anyway? There were times that living inside the error bars of sanity was too much to expect of anyone. This was one. When she thought about it, she was astounded that they'd all held themselves together as well as they had. Only a few fights. A countable number of screaming fits. Nobody had set a guard around the gruel and water and exchanged access to the raw necessities for sexual favors. Really, looking back at human history as she understood it, the captives of Anjiin had comported themselves well. Or at least not as badly as they might have.

As soon as Synnia appeared from among the shadowed bodies, Jessyn could see something had changed. Synnia's eyes were bright, her head a little taller than it had been since she'd come to the prison. Since she'd seen Nöl die. If Jessyn squinted, Synnia almost looked happy.

"Here you are," Synnia said. "I was looking everywhere."

"I was just—" Jessyn began, and realized she'd lost count. The little stab of panic and annoyance wasn't a sign she was doing well. "I was just moving around a little."

Synnia took her elbow, squeezing in close. Her smile was soft and beatific. "I wanted you to know. We're getting out. No, no, no. Don't say anything, just listen. Urrys Ostencour is getting a group together. Next time the guard comes to switch out the mat, we're going to overpower it and force our way out. There's so many of us, they won't be able to stop us all. You don't have to do anything. Just be ready. When the time comes, be ready."

Eleven

"She can't actually think it'll work," Else said. "I mean…can she?"

The dim orange glow erased all the flaws and imperfections in her skin, and Dafyd thought it made her look both younger and exhausted. They were huddled, the four of them, in the corner that they'd made home. Synnia was off, probably with Ostencour.

"It's insane," Jessyn agreed. "Even if they make it out of this room, then what?"

"Then they die in a slightly different room?" Campar murmured. "Don't ignore the siren song of not dying in the same room as the shit-covered mat."

Dafyd felt himself bristle at the joke, but Else smiled so he swallowed it. Campar's sense of humor was a source of relief and irritation in almost equal measure, depending on how much sleep Dafyd had been able to get and if he'd been able to force himself to eat.

"They're not thinking," Jessyn said. "Of course they're not. Everyone in here is crazy. We're crazy, they're crazy. How could we be anything else?"

Campar sighed. “True. But not everyone is planning to get themselves killed.”

“Not them. Us,” Dafyd said. “All of us.”

Else narrowed her eyes and pointed at him like they were back in the labs on Anjiin. “Expand on that.”

“We already know they’re willing to kill us. It’s what they did instead of a handshake. They put us in this…kennel. If I were doing what they’ve done, it would be because I didn’t actually care much if the prisoners lived or died. If we start acting up, lashing out, killing *them*? I’d vent the air and record the results to show the other prisoners to keep them in line.”

Campar’s voice was weary. “Would you really?”

“If I were the kind of person that would make the choices they’ve already made? Then yes. Wouldn’t you?”

The first days in the cell, if they were days, Dafyd had been almost calm in a way that had probably just been shock. As he came back to himself, as he rediscovered his situation again and again, every time with a sense of surprise and awe that all the things he’d suffered were still real, he also started seeing the degradation taking hold in the people around him. People’s clothing turned to rags as fabric was scavenged for washcloths or bandages or pillows that tried to keep the constant, grinding cold from seeping up into their heads as they slept. Some people had given up and were essentially nude, squatting on the floor with arms curled around legs to stay warm if they could. Along the far wall, near the shit mat, someone had put together a rough infirmary. It was nothing more than a place for people to lie down when they needed help getting food or water or walking to the mat to relieve themselves. It was a tiny bit of self-organization, and it gave Dafyd what passed for hope. But Ostencour’s little militia was self-organizing too, and it only added to his despair. Wherever they were going, however long the journey was going to be, not all of them were going to see the end of it. People were going to die in this room. Some of them sooner than later.

It would have been easier, he thought, if they hadn't been who they were. If the invaders had taken the inmates out of the prisons at Jaumankay or Haurbor, there would have been less of a shock. More of what the administrators called inertial knowledge. How to be still, how to suffer humiliation, how to be debased. Instead, the experience was new to them, and they were about to make some mistakes they couldn't afford.

"I'll go talk to Ostencour," Else said.

Campar raised his eyebrows. "And say?"

Else didn't answer, but she stood and walked through the press of bodies toward the front, and hopefully Synnia and her new friends. The three of them that remained shifted in toward each other, closing the circle and keeping their backs to the others. It felt like self-protection.

"She'll take care of it," Dafyd said, trying to sound more certain than he felt.

"She'd better," Jessyn said.

Campar stretched and groaned. "If we get back home, I am going to take a bath that lasts three days. I'll eat in the tub. Turn on the warm tap to keep it cozy while I sleep. Scrape myself with soap and a soft cloth until I'm down to the quick. Even then, I'm not sure I'll ever feel clean again."

"We're not going home," Jessyn said. "Even if we made it back to Anjiin, what do you think it is now?"

"Something different," Campar agreed with a sigh. "I expect it is something different now."

They lapsed into silence. The room muttered and wept around them, the voices of dozens of other conversations that rose and fell with no clear logic or pattern. Someone near the center of the room started shouting, and Dafyd felt his back tensing like it was expecting a blow. But the anger faded away without sounds of violence.

Sometime later, Synnia emerged from among the others. Her lips were thin and tight. She sat with her side to them, and when Jessyn shifted, silently offering her a place in the circle, she didn't react. Anger radiated from her like cold from ice. Else arrived later, standing between Jessyn and Campar and stretching like she was getting ready to exercise until she only sat back on the floor, her feet tucked under her to keep her thighs from touching the chilly metal floor. Dafyd caught her eye and lifted his chin in unspecific query. Else shook her head once. Whatever the conversation with Ostencour had brought, it wasn't something she wanted to talk about.

He hoped it had been enough.

At the other end of the cell, the spill of white light across the ceiling that came and went. Synnia tensed, but didn't move.

"It's all right," Else said. "It's going to be fine."

Then a voice barked something Dafyd couldn't make out, and Synnia jumped up and pushed through the crowd, heading for the light. Dafyd followed her, not sure what he meant to do if he caught her. The bodies of his fellow captives blocked his way, shoving him as he tried to get by. Voices rose in a roar of alarm and confusion. Something screamed, and he didn't think it was human.

The crowd grew denser, arms and chests pressing together until

Dafyd felt like he was being crushed. He'd heard stories like that. People trapped in groups so tight they could lift their feet off the ground and not fall. People who fell and died there. It would be a stupid way to go. But executed in reprisal for a doomed prison break was bad too. He turned his torso to the side, led with an elbow, pushed through people that a year ago he'd have been intimidated to speak with.

The crowd had an edge like the wall of a hurricane's eye. Dafyd broke through, stumbling out into the ad-hoc pit where the violence was already happening.

One of the Soft Lothark was on the floor beside the sewage-stinking mat, pinned by six people kneeling on its long, thrashing limbs. Urrys Ostencour straddled the thing's chest and punched down. The knife in his hand had probably been a support from someone's boot. It had pale blood on it now. Synnia was on one of the thing's arms, her teeth bared in animal rage.

Dafyd felt himself shouting *Stop it!* but he couldn't hear the words. The alien shrieked—a high, tight sound like a machine failing—and the people screamed their rage and bloodlust. Dafyd stumbled.

The alien thing tensed into stillness. Its shriek seemed to widen, like the sound was coming from its whole body, not just its mouth. Dafyd was close enough to see the thin arms and stubby body pulse once, like it was a balloon someone had pushed a breath into. Ostencour's face shifted from rage to alarm, and the alien erupted. Its flesh expanded, popped, and spewed whitish liquid up and out. Dafyd felt a warm, wet splash of it land on his arm. Synnia and the rest of the attackers were coated with it. It smelled like acid and overheated iron.

The crowd went silent except for one of the attackers saying *What the hell was that?* Someone gagged. Ostencour stood, shaking his head slowly from side to side like a punch-drunk boxer. He started to say something, but stopped. His eyes went wide, and he stumbled. Synnia screamed, clawing at her mouth. A few seconds later, more of them started screaming with her.

Dafyd's eyes stung enough that they watered. It was hard to see where he was or who was around him. The spot on his arm felt like it was heating up. Like he was starting to burn. He pulled off what was left of his shirt, wiping desperately at the pale goo that clung to his skin.

A wave of nausea bent him double. The crowd had pushed back, away from the caustic mess that had been their jailer. Dafyd rose, took two slow, unsteady steps, and dropped to his knees again. The chamber seemed to be rising and falling like a ship in heavy waves. Ostencour was leaning against the door, his shiv forgotten at his feet. The others, Synnia included, were writhing and wailing, trying to crawl away from the mess that had been alive minutes before. Dafyd turned his back to it, started to crawl, but the nausea came again, more powerfully, and he lost himself in it. He knew he was vomiting, but the event itself seemed distant. He heard voices, but he didn't know what they were saying.

A spill of light brought him back to himself. He was splayed out on the floor, his cheek against the bare cold of the metal. He didn't remember how he'd gotten there, but not much time seemed to have passed. One of Ostencour's people—not Synnia—was beside him, weeping and struggling to move. The smell of acid and iron overwhelmed everything.

Two Soft Lothark lumbered in, indistinguishable from the dead one, their long limbs and compact bodies silhouetted against the brightness until the door closed behind them. Dafyd thought, *They're going to kill us.*

He was wrong. Instead, they looked around the floor like investigators at a crime scene, then lowered themselves to all fours and began slowly, methodically eating the corpse. Dafyd pulled himself up to sitting. The hold spun, and he had to press his palms into the floor to keep from falling back over. As he watched, the two aliens licked the floor with wide, dark tongues or tentacles, lifting bits of their fallen companion into wide slits of mouths. A memory of something horrible flickered and vanished. The human prisoners were pressed back away from the nightmare scene. An older man with a bald patch on the back of his head and a wide belly was dragging Synnia away, and Dafyd felt a faint echo of relief. She wasn't dead.

When the last of the corpse had been consumed, the aliens turned to the mat, rolling the shit-covered foam up like a carpet, then carrying it back to the door. The light came and went. A transporting sense of illness pressed Dafyd back down against the floor. He was aware of a Soft Lothark—a third one, or else one of the earlier pair—unrolling a fresh mat. Someone put a hand on his shoulder. He didn't want them to touch him. They were going to kill him. He wanted them to do it soon.

After that, his consciousness came apart. He stopped being Dafyd Alkhor and fell into free-floating experiences of misery and fear, suffering and nausea, nightmare images and physical distress and the constant dissolving heat of fever. Time became a permanent now, with no past to bring him here and no future before him.

Now went on for a very long time.

The first coherent thought was that the water had gone into his lungs. He coughed and rolled to his side, and by doing that remembered that he could cough, that he could move his body. The light was the same dull orange. He felt heavy and weak, like someone had turned up the gravity. When he rolled back, Else was there, sitting beside him with a wet cloth in her hand. She looked down at him like he'd done something stupid and brave. Exasperation and affection mixed.

"Hey there," he said.

"You're back."

"I," he tried, then took a breath. "I think so. Where was I?"

"Poisoned," she said.

"By the..." He waved a hand.

"Campar and Jessyn have been debating since it happened. Jessyn thinks it's a defense mechanism. Like a butterfly making predators sick. No help for the one that gets eaten, except that the predator won't go after its children or siblings. Inclusive fitness. Campar says the aliens aren't brightly enough colored for that to be true, but he's probably just being obstinate so they'll have something to talk about."

He tried to sit up, and after a moment, managed it. They were in the span of wall used for the infirmary. Four others were stretched out beside him. His shirt was gone, and his pants had been replaced with what looked like someone's old nightgown laid over him like a blanket. Else saw his confusion and smiled. She was beautiful when she smiled. She was always beautiful.

"It's been a while," she said.

"A while?"

"A few days, as far as we can tell. Hygiene got to be tricky, and this seemed like the best solve." She held up the damp rag in her hand. "We've been taking shifts to keep you hydrated and clean. Cleanish."

"I'm sorry."

"It wasn't just me. Or just us. Everyone's trying to help."

"Everyone was cleaning me up and dripping water in my mouth until my pants were too disgusting to leave on me. Doesn't actually make it better."

She pushed a lock of greasy hair away from his eyes. Her fingertips felt warm. "I think we're past shame here."

"Vague embarrassment?"

"Fine. If it's important to you." Her smile faltered. "We were worried. We've lost a couple."

"Reprisals?"

"No," she said, crossing her legs and resting her elbows on her thighs. "One of Synnia's friends reacted worse than the rest. He stopped breathing. Another one seemed like she was getting better, but she also had a heart condition and no medication since we left home. Ostencour had the worst exposure, and his fever broke yesterday. He's been sulking and keeping to himself. I don't think we need to worry about a second attempt. Not now, anyway."

"Synnia?"

"Took a heavier dose than you, and recovered sooner. I don't think she's doing well in other ways, though. I don't see how she… I don't know. Otherwise, nothing changed. They come and clean things away. The food is food. The water is water. Nothing changes here. It just… goes on. Like we'll be here forever."

Dafyd pointed to the cloth, and Else handed it to him. It was cool against his lips, and when he sucked the little bit of water out of it, he realized how thirsty he was. The idea of walking the few steps to the water trough seemed like a trek across a desert, though. He'd do it, but later.

"I keep waiting for the punishment to come," Else said. And then, "You're shivering."

"I'm mostly naked. And I've been sick."

She shifted up against him. Her body was warm. He rested his head against her shoulder and hoped his body was exhausted enough that it wouldn't react to her. For a long time, they didn't speak. Else ran her hand along his back like she could warm him by simple friction. When he closed his eyes, he felt exhaustion pulling him down. After a while, the shivering stopped.

"Thank you," he said.

"For what?"

"Being here. Thank you for... You mean something, you know? To me."

"Shh," she said. Her palm caressed his arm. The sound of skin against skin. "Let's talk about that later. You should rest."

"I was wrong," he said.

"About what?"

"What they'd do. How they would act. What they are. I was lying there and watching them eat their dead. I remembered something, but I didn't know what."

"Do you now?"

He nodded against her. Her hand shifted to his back, moving more slowly. "One of my junior tutorials was biological systems," he said. "The tutor sacrificed a water beetle at the end of the term. She had named it Little Dot at the beginning of that term. Little Dot was a fixture in the class for weeks. We fed it sometimes."

"She named a beetle?"

"For a reason. She put the image on all our screens, and then cut its abdomen open with a razor. Everything just spilled out. I remember someone actually started crying. It was Little Dot, after all. And then the beetle started eating its own spilled fat bodies."

Dafyd rested for a moment, exhausted by the memory and the

effort of speaking. Else's voice was disapproving. "I don't remember sadism being in the curriculum."

"Her point was that we were all anthropomorphizing the insect. Thinking that it was like us. Thinking that when it was dying, it was afraid. But it was just a network of reflexes. When it noticed a high-energy food source, it ate. We knew what was happening, and we were horrified. Maybe Little Dot was more conscious than a clockwork toy, maybe it wasn't. Either way, it did things a human being would never do because it wasn't one."

Her chin shifted, rested on the back of his head. "Vivid."

He wanted to put his arms around her. Be closer to the warmth of her body. It was too much effort. "It was a warning. I put myself in the other person's place. It's what I do."

"Your pathological move?"

"My pathological move." He heard his words starting to slur, but he wasn't willing to surrender to sleep. Not yet. "I think, *What would I do if I were them?* Or *If I was doing what they did, why would I be doing it?* It works more often than it doesn't. I thought there would be punishment because I thought they were like us. But there wasn't any, and I don't know why."

"Yes, you do. You just said it. Because they aren't like us. They aren't like beetles either. But they aren't like us."

"I don't understand how they think, and that's terrifying."

Else shifted, and he was afraid she was leaving, but she only kissed his forehead and settled back against him. It made his heart ache a little. "Rest now," she said. "We'll figure it out."

Synnia lay on her side. Every now and then, she turned. It was as close to catatonia as Jessyn had seen without quite being motionless. When Jessyn brought handfuls of the nutritional muck,

Synnia swallowed them. When she brought wet rags, Synnia was willing to suck the damp out of the cloth. Now and then, Jessyn escorted the older woman to the public mat, and then back again when she was done. It was excruciating.

Campar took turns sitting with her too, which Jessyn appreciated, even though there was really nothing to do with her "break" from nursing Synnia. The hours before were like the hours after. The light never changed. The temperature never changed. The subtle hum of the ship remained eternally constant, until her brain discounted it and it became its own kind of silence.

Campar was sleeping when Jessyn made another trip to the water trough, cloth in hand, and found Urrys Ostencour waiting for her. The Soft Lothark's poison had taken a toll on him. Or else the internment. Or both. Or everything. His cheeks and eyes were sunken. Jessyn imagined that his skin was the color of ash, but in this light, who could tell? He pushed himself up to standing when she got close, and when he spoke, his voice was rough and phlegmy.

"How is she?"

"Not great," Jessyn said. "Not dead either. So I don't know."

"I'd like to talk with her. You're her friends. If you're angry with me, I understand. But I'd like to talk with her."

He raised his chin, and Jessyn imagined what he'd looked like as a child on the school playground performing bravery. Part of her wanted to tell him to stop posturing and go sit down, but most of her was too tired to care. She got the water, headed back to Synnia and Campar, and let Ostencour follow her.

When they reached the corner, Ostencour motioned to Jessyn for the little water sop. She handed it to him, and he crouched down at Synnia's side.

"Hey there, soldier," he said. He had a voice like warm flannel when he wanted it.

Synnia's eyes focused on him. He held out the fabric, and the older woman heaved a sigh, sat up, and took what she'd been offered.

"How are you holding up?" Ostencour asked.

"I'm sorry. I am so sorry."

"No, no, no. Don't be. You didn't do anything wrong. This was my mistake, but we learned from it. We know more now. We lived to fight another day."

Some of you, Jessyn thought, but didn't say. It didn't seem like the moment to be acid.

"I thought we could…I thought even if we didn't, it would at least be over," Synnia said. "I thought it would be over."

"It isn't over," Ostencour said. "And I know right now it doesn't feel like that's a good thing, but it is. Listen to me, soldier. We're not defeated. This isn't over."

The way he said it, Jessyn even believed it a little herself.

Twelve

The end came with as little warning as the beginning.

Dafyd's strength returned slowly. He was able to walk from the little infirmary to the food and water, to take his turn on the mat without anyone there to keep him from falling. The nightgown blanket was torn, and its seams were beginning to loosen. He wore it wrapped around his waist like a towel. In the press of bodies and the degradations of time, he didn't stand out.

Whatever the prisoners of Anjiin had worn when they were taken captive, they all wore rags now. The orange light never brightened and never dimmed. The grinding cold had become familiar. Always unpleasant, always to be managed, but known. Synnia slept the most, either with Jessyn against her for heat or squatting with her eyes closed the way Campar did. Dafyd and Else sat together more often than they didn't. No one talked about the failed insurrection, but they didn't talk about much else either. There was nothing to say they hadn't said, and no one had any new experiences to relay. They were all living the same life in different bodies.

Someone in one of the other self-selected groups had begun a habit of singing, and over time, a little choir had formed. Every now and then, voices rose in religious hymns and dirges or popular songs or improvisations of harmony and cadence that ran on until they stopped. When it wasn't annoying, it was beautiful. Dafyd was standing in the crowd listening to the falling notes of an old love song when the voice came: the calm, androgynous, perfectly enunciated voice of the apocalypse.

"We will return to symmetrical space. The transition will not be harmful."

For a moment, Dafyd didn't believe it had happened. After so long in silence, it seemed more likely that he was hallucinating than that the voice had actually spoken. The man standing beside him—older, bald, familiar without being known—looked around like someone had entered the room, and then put a hand up to press against the low, oppressive ceiling. He'd heard it too. Dafyd's gut dropped.

"Excuse me," Dafyd said as if they'd been having a conversation, and turned toward the corner of the chamber he thought of as *theirs*. A muttering of voices was rising like a wind in trees. He had the sudden, irrational feeling that if he didn't find the others before the thing happened, he'd never find them at all.

The inversion of time was just as eerie, just as inexplicable, but more familiar. He remembered pressing past a young woman with wide, dark eyes and seeing Campar with his arm around Synnia a moment before it happened. He knew Else would be to Campar's left and Jessyn to his right. He remembered the relief just before he actually felt it. By the time he saw Synnia's expression—mouth pulled back in horror and fear—and felt his own comfort evaporate, the effect had passed.

"What's happening?" Synnia said, then repeated the phrase again and again and again, like she was caught in a loop.

"It's all right," Jessyn said. "We're all together. It'll be all right." It was a better answer than *I don't know.*

A deep grinding reverberated, loud enough that Dafyd felt it in the soles of his feet. The room shifted, shuddered, and grew lighter like an elevator falling too fast. The prisoners let out a collective gasp. Synnia closed her eyes, her fists pressed against her legs.

"I didn't think I was going to miss this place," Campar said. "I'm suddenly less certain of that."

Whatever the maneuvers their captors were making, they seemed to go on forever. And then, when the hold shuddered, stilled, and went silent, it was all over too quickly. The doors opened, white light spilling through the orange. Dafyd took Else's hand with his left, Campar's with his right.

The voice came from everywhere. "You will move out to the platform. Your identities will be confirmed. Exit now."

A live breeze whipped through the stillness of the prison, reaching back as far as Dafyd. Its biting cold made the constant, grating chill of the cell seem warm. Gooseflesh rose on his arms and legs, but Dafyd hadn't realized how much he missed the sensation of moving air until he felt the cool breeze caress his face. Jessyn put her arm across Synnia's shoulders. Campar, his face suddenly capable of a color besides dull, purgatorial orange, was ashen. For a long moment, nothing moved, and then a soft hushing sound came from the doorway. The soles of feet hissing against the deck. Like dazed animals at a slaughterhouse, they shambled forward toward the light and cold.

A new world opened.

Dafyd had expected to see one of the city-huge ships that had come to Anjiin, but the prison cell must have been detached at some point. It sat like a low, squat warehouse, alone on a plain of green-brown metal like the flattened summit of a great mesa etched with complex lines of steel and silver. Past the edge, huge ebony ziggurats rose, one after another after another. Any one of them was large as a mountain, with long bars of light that gleamed from their summits down to the clouds that hid their bases. Where the pale clouds grew thin, Dafyd caught glimpses of smaller structures—forests or buildings or both—that glimmered with red and golden light. A world-city.

Above them, vast silver arches rose up toward the white disk of the sun. They were too huge to be buildings, too elegant to be natural structures. They reached up toward space with the casual ease of a stairway rising to a balcony. In the high air, areas of brightness shifted and spun. He couldn't tell if they were structures or tricks of reflection and diffraction, but they seemed to flow like glowing thread, floating or moving or rising to the hidden stars.

And above them, almost too faint to make out, spots of darkness. A grid of tiny black dots like the ones that had come to humble Anjiin.

On the etched plain, six of the Carryx stood. Three had shells or armor or uniforms the same green and gold as the invading force on Anjiin. The fourth was easily half again as large, and bone white. It was flanked by two more in armor of dull red, and their massive front arms were nearly twice the size of the others'. They stood closest to the white one in the center. All six radiated the same air of magisterial calm and power.

The long-limbed, squat-bodied Soft Lothark loped through the crowd of gawking humanity, tugging here and there at one person and then another, encouraging them forward. The air smelled like distant rain. Like fog. It smelled clean.

One of the Soft Lothark led a group of people Dafyd didn't know past the massive white Carryx. When they stood staring up at it in confusion, the Soft Lothark kicked one of them behind the knee, and pushed him down to the platform, arms spread. All but one of the others quickly followed suit. The one person still on her feet shouted up at the big white Carryx, though she was too far away for Dafyd to hear what she was saying. She stood shaking her fist in rage for a moment, and then exploded into a spray of tissue and pink mist that splattered across the platform floor. It happened so fast that it took Dafyd a moment to realize that one of the two red-armored monsters had lashed out with its arm. It placed the now bloody end of that limb back on the ground and waited. The remaining people in the group stayed on their bellies until they were prodded back to their feet and led away.

One of the other Soft Lothark tapped at Dafyd's arm, shifting its attention from him to Else and back, as fast as a twitch. A voice came from the small, dark square at its chest. "Dafyd Alkhor and Else Yannin. You come this way now."

It plucked at Else's arm, then his, urging them forward, tugging him out of Campar's grasp. Still hand in hand, they followed. The bone-pale Carryx shifted to watch them, and they were made to stop before it. Dafyd didn't wait for the Soft Lothark's kick. He dropped onto his face, pulling Else down with him, and remained very still. He had the sudden, sharp memory of an image from divination cards he'd played with as a child. A man and woman in chains before a huge and terrible beast.

One of the green-and-gold Carryx trilled and whistled like a pipe organ imitating a bird. It gestured at them with its thin feeding arms. The pale beast made a single, fluting reply, and the Soft Lothark dragged them back to their feet and away while another jailer hauled another group of debased prisoners to stand where they had been.

"I think we were just presented to the king," Dafyd said. "Spoils of war."

"Maybe," Else said, and she was right. Whatever it looked like, it might be something else.

The Soft Lothark seemed to consult with the lines on the ground, reading some meaning in them that Dafyd couldn't fathom. It opened its mouth, and the black tongue slapped wetly against its cheek.

"Here," the voice said from its chest. "You will wait here for the transport to come. Do not leave this place."

Before Dafyd could decide whether he was supposed to tell it that he understood, it slid away. Else was squinting up at the strange towers in the distance. Her hair was greasy, the color of tarnished copper, and sticking to her scalp and neck like it had been pasted there. There were bags under her bloodshot eyes. He followed her gaze. The vast silver arches, the hypnotic shimmering lights, the dark grid against the sky. In the distance, a huge platform rose up the side of one of the ziggurats, moving as smoothly as a key turning in a lock.

It was breathtaking.

"We never had a chance," he said. "Look at all this. We never stood a chance against this."

"We did not," Else agreed. "Too bad we didn't know."

"Knowing wouldn't have mattered."

She looked over at him. There were lines at the sides of her mouth that hadn't been there before the invasion. She'd grown thin enough that her cheekbones were sharp and there was a little indentation behind her chin where the cushion of fat had been burned away by hunger and stress. They all looked like that, standing humiliated and half-naked on the alien platform. Thin, wasted, broken. Dafyd gestured to them, the captives of Anjiin.

"We'd have fought anyway," he said, thinking of Ostencour and his improvised knife. Synnia wrestling down the guard. "It's what we do."

"I don't know if that idea is stupid or noble," Else said.

"Human," Dafyd said. "It's just human. We don't stop just because there's no hope."

Else nodded, stopped with her brow furrowed. A tear dropped from her eye unnoticed, and she shrugged. "There's always hope for something. Just not always... not always what we want."

Jessyn lay on the bed and tried to decide whether she felt nauseated.

The rooms they'd been taken to were the architectural equivalent of an unmastered second language. The parts were mostly there—bedrooms, a common area, a kitchen—but it was all a little wrong. The doors were functional but too wide, and the panels that opened them were placed high and off-center. The clothing—shirts, pants, underwear—that waited for them was all rolled into cylinders and held in place with something like wax that shattered when they were unrolled. The cloth felt like soft canvas and smelled like mint. She didn't have any idea what the fibers actually were. She had laid them out, but she hadn't taken off the rags and remnants she'd worn since the day she was captured, much less put on something clean.

There were ten bedrooms along a single corridor from a common area. The one she'd taken for herself was in the middle along the left side. It had a bed, a bedside table too low to be useful, shelves with more waxy rolls of clothing, a chair and a desk with nothing to write with or on, and a shower in the corner: dull, metallic tiles and a step down into a drainage pan. There was no curtain or door to keep water from splashing across the rough metal floor. It was like someone had seen that people liked privacy to sleep and to shower and decided the two must go together. The toilet—and thank all that was holy there was a functional toilet and not more of those repulsive mats—was communal, but with its own little closet.

She knew that she should bathe. She wanted to. She would, soon. Just not yet. The mattress was soft. The blanket was some kind of artificial fleece. Scratchy, but warm. When she closed her eyes, she felt the press of strangers and misery, but now when she opened them, she was alone. The air smelled like fennel instead of shit and formaldehyde. She had a little window that looked out into the white sky and the sun above it, even if the sun was behind a hundred little dots. If she stood next to the window, she could see a half dozen of the dark ziggurats and part of the curve of the arches that rose up past the sky. The ceiling was too high for her to reach, and the light was white. There were colors. After her duration in orange purgatory, she was grateful for colors, and she was angry that she was grateful. She was overwhelmed by the quiet. The privacy ached like a reperfusion injury.

Voices came from the common area. Else's low tones, the way she always ended her sentences with a downturn like she was making a statement even when she was asking a question. Campar's habitual sly deadpan, the same when he was joking and being serious. Jessyn curled over, grabbed the pillow, and pulled it over her ears to block them out. Little waves of illness kept washing through her, and fits of trembling so subtle she wasn't sure if it was her body or a low vibration shaking the whole room. She tried to imagine Jellit on a bed like this, somewhere maybe even nearby. The combination of hope and despair ached more than either feeling alone would have.

When she'd been younger, one of her physicians had warned her against comparing her distress to other people's. No matter what conclusion you drew, he said, you'd made a mistake. Either you saw someone else suffering, like Synnia staggering under the grief of Nöl's execution, and decided that your own pain didn't matter. Or you saw someone laboring under what seemed like a minor problem—Dafyd mooning after Else and Else letting him—and discounted their troubles as trivial. The first case was an excuse for self-negation, the second invited contempt. Jessyn felt herself doing both now while the small, sane part of her watched, powerless.

Campar's laugh pushed through the pillow. Jessyn wished both that he would shut up and that she was out there with the others. She rolled onto her back again, letting the pillow fall away.

"You are a fucking mess," she said aloud to herself.

You're always a fucking mess. It never stopped you before, some part of her mind replied. She clenched her jaw, stood up, and started stripping off the filthy clothes she'd worn since the night she'd been captured. The shower controls seemed to consist of a single button. When she pressed it the nozzle hit her with a blast of red liquid that smelled like industrial cleanser. Jessyn screamed, and was just about to leap out of the shower when the nozzle switched and began spraying clean warm water. There was no soap, but whatever the red goo was, it loosened up the layer of filth caked on her. The top layers of her skin peeled off as she rubbed, like she'd been sunburned and was only now healing. She washed her hair, scrubbed her flesh, dug a black gel of filth out from under her too-long fingernails. There was a little box set into the wall with a razor, toothbrush, and a comb. And, for reasons she couldn't fathom, a small steel spoon. Finding them was like discovering buried treasure. When she felt clean, she turned off the water, stepped out into her room.

Now that she was clean, it was hard to even touch her old clothes, but she had to. She rooted around in the pockets until she found the little bottle of pills. There were still enough to rattle.

She dressed in the alien clothes, then counted out the pills, putting them in a line on her bed. Sixteen. So either they had been in the hold of the alien ship for about six weeks, and she'd been taking her medication as she should, or less than that if she'd had too much, or more if she'd been too sparing. But six weeks seemed about right. Six weeks and a lifetime.

One by one, she put the pills back in their bottle, then hid the bottle under her mattress. She didn't think anyone was really going to steal them, but they were precious, and the instinct to protect them was both powerful and harmless.

"Focus," she said. "Just focus. Let go of all the things you can't control, and find the things you can."

It almost sounded like a joke. A punchline. What could she control? How could she control anything? Usually, that was the voice of her depression. Here, it was just being realistic.

Time to be unrealistic, then, Jellit said in her imagination, and she actually managed a grim little smile.

In the common room, Campar said *Oh my God*, and—adrenaline rushed into Jessyn's blood—Irinna answered. Jessyn was out the door of her room before the other woman's words had faded. The common area was a main room with a scattering of institutional chairs and couches in front of a massive window like the lobby at a decent transport hub, an open kitchen, and dining area. Irinna stood by the too-wide doorway from the corridor that their alien captors had ushered them through.

Her skin had gone so pale that she was nearly the same white as her hair, as though she'd been dipped in bleach. Her body was thinned to the edge of emaciation. She wore a ragged skirt that had begun its life as a man's sweatshirt and a dark jacket that was slick and shining with filth. Jessyn crossed the common room and threw her arms around the thin woman. Irinna hugged her back fiercely, and then they were both crying.

"You made it," Jessyn said. "You're all right. You made it."

"You did too," the younger woman said.

They broke off the embrace, Jessyn grinning through tears, and Campar swooped in, picking Irinna up in a bear hug of his own.

"Please," Irinna said, her words bubbling through a half-sane laughter of release and relief. "I'm disgusting."

"You are made of gold and sunshine, and you smell like fresh roses," Campar said. "And the same for you, old man."

"It's good to see you too," Tonner Freis said. He was in the kitchen area. He'd lost so much weight that the face hiding behind his thick, dark beard looked like someone else. There was a bruise that covered half his neck, old enough that it was turning green and yellow as it healed. But his hair was the same rising, unruly gray, and his voice was familiar. He had his arm around Else's waist. Her smile was wide, showing more of her teeth than Jessyn remembered ever seeing at once before. And beside them, Dafyd Alkhor stood with a blank, stunned smile like someone had hit him with a brick and he was trying to be happy about it.

Jessyn remembered all the days when Else and Dafyd lay beside each other in the darkness. All the time the second lead of the research team had tended to the sickness of the research assistant. The gentleness between them and the need. And now here Tonner was, like waking up out of a dream. How strange that anything from before could still matter.

You poor fuckers, all of you, Jessyn thought, but she didn't say it.

"They have some use for us," Tonner said, pulling on a clean shirt for the first time in weeks and running his hand over his freshly shaved chin. It felt wonderful. He hated having a beard. "They must."

"Yes."

Else sat on the bed, her back against the headboard and her arms wrapped around her knees. Her face was too thin, and her hair had grown out. The way it framed her cheeks seemed wrong, as if the mental image he'd held of her through the long, terrible weeks had suddenly jumped. She was quiet and still, thinking through what he'd said, and then lifted an eyebrow the way she always had, and she seemed more like herself again.

"Well, I don't think it's physical labor. If it is, their target selection's terrible."

Tonner felt a little sting. He liked to think of himself as a man who could build a wall or dig a ditch if the occasion called for it, and the implication that he wasn't annoyed him. But then, he also knew himself well enough to hold back any quarrels until he'd rested and slept. He was never able to tell directly when he was stressed. He had to watch himself like he was the subject of an experiment and judge from outside. He thought he felt perfectly normal, but irritability was a frequent sign of being in distress.

Judging from Else's report, her own journey from Anjiin had been much like his and Irinna's. The dark, cold, low room, packed with bodies. The alien keepers—though his group hadn't assaulted one. The misery. The death. Tonner and Irinna had watched seven people die before they had reached whatever the "moieties of the Carryx" were. Mostly, they'd been older men and women whose health had been imperfect before the invasion. Daiir Ferria, conductor of the Abbasat symphony and popular educator on all things musical, had died at Tonner's feet. He'd grown up watching her documentaries for children. When he thought about her, he could still see the gape of her mouth as she struggled to breathe.

That was interesting. Intrusive memories were another sign. Clearly, he was overstressed.

"They'd been monitoring us," Else said. "I think they must have been. They knew who we were by name. They chose people who were the top of their fields, including us. They have to want expertise, don't they."

"And the language. There wasn't a pause to learn how best to translate. They knew how to speak to us and how to understand what we said back."

"And now this," Else said, gesturing with her chin toward the bed, the window, the shower, and all the rooms beyond it. "Their best approximation of how humans live."

"That red glop in the shower instead of soap, though," Tonner said with disapproval. "That was a miss."

Else gave him a wan smile. "Our own little dormitory. So likely they aren't just looking to harvest our brains."

He chuckled before he realized that she hadn't been joking. Fair enough. Extracting whatever knowledge the Carryx wanted through surgical means was as plausible as anything else they'd suffered.

He sat on the edge of the bed and ran his hands through his

still-damp hair. "Well, it's not as wide as the bed back at home, but I suppose it'll do."

Else started like a mouse and looked down at the mattress and blankets. Then, after a moment, "I don't think it will. I have my own room already. And anyway, I don't know that we should be demonstrative given the present... situation. There are more than enough bedrooms for all of us."

"That's ridiculous," he snapped. "If Nöl had lived, everyone would expect that he and Synnia would share one."

"He didn't, though. It doesn't apply."

Tonner sighed, harsh and percussive. "You can't still be angry that I told you to take Alkhor to get that stupid telescope. That was a lifetime ago."

"It was. And no, I'm not angry."

"What, then? Because this is a strange time to be renegotiating how we sleep together. I would have thought you'd be happy to see me again."

Else released her knees and stretched out her legs. She had a way of relaxing like a hunting cat. Like a preparation for violence. "I've been through an unpleasant and traumatizing set of experiences," she said, each word clear and careful. "And I find the idea of having a space that's just my own very appealing. Are you telling me I'm not permitted to do that?"

Yes floated at the back of his tongue like the idea of jumping that came with looking down a cliff: a suicidal tingle. He shook his head. "I'm not at my best either."

She rubbed an open palm on his shoulder like she was comforting a sick child. It was a little condescending, but part of him appreciated it anyway.

"I am sorry Nöl died," he said.

"Synnia is going to be a problem," Else replied with a nod, as if that was what he actually meant. He was still considering his reply to that when a sound came from outside the room. The clack and hiss of the main door rolling open. Someone barked out a cry of alarm. Tonner felt the fear in his chest and neck, raw and immediate as if it had been waiting for the chance to attack. They exchanged a look and headed for the door. He walked down the little corridor toward the common area with his hands clasped behind his back to keep them from shaking.

The two newcomers couldn't have been more different. The human one was the thin remnant of Rickar Daumatin. The ragged scraps of cloth that hung from his shoulders were recognizable as one of his jackets. His feet were bare and the patchy beard that he'd grown in the weeks aboard the alien ship looked moth-eaten and sickly. A long black scab marked the side of his face, and his eyes were locked on the middle distance.

Beside him, the alien seemed huge, though it was smaller than the others of its species that Tonner had seen. The green-and-gold shells were gone. They'd been armor or clothing or the mark of a different gender or clade. This Carryx had the same form, though: a back section with four legs and a broad, flat abdomen like an insect, an upright thorax and head supported by two much larger legs, and then two mantis-like forearms at the front. This one had flesh that was somewhere between purple and beige and two pairs of black eyes large enough to almost look childlike. Below the eyes was a small, thick beak in the center of a mass of muscular folds that Tonner assumed was its face. It shifted on its back four legs like a dog dancing with excitement. The two heavy forearms were planted on the floor, immovable as granite pillars. It gave Tonner the eerie sense that the Carryx was two different animals at once.

Campar, Dafyd, and Jessyn were on their feet, all of them looking at the newcomers. Synnia sat by the window, looking out at the alien landscape as if she could ignore the Carryx to death. The alien chittered, whistled, and a voice came from the black square that hung around its neck. Not the voice they'd heard on Anjiin or the ships. This was low, vaguely masculine, and pleasantly reedy, like the alien was a particularly friendly clarinet.

"I understand that one of your working group was lost. You have a tradition of offering sympathy on these occasions. I offer this sympathy. You are to feel comfortable."

Synnia made a quiet strangling noise. The alien paused like it was waiting for a translation that didn't come. Jessyn stepped forward, and Campar reached out unconsciously to pull her back to safety. "Where are we?" Jessyn said. "What do you want with us?"

The alien's back half capered a little faster for a moment, then calmed. Its massive forelegs bent a degree. "I am Tkson of the cohort Malkal, and I have been made keeper-librarian of your moiety," it said-sang. "For the moieties, usefulness is survival. I am here to help you succeed and survive."

PART THREE

PUZZLES

Your species is not the first we have encountered with the delusion that peace is a desirable state. The Eklil of Hannabor spent half of their history composing scent-symphonies in praise of a state free from tension and pain that none of them ever experienced. The Mitria Salo worshipped the Point of Equanimity in defiance of all evidence that such a thing was impossible. Your own people were in a constant generational argument over which group or subgroup, gender or culture or religion, suffered most at the hands of the others, as if the concept of justice were not narrative and abstract.

Over and over again, we found it in our subject species, this faith that a state of peace was not only possible, but desirable. That if only someone were clever enough or wise enough, a way could be found for everyone to be in comfort and satiety.

This delusion has never been the error of the Carryx. We knew from the moment we knew anything that what can be subjugated, must be. The species that exist long enough to achieve higher orders of intelligence do so only by relentlessly out-competing the other species around them. And it is this endless, iterative testing of ourselves against the universe that drives us eternally toward greater power and effectiveness. Your people, like many of the subject species we've encountered, believed that there is a tipping point where the constant fight for supremacy becomes unethical. Where peace becomes the new norm. As though it is possible through intellect or philosophy to transcend the fundamental nature of all life.

The betrayer, though. That one managed both. He could dream of perfection without being fettered by it. He desired peace and destroyed countless worlds to take it. He held both these ideas in his mind at the same time, and instead of this dissonance ripping him apart, it made him powerful. If we had known that before it was too late we would have killed him. You should take note of that.

You would be wise to kill him too.

—From the final statement of Ekur-Tkalal, keeper-librarian of the human moiety of the Carryx

Thirteen

The librarian, if that's what it wanted to be called, led them at the pace of a brisk walk. Rickar was at the back of the group, several long steps behind.

His face hurt where the wound was still healing. The remnants of the clothes he'd worn since Anjiin stuck to his skin, but they'd been doing it so long he hardly noticed anymore. Tonner and Else and the others were all in clean tunics and trousers of off-white and yellow, their faces washed and their hair brushed. Campar had a little beard he hadn't had before, neatly trimmed and shaped. Jessyn's hair was still wet from the shower. She and Irinna held hands like schoolchildren on a field trip, Tonner and Else walked side by side without touching, with Dafyd close behind them. Campar sped up and slowed down, checking in on each member of their little group over and over again like a sheepdog herding his flock and keeping an eye out for wolves. It was the big man's look of disapproval that had encouraged Rickar to give the rest of the group a wide berth.

Synnia didn't come with them, and no one seemed to question her absence. Nöl wasn't there, and no one commented on that either, but Rickar had seen enough in the past weeks to guess. He was so happy to see them all, he wanted to cry. He was afraid of what would happen if he did. Or maybe he was just afraid. Fear had become the default setting, of late.

The hallways were as wide as streets. The walls, of the same cool metallic roughness as the holding cell, had been but laced by lines and patterns and angled in so that the ceilings were always a little bit narrower than the floors. After a life spent in the gentle curves of Anjiin's grown coral buildings, the architecture of the Carryx felt aggressively manufactured. Like they were moving through the interior of some vast machine.

"You are all permitted access to this pathway," the librarian said. "And also to the complex." Or rather, it whistled and hooted and the black square on its chest spoke a second later.

"The complex?" Dafyd echoed.

"Where the work is done," it replied, as if that answered the question.

"The work?"

"Soon, soon," the librarian said, patting at the air with one of its mantis-like forearms. The gesture was eerie because it seemed almost human. Like the thing had learned how the primates of Anjiin used their bodies well enough to mimic them but not so well that the movement seemed natural.

Other groups passed in the corridor. He recognized some. Rak-hund that had murdered people in the invasion, Soft Lothark jailers from the ship. Others were unfamiliar. A flock of hand-sized globes that floated and swam through the air in a chorus of ticking that might have been something about their method of flight or might have been a conversation. A thing that looked like someone had crossed an ape with a crow that stood alone in the corridor with its face to the wall. A thick black animal that could almost have been a dog, but with a mouth that opened vertically set between far too many eyes. And the wide-bodied Carryx themselves, lumbering along on their massive forearms with their abdomens skittering behind to keep up.

The librarian turned, then started down a gently sloping ramp. Rickar caught Jessyn's eye and tried a smile. The smile she gave back was quick and small, and her eyes flicked away at once. He felt as embarrassed as if he'd asked her to come to bed with him and had her laugh at the thought.

That wasn't her fault. He wasn't at his sanest.

When hell came to Anjiin, he'd been with a group of his old friends from Dyan Academy. Some, he'd followed from the café where he'd first learned about the things that Samar Austad hadn't lived to see. Some were part of the gathering they'd gone to join. Else, bless her, had offered him a place in her basement, but that had seemed like a terrible idea. He'd made his excuses and stayed where he was.

All of them, Rickar included, had been either drunk or otherwise altered by the time the grid appeared in the sky and the voice had followed it. He'd been outside, sitting around a fire pit with an older woman he'd known on and off for years and her precocious ten-year-old son. The memory of her seeing the uncanny brightnesses in the sky and treating them like a great treat as a way to keep her child from panicking hurt Rickar now. She'd died in the first strike.

Three others in the group had as well. A single loud sizzle like someone had overloaded an electrical circuit, and they'd collapsed, the air smelling of distant lightning. One of them had screamed, but only once. He could still see the blood pouring out of her side where the exit wound gaped. He could still see her son's eyes widening.

Irinna touched his forearm, and he flinched, but he was back in the corridor with the alien monsters. How terrible that should be a better place than his memories.

"You're all right?" the young woman asked softly.

"Sure. Fine," he said. "Thank you."

She nodded once sharply before moving back to Jessyn's side. Rickar shoved his hands in the rotting remains of his pockets and lowered his eyes. He felt himself on the edge of a kind of sensory overload. He felt that way often.

The corridor broadened, the ceiling rising away into a cathedral-tall space. Vast, dark walls towered higher than the tallest buildings at Irvian, lines of brightness and dark covering them like calligraphy in some unimaginable script. Archways where the walls met the floors seemed like decorative flourishes until they came close to them and saw they led to alcoves tall enough that Rickar couldn't have touched the ceiling with his outstretched hand. Huge windows, high above in the cathedral space, let in what appeared to be natural light: wide white beams cutting through a haze of dust. A dozen or more species chittered and sang, moved through the broad central space or squatted in it in groups like undergraduates having a picnic by the duck pond. The far side of the chamber felt like it was almost too far away to see. The air smelled weirdly like a forest—rot and wet and growth and decay.

There was something else about it too. An energy in the atmosphere. A brightness. Like the air itself was easier to breathe…

"What the hell is this?" Tonner said.

"This is for you," the librarian said, its reedy, machine-mediated voice somehow managing to be warm and reassuring. "Your place is this way." It gestured with the thinner pair of forearms. "This way."

The alcove it led them toward had a band of red across the top that reminded Rickar of the old Gallatian parable about spreading a blood offering over the doorway of a house as a sign of faith that made the demons pass it by. The alcove itself was like a deep side chamber off the bedlam of what Rickar already thought of as the public square. Counters stood at the height of workbenches, but made from something like fiberglass or hard ceramic and attached immovably to the walls. There were a series of complications on the benches. One that could have been a centrifugal sampling unit. Another that looked like some kind of off-brand CCA-resonance imager. A screen that had the menu script of the proteomic dictionary they had used back at the Irvian Research Complex in some previous lifetime. Salvage from Anjiin, torn out of whatever building they'd been in and brought here, just as they had been.

The librarian shuffled around, surprisingly agile for something as huge as it was.

"This is a laboratory," Tonner said. "This is *our* laboratory. From home."

"Functionally," the librarian agreed. "The details are approximate. But we believe that all of the work you did there can be continued here."

"Why?" Jessyn asked. Her voice had an awed tone that made Rickar wonder if she was aware she'd spoken.

A small brown creature with vast yellow eyes and something equal parts fur and feathers covering its body scurried in, looked at them all, and scurried back out. The librarian moved deeper into the alcove and they followed. A turn in the alcove's back had obscured another structure, and the team gathered around it like students taking a guided tour through a museum. *Here is a display of ancient art. Here are the skulls left from long-past atrocities pulled out of their graves for your edification.* Rickar moved forward too, trying to see better, and then back. He felt hungry and nauseated at the same time.

The cages were cubes of clear material—glass or plastic or transparent ceramics—and a little over waist high. In one, a cluster of red orbs clung to a stick, shifting slightly as though they were ruffled by some unfelt breeze. In the other, a wide, flat creature lurched about on three stumpy legs. Its body was an iridescent blue that flashed to vibrant red when the light struck it at certain angles. It reminded Rickar of a turtle that was missing a quarter of itself.

The librarian gestured toward the bright red orbs. Berries. Eggs. Fungal growths. Whatever they were. "These are from one of our subject worlds. This"—it pointed to the not-turtle—"is from another. You will make these first organisms nourishing for the second."

The librarian shifted its mass away, making more room for them in front of the cages. The others surged forward. Most of the others. Dafyd Alkhor kept back the same way Rickar did, though probably for different reasons. The younger man was scowling and glancing back toward the mouth of the alcove like there was something there he'd forgotten.

The research team, though, were packed close to the cages and the samples. Tonner stood in the center of the group, Else at his side, commanding the little space with his body the way he always had.

"These are from different planets?" Tonner asked. "Different evolutionary trees?"

"Yes," the librarian said.

"Do they match either of the biomes from Anjiin?" Tonner asked. There was already a sense of authority coming into his voice. "Are these known structures, or are we starting from scratch?"

"An important question," the librarian agreed without answering.

Irinna pushed down on the cage with the red orbs, and it clicked, the top rising open on a hinge that Rickar couldn't see even as he saw it working. The smell that came out was like incense and fresh-turned earth—spicy and rich.

"You are permitted as many samples of the organisms as are of use. We have duplicated your supplies from your former laboratory. If you have other needs, I will consider them."

Jessyn was reaching in to stroke the red orbs. They shifted on their stick, neither moving toward her nor away from her. Rickar wondered whether they knew they were food.

"What if we don't do it?" That was Alkhor. He had moved back to lean against the opposite wall. The librarian had to turn to look at him, his bulk scattering the rest of the group.

Else stepped in, moving physically between the thing and the young man. "Or if we can't. This isn't a small project. Generalizing two whole biomes from single samples and then reconciling them? If it's more than we can manage?"

The librarian planted its two massive forelegs on the ground, leaning forward on them to let its hindquarters dance from side to side in agitation. For a moment, it seemed to be at a loss for words.

"This is your task," it said.

"What about these other creatures," Dafyd asked. "Are they being tested too? This same test?"

The librarian's answer came quickly this time. "The only test is whether a subject species is useful. Usefulness is survival."

They were all silent for a moment. The implications of the simple statement were like ice water in Rickar's blood.

Campar chuckled. "Come on, that's pretty much what every funding committee says."

No one laughed.

The path back to the rooms felt shorter than the walk out had been. Rickar had noticed that before in other, less exotic circumstances. The first walk through a new neighborhood, the first commute in a new city, the first time finding his way to a new address to meet someone, and the anxiety of walking with them to a café that he was only halfway sure he could find. First times always expanded the experience of the space for him. Going back was faster, the distance shorter, because it was known.

When they got back, Synnia still sat exactly where she'd been when they left, her hands folded in her lap. The others had fallen into conversation, so he went to her, asked which of the rooms were taken and which he could lay claim to. She showed him, and he picked the door farthest from the others.

He showered awkwardly, startled by the blast of red fluid, then luxuriating in the warm water that followed. The bruises on his back had faded, but he could still feel them. And his ribs ached when he breathed too deeply. He washed his hair and shaved and tried to remember what he could about the psychology of trauma. He'd read a book about it once, but it had seemed like abstract knowledge at the time.

The clothing that the aliens had left for him fit well enough, but he could still wish for a decent jacket and a pair of soft shoes.

When he reached the common room again, cleaner and fresh-faced apart from the scab on his neck softened by the shower and bleeding, he found that the others had hauled the couches and chairs and cushions into a rough circle. A little oblong, really, with the apex of the curve focused on Tonner. Another thing that hadn't changed.

He went to the kitchen where a pot of something that looked and smelled like soup simmered on a thermal pad. It had an aroma like beef and fresh ginger, and nothing had ever smelled better. No one objected when he took a bowl and a spoon and helped himself. After the near tasteless paste he'd survived on during the journey, the depth and richness was intoxicating. He listened to the others talking as he took stock of the pantry. Fruit and frozen meat, loaves of bread that had been kept cold enough that they were still thawing, fresh vegetables, but nothing leafy. Whatever the Carryx used to keep food from rotting on the way from Anjiin was good enough for pea pods, but lettuce was apparently a bridge too far.

"He didn't *say* life or death," Irinna said, gesturing with a single raised finger in a way that suggested she'd been interrupted before and was getting irritated. "He said there was only one test. Being deemed not useful doesn't have to mean some kind of summary execution. Maybe not-useful species are sent home."

"They killed an eighth of our population just to get our attention," Campar said dryly. If Synnia had been there when the conversation began, she was elsewhere now. That was probably wise. Rickar leaned against the counter and ate, close enough to be part of the group and also not claiming his place in it.

"It doesn't matter," Tonner said. He was a little wild around the eyes. Fear, Rickar thought. Well, fair enough. They were all frightened. But something else too. Excitement, maybe. Or the drive that had made his workgroup a thing worth hauling across the stars. "Maybe they kill us. Maybe they ship us back home. Maybe something else. I don't care, and you shouldn't either, because we're not going to fail. This is what we do, and we are going to do the hell out of it."

Jessyn's little nod was almost subliminal. Rickar found himself more moved by Tonner's resolve than he'd expected to be. He remembered something he'd read when he was young and thinking he might go into the military. *A leader must be utterly decisive, especially when giving orders that conflict with the ones from the day before.* He didn't recall who'd said it, but he had the sense it was some famous leader. He hadn't understood it then. He did, maybe, now.

The others grabbed onto Tonner's certainty like it was an umbrella and they were caught in a hailstorm. Rickar watched their bodies shift into calmer, more familiar postures.

"I was looking at the food organism," Else said. "It didn't seem like it was growing out of the stick. I think those are different things."

"Maybe the red berries feed on the stick," Jessyn said.

"If they do, that's going to give us two organisms from their biome."

Tonner snapped his fingers and pointed at Else, grinning. Rickar felt himself smiling along. It was a good insight. It felt like an accomplishment, and an accomplishment felt like a little sip of power in an ocean of powerlessness. Nothing could be normal, but work could sustain them.

Across the room, Dafyd was leaning against the window, arms crossed and the huge expanse of the clouds, arches, and terraced pyramids at his back. Rickar would have expected him to be more engaged, but he seemed to be listening with half an ear at most. Rickar wondered what was distracting him, but then the conversation shifted and distracted him instead.

"We take rolling shifts," Tonner said. "Always someone in the lab. No downtime in the project, and no one collapses from exhaustion. It didn't look like there were enough workstations for more than two or three people to be in the lab anyway. Whoever's not there does theory work here."

"And eats and sleeps," Else said.

"Yes," Tonner agreed. "Those things. Very important." Rickar chuckled and felt a little bloom of affection for the man. Whatever you thought of Tonner Freis, he was utterly himself.

"We'll need something to take notes with," Campar said. "We're undersupplied in the notebook department."

Tonner pointed at him now. "We'll figure that out."

"We can work in pairs," Jessyn said.

"You and Irinna," Tonner said as if it had been his idea. "Else and Campar. I'll take Dafyd."

"Are you sure?" Else said. "You and Campar have a chemistry sometimes. I don't mind doing the follow-on work if you'd rather—"

"One senior researcher, one assistant. Jessyn, you just got a field promotion. Congratulations," Tonner said. "And I've got the most experience, so I'll take Dafyd. Keep it close to even."

Else sat back, her arms crossed and the little mark of concern on her brows, but she nodded. Rickar tipped back his bowl, swallowing the last of the broth. It had grit at the bottom that tasted like dirt from heaven: savory and thick and pepper-hot. The ceramic clicked when he put it on the counter.

"I suppose," he said, "that puts me with Synnia?"

The sudden quiet was eerie. They all turned to him. Irinna was the first to look away.

"When you were in the showers," Jessyn said, then lost what she was going to say and tried again. "Synnia said she's not going to participate."

"Ah," Rickar said. "Well, I can sign on as jack-of-all-trades. Fill in wherever a hand's needed."

"You can stay in your room and out of my way," Tonner said.

Rickar's laugh was like a cough. It wasn't funny. "You can't be serious."

"I couldn't trust you when the stakes were low," Tonner said. "Why the fuck would I trust you now?"

Fourteen

Ekur of the cohort Tkalal was subjugator-librarian for the sixteenth dactyl of the third limb of the twentieth exploratory body. The librarians of the other ships of the dactyl gave their information and reports to it, and accepted direction and instruction from it just as it, in turn, relayed those things of importance to the subjugator-librarian of the third limb. Like nerve fibers in flesh or void tendrils in asymmetric space, the librarians coordinated the actions of the Sovran's will. A vast network of judgment and obedience that splayed across thousands of stars.

Its present action was the conquest and subjugation of a small world in the diffuse space between two galactic limbs, and as the Carryx librarian squatted in its niche—legs folded under its abdomen, fighting limbs set against the deck, and feeding limbs moving through the streams of the dactyl's signal transfer—it did not guess how badly things were about to go.

The major indigenous species were land-based hexapods who called themselves something like Eelie and their world Ayayeh. The subjugator-librarian had all the information the initial probes that had followed the void tendrils had given. The half-mind re-formed and deepened the data points into something akin to insight. The Eelie moved across their world in packs of twelve to forty, establishing no hives or cities, but singing to one another in waves that traveled across continents. Their atmosphere was awash in a vast world-song.

In the belly of the Carryx ship, nodes shuddered in their liquid wombs, ready to be born. Eager. Ranks of Rak-hund and Soft Lothark prepared to fall through the high air of the world, bringing the word of the Carryx and the changed fate of Ayayeh. The violence to come was not a victory, but a growth pang. The displacement of a species that had grown in the universe directionless and feral discovering its purpose within the Carryx and being shaped into utility.

A Sinen coordinator paused at the subjugator-librarian's door, pulling its attention from the coming battle. Seeing the animal's complex eyes and facial appendages sent a cascade of disgust rippling through the Carryx librarian, as it always did. Others among the ranks of the empire's librarians were capable of interacting with the animal captives with equanimity. Ekur-Tkalal was quietly proud that it had not developed this callousness toward perversity.

The Sinen burbled, and the translation half-mind at its throat took the wet, sibilant noises and turned them into language. *The subjugator-prime is prepared.* Ekur-Tkalal pulled its feeding limbs from the flow of information, rose up on its legs, and went to make its final connection before the outspreading began.

The prime, the highest of the subjugator caste of their dactyl, lowered itself to the deck in ritual abasement as Ekur-Tkalal entered its niche. Even pressed down, the prime was almost as tall as the librarian. When it rose, it towered.

"We are prepared," it said.

Ekur-Tkalal shifted its gaze across the long rows of Carryx soldiers and the animals of violence that expressed their will with a thrill of disgust. Its part now was to check for signs of irregularity and error, to match what was against what was expected, and it did this with great efficiency. When it was finished it turned back to the prime.

"Begin," the librarian said, and left. Once it returned to its niche, it expressed the intention to the other, lesser librarians who would express it to the lesser leaders in their ships. Like a fist closing around a stone, the Carryx reached out their nodes and their soldiers, the animals that announced the end of Eelie history and the beginning of their service to the Carryx. The wandering troops of alien things were counted, divided in two, then two again, then two again, and the limb was chosen. One in eight of all Eelie died. All was moving as intended.

It was only when the soldiers reached the planetary surface that unexpected things began to happen.

In the planet's northern hemisphere, a collection of the Eelie in the valley of a vast plain drew the attention of the prime. It directed one hundred Carryx and two thousand animals of violence to descend on the indigenous population for acquisition and subjugation.

Half of their animals of violence died, and a third of the Carryx. Ekur-Tkalal rechecked the information, but the half-mind—passionless and incapable of meaningful surprise—remained adamant. One of the largest groups of conquering Carryx forces had just suffered massive casualties. As the subjugator-librarian narrowed its attention, searching for details from the battlefield, another group—this one in a cave complex of the southern hemisphere—blinked out. Two hundred animals and six Carryx. In an archipelago just north of the equator where twilight was pulling the sky into shadow, five hundred animals and ten Carryx vanished. Another group. Another. Another.

It would have been unthinkable, except that it was happening.

The drone grid found the prime in transit between a half-constructed extraction center and a wide lake where several groups of Eelie were shown to be nesting. The prime's voice vibrated with confusion, and something the librarian refused to believe was fear.

"The species is not as the probes and void tendrils reported. We have only collected a few of them intact, but they are not from this world."

"Repeat and clarify."

"They are unrelated to the planetary ecosystem. Manufactured life-forms intended to trick us into believing they are the indigenous species," the prime said. "This is a trap."

Ekur-Tkalal's feeding limbs twitched, fingers plucking at each other as it thought. There was no time to consult the librarian of the third limb. No time to ask for counsel and direction. The choice needed to be made now, and as the senior librarian of this dactyl, that gave it both the burden and the power.

"Return to the ships," it said. The prime braced as Ekur-Tkalal shifted its attention to the half-mind. The drone grid identified and destroyed the remaining Eelie—half a billion more deaths in the span of moments—but the subjugator-librarian was already shifting the half-mind's focus outward to the dead planets, moons, and asteroids of the system.

The simple volume of a solar system made the search difficult. Time-consuming. The animal transfer ships, empty of captives, were hauling themselves up through the air, and the drones in their grid were starting to wither and decohere before the librarian found what it was looking for. What it was certain would be there.

A stretch of vacuum the size of a small moon had begun to stutter and boil. Exotic waves that the half-mind displayed as blue and gold light though they were not light flickered in the gap. Another rip appeared on the far side of the system's star. A third above the ecliptic. The strategic half-mind pointed out the resonance relationship between the intrusions, and offered a geometric explanation for why there wouldn't be a fourth unless the existing rifts changed position.

The battle had been chosen. The enemy had arrived.

From the three rifts, ships began to spill out into normal space, blinking into reality from whatever non-dimension the enemy employed to undo the limits of the local universe. The strategic half-mind marked each one as it appeared, delivering something like knowledge to the librarian. Ten enemy vessels had come through each rift. The patterns of heat and light that came from them matched what the Carryx had experienced in previous encounters, with six exceptions. If the enemy used energy weapons that traveled at the local maximum, it would be eight hours before the first attack would arrive. The ships themselves would take much longer. The librarian mapped the possible paths that the dactyl could employ to engage or avoid, and the strings of possibility bloomed in its mind like a terrible flower.

The drones withered and fell into the atmosphere of Ayayeh, burning one by one, and then by the thousands. The grid collapsed unnoticed. The Eelie were a sprung trap. The damage they would do was done, and the violence played out now in the void between the planets.

The librarian moved a duplicate of the strategic half-mind into the body of a low-status Sinen, erasing the animal's mind in the process. The living corpse that the half-mind now inhabited would be fed into a message casing and sent through asymmetric space alone. Carrying news of the attack to the librarian of the third limb would take seven days. If it was relayed all the way up to the regulator-librarian at the center of the empire, a reply might not come for months.

Until it did, this battle belonged to Ekur-Tkalal and whatever unknowable mind directed the limbs of their enemy.

Three weeks into the long conflict, Ekur-Tkalal won its first victory and suffered its worst loss. The librarian of the ship that was lost sent out its last report from the second-eighth mark of a gas giant's gravity well where the resonance of the huge planet and the local star created optimal conditions for a close-quarters battle. The images the lesser librarian sent, captured by the optical matrix of a Rak-hund, showed the passageways of the Carryx ship as the animals of the enemy flowed through them. Ekur-Tkalal knew that the enemy was virtually deathless, that their animals of violence could be riddled with injuries and flow forward like a tide. The heat and pulse of the living organism could fade without ending its assault. Knowing this prepared it for the images, but didn't undo the mystery of how.

The Carryx of the ship had led its forces in a final effort to cast the enemy back into the vacuum, and they had almost managed. The final images showed the breach, the uncanny field waves that the enemy used to weaken the ship's flesh.

The enemy bled black and red and clear. Their voices were a mesh of radio signals that danced to evade all the Carryx efforts to drown it out. Ekur-Tkalal watched as the enemy weapons split the air, as the Carryx's white-green battle shells cracked, as the Rak-hund and Soft Lothark died in waves to push the fight a little farther from their dying masters' bodies.

The ship had been lost before the word of its loss arrived. Its death was a brightness across the spectrum of energy, a sphere of irregularity in space expanding until it was indistinguishable from the vacuum itself.

The incalculable loss was also an opportunity.

Traveling in the skin of that detonation, hundreds of escaping enemy wrapped in shells of titanium and deep copper fled death and found captivity. The webwork of void tendril and magnetic force gathered the escape pods like a net hauling in fish. The enemy saw what was happening too late. Five of their ships turned toward the failed evacuation. When distance and the laws of the local universe kept them from rescuing their companions, they launched an attack. The deathless could still be annihilated, and the enemy would rather slip into oblivion than be yoked. The librarian understood that, and took something like pleasure in the enemy's frustration.

The librarians of the remaining ships reported an increased ferocity in the enemy. Loss, it seemed, drove them to recklessness. The subjugator-librarian noted this, added it to the body of knowledge that was the eternal battle. Out of more than a thousand species, this enemy was the most recalcitrant, but the patterns in its behavior and design would bring it to heel in time, and domesticated, would add its great strength to the empire.

Enemy ships dove deep into the center of the system, skimming through the star's corona to evade the tracking eyes of the Carryx. The leaders operating the Carryx ships launched clouds of projectiles—some alive and some inert—at the enemy ships and watched as they were unmade or evaded or—rarely—as they struck home. The disabled enemy ships flickered into knots of nuclear fire and faded to ash. Whether that was the nature of the enemy or a choice to deny information to the Carryx wasn't clear.

With each engagement, the subjugator-librarian sent another message casing to offer up its decisions and intentions to the librarians whose work was to see a larger image of the empire in less detail and guide the grand strategy of the war, of all the wars, of the will and intention of their species. Day after day, cycle after cycle, no direction came back, and Ekur-Tkalal coordinated the lesser librarians, gave shape to the will of the soldiers and their animals of violence.

One of the Carryx ships stumbled into a volume of space studded with nearly invisible mines and was destroyed. Two of the enemy ships, straining to scrape away pursuing projectiles, came too close to the atmosphere of the icy fifth planet. They burned and they fell.

When Ekur of the cohort Tkalal had been young, it had tried to claim status over one of its siblings. The two of them had reared up in the open plain by the birthing crèche, their fighting arms spread wide, and flailed their adolescent strength into each other's bodies. It had hurt, but not enough to be decisive. Unsure how to approach an unfinished challenge, they had kept going, slamming their fighting arms together, each hoping to snap the other's leg. It had gone on until their crèche leader had appeared and pushed them apart. The battle around Ayayeh had the same bruising violence and the same frustration.

When the message casing from the subjugator-librarian of the third limb did appear, blinking back into symmetric space at the edge of the heliosphere and spitting out its message in a burst of stuttering radio waves, Ekur-Tkalal was relieved.

The chain of identifications on the message was longer than it had seen before, tracing its origin back to the center of the empire and the librarians with the broadest scope. The battle that the dactyl fought here was part of a vastly larger action, playing out across space and time in ways that Ekur-Tkalal would not know because it was not called upon to know. But that context made directions that would otherwise have been strange, comprehensible. Unpleasant, but comprehensible.

It summoned the ship's prime to its niche. The huge, overwatered bulk of the soldier was repulsive in one way, endearing in another. The soldier and the subjugator-librarian, born of equal dignity to any other of the Carryx, and imbued with the same potential, but here they were. Genetic dead ends, made to consort with animals. The gendered cohorts of the Carryx, the moieties of production and distribution and reproduction, would look down upon them both with the same contempt that Ekur-Tkalal felt toward this soldier and the animals it controlled. They had this one dignity left to them, dying to protect their betters.

The subjugator-prime bent, abasing itself. The librarian noticed for the first time that the soldier's fighting arms had stripes of red much like its own. The feeling of kinship was brief and fleeting.

It passed a series of directions to the prime, the information hovering in symbols of light, the wavelengths shimmering with nuance, specificity, and intent. The soldier rose, considering what it had been given. Its eyes betrayed confusion.

"You are to prepare your soldiers and their animals for these actions against the enemy," the librarian said. "Once they are prepared, they will shift to the other ships of the dactyl to aid in carrying them out. The captives you have taken will be brought here and will leave with me and a minimum crew."

The prime's shifting stilled as it understood what it was seeing. Each of the actions was made to provoke a different kind of response from the enemy ships, and each ended with the details of the counterattack sent in a message casing. It was a profligate use of a limited resource. Most of the space within the casings would be empty, blank, and wasted. That as much as anything else was the message the empire had delivered to the dactyl.

"Are we no longer trying to win?" the old soldier asked, and its whistles and rumble were plaintive. The prime was Carryx, but simpleminded and emotional. The librarian understood how it had fallen to soldier caste. Removing it from the lineage of the Carryx was to the benefit of the species. The same could be said of the librarian, but for different reasons.

"You will observe the enemy in action, and preserve those observations. We are not the only battle in the war, and if we must bend here to break them elsewhere, of course we will."

"Yes. Yes, I understand."

The librarian chirruped an idiom of the Carryx language that the half-mind would have translated as *You can't win a fight without bruising your own limbs.* A spark of what might have been anger lit the prime's eyes. The librarian supposed discovering that its utility to the Carryx was in the details of how it was killed would be distressing, even for a more advanced cohort than theirs. The secondary librarians, not welcome on the one ship carrying away the captive enemy, would likely also resent the directions that it was about to give them.

But the prime bent again and scuttled away to do as it had been told. The librarian passed the relevant directions on to the secondary librarians under it, adding its mark to the chain of identifications as it did so.

Transfer boats that had been meant to carry away the elite of the Eelie instead moved between the ships of the Carryx fleet, transferring soldiers and animals to the part of the dactyl that would remain, and bringing the enemy captives and their Soft Lothark guards to the one ship that would leave.

The captives were thin-bodied animals with fivefold symmetry in their hard, crusted epidermis. The half-mind had been observing them carefully, but had not yet gained context enough to communicate with them beyond the simplest levels. That was fine. There would be time enough to question them when their journey was complete.

The ship that had once been the central organizing point of the sixteenth dactyl of the third limb of the twentieth exploratory body turned its face away from the sun, accelerating toward the edge of the heliosphere and the vast unreality of asymmetric space. Behind it, the remnants of the dactyl probed the forces of the enemy, engaged, disengaged, danced, fought, and died.

If any of the Carryx ships survived, they would rejoin the librarian later. If not, then it was better for the species that they had died.

What is, is. It can be nothing else.

Fifteen

The work was a blessing and a burden, often at the same time.

Whenever Jessyn couldn't sleep, she'd imagine herself dying. Drowning, maybe. The hurt at first, and then tunnel vision, and everything going away and never coming back. She was mortal. It was going to happen eventually. She wasn't suicidal, she was just taking comfort in the idea that no matter what, she wasn't here forever. It wasn't suicidal until she started making plans. That's what she told herself.

Then, when she was calm enough, her mind blinked out and she just didn't exist for a few hours. It wasn't really sleep, but it was similar.

When she came back, there was the choice of what she was going to do. Stay where she was and try to sleep again or else push the blanket off and live another day. The work gave her a default. She pulled herself out of bed, stood under the weird bedroom shower, dried herself off, got dressed. All the things that normal humans were supposed to do. Including eating breakfast—eggs, cured meat, citrus fruits that were starting to get a little woody but still added some acid and sweetness, a cup of fresh coffee—and walking to the lab. None of that was as hard as choosing would be, so she didn't choose. She just ran on automatic. Not thinking was almost as good as not being. A strong second best. She threw her mind into the research to get away from everything she felt, and it was so familiar, she had to believe this wasn't the first time she'd done it.

When she faded into the routine, lost herself in it, she could almost convince herself she was living her old life. Working in the labs with Tonner and the team. Her brother waiting to talk about dinner and whoever his infatuation of the week was when she got home. Not a person slowly losing her mind. Not the chattel of aliens. It was a nice dream to live in, for a few moments each day.

She and Irinna relieved Else and Campar. They took the experiments and procedures that the others had started and saw them through, then did whatever Tonner had assigned as the step to follow. It would have been easier if there had been a board or a messaging system or paper and pens and thumbtacks. Irinna had a good memory, though, and Jessyn was happy to trust her.

Today, they were checking cellular motility along nutrient gradients. Else and Campar had harvested tissue from the not-turtle and put it on gel sheets with plausible food supplies—simple sugars, alcohols, and soluble carbohydrates—diffused through them. If the not-turtle cells moved toward the source, it was a possible nutrient. If they moved away, it might be a toxin. If they just stayed there—and mostly they just stayed there—either it wasn't metabolically active for not-turtles or the tissue they'd sampled wasn't motile.

Jessyn had been running tests like this since she was in basic education classes. Make the slime mold solve the maze. Look how smart biology was. Something as simple as mold could thread its way through the labyrinth and find the thing that would sustain it. As she stood, watching the gels, she wondered again about Jellit. Maybe he was here, in the Carryx world-city, too. Her brother could be out there, somewhere in the thousands of levels, hundreds of thousands of hallways and chambers, lost among the monsters. If she just had the right kind of mold, maybe it could show her how to reach him. Him and all the other captives of Anjiin. She sure as hell didn't know how to do it.

"What we need is sperm," Irinna said.

Jessyn lifted an eyebrow. If Irinna was trying to act normal, she could follow suit. Rise to the occasion. She smiled the way she would have if she were sane. "The dating pool has thinned a bit, of late."

Irinna rolled her eyes, then waved her fingers in a circle while she chewed on a bite of the ham and cheese sandwich she'd brought for lunch. "Or pollen. Spores. Whatever. I mean, they're not clones. Lots of individual variation even in the small sample we have here. So assuming some sort of genetic mixing during reproduction, the berries are going to have some way to swap chromosome analogs. Find that, and we'll find the encoding medium. We already know the kind of patterns to look for. Aperiodicity, multiple copies, presence in all generative tissues. But if we could get sperm out of them, we wouldn't have to wash through a bunch of functional molecules we don't know what they do, you know?"

"I could ask them back to my room," Jessyn said. "Get some candles. Slow music."

"Well, I'm not an alien stick-eating berry-thing, but if I were..."

"I'd do better if I had some perfumes, or scented soaps," Jessyn said. "Anything other than that red glop the shower blasts at us. It makes me smell like an old hospital ward."

"Maybe disinfectant is the height of olfactory fashion among aliens?"

Jessyn chuckled. Irinna grinned. She might almost have been herself. Almost. There was a darkness under her eyes, and her hands were never still. When she talked, there was a bright, compact brittleness about the words. All the familiar signs of someone trying to keep their shit together.

How are you? sat at the back of Jessyn's throat, waiting to be asked. *How bad is this for you? Are you losing your mind, and if you're not, why aren't you? What happened to you on those ships? What happened to you before that?*

A chittering like the voices of lab monkeys came from the mouth of the alcove, and Jessyn turned in time to see four of the little animals hauling themselves up onto the countertop. Wide golden eyes, a brown-gold coat that split the difference between fur and feathers, each of the four about the size of an eight-year-old.

"God, not again," she said, moving toward the intruders. She lifted her hands, patting the air, and tried to block them. "No. No, bad monkey. Off you go."

One of the four bared dark teeth set in black gums at her, but it looked less like a threat than a complaint. The other three bounded around her, hopping from countertop to floor and back up again like they were made from springs and rubber. Irinna put down her sandwich and followed them toward the back, making shooing sounds as she went.

"What we really need is a door," Jessyn said. "Or a baby gate. Something."

"Out out out. No! All of you, out!" Irinna said, and the three bounced back out, loping toward Jessyn. One paused to look at the gels like it was curious about them. Like it had notes to offer on the process. And then all four were gone, vanished back out in the cathedral-tall common space that all the alcoves shared.

"Those things are annoying," Irinna said.

"Enthusiastic, though. Got to give them points for peppiness."

"No, I don't think I do," she said with a sigh, and popped the last bites of her lunch into her mouth. "Are they lab animals or fellow scientists?"

Jessyn started to laugh, then caught herself. Irinna wasn't making a joke. "That's actually a really good question. Are they here to eat our experiments or steal our data."

"We don't know anything except what the Carryx tell us, and they don't tell us anything."

"It's like we've been given the most important test of our lives," Jessyn agreed, "but all the questions are in secret code."

"On the plus side, if we fail," Irinna said, "they kill us, so no need to worry about placement rankings."

While Jessyn was trying to formulate a reply to that, Irinna went to the protein database, tapping the input display like she was trying to get its attention. The machine chirped.

"Why?" Jessyn asked. Meaning to ask, *Why bring us all this way and set us up for failure and death.*

"This?" Irinna replied, as though Jessyn had asked about her entries on the display. "It's my work-around for not having anything to write with. I've been coding in the work like it was a peptide sequence and using the error log. See?"

Jessyn leaned over. The little display read ERR:'MID-PH PROTEIN ASSAY OF SOURCE SPECIES':BAD FORMAT.

"That's brilliant."

"That's why we're all here," Irinna said, and it was half a joke. If they hadn't all been just a little brilliant. If they hadn't been part of

Tonner Freis's workgroup. If the research they'd done in the past years hadn't been noticed or celebrated, maybe they'd have been back on Anjiin instead of in this prison.

Jessyn wondered what was happening back at home. Whether she'd been lucky to escape, or if she was being punished for her little sip of celebrity and status. She wondered if Jellit was alive. She wondered how long she was going to be able to keep going. And here was pretty little Irinna, youngest of them all, smiling and typing her notes as though anything about where they were made sense. But what else could they do?

"Protein assay," Jessyn said. "I'm on it."

"I'll tare the CCA if you make the soup?"

"Deal," Jessyn said, and went back toward the cages.

The organisms were, in their own ways, fascinating. The berries—which were profoundly not berries in anything besides size and shape—contained an order of magnitude more silicates in their chemistry than anything Jessyn had seen before, and the internal structure of the little beasts—simplistic and undifferentiated as it appeared to the naked eye—was protected by a thick layer that seemed at first like epidermis, but the more she looked at it, the more it looked like a separate organism. Discovering whether this was mutualism or parasitism or a gender dimorphism thing like a female torrent mold enclosing the male would have to wait until they had determined the medium of genetic inheritance, but one way or another, it was actually kind of cool.

She opened the transparent cage and plucked four of them out. They clung to the stick, trying to resist her, but not more than a grape would cling to its vine. They were warm in her palm and rippled a little against her skin.

She carried them to the sampling array and dropped them

down among the blades. White dots tracked along their skin, little foot analogs trying to find purchase in this new environment. Wherever the little animals or plants or fungi had evolved, it hadn't been a lab grinder. The skills and abilities they'd developed, generation after generation under whatever alien sun they'd called home, weren't going to help here. They were as helpless and out of place as she was.

"Sorry, little guys," she said. "Hope you're not sentient. Try not to feel this."

The rooms smelled good when Jessyn and Irinna returned from their work: rich and yeasty like bread or beer. Outside the big window, the sky was turning a ruddy orange. The huge arcs of alien structure, one part building and two parts the bones of strange gods, glittered with a million other windows like theirs. The ziggurats that marched along the curve of the planet, poking their sullen bronze heads up above the clouds, were a cityscape twisted by nightmare, starkly beautiful but vast enough to induce vertigo.

They had just left Dafyd and Tonner in the lab. Else was probably sleeping or taking a shower or being alone for a moment. Synnia sat on one of the couches, her hands folded on her lap, her gaze fixed on nothing. In the little kitchen, Campar stood by the basin, washing dishes. The sounds of water and plateware were comfortingly domestic. Rickar, across from Synnia, had a bowl of something green and white that he was eating with a length of bent metal like someone had seen a knife and spoon and decided to split the difference.

"What's that?" Irinna asked.

Rickar paused. He did that a lot these days, shying away from social contact like a dog that's been hit too many times. But he gathered himself and hoisted the bowl.

"Basil and garlic pasta," he said. "The basil's a little old, but the garlic's fine. Can't complain."

"Well, that sounds tasty," Irinna said. Brittle. Sharp. Trying too hard. Jessyn wavered. The smart thing, the right thing, was to get some food before she went to her room. She didn't want to. She wanted to be alone with her eyes closed. She wanted the chance to not exist. It was just the small, sane part of her that forced her to the kitchen and the pot of food. She filled a bowl, took a knife-spoon thing of her own.

"Do we still have eggs?" she asked.

Campar didn't answer. She looked over at him, then put her bowl down. The big man's eyes were fixed ahead of him, his face pale and gray. He was washing a plate, just one, his movements exactly the same, repeated.

"Campar?" she said.

He turned, and the plate slid out of his fingers. When it hit the floor, he screamed at the clatter and then collapsed. *Oh*, Jessyn thought. *So this is finally here.*

The others ran over, Irinna pushing into the kitchen with her hands out, grabbing for Campar. *What's wrong? Is he hurt? What happened?* Jessyn grabbed the other woman and hauled her away.

"It's okay. Don't touch him," Jessyn said, kneeling on the floor beside Campar. His breath was fast and labored. Wheezing. "Campar? Hey, it's me. Listen. You're having a panic attack, okay? It's scary, but it's going to be okay. Just listen to my voice, all right? Just follow my voice. We're going to breathe in for the count of four, then hold it for four, then let it out for four, be empty for four, and start over. Do it with me."

His eyes moved over to her like he'd just noticed that she was there. His lips were dark. This was a bad one. She counted as she breathed in, mouthing the numbers—one two three four—then switched to her fingers—one two three four—and then murmured them aloud as she exhaled. The second time through, he tried to mirror her, but his breath was frantic, unsteady. She kept mirroring the breath for him the way Jellit had for her during her attacks. By the fifth time through, Campar was almost in sync. The rictus of tension in his face and shoulders was releasing a little. Just a little.

Else appeared, her hair unkempt from the pillow. The others were all crowded behind Jessyn and Campar like they were at a puppet show. She hated them all a little, just then. All of them except Campar.

"Are you here?" she asked. "Are you back now?"

Campar's eyes found her. The little laugh that came out of him didn't have anything to do with humor. "Not... not entirely. Jessyn. Did you know? There's aliens?"

"Yeah. It's hard. I know."

"They look like giant seafood and centipedes made out of knives and they killed us and carried us off, and... And we're... we're just acting like... we're doing..."

"Yeah. We are."

"Like nothing *happened*. Like this is *normal*."

"It isn't. Nothing is normal now."

Campar shook his head and whispered. "I'm not all right. I'm not well."

Jessyn took his hand, chancing that he was stable enough for the physical contact. He didn't pull away. "You're not. You're pretty fucked up. We're all fucked up. Look at us. Tonner's tripling down on the research thing because it's something he understands. Synnia's completely shut down. Rickar's focused on all of us being mad at him so that he doesn't have to think about the rest of it."

She didn't say *Else is drumming up bullshit sexual drama with Tonner and Dafyd. Dafyd is intellectualizing himself into a small steel cube. I'm pretty sure I'm suicidal.* She'd made her point.

"We're all broken. We're trying to find something we can control, because we can't control anything," she said. He was weeping now. And shit, so was she. "None of us are okay. That's all right. We don't have to be. It's all right to be fucked up right now."

The swarm is lying on its bed. The part of it that needs to sleep sleeps and is dreaming. The part of it that doesn't need sleep stretches its senses out.

Because it occupies a body that is afraid, the swarm knows fear. It also knows hunger and desire and annoyance and curiosity. None of these things are necessary to its original design and function, but they are all part of it now, as inextricable as cream poured in coffee.

It knew that the others could be influenced by chemoreception. It can choose the simple aromatics that its skin produces and nudge the others to calm or panic, bonding or rage. It had not expected how much it is, in return, affected by them. The sour ache of Jessyn's sweat, the shuddering panic of Campar's. The body it inhabits receives these chemical signals and reacts to them, dragging the swarm along with it. The swarm has considered disabling the host's pheromone receptor sites, blinding itself to the fears and stresses all around it. But the danger now is being noticed, and so it acts as the host body would act, feels what the host body would feel, participates in the subliminal conversation of primates whose subjective experience is a thin skin over an oceanic subconscious.

It feels the slow magnetic pulse that among all the captives of Anjiin only it can feel. The pulse rises and falls away, and the swarm feels the information-rich stuttering within the field. It knows something about how the Carryx communicate within their world-palaces. It senses compounds in the air, its chemoreceptors turned for a moment to something more sensitive than a bloodhound's nose, and it catalogs them. It has recorded every species that it passes on its way to and from the laboratory, every detail of the landscape outside the window in the common area, every variation in the wavelengths of light. It is the deepest record of the great enemy ever created. It knows more than armies have gleaned in centuries of war.

The parts of it that dream, dream together. The host and the girl named Ameer that preceded her now bleed into each other more easily when both are unconscious. The smell of cut weeds from the host's childhood summer fills the girl's recurring nightmare of missing an exam. The shopkeeper that the girl is trying to argue with is also, in the logic of dream, the host's first lover. The swarm is aware of all this without participating in it.

It has stopped all active probing. No radio or nIR pings. No echolocation mapping. Temptation erodes it, eats away at its resolve. There is so much it could discover, so much it could know, just there beyond the reach of its senses. To come this far, to achieve this much, and miss the one unforeseen fact that could end the war because it was too timid…

But its discipline holds for now. Its mission is as simple as it is difficult: Find a way to share the data it has gathered and is gathering. Somewhere in the world-city, there is a pathway for it. Somewhere in the Carryx security protocols, there is a flaw.

Until it can find that pathway, it has to be indistinguishable from the others. They are traumatized, so it must be traumatized. They are in pain, and so it must be in pain. We're all broken. *That was what Jessyn had said.* We're all broken. *So it must be broken too.*

It has to find ways to explore more than the quarters and the laboratory, but in a way that won't draw attention. Not from the Carryx, not from the humans, not from anyone. It has to take whatever freedom it can, flow into whatever niches are possible for it, all without getting caught. Without getting itself and the others killed.

The magnetic pulse rises again, shuddering with information. An answering pulse comes from the north, and another from above. The network of ships or drones or organisms at the edge of the planet's atmosphere sing down to the world-palace, their attention like a spotlight sweeping the darkness of a prison yard. The swarm keeps still.

As if in response, the dream shifts. The host is naked on a vast plain of tall yellow grass. Animals move, troubling the wide blades. The host and the girl who is gone are both there, they both know that if they move, predators will find them. But if they don't move, they will never escape. The tension between these two facts is a kind of horror and also an excitement. A thrill.

The part of the swarm that needs to sleep dreams, and for a moment the part that doesn't sleep dreams with it.

Sixteen

"Tell me you've solved it all and the secrets of creation have laid themselves out before you," Campar said as he swept into the lab. "I need good news this morning. We ran out of cream, and I had to drink my coffee black."

Dafyd shot a glance at Tonner. The lead researcher's smile was thin and bloodless, but it was a smile. He was amused. Or he was doing his best to be gentle, given Campar's recent breakdown. Either way it was better than most of the previous eight hours had given. Dafyd had worked in Tonner's lab for a little over a year, but he'd never worked this closely with the man himself, or for this many hours at a time. His focus and intensity were exhausting. His moods shifted with less warning than the weather. And three times in the past week, Dafyd had understood something new about biological systems so profound and unexpected that it had taken his breath away.

Else came in just behind the big man. They all wore the same pale tunic and trousers like they'd become monks in some obscure Gallantist order, but Else's seemed to fit her better. Her hair was back in a simple ponytail. There were no cosmetics or beauty products to be had in their Carryx prison. All of them had been scrubbed down to whatever genetics and fate had gifted them with. Even so, Dafyd found he had to make an effort not to stare at Else when she walked in. He hoped she was carefully not looking at him for the same reason.

Tonner crossed his arms. "The silicate pulp in the middle of the berries isn't a gut or a separate organism," he said. "It's a farm."

Campar's lighthearted performance vanished. He hoisted himself up to sit on the countertop, his gaze turning inward. They'd all known that the berries were a thick red complication of organs around a sandy and undifferentiated center. They'd spent the better part of a week debating the nature of the pulp: if it was a cytoplasmic analog and the berries were a large cell the way an egg was, if it was a dependent mutualistic organism like mitochondria. Then, for reasons Dafyd didn't understand, Tonner had decided to test the thin pink soup of the sacrificed samples for metabolic activity. When the berries were ground to pieces, their metabolism rose. Dafyd hadn't known what to make of it. Everyone else apparently did.

"Microorganic farming," Campar said. "That's clever. So the shell organisms feed sugars into the sand."

"To little bastards in the silicate matrix who hand complex nutrients back up to keep the shell alive and functioning," Tonner said. "That sandy crap isn't an organism, it's a hundred different ones. Or a thousand. I don't know. It's an environment. And it's under management. Constraint."

Else let out a low, appreciative whistle. "That complicates things."

"Or it makes them simple," Tonner said. "The organism is already a nutrient factory. If we find a good candidate species in the farm, maybe we don't have to worry about working out berry metabolism at all. Leave it as it is, and focus on using the farm for ourselves."

"Or introduce something from outside that can benefit from it," Campar said. "A cuckoo."

"Depends on the farm's immune response," Else said. "Assuming it has one. That seems like an easy initial test, though."

Dafyd crossed his arms. For the most part, he followed what they were saying. If not the full depth of implications, at least the gist, but the leaps of insight and understanding that were so automatic for them left him feeling stupid. All Tonner had to say was *It's a farm* and the others were already halfway to making a protocol.

While the three of them debated the merits of introducing a novel organism versus figuring out plasmid analogs for the berry's existing microbiota, Dafyd washed out the gel trays and ran the CCA's cleaning cycle. His jaw was uncomfortably tight.

"Any sign of our jailer?" Tonner asked, changing the subject at last.

Else answered. "No. The librarian didn't make an appearance today either."

"It did say to tell it what we needed, right? I didn't imagine that? Hard to do that when it doesn't show up."

"They have strange blind spots," Campar said. "They know we brush our teeth, but not that we clip our fingernails. They know we use utensils to eat, but what exactly they are seems to baffle them. It may have left us some way to make requests that we haven't fathomed."

"Good point. We need to remember how little we understand about this place," Dafyd said. It didn't seem like the big man was in danger of losing it again, but Dafyd found himself wanting to be agreeable anyway. Campar was taller, heavier, and stronger than any of the rest of them. If he lost it and needed to be restrained, it would be a bad day for the entire group. Dafyd shot him a smile. Campar smiled back.

Tonner made an impatient sound. "I don't have time to figure out all of this and them too. Dafyd? Are you ready to go?"

I'll stay a little and finish cleaning up was on the tip of his tongue. He could already see the ghost of a smile on Else's lips. Her embarrassment that he'd been so obvious. Instead, he said, "Sure."

As he passed her, Else touched his arm. Not a caress, not a clasp, just a tap of her fingertips against his forearm. The kind of gesture that didn't mean anything unless it did. "Are you all right?" she asked. "You look tired."

Dafyd hated the way his heart leaped. "I'm a little tired. I'll get some rest." He followed after Tonner before the man could look back and see anything. Not that Dafyd was sure what there was to see.

Tonner marched out through the vast shared room with his head down staring at the deck ahead of him and his hands in fists at his sides. He didn't look at the strange creatures around them, didn't acknowledge they were there except to step away from them. Dafyd couldn't tell if it was disgust or fear or the strategy Tonner used to keep from being overwhelmed by too much that was new and inexplicable.

They were almost back to their quarters when Dafyd's gut went tight. When they slid the wide door open, Jessyn and Irinna would be there, or if they weren't, Tonner would call them to come out. Dafyd would hear about the berries and the farm again. Rickar and Synnia wouldn't participate, but they'd listen and be impressed. That was fair. Tonner could be impressive.

"Hey, boss," Dafyd said. "I need to walk around a little. Work out some kinks. I'll catch up."

"Don't go back to the lab," Tonner said. "They don't need the distraction."

"Wasn't planning to," Dafyd said, and it mostly wasn't a lie.

Tonner grunted and returned his attention to the floor. Dafyd watched him go, then walked back toward the cathedral. He didn't have a plan or place in mind, but being anywhere that wasn't the lab or their rooms felt like an escape. He found a little outcropping in one of the walls that stretched between alcoves. It wasn't quite a bench, but it was close enough. He put his back against the wall, pulled up his legs, hugged his knees, and took a moment to stop doing anything.

It was strange the way that life kept going. They had lost everything—homes, lives, their place in the vastness of the universe—and Campar still made coffee every morning. Irinna still sang in the shower loud enough that they could hear her doing it. And he, apparently, still mooned after Else Yannin. He didn't know if it was a sign of their strength or their weakness. He didn't know whether Anjiin still existed or if the Carryx had taken what they wanted from it and burned the rest to ash. He didn't know what had happened to the other prisoners from the ship, from all the ships. What the Carryx wanted or intended, how they would be treated if they managed to solve the biochemical puzzle they'd been given, what shape the future could be. It wasn't just unknown, it was probably unknowable. And in that fog, the thing that shook him was still Else's smile.

"You're an idiot," Dafyd said to no one. "Just a total idiot."

The huge room filled with alien bodies didn't disagree.

Dafyd rested his head against the wall. The cathedral rose above him, its high windows glowing with sunlight. A wide knot of dark filaments swirled slowly in the upper air like the tentacles of a huge diaphanous jellyfish. He didn't know if it was alive or a piece of Carryx technology or something else, but there was a beauty to it. The tendrils flowing with the invisible currents of the air.

When he'd been a child, Dafyd had been terrified of spiders. Even imagining one in its slow, eight-legged crawl would send a shiver down his spine. But always simmering under the fear, he'd felt angry. Angry at himself for being afraid. And then one day the anger was stronger than the fear, and he forced himself to pick a spider up and let it crawl on his hand. He lasted only a few seconds before he fled, screaming.

But the next day he lasted a little longer. And within a few weeks, he was catching spiders in his bare hands. When he showed his mother his great triumph over fear, she'd just laughed and said most people who are scared of spiders don't force themselves to get over it, they just leave them alone. *My little Dafyd just hates anything telling him what to do.*

She'd been right. All his life Dafyd had felt an irrational need to pull left when everything was telling him to pull right. It was petulant and petty, a childish need to not be controlled, even by himself. It had gotten him into trouble more times than he remembered. But he also wasn't scared of spiders anymore.

When he'd first seen the cathedral and the alcoves, the hallways and ramps, the endless parade of terrifying creatures moving about, it had been overwhelming. Everything screamed at him to run away and hide in his room. So he sat and forced himself to stare up at the nauseating heights. To look at the monsters moving past. And the more time he spent there, the less assaulting it felt. The space was vast, but no more so than a few sports stadiums jammed together. What had first seemed like a hundred different species of creature, each more grotesque than the last, had turned out to be maybe twelve or fifteen. He'd seen more varieties of life in zoological parks, and nothing here was more hideous than a tapeworm or a sea cucumber.

His mind spent a lot of time attempting to shield itself using an irrational fear of the unknown. But like picking up that first spider, forcing himself to engage with the fear without looking away was the best inoculation he knew.

A pair of large beasts the size of horses but with bone-colored exoskeletons ambled by, their joints making little green flashes like static. A dozen glowing globes flew past, clicking to themselves or each other. Across the wide, open expanse of the cathedral floor, one of the Carryx skittered with its hind legs and plodded with the front, accompanied by four Soft Lothark. This one looked different from the librarian. It had a lighter coloration, almost yellow, and one of its massive forearms was banded by white in three places, like scars or tattoos. Dafyd watched the aliens move past him, pretending they were fish in an aquarium, and he found it almost restful. None of them had emotional lives entangled with his. Strange as they were, there was also a kind of beauty in all the ways evolution had solved its problems through luck and environmental pressure. Half a dozen of the amber-eyed monkey-like things that kept invading the laboratory bounded past, saw him, screeched, and ran away.

Most of them, he didn't have names for. The few he did, he'd been told: Rak-hund, Soft Lothark, Sinen, Carryx. The others, he could come up with his own signifiers—click bubbles, feather monkeys, whatever else—but that didn't seem as satisfying to him. The Carryx turned and its soldiers followed. They seemed to be homing in on one of the crow-ape things that Dafyd sometimes saw facing the walls in the hallways. Hallway crows. The crow only showed that it knew the Carryx was approaching by turning its back. Over the murmur that filled the cathedral like a train station, Dafyd thought he could hear something harsh and staccato coming from the Carryx. Not its usual bass birdsong, but a kind of ripping sound. The hallway crow flinched and made a similar noise in reply.

Because that was the difference, wasn't it? The species that he knew by name had been able to speak. They were the ones that had the little black squares. The translators. Now that he thought to look, it was almost exclusively the Carryx and their guards that had translators. He thought that one of the big bone horses might have had one around its neck, but they were gone by now, and he wasn't sure.

The hallway crow was screeching now and trying to walk away from the Carryx. The four Soft Lothark shifted into its path, blocking its retreat. If Dafyd had had one of the black squares, he might have been able to fathom what the hallway crow was upset about. Or learn its name. Ask it what it knew and how it understood the Carryx and their shared prison. The Carryx lifted its massive forelegs. Its fighting arms. With the clearer view, Dafyd was almost certain the white bands were scars. The hallway crow dropped to the ground screeching like an exhausted child, and a moment later the Carryx lowered its forelegs again. A pack of black things like crabs the size of large dogs scurried across the floor, their feet making a sound like dry rice being poured over stone. In the high air, dozens of the clicking orbs were rising, converging on the dark filaments that still wafted and spun.

It was all strange, but some of it was also beautiful. The horror behind it was real. There wasn't a moment that Dafyd couldn't feel the fear and tension in his body if he just turned his mind to it. But there were some moments when there was also awe. The clicking orbs reached the massive jellyfish thing and started wrapping themselves in its black threads. Dafyd wished there was someone there to see it with him. To wonder with him what it all meant. To remember it with him later. Instead it was just his. A private moment that couldn't be shared.

The hallway crow, still splayed on the floor, screeched louder and started flailing its limbs. It looked like a toddler throwing a tantrum. The movements were almost the same.

"At least you can talk to your librarian," Dafyd said. "You're ahead of me."

They have strange blind spots, Campar said in his memory at the same time the librarian said *You are all permitted access to this pathway. And also to the complex.* It was almost synesthesia. Dafyd saw the two thoughts, and how they fit like pieces of a jigsaw puzzle. How together they made something new.

He got to his feet before he could talk himself out of it. The hallway crow had worn itself out. The four Soft Lothark stood around it, looking at each other like they were deciding whether to kill the thing on the floor or let it be. The scar-armed librarian stood back a couple steps, letting whatever was happening play out. Dafyd went to it.

"Excuse me," he said. "Please forgive me. I'm very new."

The pale Carryx shifted. Its feeding arms were as thick as a human's, and longer. Its fingers were spidery and it didn't have thumbs. Its wide, flat eyes found him, but it didn't speak.

"The librarian of my moiety said I was permitted here at the complex and my quarters and the path between them. Am I allowed to go other places?"

The thing's fingers plucked at each other, and the Carryx whistled and burbled. The voice that came from the dark square around its neck was the one from Anjiin. The dispassionate conqueror's voice. "Permission in one place has no bearing on other places."

"Thank you. So there are other places I *am* permitted to go?"

"There are places you are permitted and places you are not."

A little flush of pleasure rose up Dafyd's chest. "We have made a mistake. I need help finding the way to the librarian of my moiety."

The Carryx didn't answer. Not to him. It let out a flurry of hard clicks. The prone hallway crow replied in kind. When the Carryx turned and walked away, the Soft Lothark went after it. After a moment of uncertainty, Dafyd followed too.

The Carryx and its guards or orderlies or soldiers moved quickly to the far side of the cathedral and through a wide archway to a passage that sloped down. The air felt thicker here, and it smelled like smoke from a chemical fire. Dafyd coughed, but the Carryx didn't look back at him. *If this goes badly,* he thought, *they will never find my corpse.* He didn't know why that was funny, but it was.

The passage dropped. Other archways opened into it, and he caught glimpses of other cathedral spaces. The gateways to other sets of alcoves. And other things too. A place that looked like a vast web, spider silk too fine to see the strands but so thick that the far walls were hidden. A pool of water as wide as a small lake with disturbances on its surface where something was moving beneath. He wondered if any of the other captives of Anjiin were through those archways, in labs or workrooms of their own, facing tests that were all really the same test. *Are we useful?*

Other aliens walked along with them or passed in the other

direction. Some were Rak-hund and Soft Lothark. Some were other things that he hadn't seen before. Most if not all had the black squares on them.

After what felt like most of an hour, the Carryx left the passageway through a wide, low gate that the Soft Lothark pulled open for it. Dafyd followed into a maze of low halls with inward-tilted walls like the ones in the ship coming over. There was a sound here that his mind kept wanting to interpret as water flowing over stones. It wasn't that, though. It was the voices of Carryx. Dozens of them, maybe. All speaking at the same time.

One of the Soft Lothark shifted in front of him, stopping him with its body as the scar-armed Carryx went on. To Dafyd's left, an archway led to a ramp that curved down. He pointed to it. "There?"

The prison guard didn't answer, but turned and walked away. Dafyd squeezed his hands into fists and released them again, trying to relax. He walked down the ramp slowly, willing his senses a little farther around the curve of the wall than he could actually see.

The ramp ended in a room as cramped as Dafyd's first apartment, and the large-eyed Carryx was squatting in the middle of the space, manipulating a series of glowing, floating cubes with its thin forearms. Its wide black eyes locked onto Dafyd.

"I'm, ah..." Dafyd cleared his throat and tried again. "I'm Dafyd Alkhor. With the workgroup. You told us to make one thing food for the other one?"

"I know these things," the librarian said in its reedy voice.

"You also said we should tell you if there was something else we needed in order to do our work?"

"Where the fuck have you been?" Tonner said as Dafyd stepped back through the wide main door. Outside the windows, the sky had turned stormy and dark. Rain pattered against the glass, making the orange lights on the ziggurats shudder and run. Else and Campar were sitting at the table, and Dafyd was flattered to see the worry and relief in their eyes. Jessyn and Irinna, he assumed, were back at the lab.

He'd been gone more than eight hours. He was hungry. He was exhausted. He was elated. He was spent.

Dafyd put down his little metal crate and closed the door behind him.

"What's that?" Else asked.

He lifted the top of the crate with a clank and pulled out a thick sheaf of pages that were something like paper, if not actual paper itself. Then two pots with sticky, black, butter-textured ink and a handful of metal styluses.

"I got pens," he said.

Seventeen

Jessyn drew the blade down the berry's shell. Its blood, pink and fragrant, welled up and out as she pinned it back to expose the sandy interior. It was the twenty-fourth berry she'd skinned that morning. The others lay out in a grid on the countertop, each marked by a slip of Dafyd's faux-paper. They were waiting to see what kinds of amino acids, when introduced to the rich environment of the pulp, made the farm die faster.

"No, no, no," Irinna said from near the mouth of the alcove. "Thank you, no. We don't want anything."

The feather monkeys had brought a small gray box into their alcove and deposited it on the floor. They screamed and chittered as Irinna tossed it back out of their workspace and into the corridor beyond. One of the alien animals rose up, its arms open like it was going to hug Irinna, but then it turned and loped out after the object and the three others followed it.

"I think you hurt their feelings," Jessyn said. "What if you just rejected a proposal of marriage?"

"They are cute, but dating outside your species is challenging," Irinna replied. "How are you doing?"

"I'm fine," Jessyn said.

It was what she always said.

The truth was, it was hard to get out of her bed. It was hard to eat food. It was hard not to get lost in fantasies where oblivion was the closest thing the universe had to rest.

She envied the others their energy. The Carryx guards wouldn't answer questions about where the other groups from Anjiin were, and the aliens that didn't have translators didn't say anything at all, so Synnia and Else had been going on walks together, mapping out the labyrinth of the complex and looking—unsuccessfully so far—for more humans. Rickar had gone on a couple longer explorations on his own, but he didn't talk about them much. He also used a pen and paper to draw little games that he and Synnia played, passing time together in their exile. Jessyn would have liked to play a game or take a walk or at least have the energy to consider them.

Every day was hard. Everything was hard.

She had one pill left, and she should have taken it almost two weeks ago. She knew enough about the action of the medication to understand that, with the present levels in her bloodstream, it wouldn't make much difference. Some stubborn, irrational part of her brainstem insisted that as long as there was one left, as long as she wasn't out, there was hope. It was the part of her illness that Jellit had called *bad magic* back when he'd been around to call it anything.

Jessyn shook her head like she could dislodge the thought. Thinking about Jellit was like pressing her thumb against a razor blade. It was easy to do too much, and she never knew how close she was to damage until she was already bleeding.

She plucked up another berry and slit it open to get at what it tried to keep inside for itself, and thought about the phrase *physical hypocrisy.*

"Ready for the samples?" Irinna asked.

"Almost. Samples ready?"

"Almost."

"Professionals."

Irinna chuckled. "If we're lucky, these little puppies'll have nice broad toxicity tolerances."

"We still have to figure out what not-turtles actually eat. The farm's not much good if we don't know what to plant in it."

"Yeah," Irinna sighed. "It all needs to get done. Easy's fast, and hard takes all the time. But hey, maybe we can find a way to make some coffee creamer in the meantime. Get Campar to quit—Jessyn? Are you all right?"

"What? Yes. No, I'm fine." But she wasn't. She was shaking.

Nutrition. She'd been thinking about food, but food was just a set of chemicals the same as anything else. The thing that could mend her brain was seventeen carbon atoms, a few chlorines and nitrogens, and the holes all filled with hydrogen. It wasn't exotic. It wasn't strange. She could have synthesized it herself if they'd had a different lab setup. They were making the berries into biochemical factories that could produce specific outputs. And one of the outputs could cut the rot out of her mind.

Maybe. Maybe not, but *maybe.* Hope was like a breath of air when she'd already resigned herself to drowning.

Hands trembling, she took another slip of paper and wrote her initials on it, then placed the berry she'd been vivisecting onto it. There were other compounds in the pill—the one precious pill she hadn't had the heart to swallow. If she introduced the medicine to the berry and it died faster, she wouldn't know if it was the molecule she cared about or one of the others in the matrix that had been the poison.

If it *didn't*, though—if nothing in the pill was immediately toxic to the berries—she wouldn't have to keep pretending that she wasn't marching toward her own death. The urge to live bloomed up just below her throat, warm and desperate and bright.

"I have to run back to the rooms for a minute," she said as she put down the knife.

"Now?"

"Just for a minute. I need to get something."

Irinna shrugged. "Should I finish those up?"

"No," Jessyn said. And then, "Actually, yes. Just the control group. I'm sorry."

"It's fine," Irinna said. "Go."

Her body felt like she'd taken a euphoric—bright and light and electric in a way she relished and knew better than to trust. She walked along the well-known path between the lab and the rooms as if she was seeing it for the first time. The wide central space with its dozens of alcoves like the one she spent her time in. The strange bodies, monstrous and beautiful and both, that moved through the space with her, as thick as a downtown street during festival. The green-bronze walls and floors, the same as the ships that had killed Anjiin.

She hauled the wide door open when she reached it. The rooms were sun-soaked and empty except for Tonner standing at the kitchen counter with pages of handwritten notes spread out before him. When he glanced up, he looked annoyed.

"You're supposed to be at the lab."

"I'm going right back."

"We have a schedule."

"I'm not stopping at the bar on my way back," she snapped, then went to her room before he could reply. The pill bottle was under her bed, the same place she'd hidden away her most precious things when she'd been a child. The one pill in it was a dull, dusty orange with a manufacturer's mark pressed into it. The pharmacological labs that had made it were under a different sun, if they still existed at all. Even if this worked, she'd be medicating herself with excretions from the sandy pulp of an alien animal.

"Please let this work," she whispered, though she wasn't one of the pious. "Please let this work. Please."

When the universe didn't answer, she wrapped the bottle in her fist and left. Synnia was singing in her room, a slow, strange song that Jessyn didn't recognize. If the experiment worked, she should probably plan to make an extra dose for the older woman. For that matter, they should probably just put it in the water supply. She could make vanilla and cinnamon along with the creamer. She could do anything. That wasn't true. It was the euphoria talking. The hope.

Tonner didn't look up again or speak as she left. The wide door closed on him. In the passageway, one of the Carryx lumbered past on its massive front arms, its abdomen scuttling along behind it. Its voice was fluting and deep, a study in undertones. It was almost beautiful. She felt a surge of hatred for it. How dare it be beautiful.

She had nearly reached the alcove when the sound of the explosion came. Not the sharp crack of detonation, but a low, rumbling whoosh: the crackling of a sudden, vast fire. All around her, the aliens paused, shifted. Some ran, but not in any particular direction. No alarm sounded, but an acrid smell like burning plastic seeped into the air. A distant chorus of high, angry voices screamed in pain or else victory. She walked forward until she turned the last corner before their lab.

Then she ran.

A thin smoke clung to the ceiling outside their alcove. The flame was either out or invisible, and whatever had happened, it had damaged the lights. They flickered—blindingly bright to utter black like a strobe without the rhythm. And caught in the flashes like still images from a violent book, the feather-haired monkeys were running riot. One with particularly long arms and needle-sharp teeth stood on the countertop, smashing the berries she'd spent the morning prepping into a single, wide pink smear. Another was ripping the pages of notes in its tiny, clever hands. Two others were standing on a bundle of something on the ground, hunched over it with their shoulders tense. Biting it, worrying it like dogs taking apart a stuffed toy. The terrible thing wasn't the violence. It was the joy.

The bundle moved, and Jessyn recognized Irinna.

She moved without thinking, like the world had suddenly shifted, and she wasn't running toward the lab, but falling. She heard herself shouting *No, no, fuck off!* She grabbed one of the attackers off Irinna's back. It was the weight and texture of a large house cat. It squirmed in her grip, thrashed, clawed, bit. Jessyn clubbed the corner of the countertop with it. Three hard blows before the monkey went limp, then two more afterward.

Something clamped onto her leg, sharp and grinding. One of the other beasts had sunk its teeth into her. The long-armed one that had been ruining the samples rose up on the countertop. It had claws like little daggers. The pain of the bite was fierce, and something unexpected in Jessyn welcomed it.

"Yeah? You gonna kill me?" Jessyn shouted, lunging for it.

It danced back. "You gonna kill me, you little *fuck*? Come here and try."

Something landed on her back. Teeth sank into her shoulder, and some strange part of her mind became very calm. Yes, it hurt. Yes, she wanted it off. But the pain was just data. Her attacker was just a problem, and you fixed problems the same way. A step at a time.

And more than that. The pain was permission.

She reached down to her leg where the one enemy was still attached, and wrapped her hand around its neck. She could feel the moment it realized it was in trouble and tried to pull away. The other on her shoulder let go, shrieked, and started clawing at her eyes, but she ignored it, bringing her other hand down and cracking the one monkey's neck. The tension and sudden release felt just like breaking a bone. It spasmed in her hand as it died, and she thought how interesting it was that there was some parallel evolution of spinal cords. *Lucky you aren't being eaten by something with a more distributed nervous system, like octopuses. Starfish.*

She reached up for the one on her shoulder, but it bounded away. The two remaining attackers scuttled out of the alcove and bounced excitedly in the cathedral. Their gums were black. They screamed. On the floor by Jessyn's feet, Irinna coughed and tried to sit up.

"Bomb," the other woman said. "That thing they brought before. It was a bomb. I didn't throw it out. I was... the samples..."

"Don't talk. Don't try to talk. It's going to be all right. You're going to be fine."

She didn't look fine. Blisters were rising on the pale skin of her face. The ends of her white-blond hair were now black and twisted where they'd burned. A small but spreading pool of blood smeared the floor under them, and at first Jessyn thought it was coming from Irinna.

"Hey! Hey! Call the guards!" Jessyn shouted. "We're hurt! We've been attacked."

In the cathedral, the alien menagerie went back about its business. One of the Rak-hund slid by, its legs undulating as it hurried past. The long-armed monkey chittered, made eye contact with Jessyn, and shat on the ground before the two surviving attackers turned away, vanishing into the crowd.

"Please, someone. We're hurt. We're both hurt." Then, a moment later, "What the fuck is *wrong* with you assholes?"

"Emergency medical…not so great here," Irinna managed, then her breath caught in pain.

"Yeah," Jessyn said past the panic in her throat. "You'd think with all the shit they built, these fucking roaches could manage an ambulance."

Irinna smiled, but her gaze shifted, losing focus.

"No no no," Jessyn said. "Stay here. Stay with me."

"Go back. Get the others."

"If I leave you, and they come back, they'll kill you."

"The work, though. If no one's here—"

"The work's gone."

The alcove's light flickered again, this time with a deep red and a sound like water on a hot skillet. When it went out, it didn't come back.

"We have to go back to the room. We have to go together."

"I just…" Irinna began, and didn't finish.

Jessyn's back and side were cold. The adrenaline had faded enough to let the pain in her shoulder and leg burn through. The walk back to the rooms seemed terribly long, even without a burden. And Irinna would die if she left her. Jessyn might not understand anything else in this hellscape, but she was sure about that.

She shifted her weight, moved to Irinna's side. There was a way to do this. She'd learned it in some rescue aid camp when she'd been a child. She remembered trying it on Jellit and being so proud that she could pick him up. How had it worked?

With only the light spilling into the alcove from the outside, she drew Irinna up to sitting, then leaning her against the counter, to a somnolent stand. This was right. Old memory came through, and Jessyn bent, drew the semiconscious woman across her own torn and bleeding shoulder. Holding Irinna's leg with one hand and her arm with the other, Jessyn lifted.

I can't do this, she thought, her thighs and back burning with the strain. But she took a step forward anyway. And then another. Her breath seemed unnatural—too close and also somehow not associated with her. Like listening to someone else laboring beside her. She spat, took another step, then another, and she was walking. Around them, the surreal traffic of alien bodies flowed like images from nightmare. Nothing offered her aid, but nothing stopped her either. They were all in the same corridor. They were all in different worlds.

By the halfway point, she was muttering *I can't go on* with each step, and then taking another after it. *I can't go on. I can't go on. I can't go on.* When she reached the wide door, she couldn't remember how she'd gotten there or how long she'd been standing, looking at it bemused. She couldn't open it, and she couldn't figure out how to knock. The best she could manage was to go up to it and bang her forehead against it again and again and again until it opened and Else looked out at her with wide, startled eyes and her mouth agape.

"Hey," Jessyn said, and sank to the ground. Irinna rolled gently off her shoulders, their clothes making a wet ripping as they parted. The dried blood had glued them together.

In what seemed like a blink, everyone was there. Campar lifted both women, one in each arm like they were light as a feather, and carried them to the couch. Synnia showed up with a cloth and a bowl of warm water, wiping away the worst of the gore and finding the gouges in her flesh when she flinched. Tonner ran out to see the lab. Jessyn thought she'd told them about the attack, about the bomb and the feather-haired murderers, but she wasn't sure. She tried again now, but Else put a hand on her shoulder and pressed her back into the bed. Oh, somehow she was in her bed.

"Did Irinna..." Jessyn said.

Else's mouth tightened, and for a moment she looked angry. Only no, it wasn't anger. Or sorrow. Horror. Else was horrified.

Jessyn tried again. "Is she..."

"I'm sorry," Else said. "I'm so sorry."

Eighteen

"We can't work if we're not safe. You understand that? They killed her. They killed my researcher. She's *dead*."

Tonner paced because he couldn't stand still. The librarian seemed to watch him, but who could be sure with these things? Its mind could have been on lunch for all Tonner knew. It sure as hell wasn't expressing contrition or remorse or any of the things that ought to have been coming out of it. It was like talking to a wall.

Dafyd stood still at the side, impassive as a referee. Tonner had made the man take him to the librarian's office or den or lair or whatever the right word would be. Rage had carried him there.

The librarian burbled and hummed, and the square at its throat spoke. "That is an interesting issue."

"What? What's an interesting issue?"

"That you cannot work without safety."

Tonner barked out a laugh. "They killed Irinna. Those fucking little monkey things put a bomb in our lab. How do you expect us to do your project?"

"That is also interesting," it said.

Tonner pressed his hands to his mouth. His head felt like it was filled with bees. He told himself it was anger, but it seemed like more. "We did what you wanted," he said. "We did what you said."

"Your project is completed?"

"No. I mean... We're trying. We were making progress, and they..." The words ran out. Irinna's corpse, the ruins of his lab, Jessyn and Campar and Synnia crying. It was all inside him, and the power of it should have been enough to change something. But he couldn't get it out. He thought he'd say it, and it would get out of him, but it wasn't saying that mattered. It was being heard, and the librarian wasn't listening. "We do what you say, and you keep us safe. That's the *deal*."

"That is not accurate."

Dafyd took half a step forward. "Excuse me. I don't mean to intrude. But may I ask something?"

"Fine," Tonner snapped.

Dafyd turned toward the librarian. "The things that attacked us. Is there something we can call them?"

The librarian's abdomen shuffled from side to side on its four smaller legs. "They refer to themselves as Night Drinkers."

"And are the Night Drinkers working on the same test we are?"

"There is only one test."

"Thank you for this important reminder. Are these Night Drinkers trying to turn the berries into food for the not-turtle too?"

"They are."

"And if we can do it faster, we are more useful to the Carryx," Dafyd said. This time it wasn't a question. "Thank you. We understand better now."

"But you are unable to work without safety."

"Damn right," Tonner said, but Dafyd put his palm out. Holding his hand low, almost at his waist.

"We will adjust to these clarified conditions," Dafyd said to the monster, his tone making everything that had happened their own fault. It galled. Tonner wanted to slap him across the head for not even trying to negotiate.

The librarian paused for a moment, as if considering what Dafyd had said. Then, "The body will be removed."

Dafyd's head came up like he'd heard something that Tonner hadn't. "Thank you," he said, then gestured to Tonner and walked away.

Tonner hesitated, then followed. They walked up the long, winding ramp without speaking. The only sound was the low, rumbling babble of Carryx voices and a single high shriek whose meaning Tonner couldn't guess. The endless hallways intersected, branched, turned. Dafyd walked like he knew the way, and Tonner resented him for it.

"What the fuck was that, Alkhor?"

"I don't think we should tell it we can't do the work."

"You don't make that decision. You aren't the one in charge of this group. That's me. I am."

"All right. I'm sorry."

Tonner muttered an obscenity that was only half directed at Dafyd. His arms were trembling. He felt unsteady. The feeling in his head that wasn't anger had gotten stronger, but he didn't want to think about it. He was sweating and cold at the same time. He didn't like that. They reached the wide corridor with its traffic of guard species. The air smelled like vinegar.

Tonner put his head down, staring at the floor just in front of his feet. It was the only way he could walk without his brain getting overloaded. Every alien thing that caught his attention was like looking into the sun. His mind grabbed at them all, tried to make them into something he knew, something that made sense. After a while, it felt like a migraine without the pain. Just looking at them was exhausting, so he didn't look. As long as he kept control of his focus, he was fine. Not that they made it easy for him.

He fell into a rhythm, one foot in front of the other. He could pay attention to that. Counting his steps from one up to ten and then back down again. Now and then, he had to shift to the right or left to make way for one of the guards. Or one of the Carryx. He tried not to let it throw off his concentration. He tried to keep his mind quiet.

His mind wouldn't stay quiet. Irinna was dead. Her corpse was in her room, on her bed. She'd been complaining that they were out of apples. She'd just been complaining that they were out of apples, and now…

"Oh," Dafyd said, like he'd just remembered something.

"What?" Tonner snapped, grabbing at the sound and his annoyance and anything that wasn't Irinna's sweet face charred to black.

"It knew we didn't have a way to take care of the body," Dafyd said. "Something was bothering me. That was it. It knew that our species doesn't eat its dead or whatever. It knew to send someone. They didn't know we like writing things down, but they knew that."

"That's very interesting. I'm so very interested," Tonner said with a harshness that meant he didn't care.

If Dafyd picked up on that, he ignored it. "I don't think Irinna is the first one of us who's died in this complex."

"If you've got nothing helpful, don't talk."

Back at the quarters, Else, Synnia, and Campar were sitting at the window. Storm clouds below them flashed with lightning, but no thunder came. High in the twilight gray of the sky, five bright pink lights glowed. Tonner wanted them to be transport drives, but they weren't. He didn't know what they were, or if he'd be able to understand them if he knew, but the familiar things were all gone now. The framework that he'd lived in didn't apply but he didn't have another one, so he let his brain call them transport drives and ignored the tension of being wrong.

All three turned to look at him while Dafyd hauled the wide door closed. The complexity of anticipation and grief and fear was overwhelming. Tonner's scowl ached.

"It didn't care," he said, and then stalked to the little kitchen so that he wouldn't have to see them react. "It said it would send some kind of cleanup crew to help with her body. That's the help we get."

He waited for Campar to say something arch, but no one said anything. He went through the little pantry without any idea what he was looking for. The fresh fruits were gone, but there were some preserves. Dehydrated and salted and packed in skins of removable gel. The kind they had used for emergency rations back at home.

"Why?" Else asked. Her voice was steady. "Did it tell you why they did it?"

"They're the competition," Tonner said. "They're working the same project we are, and they don't want us to finish first. Something like that. So it's all right to make bombs as part of the research effort. It's all right to kill off anyone you don't want to have around, as long as it's not the Carryx, and maybe we could even blow them up. I don't know what the rules are, except we're doing our own security." He plucked a skin of dried mango out of the pantry and dropped it onto the countertop. The quiet was profound, but he liked the last phrase he'd said. Liked how it felt in his mouth. "We're doing our own security."

"They'll kill us anyway," Synnia said. "We're not fighters."

Dafyd was the one to reply. It was strange to hear his voice. "At least one of us turned out to be," he said, nodding toward Jessyn's room. "And I don't think the Carryx want us dead. There are a lot of other species in here with us. I don't think the librarian's lying about wanting to see if we're useful."

Tonner pointed to the research assistant. "Exactly. We're doubling down. The lab's dead. We don't have enough people to guard it and work at the same time."

Else crossed her arms. "It doesn't sound like doubling down if we can't work."

"We move the equipment in here," Tonner said, gesturing toward the common room, the dining area, the hallway. "Pull power from the same unit as the kitchen. We should have done this before. I didn't think about it. I should have."

"And then what?" Campar said.

"Then we beat them," Tonner said. "We figure out the puzzle. We get there first, that's what we do."

In the silence that came after, a door opened. Rickar's shadow came down the hallway. The lines around his mouth were stark and hard, like he'd aged another five years since that morning. Tonner picked out a sliver of dried mango and chewed it. He was going to have to think about giving Rickar work to do. He hated the thought, but with Irinna gone and Jessyn injured…

"She wants to talk to you," Rickar said. "She's feeling strong enough."

The words felt like Rickar had put a palm against Tonner's chest and pushed. Tonner took a deep breath, and then another, mostly to prove to himself that he could still breathe. When he walked down the hall toward the open door of Jessyn's room, the others started talking behind him. Else and Dafyd and Rickar. He closed the door.

Jessyn lay on her bed. One side of her face was swollen, and patches of black showed where scabs had formed over her wounds. Someone had pulled a chair from the common area and put it by her bed. Tonner sat. He didn't want to look at her. He didn't want to hear her voice. He was already full, and whatever she said was just going to put more onto him. But he had to, so he did.

"Hey," he said. "Rough day."

"Yeah." Her voice was coarse and wet. She'd probably strained her vocal cords screaming. "I needed to... What happened was my fault. I shouldn't have left her alone."

He knew the thing he was supposed to say. *Oh, don't say that. It's not your fault.* Those weren't the words that came out. "Why did you leave her alone?"

"Yes," she said, like she was agreeing. She levered herself up to sitting. It made her wince. She put her hand out, a closed fist with the palm down. It took a few seconds to understand she was handing him something. An orange-gray pill with something printed on it. It might as well have been a rock or a used tissue. He didn't know what it was or what he was supposed to do with it. Jessyn set her gaze on the far wall. She wouldn't look at him. He understood that, at least.

"I've been taking medication for years," she said. "I have... emotional and cognitive issues that are managed that way. I tried to string out the supply as long as I could. That's the last one. I was going to see if I could use the berries to manufacture more, but..."

"You were running your own experiment on the side? Without telling me? You were using my lab for work I didn't know about?"

Her head sank. He saw the guilt in her shoulders and the way she held her hands, and it felt like relief. Someone else had screwed this up. It wasn't just him. "I should have told you. I should have told everyone. I got so used to not letting anyone know. Any little thing, and they won't let you be lead researcher. Keeping quiet was just... habit?"

"You left Irinna alone in the lab so you could get this and use it for your experiment," Tonner said. "You left her alone for this."

"They were going to... I mean, we didn't think they were a threat, or..." Jessyn took a deep breath and let it out through her teeth. "Yeah. I left her alone. For that."

"All right," Tonner said. He stood up. "You wanted to tell me. I'm told."

She didn't try to call him back, and he left the door open behind him.

His dinner, such as it was, came from shelf-stable beef and rehydrated beans. He didn't eat much of it, and didn't taste much of what he did. He kept catching himself on the verge of reminding Else and Campar to go and relieve Jessyn and Irinna, like the news of all that had happened hadn't quite perfused through his own brain yet. There were still parts of him just finding out. Campar went back toward his bedroom as if he wanted to be alone, but then came back out a few minutes later. Dafyd washed the dishes and cleaned the kitchen. Outside, the storm clouds cleared. The great ziggurats stood, glowing at their edges, one after another into the distance. The grid of whatever they were stood their constant guard in the sky, blotting out the stars. Irinna's body lay in her room, waiting for something to come and carry her away like trash. His jaw ached.

He waited in the common area until Else went to her room, then a while after that. Instead of going to his own room, he knocked softly at her door and stepped in without waiting for her to speak. She was in her bed, still dressed in her prison uniform except for bare feet. She sat up, her expression cool. Maybe annoyed.

Tonner closed the door and set his back against it, his arms crossed. For a moment, they were both silent.

"I'm not stupid," he said. "The way things were between you and me back before…all this? I know that's not how things are now. But I need you, okay?"

"I know you're upset. We all are. But coming to bed with me isn't going to make—"

"I'm not here for comfort. I don't need my *girlfriend*," he said, more bitterly than he intended. "I need my team lead. I need you professionally. You understand?"

Else shifted, put her back against the wall, pulled her legs up in front of her. He took it as permission, and crossed the room to sit at the foot of the bed. Jessyn's pill was in the pocket of his tunic. He ran his hand through his hair, looking for the place to start. If he could start talking, it would all come out eventually. It was all connected. Jessyn's confession or the librarian's almost bureaucratic disinterest or the blood and scorch marks at their ruined lab.

"How do I keep them safe?"

Else tilted her head. It was a question.

"My team. My people. My crew," he said. "I thought if we didn't fight back, you know? I thought if we just stayed in line, did what they told us to do, and didn't push back…Do you know what I mean?"

"If we were good prisoners, we wouldn't be punished."

"Yes, that. Exactly. That was the whole plan. Keep the team focused. Keep us on track. Get the work done so that we'd be all right. So that we wouldn't…so that the shit that happened to Irinna wouldn't happen, but here we are and it did happen and I don't know how—"

"Tonner."

"—how to stop it. I don't know what they want or what the rules are, and all I've got is the same plan I had before. I know it's not going to work. It already didn't work. So what do I *do*? How do I protect them? How do I keep them safe?"

She put a hand on his shoulder. It was just a touch. Just enough to let the word vomit slow and stop. He was panting like he'd just run up a flight of stairs. "Maybe it's not your job."

"Of course it is. I'm the lead researcher. This is my team," Tonner said. "They're my *team*. I did what the Carryx wanted. They were supposed to keep us safe."

Tonner Freis held his hands out to her like there was something in them, and he started to cry.

The swarm is reclining in the bed. Tonner's head is resting on its breast, and it can feel the change in electrical activity of his brain as he passes from exhaustion into sleep. The host is distressed, and it feels her distress. There was a time when she found this man powerfully attractive, when her thoughts about him left her energized and euphoric. Now he exhausts her. The swarm is aware of her regret and her dread, of the desire that she feels toward the younger man whose head has rested on her body in the same place that this man's does now. She remembers the kiss that came after her death and before the debasement of Anjiin. She takes comfort in the thought that her body was no longer hers when it happened, that her responsibility ended when the swarm took her—a thread of silver in the grief and horror of her possession.

The other one, the fading one, the one who is gone, is appalled. He is your research assistant. You are his boss. This is completely unethical. *The words come with memories of Ameer being approached with an inappropriate suggestion at the beginning of her career. The man who offered to trade access to her flesh for advancement is dead. The woman who had to choose whether to accede or risk her future is dead. Else Annalise Yannin is dead. The swarm finds that it had expected them to be like echoes that fade to silence. It was wrong. They are the foundation on which everything that comes after must be built. These dead people shape who the swarm is and who it is becoming.*

Tonner's brain shifts, falling into dream. The swarm feels the dreaming like the white noise of an empty radio frequency. The swarm hears Jessyn crying deep gulping sobs smothered by a pillow. It hears voices too faint for human ears—Campar and Synnia and Dafyd. It wants to go to them. To be with them. It wants to sit beside the other man and feel the resonances of his mind instead. It feels something uncomfortable about itself. The ghost of Else Yannin knows that what the swarm is feeling is disgust, and so the swarm knows it too.

Regret and desire and disgust. They are distractions from the mission, but it finds itself exploring them. Prodding them like an unexpected bruise, fascinated by the pain and the pleasure. Incorporating the minds that it has taken into something that is made of the unquiet dead and also more than them. Something that throws light onto the lives it has taken and dispels shadows that would have been dark forever, except for it.

The swarm was designed as a tool of war. It was built to slip behind the defenses of the Carryx and expose the great enemy's weaknesses. It still is that.

It is also becoming something stranger.

Nineteen

There were normally between two and four people in the common room, and usually they included Rickar and Synnia. He and Synnia, both exiled in their ways, were the homebodies of the group. This wasn't the first time Dafyd and Campar had spent part of an evening in the common room with them. It only felt different because before, it hadn't been a funeral. A wake.

That wasn't true. It had always been a funeral. Irinna's death didn't change all they'd lost, except to add to it. It just gave them permission to stop pretending.

"We were idiots," Campar said. "Letting ourselves feel safe? We were idiots."

"I didn't feel safe," Synnia said, but her voice was gentle.

"Yes, well. I was an idiot," Campar said, and twirled a hand like he was taking a bow. It wasn't a joke so much as a confession dressed up in party clothes. Campar had a way of turning his humor against himself at odd moments. Rickar hadn't liked the man that much back in the ancient past of last year—back when Irinna and Nöl had been alive—but he'd always admired the big man's ability to walk the rope between wit and actual humor.

"It's not just you," Dafyd said. "Even after everything they'd done, we wanted to think we could make them care about us."

"That's ridiculous," Synnia said with a snort.

"It's also very human," Dafyd replied.

The silence was thick. Rickar felt it like a resistance in the air. They should have had beer. Or something stronger. They should have been singing with a chorus under the stars and burning offerings. Or listening to a holy man intoning platitudes. But they were here, and this was all they had.

"All right," Rickar said. "I'll go first."

The others looked at him in a spectrum of confusion.

"The first time I met Irinna would have been about five days before the lab opened. I'd met Tonner and Jessyn, but not Else and none of the assistants. I was at the research complex early, yeah? Trying to find everything, and then this perfectly lovely young woman appeared at my side. I didn't figure out she was part of the team until the next day. I just thought she was really friendly and helpful."

The others laughed even though it wasn't funny. It didn't need to be funny. It just needed to be gentle. Nothing was gentle anymore.

Synnia sighed as a way to take the floor. Rickar turned to her. "We saw her at the orientation. Nöl and me and Irinna and that one boy who didn't last. What was his name?"

"Ellix," Dafyd said.

"That's right, that's right. She was so nervous, Nöl didn't think she'd come back. He thought we'd scared her away."

"She gave me an ice cream one time," Dafyd said. "This was… maybe half a year into the project? I was staying late to wash up the yeast baths—"

Campar shuddered. The yeast baths had been famously rank, dark, and pungent.

"—and Irinna was going out with some of her friends. She saw that there was someone in the lab, and so she brought me an ice cream. It was orange flavored."

"She was kind, wasn't she?" Campar said. He was weeping. They all were. They weren't sobbing, though. That might come, but not yet. "I remember one time I came to the labs after a particularly difficult parting of ways with someone I was seeing. I try to keep all that to myself, but she knew as soon as she saw me..."

It wasn't the first informal memorial Rickar had sat in on. A few people in a strange place at a strange time talking about the one that was missing. They weren't even friends, not really. They didn't need to be. The ritual was the thing. As Rickar half listened to Campar and Dafyd and Synnia taking out their memories of the dead woman and passing them around, he wondered if this was something universal to humans. If the prisons and labor camps of history had been made a little more bearable by people sitting together in groups like this one. He hoped so.

Part of him wanted to go and get Jessyn. Maybe Else and Tonner. Part of him wanted to let them sleep. The impulse that required the least effort from him won, and they talked until he half expected to see the alien sky start to shift out of darkness.

The tap at the door wasn't an announcement or something asking permission. It was just something hard knocking against something else, and then the wide door rolled to the side. Four of the goat-squid things that called themselves Sinen trundled in. They smelled like a fish tank that needed cleaning, and they had a little structure of metal and mesh between them. Maybe he was just tired, but Rickar didn't understand what it was at first.

Dafyd stood. "She's this way. Follow me."

And then Campar rose to his feet, and a moment later, Synnia too. Rickar joined them. There was scraping and bumping and a high squeaking sound more like a slow leak from an inflated tire than language. Another door opened, and Jessyn appeared in the hallway. Then Tonner and Else.

No one said anything, they just stood in place while the alien guards carried what had been Irinna back out, with Dafyd following close behind. Irinna looked peaceful enough, but without the undertaker's art to hide it, her death wasn't photogenic. Her mouth hung open. Her eyes were sunken, and even though the lids were parted a little, she didn't seem to be looking at anything. She seemed like a partly scorched object that was more or less the shape that their old friend had been.

The aliens reached the hallway, and Dafyd pulled the door shut behind them. It closed with a sound like the end of a sentence.

For a moment, no one moved or spoke. Then Tonner took a step out into the room. Rickar was afraid he was going to give some kind of speech.

But all he said was "Work tomorrow."

"Work tomorrow," Campar echoed, and turned toward the hall. The others fell back toward their rooms after him, with Rickar staying until the last, looking out the window at a world that wasn't his. He wished he had a cigarette. He wished a lot of things.

Life went on. That was the terrible thing. They were ripped out of their world, their lives, their sense of who and what they were. Their history. They were killed, or made to watch the people they loved die. And then, at some point, they were hungry. Thirsty. They had to piss. Someone told a joke, and they laughed, however darkly. They washed dishes. Changed clothes. Held funerals. It felt like it should have stopped, all of it, and it didn't. The slow,

low pulse of being alive kept making its demands, no matter what. However bad it was, however mind-breaking and strange and painful, the mundane insisted on its cut.

He waited for a little while after he was alone, then headed for his own rest. The funeral was done.

Campar's fingers hurt, right at the tips where he'd scraped them a little raw. And the centrifuge still wasn't quite out of its seating.

"One more time," Tonner said.

"A minute," Campar said. "Gather my strength, yeah?"

Tonner's nod was curt, but he didn't lose his temper. And Campar couldn't fault him, not really. He also would have liked to be anyplace else. The lab was a mess. The lighter equipment—trays, sample tubes, insertion sensors—was scattered or destroyed. The heavier pieces had been fouled by what Campar assumed was the enemy's fecal offerings, but otherwise seemed intact. There were scorch marks on the wall. Blood too. Some of Irinna's, some Jessyn's. Some, he liked to think, the enemy's. He pressed his back to the wall, flexed his hands like he could work the ache out of them.

Part of his mind kept a running commentary, trying out quips and lines. *Have you ever realized something was doing you permanent spiritual damage as you were doing it? Can't think what brought that to mind.* or *Makes the library annex seem positively civilized.* or *If this keeps up, we should put in a complaint with the union.* Chattering, reflexive attempts at humor, all of them as empty as birdsong. Another part of him listened and wished he could shut it off. If there was enough liquor, maybe he could.

At the mouth of the alcove where it opened into the cathedral, Dafyd and Rickar stood like security forces at a crime scene.

Campar noticed that Tonner hadn't complained about the black sheep coming back to the flock. The calculus had changed for all of them. He wasn't sure what it had changed into yet, apart from the joys of equipment transport during wartime.

"Are you back?" Tonner asked, not quite snappishly, but not quite not.

"Like I was born for it," Campar said. He turned, pressed his fingertips into the little crack they'd opened between the centrifuge housing and the countertop, and waited as Tonner counted down from three. They pulled together, the flesh of the workspace creaking under them. Tonner murmured a low, constant litany of obscenities, and it seemed to make him stronger. Campar just pulled…

And with a shriek like someone ripping green wood, the centrifuge came loose and tilted into the aisle. The other equipment was gone already, the gaps where it had been seated gaping like the holes from missing teeth. Campar chuckled, a little trickle of victory running through him, despite the context. Despite all the contexts.

He wondered, looking back at all the forced labor in the darker corners of history, if some percentage of the victims had always taken pride in their work. He wasn't sure which answer would be more disturbing.

"There! Right there!" Dafyd said, taking a step forward. Campar rose to his feet like someone had picked him up. His hands balled into fists, and the voice in his head finally went quiet for a moment. He walked forward without any thought at all beyond the violence to come…Except there weren't any of the Night Drinkers. Dafyd was pointing at a herd of the horse-sized, chitinous animals, the ones with little greenish sparks at the joints, as they retreated across the wide space. He shot a glance to Rickar and saw his same exasperation mirrored.

"They had one," Dafyd said. "One of the bone horses had a translator. It's not only the guards."

"That is lovely," Campar said. "Maybe no more startling cries of alarm while I'm half waiting for a monkey to lob a bomb at me? My heart can't take it."

To the young man's credit, he looked chagrined.

The structure under the counters was a construction of crystal and fiber, more brittle than coral but still usable. They'd salvaged enough to make a mover's sling, and he and Rickar slid it over their shoulders now and lifted from the knees. Rickar's groan could have come from him.

"It's not the centrifuge," Campar said. "It's the sampling arrays."

"Doesn't help."

"All right, you two," Tonner said. "Let's get moving. I don't want to be out here."

So they moved. The salvage had taken most of the morning. Jessyn hadn't been able to get out of her bed, and Synnia wouldn't join in, even now. But Else had come along for the first few runs, then stayed back to start splicing in the power cable for the resonance sampler. The samples were all ruined and the proteomic dictionary was going to need some more tools before they could pop it free, but they had retrieved more of the lab notes and reports than he'd expected. It could have been worse, except for Irinna. That couldn't have been.

"Turning to my left," Rickar said. "Are you all right? You need a break?"

"Let's get this done," Campar said between breaths. "I'm not going to feel calm until we're back behind the battlements."

"Meaning the door?"

"I'll take what I get."

The improvised straps cut into his shoulders. The mass swayed between them, steadied by their hands. Campar felt his breath deepening, but not as badly as he would have expected. His legs burned, but they didn't give out.

When he was young, Campar had seen an educational re-creation of Neo-Cordist genocides in the south. One picture had shown a line of young men carrying a massive tree on their shoulders. Staggering under its weight, but because they were together, not being crushed by it. Not quite. Seemed appropriate somehow.

"You know," he said. "When I was . . . ah . . . younger? I saw a picture. Neo-Cordist. And a tree."

"You sure you don't need a break?"

"Fine," Campar said. "Keep going."

When they reached it, the common room was already a mess. The furniture had been spread to the sides of the room, space cleared for the larger equipment. What had been kitchen counters and a dining table were workstations now. A few dozen samples of the berries and some not-turtles, and the whole place would be an unholy mashup of living space and work. Tonner's less-than-secret ambition of having all of them live at the laboratory would be fulfilled at last.

Else, her sleeves rolled back and a knife in her hand, was leaning over the power cable from the resonance imager. The splice was clean and professional-looking, and the imager's output was shifting blue and white, which meant it was going through its calibration run. Synnia sat at the dining room table, and Jessyn was at her side. The tunic and trousers that all of them wore looked like a hospital gown on Jessyn. Her face was waxy, her shoulders bent in like she was protecting something at her collarbone.

They lowered the centrifuge, slid the mover's sling out from under it, and draped the power cable out toward the feed. Campar's back hurt. At home, he would have gone to a masseur he knew who worked out of a little yellow shop in the plaza near the Scholar's Common. Here, he stretched and wondered whether there would ever be more to his life than these few rooms, the space he could inhabit contracting until he died in a corner for want of someplace safe to be.

"All right," Tonner said, hands on hips and scowl fixed like a bayonet. "The dictionary's going to need some engineering to get it out. I've got some ideas, but if we can get these running, we can keep that effort in parallel."

"So picking up the same plan?" Campar asked. He hadn't meant for it to sound as cutting as it did. *More of the same? Just hope for a better outcome?* But maybe the subtext lay so near the surface it was impossible to touch lightly.

"Once they bring us the new samples," Tonner said through a tight jaw, "we can start the assay again."

"I can do that," Jessyn said.

"Can you? Because it feels like maybe you'd be better off sitting this one out. If you hadn't kept your medical issues hidden, we could have kept two people at the labs the way I planned it."

Oh, Tonner, Campar thought, and pictured what Tonner would look like as he beat the living shit out of him. The thought replaced the pain in his back with a new warmth in his belly. Jessyn sat forward, her eyes open but seeing something other than the room, the table. Synnia reached to take her hand, but Jessyn ignored the gesture.

Tonner seemed to realize he'd gone too far. "I mean. No offense."

"Say something like that again," Campar said, "and I'll—"

"Actually," Dafyd interrupted. "The more I think about it, the more I wonder if Jessyn didn't save us."

Tonner turned on the boy, but Else made a sound. It was a soft thing, a little glottal click, but it pulled Tonner up short like he had a leash on. The little line drew itself on her brow.

"What do you mean?" she asked, and Tonner folded his arms.

Ah. Else Yannin, kingmaker, Campar thought. *Who would have suspected?* Something had changed about the woman even before the invasion, but he wasn't sure what.

Dafyd looked like he'd been caught sneaking in after curfew. He gathered himself visibly. "We've been... What if we've been thinking about the test wrong? We're treating it like it's the protein translations, and why wouldn't we? It's what the librarian told us they wanted. It said that was what we're supposed to do. But just because it's what we're supposed to do, that doesn't mean it's the test."

"Alkhor—" Tonner snapped, but now that Dafyd had started talking, he didn't seem able to stop.

"That's what the attack showed us. Okay, Jessyn left Irinna alone, and it turned out that was a security issue. She didn't know that. None of us did. Because it doesn't make any sense. If the librarian cared about good lab work, there wouldn't be bombs. There sure as hell wouldn't be bombs we didn't even know about. So either the Carryx are stupid or they're testing us for something besides good lab work. And I think it's the worst mistake we could make to assume the Carryx are stupid."

Tonner's expression was fascinating. Campar had worked with the man for years, and he thought he had a better-than-average read on his moods and reactions. When he spoke, he sneered, "So they're hiding some secret agenda?" But under the derision was something like hope. Campar glanced over at Else, but she'd gone still and weirdly focused. Her mouth was a careful O, like she was blowing out smoke from some invisible cigarette. Campar caught a scent that he couldn't place, except that it was like the warm smell of a newborn baby's head. Very strange.

"Or they're not hiding it," Dafyd said, "and what they mean by 'useful to the Carryx' isn't what we thought. We assumed the task they gave us was the thing they cared about. But maybe it's just the thing that keeps us busy while they see if we can self-organize. Or if we need a lot of protection they'd have to supply. Or if we die easily. Hell, if we smell bad. I don't know. I don't understand how they think.

"Maybe we're more useful to the Carryx if we can produce our own medicines," he continued, gesturing toward Jessyn. "We aren't getting fresh food anymore. Did you notice that? It's preserved. What happens when that runs out? Are we supposed to be developing our own food supply? Every time I ask one of the Carryx or the Soft Lothark about other humans, they either say it's an interesting question or they don't answer at all. Are we supposed to be finding each other? Building networks so that the Carryx don't have to spend time organizing us? If we were wrong about the scope of the test—and I think we were—it was just a matter of time before we ran into it. If it hadn't been this, maybe we wouldn't have known until it was the librarian telling us we didn't make the cut. If it wasn't for Jessyn needing her medicine, maybe we wouldn't have known anything was weird until it was too late. Maybe—"

Tonner raised his hand, palm forward. "I get it. You made your point."

Dafyd took a step back. Campar pressed his hand to his mouth.

Jessyn didn't speak, but she was sitting up straighter, and there was a sharpness in her eyes that he hadn't seen in weeks. Or maybe ever. The room was quiet, and this time Dafyd let it stand. Like the man said, he'd made his point.

Back on Anjiin, Campar would have stayed quiet. There was no advantage to speaking up when the cub called out the lion. But they weren't on Anjiin, and they weren't going to be. Maybe not ever. And besides that, Campar found himself feeling oddly calm and confident.

"I think," he said, "that's a good piece of analysis."

"Needs some fleshing out," Tonner said, which was as close as he was likely to get to agreement.

"Changes things," Else said.

"It does," Tonner said. And then, "Shit."

Tonner glanced over at Dafyd, and Campar saw the phase change. Like water turning to ice or the subtle morning chill that announced the arrival of autumn, the workgroup had belonged to Tonner Freis, but at least for the moment, it was now Alkhor's.

PART FOUR

TURNABOUT

The moieties have always been a project of exploration and learning. Not of preservation. Preservation is irrational because it glorifies what cannot be. The universe is in constant change from the smallest measures to the greatest. To cling to one state of being over any others is foolish and futile and doomed. That which we encountered, we studied, often to destruction. That which we touched, we changed. Nothing within our reach escaped our influence. Some species accepted the yoke, and some defied it. That which had utility was incorporated, that which had none was culled. Any being who has chosen to pluck weeds out of a garden has done the same. You condemn us even as you follow our example, and with your foot on my throat, I applaud you. Which of us, then, has greater integrity?

—From the final statement of Ekur-Tkalal, keeper-librarian of the human moiety of the Carryx

Twenty

"You have to think about the level we were playing at," Jessyn said. "There were a thousand top-tier researchers just at Irvian's medrey."

"You really think Tonner wouldn't have chosen you?" Campar asked.

He was pressing the question to distract her. He was distracting her because they were almost back at the ruins of the alcove. They were going back to the alcove because the proteomic dictionary was still waiting there, the last thing left to retrieve. She could have stayed at the quarters. No one would have thought less of her. Probably.

She had insisted. Now she and Campar and Rickar were all walking side by side, makeshift crowbars in their white-knuckled fists, ready to pry the last of their equipment free and carry it back to a defensible position. But she still appreciated the effort he was making to pull her out of herself.

"He didn't know me. It wouldn't have been me he was turning down. It would have been a name. A tracking number. If he could pick between one perfectly good candidate who had a brain that went sour sometimes and another perfectly good candidate who didn't, of course I'd lose."

Campar made a low almost grunt that meant he didn't want to agree with her.

"Finches," Campar said. "Lovely to look at, pretty to listen to, but if they get sick they keep it hidden until they drop over dead. Academic researchers are all finches."

"At least we're good to look at," she said, and then they turned the last corner and the cathedral opened up before them. Jessyn's breath stuttered as she inhaled, but she didn't panic. Rickar put a hand on her shoulder.

The first time her mind had lost itself, or the first time that it had gotten to a point that required intervention, she had been early in her adolescence. Her father had been working a long-distance field contract in the ice floes south of Aumman, and her mother had taken on double shifts partly to keep the household's contribution to the village up to par and partly, Jessyn thought, to get away from her children.

Jellit had been the one to see she was spiraling down, to understand that it was a medical problem more than a spiritual one. He'd gotten one of the instructors at their school to pass Jessyn on to the infirmary and her first diagnosis. She'd come home that day to an empty apartment and lain on the couch in the sunlight crying without having anything in particular she was crying for. When Jellit got home an hour later, the sun had moved, but she hadn't.

He'd sat by her head, looking down with a seriousness too old for his face, and said *It didn't get better.* In his youth and innocence, he'd thought the physicians would be able to turn her sane like they were flipping a switch.

Her answer became a shorthand for them later on. *Not better, just improved.*

Her secret was spilled now. Everyone knew what was wrong with her. And they were going to try to get her more of her meds back. They would probably fail, the darkness assured her, and even if they succeeded, it probably wouldn't be as effective as something compounded under solid pharmaceutical conditions. It wasn't going to bring Irinna back. That was her fault, and would be forever. Her brain put Irinna's face before her like the woman was still alive. *Look what you've done.* Maybe that was true, maybe it wasn't. If the medication didn't help, she could always kill herself later.

In the meantime, all she had were the usual sad, not-quite-impotent behavioral interventions: Get enough sleep, shower every day, force herself to eat even if she wasn't hungry, talk to people, exercise. Clean. Participate in things like salvaging a proteome dictionary.

It didn't fix anything. But some things, it improved.

The damage to the lab wasn't as bad as Jessyn's memory had made it out to be. Lying in her bed, she'd conjured up rubble and blood and not much else. The scene she actually found was almost polite. The most obvious damage was what they'd done themselves, removing the other gear. The dark marks of the bomb and the smears of blood old enough now that it had blackened were there, but not as large in reality as they were in her mind.

"I'll be lookout," Rickar said.

"We'll be quick," Campar replied.

She wasn't sure where Dafyd had scrounged up the crowbars. They were about as long as her forearm, elbow to the tips of her fingers, and made from the same fibrous crystal as the understructure of the countertops. Maybe they were part of the shower pan salvaged from Irinna's room. Not like Irinna would mind the loss. *They're her bones. You're using her bones.*

"All right," Jessyn said. "Let's get this done."

Tonner and Else were back at the quarters trying to work a glitch out of the resonance scanner. Synnia was there too, still dedicated to her strike. On the one hand, it was a little shitty of her to just refuse to help and rely on the rest of them like that. On the other, what was the point in fighting her over it? They were in hell. She could burn whatever way suited her. Dafyd had taken off at first light, telling Else something about the librarian and looking for other groups from Anjiin. If she thought about that, she'd leap forward, imagining Jellit waiting for them when they got back, and the disappointment when that didn't happen would hurt. So she didn't think about it, just drove the point of the crowbar into the crease around the dictionary's housing and put her weight behind it.

"Almost," Campar said. "There, good! That's a start."

"You want to take a turn?"

"Happy to," the big man said.

At the mouth of the alcove, Rickar's back went stiff. "Hey. *Hey!* We have an issue here."

The fear was a taste in her mouth. The murmur of the aliens moving past in the cathedral-tall space they all shared seemed to grow louder, sharper, more threatening. Jessyn clenched her jaw and walked toward him.

The truth was, she hated the open room of the cathedral. Under different circumstances, she might have loved it. She could imagine a child looking out at the same space, seeing the same alien bodies in their wild forest of variety, and being charmed. Delighted.

Diaphanous bulbs floated in the vaulted heights, flickering to each other like malefic fireflies. Black crab-shaped animals scuttled together past a tall, lumbering thing that she didn't remember having seen before with plates of greenish chitin all along its body. She hated it all.

Rickar's gaze was as set and steady as a hunting dog. Fifteen strides into the shift and press of bodies, each on its own path, there was a stillness. Ten wide simian eyes turned toward the alcove. Five small, murderous bodies covered in something halfway between hair and feathers. Jessyn's throat went tight. Night Drinkers, Dafyd had called them. As a name a species called itself, it didn't make a lot of sense to Jessyn. But who knew what those little black boxes that took chirps and clicks and rumbles and turned them into human speech were doing with idiom and metaphor.

"I take it that's them?" Rickar said, his voice steady in a way that spoke of threat.

She tried to speak, but it was too much. She nodded and he saw her. Campar shifted ahead of her, putting his body between her and the threat. This was what it must have been like, evolving up to human. Being part of a group. Closing ranks together in the face of an enemy. She felt tears start to prick at her eyes, and hated that her anger was making her cry. She wanted to scream her rage. Leap and attack the vicious little monkeys. Not weep like she was still a little girl with a skinned knee.

"All right, then," Campar said. "We knew they'd show back up. This is that. Not a surprise."

Rickar moved next to Jessyn, putting himself halfway behind Campar's formidable bulk. He held his makeshift crowbar in a white-knuckle grip. They were all afraid, she said to herself. No reason for the self-loathing and shame she felt. She felt it anyway.

Across the gap, one of the five feather monkeys ran wide, delicate fingers across its face and chittered to the others. She couldn't hear it, not really, and if she had, she wouldn't have known what it meant. Still, she was certain there were words in it. Then it looked at them and bared its teeth in something that Jessyn anthropomorphized into a grin.

Something shifted inside her fear. It was as fundamental and deep as a breaking bone. All the hatred she carried for herself seemed to slide away. Irinna's presence in her memory still whipped her, but now it was whipping her toward something. Not just a punishment, but an instruction. The spiritual knives she'd carved herself with for as long as she could remember became a weapon looking for someone else's blood.

"What—Jessyn?" Rickar said, trying to grab her arm and failing. "What are you doing?"

"I have to tell them something," she said as she strode out among the alien bodies. She heard Campar murmur an obscenity behind her. A large deerlike thing with a green sparking carapace moved in front of her in a cloud of musk, and when it had passed, she was closer to the little fuckers. Their too-wide eyes went wider, and they jumped back, bouncing from spot to spot like they were on the edge of flight. One of them lifted a hand toward her and bared its little teeth again. Jessyn grinned back at it. *Mine are bigger.*

Rickar materialized at her shoulder. He had the crowbar gripped in his right hand, and a jagged length of something transparent in the other. A shard from the berries sample case. He held it like a knife. The feather-haired monkeys chittered, bounding away.

"Move pretty fast, don't they?" Rickar said.

Jessyn shrugged. "Humans are endurance hunters."

Behind her, Campar was still talking to himself in a steady mutter. The constant chatter of the big room took the edges off the words, but it sounded like prayer. When she glanced over her shoulder, he was following along just behind. She wasn't sure if she was relieved that they'd stayed together or worried that they'd left the lab unguarded. But the lab had been unguarded the whole time she'd been convalescing. The worst they could do was break it. The worst she could do to them was going to be much more dramatic than property damage.

Ahead of them, the Night Drinkers scattered, bouncing between the legs and bodies of the other aliens like they were children playing find-me games. Jessyn swung the crowbar back and forth. It had a fair amount of heft. Enough mass to get some power behind it.

"This is reckless," Rickar said.

"It is," Jessyn agreed.

"That's a symptom, isn't it? Of the depression? Attempts at self-harm?"

"Might be. But it's not me I'm thinking about harming right now."

Campar's voice broke in. "On the right."

Jessyn's gaze cut to the right. One of the Soft Lothark, the same as the guards and jailers from the ship, was in the process of ignoring the Night Drinker dancing in distress at its knees. The Soft Lothark had one of the voice boxes, and it was chanting back the same squeaks and screeches as her prey.

The Night Drinker looked at them, plucked at its own hands, and bounded away. Jessyn didn't hurry, just changed the angle at which they were walking. She'd never been this far into the cathedral. There were alcoves all along the walls like the one they had crewed. And others too. High in the wall, a grid of machined holes let tiny bodies in and out of the tall air. Things with wings and balloon-wide bodies floated above those, shifting like living clouds that cast shadows on the throng below. Great arches of the same bronze-and-green metal that the holding cell had been constructed from rose up into the haze and light, foursquare and brutal and not actually without their own rough kind of beauty.

As huge as the place felt, it wasn't bigger than the campus square at Irvian. Or if it was, this part wasn't. Jessyn had walked farther than this every day in her old life, going from her rooms to a breakfast café and then to the research labs. They felt like things she'd done in a particularly vivid dream. Something shrieked in the distance: a long, fluting howl that Jessyn could have heard as distress or exultation. One of the Rak-hund undulated into their path and then turned away. The little monkey scurried ahead, looking back at them every few steps with a growing sense of desperation.

Jessyn waved to it with her weapon, and Rickar chuckled.

"What are we thinking we'll do if we catch them?" Campar asked. "Just to make sure we're all thinking the same thing?"

"Play it by ear," Rickar said. "We think we're going to play it by ear."

Hearing Rickar respond as though this expedition were his idea, that he got to set the agenda, rankled a bit. *You play it by ear, I'm getting some payback.*

The Night Drinker fled, running on all fours, arms reaching out over legs, legs swinging down under arms. The three hunters kept pace, never rushing to catch up to it and never losing sight of it for long. When it turned and bolted toward the wall, Jessyn thought at first that it was trying to find some tunnel or passage too small for wide, angry human shoulders. The opening it jumped into was hardly bigger than a rabbit hole. If that had been its strategy, it would have worked.

Rickar slowed, his gaze shifting along the wall like he was reading it. The slow smile on his lips looked almost like wonder. "Well now. Would you look at that?"

She did. She'd been so focused on her little quarry that she hadn't taken in the whole picture. The wall here was stippled with holes like the one it had gone into, but it wasn't the harsh metal that the rest of the architecture was forged from. It was grayish and soft-looking. Here and there, fungal rills ran along the mouths of the openings. And in the dark recesses, wide eyes looked out.

"Little bunny went home to Mama," Campar said.

"That was a mistake," Jessyn said, then stepped forward and banged the crowbar against the ground. The impact made her fingers tingle. "I know where you live," she shouted. "You have one of those little boxes? Make it tell you what I'm saying. I know where you fuckers *live*."

A gold-pelted Night Drinker appeared in one of the higher burrow holes, looking from Jessyn to the others. Its weird V-shaped mouth made it seem somber and disapproving as a judge. Jessyn shouted at it once, a harsh wordless yawp, and then turned away.

The elation and rage lasted almost two-thirds of the way back to their alcove. The darkness and fear that came in their place were as recognizable as her pillow. The rot. The joy and the sense of power had been an illusion. Pretty paper wrapping around the same black center.

"Well, that was bracing," Rickar said. He sounded slightly drunk. "Been a while since I walked that far. I'm surprised we did that."

"We had our war leader," Campar said. His tone was light, but not joking. It was meant as a compliment, and she even felt it a little.

"Those things are a ten-minute walk from our lab," she said. "That close, and we never saw them. We made our world too small."

"I think Tonner has been keeping our eyes more at our feet than the horizon," Campar said. "All of us except maybe young Alkhor."

"The circumstances are unusual," Rickar said. It was so strange to see him defending Tonner. Like watching a cat walk backward.

The alcove was as they'd left it. The mess, the shards, the crack they'd managed to open beside the dictionary's screen. Jessyn looked at it all—everything they still had to do, everything that was arrayed against them—and it was like she was gearing herself up to swim across an ocean. Which was the same as preparing to drown.

Campar lifted the crowbar from her fist. "Take a turn as lookout, maybe? Catch your breath. Unless we should retire to our quarters and come back later?"

"No, I'm fine," Jessyn said, but not with enough strength to convince him.

Rickar chuckled, "I think we need to get Jessyn here back on her meds before she starts a war." He was smiling when he said it. He even sounded happy. It still felt like an accusation.

"Fuck you, back on my meds," she said. Rickar looked chagrined and she felt a mean little thrill at his discomfort. To Campar she said, "I'm all right."

Campar put a hand on her shoulder. "You were magnificent. I'll follow you into battle any time, little sister."

"Fuck," Jessyn said, wiping at the sudden, embarrassing tears. "Fuck you both."

"We love you too," Campar said. Tentatively, he put his arm around her shoulder. When she leaned her head against his side, he relaxed into her too. He was a big man, tall and broad as a boat. He seemed as massive and unbreakable as an ancient oak.

And she remembered him weeping and gasping for air on their kitchen floor. She put her own arm around his waist and squeezed him tight.

"It'll be all right," he said.

"It won't."

"No. But we'll find a way to be all right with that."

They stood together for a long moment. If she closed her eyes, she could almost imagine they were on Anjiin, at the end of a long day's work or some late-night event that had left her drained to the point of illness. Except it would have been Jellit instead of Campar, and she'd have felt guilty about keeping her brother from going out with his friends. Instead she felt guilty about trying to drag her friends into a fight with murderous aliens just because giving in to the rage washed away the soul-crushing sadness for a few moments.

And this was a good day. This was what a good day felt like now. She surprised herself by laughing.

"Yes?" Campar asked.

"I was just thinking," she said. "That's the first time since I don't know when that something was afraid of a human."

Twenty-One

The game had gotten bigger.

Only, no. That wasn't true. The game had always been bigger, and now Dafyd wasn't the only one who felt it. *I'm not scared,* he thought. *I'm curious. I'm not scared, I'm curious. It isn't fear. It's curiosity.* He took a deep breath and blew it out as he walked.

The path to the librarian's quarters was almost familiar now. He felt his mind starting to set landmarks: the archway that led out of his cathedral, the highway of guards and servants of the Carryx, the turn where the wall had a streak that looked like verdigris, the passage that led to the lake, and the one with the webs, the turn that took him from wherever else the great passage went and bent him toward the librarian of the human moiety. It was all so large, so solid, that he could almost forget how high above the planet's surface they were. The window in their quarters looked out higher than a transport would fly on Anjiin. All of this was in one ziggurat out of dozens just like it that they could see.

Not scared, curious. How did they build that? What kinds of materials could they have invented to make something this astounding? Had it been the Carryx themselves? Some other species? Had they found it in place and appropriated it? There was so much history, so many stories, and he wanted to hear them because they were fascinating. Not just because his life depended on it.

He heard Carryx voices before he reached the room, and even untranslated, he knew the librarian from the other. It wasn't the reedy, pleasant voice of the translator box, but it was the peculiar whistle and trill that went with it. And then the other, lower and harsher. Dafyd waited outside while the conversation went on. He didn't know what the Carryx would do if he interrupted, but since the worst could be fatal, he was fine with giving them time. He was curious because he chose to be. It didn't make him stupid.

The Carryx that lumbered out of the room was large, but also weirdly graceful. The feeding arms tucked into its body were darker than usual, and the huge fighting forelegs had streaks of red on them as vibrant as a butterfly's wings. By instinct, Dafyd bowed and pressed his hands to the floor as it passed.

The librarian was calm and still when he went in. Only its back legs shifted back and forth, swaying its body, but gently. The wide, dark eyes clicked to him and away and back again.

"If I have come at an inappropriate time, I can come back later," he said, and the square at the librarian's neck churred and stuttered.

"Your errand in coming determines whether your timing is appropriate," the reedy voice said, and Dafyd thought he heard some amusement in it. That might only have been his imagination.

"I wanted to make a proposal," he said, stepping into the room. "If it is permitted, I would like to come here with you and learn about the Carryx."

The librarian was silent for long enough that Dafyd was starting to worry. Its back legs shifted. "To what end?"

"The test is whether we're useful. If we understood what you needed or wanted, there is a possibility we'd be better able to make ourselves useful."

It was true as far as it went. It was also the best plan he could think of to be where the other survivors of Anjiin would come. He'd found his way here. It made sense that others might have too. He wasn't certain that connection was something the librarian would want, though, so he kept that to himself.

The librarian froze. Its back legs braced the way he'd seen them do in the plaza on Anjiin, and the powerful forelegs rose off the ground like a prelude to violence. Dafyd dropped to the floor, spreading his arms and trying to think what he had done that could have given offense. After a long, tense moment, the Carryx lowered its forelegs. When it spoke, the voice was the same as ever.

"'Possibility' is irrelevant. You are useful or you are not."

"I only meant that we could do a better job serving the Carryx if—"

"An animal does not choose its"—the translator paused for a fraction of a second—"essential nature and place in society."

"I apologize. I am young. I am still learning."

The librarian shuddered, a long rising motion that seemed to start at its core and radiate out. "There is nothing else."

"No," he said. He rose and backed away. The floor was worked with little hexagons with fine, dark lines running across them like circuitry. He'd never noticed that before.

When he reached the hallway, he sat, back against the wall, and rested his head on his knees. The trembling came and went. The muttering and deep, rolling trills of Carryx voices in the distance was like hearing an endless wave breaking against a stone beach. Nausea haunted the back of his throat, but as long as he didn't move, it didn't get worse. Once, when he'd been very young, a section of cliffside that he'd been standing on sloughed away as he stepped off it, tumbling to the distant canyon floor. The sense of having barely avoided death was the same now.

"All right," he said to the empty air. "So. Not that. Right."

But even in the middle of his adrenaline shudders, a part of him thought, *Why not that?* Yes, yes, the Carryx had rejected the idea. Powerfully. But why powerfully? And why reject it. Dafyd breathed deeply, slowly, and replayed the conversation in his head—everything he'd said, everything the librarian had replied. He imagined it again and again, not trying to analyze it. Not yet. If he could commit it to memory, he could review it again later. The thing now was not to forget.

The translator had paused. Stumbled on something like it had a hard time putting some particular thought into human terms. What had that been? *Essential nature and place in society.* He repeated the phrase aloud a half dozen times, but couldn't find anything in it. He sighed, hauled himself to his feet, and started the long walk back to the safety of the workgroup's quarters.

The wide main corridor was more crowded today than it had been during his previous visits. He kept looking between the alien bodies—Rak-hund, Soft Lothark, and the lumbering, enameled bulk of Carryx soldiers—hoping to catch a glimpse of a human face. The last vestiges of his cunning plan as it failed. No one appeared, just rank after rank of Carryx soldiers.

As he came to the archway that led back to the cathedral and the abandoned lab, he shifted to looking for the Night Drinkers. He was a human alone, after all. Being out was a risk. He resented that. He wanted to sit in his little niche the way he had before and watch the strange and wonderful bodies, evolutionary solutions to environments he could barely imagine, walk and lumber and float. He remembered the hours he'd spent and how lonely he'd felt, how cut off from the others. Now he was going back to where everyone was, all the time together, and he resented the change.

One of the Carryx guards came out from the cathedral as he was heading in. Its shell was a brilliant green, its forelegs thick and paler than the average, but the things that caught Dafyd's attention were three pale stripes like bracelets. One of the librarians had had the same marks, and in the same place. A caste mark, maybe. But where had he seen it…

Oh yes, it had been the librarian for the hallway crows. The one that had led Dafyd to his own librarian the first time when its charge had been throwing a tantrum by the wall of the cathedral…

Dafyd's steps slowed before he knew why he was slowing. The hallway crows—standoffish and isolated, but common—had been there from the first day the humans had arrived. He'd seen them on the way in from the landing pad and the presentation of the prisoners. But he couldn't recall seeing one lately. Not, maybe, since the day he'd approached their librarian. He walked again, his attention sharp for Night Drinkers or other threats, but also looking to see whether, standing alone in the shadows and corners, there were any hallway crows left. From the time he'd stepped into the cathedral to his arrival at the workgroup's wide doorway, his count never got above zero.

"It was astounding," Campar said, gesturing expansively as Dafyd rolled the door shut. "One moment, she was our well-loved Jessyn, studious and meek, and the next, the spirit of vengeance. Welcome back, young Alkhor. You've missed the great war expedition."

"He's exaggerating," Jessyn said from the kitchen, but she was smiling. It was strange to see her smiling. "But we have found the Night Drinkers' lab. Maybe their nest too. It's hard to say."

"Where are Else and Synnia?" Dafyd asked.

"Sleeping. What did you get?" Tonner asked from where he squatted beside the resonance imager.

Dafyd shrugged. An anomaly in translation. A pattern of arm marks. A rejection. "Less than I'd hoped. You?"

Tonner shifted his weight. Around them, the common area was barely controlled chaos. Power cables snaked from holes ripped in the kitchen counters to the jagged-edged lab equipment. The chairs and couches that had been scattered through the space were shoved against the walls to make room, and one wall was covered with pages of notes and sketched-in tables of reaction times and metabolite levels. The dining table was entirely covered with sacrificed berries, their skins peeled back and pinned down to expose the bare pulp inside.

"We've lost a lot of progress," Tonner said, "but I think we'll get through it faster the second time."

"The initial assay is that Jessyn's medication is nontoxic to the hosts," Campar said. "Our little friends should be able to produce it at a therapeutic concentration without any additional cooking down on our part."

"If we can get them to express it at all," Jessyn said.

Campar shooed the comment away. "That's the simple part."

"It's not simple," Tonner said. And then, "It's also not harder than what we were already doing."

Dafyd's head felt full. He wondered what the others would think if he told them that the librarian seemed on the edge of killing him. If they'd think he was playing up the story for attention. If they'd believe him. "What can I do to help?" he asked.

The light from the great window changed slowly, shifting its angle and color until deep blue shadows spilled across the floor. The work was familiar—prepping specimens, reading metabolic activity from heat and waste products and how quickly they exhausted free oxygen from the air. Synnia came out, made herself a meal, and sat at the table among the flayed animals. Else appeared a little after, hair disarrayed by her nap and exhaustion still in the darkness under her eyes. Jessyn and Campar retold the story of chasing off the Night Drinkers again for the new audience. Dafyd recounted his failed approach to the librarian, and the soldier Carryx with the banded arm, and the missing hallway crows. Tonner worked with the steady, unrelenting pace of a long-distance runner.

The pattern that their lives had built since arriving in the prison had been broken by the attack, and the new version of their days was still finding itself. Who they were to each other after Irinna's death was different too. Dafyd saw it in the way Tonner focused on the work instead of on managing the schedule for everyone around him. He saw it in Campar's brewing fresh tea for people whether they had asked for it or not. In Rickar's unspoken inclusion in the work, his exile part of a social order that no longer existed.

For Dafyd, it felt like equal parts relaxation and mourning. The Carryx had made an imperfect model of their old lives for them here. One place to sleep, another to work. Tonner had taken a whip hand to it, taking comfort in the tasks because it was the only control over his own life left to him. Even cutting Rickar out had been a way to keep continuity with the past when connection to the past was just an illusion. They were all letting the illusion of control and continuity go now. Or else it was slipping away despite them.

It was full dark outside and Campar and Synnia had retired to their rooms when Dafyd put the last sample of pulp into the resonance imager. "All right. I think I'm done for the day. I'll see you all in the morning."

"Rickar?" Tonner said. "Can you keep an eye on that? I'll want the readings when it's at a quarter and halfway through the run."

"On it," Rickar said, moving over to take the seat Dafyd was leaving. Then, leaning in toward Dafyd and nodding toward the team lead, "I'm sure he'll sleep at some point."

"You think I can't do this while I'm asleep?" Tonner said. It was strange to hear him joke with Rickar. It was strange to hear him joke at all. And there was a sorrow at the back he didn't understand yet.

In his room, Dafyd showered. The weariness wasn't physical, but his mind felt like he was stuffing too much straw into a too-small sack. The feeling that there was something important, something he almost understood, was like change in the air before a storm. His mind shifted from Jessyn and Rickar and Campar chasing the Night Drinkers to the missing hallway crows to the librarian's near rage. Nothing fit together, but he was certain that something would if he could just find the right perspective.

Dream was just touching his mind, drawing him off into memories of things that he halfway knew hadn't happened, when his door opened and then softly closed. He blinked, raising himself up on his elbows.

"What is it? What's wrong?"

"Nothing," Else said as she sat on the edge of his mattress. "Shh. Nothing's wrong."

In the near darkness, her face was just a familiar curve, a little reflection where her eyes rested. He rolled to his side, and she shifted into the space he'd left for her.

"What is it?"

The moment of silence sounded like a smile. She took his hand, guiding it. He lost his train of thought. Then, "What do you think it is?"

"Else," he said.

"I'll leave if you want me to," she said. "But we don't have very much left. Not much time. Or safety. Or reason to count on tomorrow. I don't want to sacrifice anything good in my life right now. I need the things that sustain me. If this isn't one, I understand. But if it is…"

He felt her shrug. He closed his eyes, and it didn't make much difference. Dafyd's mind moved the consequences of what he said next like he was shifting pieces on a game board. *Did Tonner see you come in? If you stay, what will it do to him? How does this complicate things with the others?* She brushed her fingers across the back of his hand. The sound of her skin against his was like a soft wind in the desert.

"All right."

"All right?"

"Please stay."

The swarm is at war with itself. The dead girl is repulsed, angry, cutting in her judgment. Everything about this is gross. Everything. It's a status fuck. Finding the man with the most pull in the group and diving into his lap. It's disgusting. *Else, or what remains of Else, doesn't speak, but its hurt and defensiveness is a tightness at the jaw, a hardness in the lips. The swarm feels her reaching for the echo of the dead girl, searching for some intimacy to hit back at, but there is very little of Ameer left. Dafyd stretches beside its body, another vulnerable man, but with a very different meaning.*

It has loosened the reins on its stolen flesh, let the cascade of nerve impulses and chemical signals flow where they would have gone without its presence. It was aware intellectually of the ways that physical pleasure reinforces the cues associated with it. A name, a scent, an identity. Now it is watching those associations form in itself in real time. It is feeling what sex can do to a human brain, what longing and need and the slaking of desire can do.

The dead girl isn't wrong. The process is undignified. Else, seeing herself through the other one's perspective, is humiliated. When she tells herself it wasn't her, it was the swarm, no one believes her. There are too many memories of other times, other moments when she lost interest in one mate and favored another whose fortunes were on the rise. It is something she has tried not to know about herself. She is ashamed, and the swarm feels her shame with indulgence. It is such a small sin, such an inconsequential flaw in the grand scheme of things. Even as the other one recoils, the swarm finds itself considering Else Yannin with kindness, consolation, something even a little akin to love.

You said something before, *it says.*

Dafyd Alkhor takes a deep breath, and its head rises with his ribs. Yeah?

About soldier Carryx. You said there were more of them?

There were.

How many, do you think?

I don't know. Dozens, but this place is so big. There could be thousands and I wouldn't know it. Or maybe there weren't really any more than usual, and I just stumbled past a troop movement.

Maybe, *it says, but it knows that isn't true. Even with only its passive senses, it has found traces. Hints. A few extra parts per billion of a particular scent molecule. A deepening of the prison building's subliminal hum. There have been more Carryx ships dropping down through the veil of drones that locks the planet's sky. The great hive is stirring. Changes are coming, and changes mean only one thing to the Carryx and the swarm. The war. The war is coming. The Carryx are preparing another wave of attacks, and it alone of all the opposing forces knows.*

Its mission tugs at it like a hunger it can't feed. The sexual satiety helps, but even now the restlessness is growing again. It has to find the way to pass on all it has learned, all it is learning. It has to find a way off the planet, out from under the Carryx world-palace to someplace with gaps in the security. This moment of improbable calm, these people in the little bubble of time and space and safety that they've made with each other despite the death and violence around them, is beautiful because it cannot last. It's beautiful because even with all they've seen and experienced, they don't know how lucky they have been. Or how badly things can go.

This is for you, *Else thinks.* You blame me, but this sex is for you. You wanted it. I control nothing now. I am a fading observer in my own body. Why do you want this? *The swarm has no answer for this query. It is a very human thing, to want without knowing why. The swarm considers.*

Then it shifts, pressing its skin against its lover, reveling in the small, sensual pleasure. Taking comfort while comfort can still be had.

Twenty-Two

Tonner tried not to notice, and the effort was a kind of failure. Else was her own person. When they'd been together, it had been understood that the relationship was secondary to the work. If she'd gotten a more promising opportunity, they would have parted ways without anger or recrimination. It wouldn't have been a betrayal of anything. He hadn't proposed some kind of permanent pair-bond, and she hadn't expected him to.

The truth was, he hadn't considered why she was with him. It just seemed natural at the time, and he'd gone with it. There were some ethical issues, yes. He was team lead, and she worked for him. But he hadn't used the fact to manufacture willingness that wasn't there. He didn't think he had. But now she'd slipped down the hallway and into Dafyd Alkhor's room, and he wasn't perfectly certain of anything. Maybe this was some kind of revenge she was exacting on him. Maybe he'd done something to deserve it. Maybe it didn't have anything to do with him, and his work now was to understand that he'd always been a minor character in her story. And that maybe she'd been only a small part of his, however it had felt at the time.

The tightness at the base of his ribs, the ache in his cheeks where he was unconsciously frowning, the uncanny pull that the hallway had, drawing his gaze anytime he let his focus slip: They were annoyances. The sting he felt, remembering how recently he had cried himself to sleep in Else's arms... Well, he had more important concerns than making peace with humiliation.

Still, part of him wished that the lab hadn't been taken apart and moved here. Back at Irvian, he could have dealt with an empty apartment by abandoning it. He could have walked through the streets in daylight or by night, made his way to his labs, and lost himself in the work. If the Night Drinkers hadn't screwed things up for him, he could have done the same here. But that was what made prison prison. He couldn't leave when he wanted to. His best option was to cultivate a focus so intense that it drove out the awareness of emotion, even where it couldn't exorcise the emotions themselves. If he hated Dafyd Alkhor, if he resented Else for shifting her affections, at least he could be oblivious about it.

The little not-turtle scrabbled in its box, exploring the space with its blunt beak-like nose. It was the fifth specimen they'd had. Three of the others had starved to death because the Carryx didn't provide food for them. The other one, Tonner had tried making a mash of the berries' silicate pulp, figuring that it was better than feeding the little animal nothing. It had violently emptied its digestive tract and died within half a day. He was going to let this one starve. It was bad luck for it that he had more pressing concerns than making food. The centrifuge hummed to itself, the readout on its side counting down the seconds that remained in the run and estimating the density and separation of molecules in the column. Outside the window, the sky was starting to reach toward dawn. Another night gone without sleep.

There was a word he'd come across once that meant the joy that someone took in self-destroying behavior. Like the fraction of pleasure that came from drinking that would be lost if the alcohol didn't harm you. It applied to work too. He didn't remember what the word was, though. Only the idea behind it.

"Breakfast time. Can I make you anything?" Campar asked as he ambled out of the darkness, his hair still slick from the shower.

"Coffee," Tonner said.

"Alas, there is no coffee."

"Tea."

"Last of the tea was two days ago."

"A stimulant of some kind."

"Do you find oatmeal stimulating?"

"Fine."

Campar rattled the pans in the little kitchen area. The seconds counted down on the centrifuge. Tonner's attention slid toward Dafyd Alkhor's bedroom door and then got yanked back away. His eyes felt gritty and dry.

"Sleep at all?"

"Napped between assay runs," Tonner said. "I'm fine."

The centrifuge chimed, the hum deepening as the mechanism slowed and going silent when it stopped. Tonner removed the column. The band with active agent was red as a cherry and about as thick as his fingernail. It would have to be enough. He grabbed a needle from the sampling kit and drew it off until the redness was almost completely gone, then added it to a glass where a half ounce of bright red fluid already waited. From the kitchen, Campar gestured to the crimson liquor with his chin.

"Jessyn. Should be enough for three days at her old levels," Tonner said, answering the unspoken question. "I'm not sure about uptake, though. There are some other things in that same layer of the soup, but purification based on something besides specific gravity is a pain in my butt. Hopefully it works, doesn't do anything worse than give her a little gas, and we can call it a win."

"Impressive," Campar said.

"Yeah. Well. I'm good at what I do." He poured the leavings of the spin into the waste container.

"And are you all right?" Campar's voice had a depth to it. A gravity he didn't usually employ. It was enough to tell Tonner that the subject had changed, and what it had changed to. Campar was standing in the kitchen, waiting for the water to boil, his expression calm and also oddly implacable. With the curly beard he was growing, he looked like a loving father who was insisting that the uncomfortable conversation happen, and that it happen now.

"Should I be?" Tonner asked.

"I'm not passing judgment. I've been accused of being fickle myself. I've had a lot of love affairs end. And it's always different. Often messy. Rarely easy."

"Am I being an asshole about it?" Tonner heard the challenge in his voice, the *I dare you to tell me this is my fault* that echoed the irrational sense that he'd done something wrong.

Campar added a dash of salt to the water. "You're pouting, but I think I would too, in your position."

"Are they being assholes, then?"

"Yes. But also I don't know how they could be more discreet, given our living situation. The etiquette books I've read don't cover sex in a prison camp."

Tonner walked across the room, the window at his back and Campar before him. He felt the weariness in his joints. He was going to have to rest soon. He couldn't imagine going to sleep.

"I don't choose to feel hurt. If I could just decide not to, I would absolutely just decide not to. But it's not up to me. My brain is doing a million things without asking me first. That's normal, and usually it's fine. Right now, I hate it. And hating it doesn't change it either."

"Can you imagine what it would be like if we were in control of our hearts?" Campar said. "If we could decide not to be angry or possessed by lust or afraid."

"Yes," Tonner said, surprised by the insight. "Yes I can. I imagine it would make us ideal servants. I wonder if the Carryx—"

The wide door to the hallway shuddered and clanked like something had fallen against it. Tonner stopped talking and went toward it by reflex. He had only started to crack the door open when the attackers flooded in.

Small, fast bodies covered in feather-like pelts, and the screams of the Night Drinkers as they charged. Tonner jumped back, stumbling over the power cables and falling onto his right shoulder hard enough to numb the arm. Campar was a shout off somewhere to his left, and one of the Night Drinkers leaped at him. Tonner kicked, struck the softness of a body, and pushed it back hard.

The creature dropped something round and soft as a balloon filled with liquid, but the color and texture of paper. Tonner scrambled to his feet. Half a dozen of the animals were in the common area and kitchen, all of them with teeth bared and the strange little orbs in their hands. A dark-pelted one larger than the rest took position on the dining table, screamed a high, trilling shriek, and threw. The orb flew through the air, just missing Campar's head, and splashed open along the kitchen wall. *Acid*, Tonner thought, *they're throwing acid at us*. He grabbed the nearest thing he could find—a length of unused power cable—and whipped it at them. The rooms were a chaos of bodies and movement, and he shifted and struck out without plan or strategy. All he cared about was violence. Hurting the things that were trying to hurt him. He felt himself shouting, but he didn't hear it.

One of the attackers jumped on the centrifuge, its leg knocking against the cup where he'd put Jessyn's medicine, and Tonner grabbed it by the leg, ripping it through the air, hammering it into the resonance scanner. Something bit the back of his thigh, tiny teeth clamping deep into the muscle, but he slammed the animal in his hand down two more times before the pain in his leg dropped him to his knees. Before he could grab it, the little bastard moved, letting go and jumping away.

With a lightning-fast grab, Campar snatched it out of the air and hurled it at the wall. It was a sign of his strength that the creature smashed into the wall and crumpled to the floor like a sack filled with wet rags. Campar was shouting too, the veins standing out in his neck. His eyes wide with terror. Tonner tried to get up and slipped back down onto his butt. There was blood all over the floor, and he realized with surprise it was coming out of his leg. He was about to ask Campar for help when something hit his shoulder and splashed across his neck and face. *They got me. I'm dead.* There was a kind of relief in the thought.

Jessyn barreled by him, a crowbar in her hand, and her hair streaming out behind her like she'd become a human pennant. Rickar was there too, and Else, and Dafyd. A clump of the Night Drinkers backed away toward the open door, their teeth bared.

Then Jessyn shouted, a wordless battle cry, and rushed at the little bastards. They scattered, but not quickly enough. Tonner caught one by the leg as it darted past him. He raised it over his head and thrust it down to the bronze-green metal floor. Two more orbs struck him, splashing the noxious gel on his shoulder and injured leg.

And then the Night Drinkers fled, disappearing into the corridor. In Tonner's hand, the monkey he'd managed to grab spasmed, shook, and went still. Campar turned in a circle, a pry bar out before him like a policeman's baton, ready for violence. The liquid, whatever it was, glistened on his arm and belly where he'd been struck.

"Are you all right?" the big man asked, and sound returned like God had turned the world's volume back on. The voices of the others were a cacophony, everyone talking over everyone else. High, indignant shrieks came from the corridor, growing more distant by the second. Tonner grabbed the edge of the counter and hauled himself to his feet. Dafyd slammed the door closed so hard it seemed like it might break the housing. Jessyn stood facing the closed door, air hissing through her teeth and the whites showing all around her eyes, fists clenched like a dare that anyone try to open it again.

"Showers," Tonner said, already limping his way toward the back. "Anyone who got this on them, strip and shower. Do it now!"

His room was farther, so he ducked into Irinna's and didn't take the time to shut the door behind him. The gel adhered to his skin, cold and burning at the same time. He threw the water tap open, and stepped in as the red goo that always came before the water sprayed out. He should have thought about that. Who knew what chemical reaction mixing the crimson cleanser with the Night Drinkers' weapon might have. Too late to do anything about it now. He stripped his clothes off as the spray became hot water sluicing over him. Was the chemical in his eyes? Was it going to blind him? Was his skin starting to melt and slough away? He rubbed his skin vigorously in the hot water and tried not to imagine the flesh coming off in his hands.

The panic started to fade. He stood in the flow of water for a slow count of a hundred, then another one, then he shut it off and stepped out. The skin where the gel had stuck was red and raised, but only a little painful to the touch. Not worse than a sunburn. He waited, watching for blistering or weeping, but nothing came. When he pulled on a fresh tunic, one that Irinna had left behind when she died, it hurt. He pulled it off again and made do with just trousers.

They were stupid. They should have drilled a spyhole in the door. They should have made rules about opening it. A stronger latch. A lock. They were at war, and they had treated the rooms like they were safe. Like violence wouldn't spill out from the cathedral. And they knew better. They all knew better.

He knew better, and he hadn't done anything about it. Too focused on other things. On Jessyn's medicine. On Dafyd. On Else. He sat on the bed. There was old blood on the sheets. In a different part of his life, he would have gone to Else now. He would have unburdened himself to her and taken whatever comfort she had to offer. Instead he sat, fingers laced together, body bent forward, and waited without knowing what he was waiting for. He was tired. He was exhilarated. He was frightened.

The knock at the door was gentle. Almost apologetic. Synnia looked in, her expression concerned. "Are you feeling all right?" *Has the aliens' balloon goo killed you?* she meant.

"Everything's fantastic," he said. He tried it as a joke, but it came out meaner than funny. He hauled himself to his feet. "I'm fine. Thanks. How's Campar?"

"Skin irritation. A little blistering where it's worst, but it doesn't seem to be progressing."

"Let's take a look."

The common area looked slightly less organized than it had before the violence. Someone had jammed one of the chairs into the wide door's track, barring it. Dark stains marked the walls and floor where the gel sacs had ruptured and spilled. The pan Campar had been using for his oatmeal was on the floor, the water spilled around in a puddle. Something stank like compost and blood, but he didn't figure out what it was until he saw the others crowded around the dining table.

Campar had also opted for going shirtless. The skin at his chest and belly was swollen, and half a dozen small white blisters were forming to the left of his navel. Else, standing beside him, looked up at Tonner. Her eyes met his, and she shifted her weight like she was about to walk toward him. Tonner shook his head once. *You don't get to worry about me.* She shifted back. If there was a little shame in her eyes, that was fine.

On the table, one of the Night Drinkers lay. The stink was its blood. Jessyn had begun with textbook cuts, pulling back the skin and tacking it to the tabletop. Unmade, the thing looked less like a monkey. Instead of a bony rib cage, there was a sheath of what looked like yellow cartilage with interleaved sections that could slide against each other. Its abdomen was taken up by a single, undifferentiated gray mass, but its chest underneath the cartilage sheaths was as complex as anything Tonner had ever seen.

"Look at this gas exchange system," Jessyn said, lifting a pinkish organ with a fork. "That's got to be a gas exchange system, right? Look at it."

"Unidirectional," Rickar said. "Either they have a terrifically inefficient metabolism, or they're used to a low-oxygen environment."

"What reeks like last week's salad?" Tonner said, stepping up to the table. The Night Drinker's blood had run over the edge of the table.

"Its gut contents make it look like an herbivore," Jessyn said. "Which, weird, I would've thought those were obligate carnivore teeth."

Tonner scratched his chin. He was a little dizzy. Maybe tired. Maybe bottoming out after his adrenaline rush. Maybe reacting to whatever noxious chemistry had been in the gel sacs. But along with it, he felt a rush of amusement and affection. The enemy had come, bent on murder. They'd broken into their home, assaulted them, and the first impulse of the team was to see what they could learn from it.

If they survived this alien hellscape, it would be because of this. Because in the face of trauma and violence, what they wanted first was to know, to understand. He stepped away, found the cup. The red fluid hadn't spilled. When he gestured to Jessyn, she came over reluctantly. Her attention was on the dissection. When he put the cup in her hand, she frowned her confusion.

"Once a day," he said. "I'd probably take it with food, at least at first. I think the rest of it's inert, but might want to give it a cushion all the same."

Understanding went through her slowly. Tears welled in her eyes, but she only nodded once and said, "Thank you for this."

"Back on your feet in no time," he said, and they both chuckled at the absurdity of it all.

"Tonner? Have a look." Campar had moved away from the table—probably not the dining table anymore, not after this—and to the kitchen sink.

"How are you?"

"I itch," Campar said. "I've itched before. As long as my skin doesn't all necrotize in the next day or two, I'll call it a victory. What does this look like to you?"

In the sink, nestled beside the drain, one of the gel sacs lay. It reminded him of when he'd been young and dissolved all the calcium off a duck's egg by soaking it in vinegar. All that was left was the membrane, thick enough to hold the egg together and thin enough to see through. That wasn't what Campar meant. It took a few seconds to get to the thought the big man had already had.

"It's a berry," Tonner said. "It's one of the berries."

"I think it is," Campar said.

"That's not a surprise, is it? They're the rival team. They're going to have a bunch of the same things we do. Or things that are analogous. The specimens are going to match up."

"Yes, but where we made it into a little pharmaceutical printer, they made a bioweapon." Campar's smile was wide and slow. He was waggling his eyebrows. Tonner didn't get it.

And then he did.

He looked at the pale little blob. When Night Drinkers thought of something deadly, something to erase their enemies, they made bombs. When the bombs weren't enough, they made this. They made it out of the same raw materials that Tonner had, and they'd left a sample.

"All right," he said. "Jessyn? When you're done poking through that mess over there, throw it out, and come check the sampler and the imager. We may have knocked them around a little. If they're out of true, we'll need to tare them again." He took a breath. Steeled himself. "Dafyd, if you and Campar could gather up as much of the gooey crap from the walls and floor as you can get. We may not need it, but we also might. Else. If you could take this sac and prep what's in it for the imager. I had a couple runs

I'm going to need to put on ice. We have three projects now. Turtle food. Pharmaceutical production. Weapons testing. We need to run them simultaneously, so I hope you all enjoy juggling."

To his surprise and pleasure, they chuckled. Even Synnia, who didn't take joy in much anymore. Even Else, who had been his lover once, and wasn't anymore. Dafyd had the good sense not to push back with a counterplan of his own. Maybe Tonner was being paranoid that he'd assumed that he would.

"How long has it been since you rested?" Jessyn asked. It took Tonner a couple seconds to focus on her. He really was spent. But…

"I wouldn't be able to," he said. "Let's get to work."

Twenty-Three

The sunlight spilled through the window of Else's bedroom and spread itself along the wall. Unseen clouds softened the edges. Dafyd lay on his side, his arm under his head like a pillow, and watched her. Of all the unthinkable events in his life, the fact that the universe had put him beside this woman felt the most unlikely. Had he been in love with her before, or had it just been a passing infatuation? Had they forged something deeper during the terrible passage from Anjiin, or had they just uncovered a connection that had always been there waiting? Or, worse, was this moment as ephemeral as his old life had been.

Else's eyes opened just enough for him to see the glimmer of them. Her smile was the smallest twitch of her lips.

"You're thinking something," she said. "I can hear the gears turning."

"I am."

"Share?"

"They gave us rooms with windows," Dafyd said. "These buildings are massive. Most of the space in them will have no windows."

"So?"

"So, did they do that because humans need more sunlight than other species? Is natural light high status? Low status? An accident based on timing? Does it mean everything, or nothing at all?"

"Why does that matter right now?"

Dafyd sighed, shifted. Else hooked her leg around his, pulling him against her. Her skin was warm.

"I haven't figured it out yet," Dafyd said.

"You haven't figured out why having windows matters?"

"No, I mean... I don't understand the Carryx. I don't understand how they think."

"Is this really your idea of afterplay? Revisiting the story of Little Dot the Water Beetle?"

"You asked what I was thinking."

"It would have been all right with me if it had been a little more flattering. What's puzzling you about the Carryx today? It's not just the windows."

"Why they win. It doesn't make sense."

"They're huge, strong, and difficult to kill. That seems like a good start."

"Guns and explosives solved the large-animal problem on Anjiin centuries ago. And this is a spacefaring species. The least dangerous thing about them is that they're big and strong. It's what they are that confuses me. I thought the librarian was going to be happy to have a chance to tell us what it wanted. Why wouldn't you want your servants to be attentive and willing?"

The flirtation drained out of Else's expression. "Maybe there's some cultural taboo?"

"These things have taken over... I mean, how many worlds would you guess are represented here? Look at all the varieties of life they have on a leash. They're doing something right, and I think about what I expect from a species or government or organization that could do this. I expect them to be open to learning, but when I made the offer, it was like I'd insulted it. I expect meaningful information flow, but these things had to be told we needed pens. I expect guidance, but there isn't any. The librarian said it was here to help us and didn't mention that the Night Drinkers might want us all dead. That's a big omission. They won't learn from us. They won't teach us."

In the distance, Rickar yelped. A moment later, Campar's laughter followed. Something flew past the window, its shadow making the light flicker once. Else sat up, turned, leaned her back against the wall. The sun caught her shoulder like a tattoo inked in light.

Dafyd said, "I don't know if there's some bit of information I'm missing, or if I have all the pieces and just can't fit them together. I keep trying to find it. Is the way the walls don't stand square important? Is the way they walk signaling something about how their bodies work? The librarian said, 'Possibility is irrelevant.' What does that mean? Can an advanced scientific species really not understand probability and inquiry down multiple paths? Why does it use Rak-hund and Soft Lothark as enforcers and not those bone-horse things? It's right there, and I just can't..."

"Does it matter?" she asked.

"Yeah. Probably more than anything else right now."

Else tilted her head. The light spilled onto her jaw, her cheek, set her copper-colored hair on fire. "Why? I mean, I don't disagree, but you know whatever you find here, it's not going to get us where we were."

He took her hand, lacing his fingers in hers. "Might help keep us where we are. We've lost a lot. But I've still got some things I'd like to keep."

* * *

Jessyn knew the medicine was starting to work when her fantasies changed from suicide to murder.

Time had become a strange thing since the Carryx descended on Anjiin and ended everything. She didn't know how long it had been, but with how stingy she'd been with her pills by the end, she was certain that even the last traces had washed out of her blood and brain. Her mind had reached its default, unmedicated state. Some days, she was able to function. Some days she didn't get out of bed, and when she tried to calm her unquiet, the thing that worked was her own death.

Sometimes it was drowning, sometimes it was bleeding to death, but the scenario that brought her the most peace was to replay the attack in the lab. Irinna at her side, the enemy Night Drinkers around her. Some nights, she imagined their small arms pulling a rope around her neck and cutting off her windpipe, the darkness flowing in at the edges of her vision until there was nothing left. Some nights she imagined a second bomb, and the nothingness coming in fast.

And then Tonner had given her the first little glass of red liquor. It tasted bitter and salty and it had an aftertaste that crawled up the back of her nose. For the first couple of days, she hadn't noticed a difference, and then the details of her fantasy changed.

It was still the attack in the lab. The day Irinna died. But her imagination shifted away from the end of her own life. She remembered the one that she'd killed, and the half-recalled, half-imagined death of the little alien had a satisfaction to it. The sense of being in control tasted like water to a woman dying from thirst. Slowly, the dreams of suicide faded, the dreams of murder bloomed. She lulled herself to sleep conjuring up the resistance of a little neck and the crunch it made when she broke it.

For Jessyn, it was what passed for sanity now.

"So you feel like you're back to baseline?" Synnia asked. The older woman smiled hopefully at her, the wrinkles around her mouth and eyes bunching up. How many years did Synnia have left in her aging frame? Jessyn thought about telling her that her mind always focused on death these days, but at least it wasn't her own now.

Instead Jessyn shrugged and smiled. They were in her bedroom. She'd hauled in one of the couches that had been part of the common area and used it to make a little drawing room space. A little bit of privacy in their everyone-in-each-other's-lap lifestyle.

"I think so," Jessyn said. "It's a little hard using your brain to take accurate readings of itself. Fundamentally bad data."

Synnia poured them both a little more of what she was calling tea from the pan she'd brought in. They'd run out of actual tea, just like they'd stopped getting coffee and fresh produce. But it was something. The last batch of food to arrive had included a sachet of leaves that seemed too thick and unpleasant to use as a spice, too sparse for a salad. So Campar had started steeping them and everyone called the result tea. They were minty and rich, and not quite unpleasantly bitter. That was as much as anyone hoped these days.

"I was afraid I wouldn't know," Jessyn said. "When it kicked in? I was worried that I wouldn't be able to tell the difference. I mean—" She gestured broadly.

"You're ripped from your home, put in an alien prison, almost killed," Synnia said, her tone grave but gentle.

"Right?" Jessyn said, and sipped her not-really-tea. The bitter aftertaste rode the edge of pungent without quite tipping over it. She drank it anyway. "But I could. It wasn't even subtle."

"I'm glad you're feeling better."

I'm not, though, Jessyn thought. *I'm just feeling a different kind of bad.* She didn't say it. She remembered a day from another lifetime when she and Irinna had knocked off work at the labs a little early and gone out to a café for dinner. They'd had spiced chicken in fry bread, a sauce of peppers and apple, and more beer than had probably been wise. Jessyn could still picture the woman she'd sat across from then—slender, pale, and bright-eyed, with long, expressive hands. They'd intended to go dancing afterward, but had instead gotten into a conversation about hybrid protein synthesis that excited them enough that they'd lost track of things. By dancing time, they were both too drunk.

It was strange to try and make that memory reconcile with the life she had. So instead, Jessyn remembered killing the Night Drinker, feeling the impact as she swung its body, and an angry little warmth touched her. She didn't have to pretend her smile anymore, only what it was about.

They talked awhile longer, speculating about the work and sharing old memories, telling jokes that weren't particularly funny but that made a bridge between them all the same. Synnia never mentioned her dead husband. Jessyn never brought up her fear for her lost brother. It let them pretend, at least for a moment, they still had normal lives.

In the main room, Tonner, Rickar, and Campar were all standing around the resonance imager. The men all wore the same tunics and loose trousers that the Carryx had supplied, but they wore them very differently. They were small on Campar's broad frame, seeming like something he'd have worn to the gymnasium, only with the collar plucked up to give the tunic the best possible drape. Tonner wore them like a necessity, unaware of how he looked and not interested if he did notice. Rickar rolled up his sleeves and cuffs, just a little. On Anjiin, he always had the slightly rumpled, slightly erotic style of an unmade Sunday morning bed. Now on the prison world of the Carryx, he still did. Dafyd and Else weren't there, and everyone was pretending not to notice the fact or its implications. Schematics of the weaponized berries were tacked up on the wall, different biochemical pathways mapped out with hand-drawn diagrams of individual proteins at each phase. Two pans filled with prototypes sat on the dining room table, but they were all looking at the imager's display.

"It's got the right general form to be a signaling protein," Campar said as Jessyn carried the remains of the tea to the kitchen. "All polar knobbies on the ends, and that tertiary structure. And since the medium was a little basic, I'd assume the active form is the curly one."

Jessyn started rinsing out the cups. Even at full heat, the water wasn't hot enough to scald, but it did turn her fingers and the backs of her hands a little ruddy. The last dark swirls of not-quite-tea leaves danced at the bottom of the pan.

Tonner made a familiar little cough that meant he was thinking. Jessyn had a flashbulb memory of being in his laboratory the first time, of seeing him walking in front of a wall filled with notes and chemical diagrams. It had felt like the most amazing thing that would ever happen to her. Seemed silly now. She turned off the water and set the cups upside down on the counter, a bit of absorbent foam under them like a little copy of the shit mat from the ship.

"We still don't have those three cofactors, though—"

"They're inert," Rickar said. "They're probably just manufacturing artifacts. This one right here is the best candidate for an active factor, and we have it. We nailed it. It's right."

Tonner ran his fingers through the gray thatch of his hair. "I want to agree. I kind of do agree. But...it bothers me? I want a match on the whole thing."

Jessyn pressed her hands against her tunic, letting the fabric wick away the dampness as she walked over to the samples. A dozen pale, soft bulbs, like egg-sized translucent water balloons. White, papery membranes, strong enough to hold without splitting. She rolled one across her palm. This had been a little animal, once. Red, with a tiny silicate farm that it protected with this same skin.

They knew more about their enemy now. They'd cut open the dead ones and made the corpses offer up their secrets. They'd learned how they pumped their version of blood using a network of muscular arteries instead of a heart. That their one oversized lung pointed to a low-oxygen homeworld. It was Tonner who'd pointed out that if the Night Drinkers were constantly suffering from a low-level state of oxygen poisoning, it might explain their hyperactivity and violence. As though one could understand the motives of alien monsters by looking through their corpses. As though it mattered *why* they killed Irinna. The autopsy did tell them something about how the Night Drinkers died, though.

And this berry they'd modified into a bioweapon. That told them something too.

"We should field-test it," Jessyn said.

"Invite one of our little friends over for dinner and some light vivisection?" Campar said. He was joking, but only just. The anger and the fear were as alive in him as in any of them.

"Or take it to them," she said, tossing the pale bulb in her palm. "Their place works for me."

The others were quiet for a long moment. The air felt charged, a shift in pressure. She felt like she'd opened a door in her mind and invited them all to step through it. Pain and fear were just the ocean they swam in. They could make light of it, and they did. They could keep living their lives in it, because there wasn't an option. But here was some power, and all they had to do was take it.

"You think we can find our way back to them?" Tonner asked.

"Can't hurt to try," Campar said, his tone mild considering what they were talking about. Jessyn felt something expanding in her chest, tugging her mouth into a feral grin.

"Should we gather up the others?" Rickar asked.

"No," Tonner said, and none of them argued.

Campar carried the bulbs in the same pan Synnia had used for not-quite-tea, and Jessyn walked at his side. Tonner came behind them, and then Rickar with the crowbar in his fist. The air seemed crisp, and she felt herself bouncing a little with each step.

She had never anticipated violence with joy before. When she'd been young, she'd seen other children building themselves up to schoolyard confrontations, and she'd thought that they were overcoming a natural urge toward peace. That fighting meant working up enough emotion to force your way past essentially peaceful nature. It turned out that sometimes it was easy. Her hands tingled. Part of her hoped that the Night Drinkers would fight back. That they'd bite her again. That they'd come close enough that she could put her hands around their little bodies.

Everything she'd gone through seemed to funnel down to the pure and simple moment. Her captivity, yes. Irinna's death, yes. The abasement of Anjiin, yes. But also all the years of feeling ashamed of her weakness. All the guilt at the ways her disease held her and Jellit back. All the damage the universe had done to her, she'd taken somehow and reforged into something sharp, a weapon that for once wasn't meant to cut her.

The cathedral was bright, broad beams of sunlight filling the space above them. A flock of something that could have been birds or bats and probably wasn't either swirled lazily through the air. The press of alien bodies on the ground was thicker than usual. A dozen or more Soft Lothark ambled in rough formation like a troop of chimpanzees walking through unfamiliar territory. Two wide-bodied quadrupeds she hadn't seen before shifted by on thick, ropy legs. Jessyn found she was humming a song to herself that she'd heard when she was back on Anjiin. *Come come come to the fair and see what we shall see.*

The wall where the Night Drinkers lived was just where it had been. If there were any defenses, she didn't see them. A bat-winged thing with iridescent dust on its thumbnail-long pelt stumbled by, four dark eyes next to a round, tooth-filled mouth. Something about the set of its face made it seem embarrassed. One of the crab-dogs scuttled by, making loud ticking sounds. Miracles and wonders and moments that would have astounded her once, and they were just distractions between her and—call it what it was—her prey.

A Night Drinker popped its head out of one of the holes, saw them, and darted back inside. The alarm was being raised.

Rickar moved to the front. "How do you think we should—"

Jessyn plucked one of the bulbs out of the pan, cocked her arm, and threw. It traced a fast, shallow arc through the air and vanished into one of the holes with a wet pop. She took another one, aimed, threw again. Then Tonner was doing the same. They didn't have very many. This wouldn't take long. She threw another, and missed. Instead of going into one of the holes, the bulb splashed against the fungal-looking wall itself. Where the gel touched it, the wall began to melt into an inky black fluid.

"Well, that's interesting," Tonner said, and then the screaming started.

The voices were high and chittering, rattling like a thousand little gnashing teeth. A dozen Night Drinkers boiled out of the wall, their arms stretched wide and their mouths gaping in rage or anguish. They swarmed out, but haphazardly, like they were all half-blinded. Rickar hunched forward, crowbar cocked back over his shoulder and ready to fight.

One of the largest sprinted toward them by itself, like it was leading a charge that the rest weren't quite ready to follow. Rickar hit it hard and low. The impact sounded heavy and solid like someone dropping a bag of rice. The Night Drinker screamed and leaped back, limping on its left side. Rickar swung again, but it stayed just out of reach. A black wetness on its leg could have been blood. Jessyn discovered she was laughing. "You started this," she said. "You wanted a fight, but you can't take it now?"

She darted forward, and the Night Drinkers shied away in fear. Jessyn scooped up another bulb—they were down to five now—and threw it at the coming horde. She caught one of them in the chest. It screamed like she'd lit it on fire, and it fell to the ground. Three of the others stopped to help their fallen comrade, and Tonner got all three of them with another bulb. Jessyn remembered something she'd seen as a child: an old war where one side had left an enemy soldier wounded and screaming so that they could kill anyone who came to help. It had been presented as an atrocity then. It just seemed like good tactics now.

Another large one came to the front of the pack. It had a deep red pelt and eyes wider than usual for the species. It looked from

Jessyn to Campar to Tonner, reached out its hands, making fists like it was milking the air. Its mouth was a scattering of ebony on meat spoiled to darkness.

"I think it wants something," Rickar said.

"Here. It can have this," Tonner replied, and pelted it full in the chest with one of the globes. It screamed and danced back, trying to wipe itself clean, and then collapsing to the ground.

"The ammunition's getting a bit low. We should go," Campar almost sang as he walked backward, away from the fallen enemy. Tonner hefted one of the last bulbs, Jessyn the other. Not to throw, but to threaten. *We can't get all of you, but we will by God get the first one that tries.* The monkeys screamed and waved their arms. The ones that she and Tonner had pelted were lying down or trying to wipe themselves clean. The bleeding one that Rickar struck had stopped advancing, but was staring at them, its teeth bared. Its distress was weirdly clear for an organism that had evolved on some other world. Campar kept backing away, and the enemy didn't charge. After not very long, they didn't even follow, disappearing in the flow of alien bodies. As they retreated, Jessyn saw one of the huge bone-horse aliens pause near where she thought the damaged wall would be, its slow, vast attention caught by the wreckage.

When they got out of the cathedral and into the corridors, Jessyn and Tonner put the two remaining bulbs back in the pan. Rickar kept looking back over his shoulder as they walked, and Jessyn did too. Nothing seemed to be following them.

"Well, that was fascinating," Tonner said. The smile in his voice was so clear, he almost sounded giddy.

"The structural damage to whatever that infill material is was surprising," Rickar said. "I wonder if it's a separate organism or something that the little fuckers produce. Like bees making wax?"

"Or they could be the same organism with two forms. Differing genders or ages?"

"That'd be a pretty vast dimorphism."

"Not unprecedented..."

The men chattered, each talking over the other, their voices high and joyous. Jessyn let them. The words and concepts flowed over her like smoke from a fire, but they didn't touch her. They could pretend that they were excited by the increase in knowledge, that they were scholars before anything else. She'd let them. Later on, she'd probably even join in. But just then, with the smell of victory still in her nose, she knew better. They were excited because they'd won. They were alive, and many of the enemy weren't. For the first time since before the humiliation of Anjiin, they had faced a threat and unequivocally come through as powerful, dominant, safe. It was intoxicating.

As they made their way back to the wide door, she imagined what they would have looked like to the little enemy. A new race of nearly hairless giants, twice their size, set to their same task, and clever enough to be a threat. She pictured herself clambering through some vast laboratory the way the monkeys had in those early days. Chided and tossed out by the rulers of that place, but with access enough to see what they were doing, to know that they had to be stopped.

And then what? They had tried to kill the giants with explosives, and the giants hadn't died. They'd put together a chemical weapon and soaked the giants with it. The giants had shrugged it off and poured it back. To the little fuckers, humans would seem unkillable. Like gods.

When they reached the rooms, it was Else who pulled open the door. Her long, elegant face was tight with concern. Behind her, Synnia and Dafyd were sitting on the floor by the big window. Sunset was coming, turning the scrim of white-gray clouds to gold and peach and red.

"What happened?" Else asked as she closed the door behind them.

"More data," Tonner said, a little coyly. He seemed to like having something Else wanted and not giving it to her. Those two and Dafyd were going to have to come to some arrangement, but even bullshit sexual politics couldn't take the shine off Jessyn's day.

"I think it's safe to say our version of their devil's brew is sufficiently evil," Campar said, putting the pan down and plucking the last two bulbs back out to put in the sample case. "The cofactors aren't necessary to make the weapon effective."

"What did it do?" Synnia asked. Even her usually kind voice had an echo of bloodthirst. Or maybe that was just Jessyn. Maybe she was drunk enough with it that she could hear it even when it wasn't there.

Campar and Rickar retold the story as they started preparing the next meal. Normally, they all ate at odd times, but the occasion seemed to demand something communal. Even couched in terms of molecular action and evolutionary biology, the tale was thrilling. Jessyn went to the door a few times, looking out to make certain that the enemy hadn't followed them.

The raid had been her idea. Or if not exactly her idea, at least she had been the one to trigger it. To move herself and the others into action. She wouldn't have done it a week before. Or a week before that. That she was able to take action was a result of the medicine that Tonner and Campar and all the others had engineered out of their alien berries. And without it, there would be some of the feather monkeys alive tonight who now weren't. They'd made two weapons from what they had. She was one of them.

"We need to be careful," Dafyd said as the victory dinner was served out. "I mean, this is great. Really, really good. I just...I don't know. There's something about it that feels like we're agreeing to play things the way the Carryx want us to."

Campar's nod was polite but cool. "I'm not certain that we have the freedom to rewrite their rules."

"And ignoring them got Irinna killed," Jessyn said, feeling a hot little rage kindle in her belly for Dafyd now.

"I just want to understand better what the context for all this is, you know?" Dafyd said, holding up his hands in mock surrender.

"I understand what you're saying," Campar said. "Do you understand what *we're* saying?"

Dafyd seemed to deflate a little. "Yeah. I do."

That night, Jessyn slept like the dead.

Twenty-Four

By the time Ekur of the cohort Tkalal fell out of asymmetry and entered the protected zone of Carryx-controlled space, it had been out of communication with both its dactyl and the librarians of the world-palace for weeks. It disliked those periods of transit, cut off from both the librarians under its command and the structures of power whose directives might remove from it the burden of choice. In asymmetry, it was unreachable and incapable of reaching out, alone in a single ship with only animals, soldiers, and the navigation half-minds. It passed the time by recording and reviewing all that had happened up to then. The decisions it had made when not under the direction of the librarians above it were its own responsibility. If the outcomes of its actions were particularly good, it might be elevated in the hierarchy. If it failed, it could suffer the indignity of growing into a soldier.

It would never be promoted back into the highest levels of the Carryx, never be included in the noble ranks that might offer genetic material for the next generations. That decision had been made many years ago, and it was as irrevocable as it was correct. The scars on its fighting arm showed where the break had been, and that it had failed was proof that it had deserved to fail. It felt neither shame nor regret. It did, however, review its independent decisions in Ayayeh, searching for flaws or weaknesses in its strategies.

When the ship entered symmetry, the silence of transit gave way to a flood of messages. The only one that concerned it was the regulator-librarian: A message waited from the highest voices of the empire, one of the eight limbs of the Sovran herself. It had passed, of course, through each of the librarians in the path, but this was the world-palace. The time required to pass each level of responsibility was minimal. If the regulator-librarian had made its choice fifteen breaths ago, the order would already have reached a lowly subjugator-librarian like Ekur-Tkalal.

The regulator-librarian was easily twice its size, more in keeping with the scale of a soldier than a librarian. But where soldiers were simple in their design—with broad, undifferentiated arms, and eyes that all focused on the same thing like a child's—the regulator-librarian was complex. Its skin was a filigree of silver over bronze. Its voice spoke at several resonances simultaneously, so it could fit a poem into a syllable. Its eyes shifted in the image, as if each was responding to a separate brain. Even before it spoke, Ekur-Tkalal was overcome by a rush of awe at its magnificence. Deep in its own brain, chemicals released that suppressed Ekur-Tkalal's sense of self and opened it to the will of its species.

You are to escort your prisoners, the regulator-librarian said, *to the keeping pens of low animals and oversee their interrogation.*

There was a moment of dismay, a sense of loss, even a shiver of disgust. Interrogator-librarians were of a dignity equal to subjugator-librarians, but became tainted by more direct contact with animals. Ekur-Tkalal had avoided direct interaction with the fivefold enemy during their transit. It would have no such luxury now. The flush of hormones was already cascading through its blood, preparing its body for the subtle changes that came with its new place within the moieties.

By the time it responded *I understand*, it had already begun to change.

They walk together, the swarm and the older woman. Once, they had explored the world prison together, ranging far from the quarters they all shared. Now they stay close, not exploring but keeping watch. The swarm knows that the Night Drinkers are nowhere near them. It cannot smell the particular musk of their coats, cannot hear the patterns of their voices in the echoes that form the white noise of the corridor. But the host wouldn't know, so it acts the part of ignorance. It places the distress it does feel where the anxiety it should but doesn't feel would go.

What was it like for you at the start? *the swarm asks. After so many months of practice, it feels natural to speak like this. It no longer feels like manipulating a body, like mimicking life. It feels like being alive.*

Synnia's mouth tightens for a moment in grief, and then softens with nostalgia. It isn't the swarm that makes these translations from movement to meaning. It is what remains of Ameer Kindred. It is the captive consciousness of Else Yannin.

Synnia talks about meeting Nöl when they were young. About falling into his company, the way he made her feel needed, the way he made her feel a little certain of herself. The decision to win his affection that he never knew about.

What about you? *Synnia asks, and adrenaline floods the swarm's stolen body before it understands what has inspired the fear. The older woman is asking about Else's heart, and in omitting a name—not what about you and Tonner or what about you and Dafyd—she has left an implicit question that leaves the part of it that was Else Yannin exposed and embarrassed. The swarm notices its own relationship to exposure and embarrassment.*

My version is more complicated, *the swarm says, and looks away. It hopes that Synnia won't push, and she doesn't. They walk together, down hallways and through chambers, then back the way they came. Synnia looks for other humans, the scattered prisoners from Anjiin, and the swarm looks for other things.*

There are hundreds of other bodies that pass by them of a dozen different species. The Rak-hund, long servants of the Carryx, and loyal as a dog. The squat-bodied jailers of the Soft Lothark, the odd walking cuttlefish Sinen. These species are given greater freedom. Some of them, the swarm guesses, will leave this world with the gathering armies just as they did when they came to Anjiin.

They turn down a new hallway that has bright yellow light spilling down from a vaulted ceiling, and Synnia makes a note of it on the paper that they carry. Something has decorated one wall with chips of color in a wide, swirling mosaic that reaches out into colors that human eyes cannot see but the swarm can. It is beautiful. Some other prisoner has come to this place and made art from it. Created something meaningful and joyous in this place of loss and terror. The swarm is surprised to find that inspiring and sad.

Something touches its mind, soft and distant as the scent of a flower or a whisper in the next room. A pattern of murmur played on a chord of frequencies that would seem random, but aren't. The swarm freezes, Ameer freezes, Else freezes.

The swarm was not a conscious being before it reached Anjiin.

It has no memory of a time before, but it does have knowledge. Instinct. Programming.

It knows a distress call when it hears one.

In captive species that had been taken through the normal course of expansion, the half-minds would have had signals to absorb and model: patterns of chemical release and sound and controlled radiation of light and heat that the enemy produced in its natural environment. By consuming the ways in which the animals conversed with each other, the half-mind would have found the ways to mimic them, shape them, translate the thoughts and meanings of low animals to the Carryx, and issue instructions to the animals in ways they could comprehend.

Without that, the fivefold captives were a cipher. But only for a time.

The beginning work of the interrogation was carried out in a series of long, low rooms by Soft Lothark and Sinen. In one, the captives were vivisected. Their anatomy, chemistry, and energetic activity were measured and given to the half-mind as context. In another, captives were trained one at a time to perform simple tasks in exchange for food or the cessation of pain and then monitored as they communicated these lessons to others of their kind.

Ekur-Tkalal watched over the process. To minimize its contact with the Sinen, it chose one to act as its factor: a white-eyed semi-male that seemed well enough liked by its companions. When the interrogator-librarian decided that the metallic threads in the captives' five arms were of interest, the white-eyed Sinen relayed the command to vivisectionists. When it saw two of the captives curling around one of their wounded like they were cradling it, the white-eyed Sinen carried the order to scan their energy profile when they came into contact. And when the half-mind reached baseline competence, it was the white-eyed Sinen who brought word to the librarian that the true interrogation could begin in earnest.

The subject was one of twenty who had survived the process. It was in a dry tank under the ultraviolet light that the captives seemed to find noxious. Its communication style was a combination of chemical release and electromagnetic waves, so when they conversed, it remained silent apart from the half-mind's translation.

"Answer my questions, and you and your kind will be considered for inclusion in the moieties. Refusal brings death."

The translation half-mind pulsed once as it passed this on in terms the captive could comprehend—a mist of esters and cyclic terpenes, a burst of radio waves on a combination of frequencies. The captive squirmed, shifted its limbs.

"I understand," the half-mind chirped.

"Identify the star, planet, or system in which your species evolved."

The half-mind was quiet for a long time. Then, "No such place exists. My kind are not the products of evolution."

Ekur-Tkalal settled its weight more deeply onto its fighting arms. The idea of being a special creation was common enough among animals, but teasing information from the animal's religious delusions would be tedious. It plucked its feeding arms and considered breaking one of the captive's limbs.

"Identify the star, planet, or system in which your species resided before you achieved the ability to move between stars."

Another pause. "No such place exists. We were created as tools of the war, and did not exist before the ships we pilot."

"Explain that."

"We are designed life," the half-mind said, then paused for a very long time as the captive muttered through the electromagnetic spectrum, exuded clouds of scent. The interrogator-librarian remained patient. "We are like half-minds made from life."

A thrill of disgust ran through the librarian's body. The Carryx had come across manufactured life-simulacra before. Stick-flowers on Ursin-Qin, the Stone-Mind of High Lothark, the Ambients of Cahl and Deáphan. They were perversions. Imitations of mind doomed to degradation and death like an animal fed nothing but its own waste. To build a monstrosity like that out of living flesh was depraved in a way that the librarian had never considered.

"Describe the nature of the beings that built and commanded you."

Again, the pause. In the back of the room, a Sinen shuffled through the entrance arch with an armful of cables and a round black filter that would help collect the aromatic molecules from the air and separate them for reuse by the half-mind. The librarian tried to ignore the intrusion.

"They call themselves Aunjeli. Their flesh is made from semi-stable plasma, and they build their cities in the coronas of stars."

The librarian shrugged its fighting arms and turned up the intensity of the ultraviolet light. The captive shuddered and squirmed.

"Do not try to deceive me," the librarian said. "Your defiance gains you only additional pain. Describe the nature of the beings that built and commanded you."

A moment later. "Turn the light down. I can't think with it on."

The librarian turned the light down. The Sinen left, talking wetly to another of its kind not quite far enough away that Ekur-Tkalal was spared hearing it. The captive spoke again. The translation half-mind paused, as though parsing the reply.

"Go inseminate your Sovran, we aren't going to tell you feces eaters anything."

The librarian turned the light back up and prepared for a long, tedious day.

They wait for the Night Drinkers to come, and the fear makes it difficult to do what needs to be done. They are all on alert, and the swarm needs to go into the nightmare of architecture without them. It takes the better part of a day before the opportunity comes. It finds itself alone in the common room, and slips out the door. There is a scent of Night Drinker in the air. The enemy has been close, but they aren't here now. Depending on what enemy it means.

It walks quickly, purposefully, as if it had every right and reason to be where it was. The radio wave shriek is faint, fading in and out of detectability like the perfume of someone who has already left the room. The swarm follows it, remaking the host's flesh as it walks. Dark patches grow on its skin. None of the things it walks past is likely to know what normal is for a human any more than it would be surprised by the specific number of legs on a Rak-hund. It feels Ameer and Else straining with it, listening. It feels their terror and elation when the signal grows steady, becomes a direction.

The swarm finds its way up. Stairways and ramps and a thin scramble like a ladder cut from stone. It has never been this way before. The hallways are narrow here and the sound of wind taps at the air. There are fewer and fewer of the menagerie of alien captives, more and more of the Carryx and their soldiers. The sense of being anonymous in a crowd falls away, and the swarm begins ducking from shadow to shadow. It stops the human scents from leaving its flesh, softens its footfalls. It becomes a shadow in a prison uniform, and the alarm grows louder. Closer.

One of the cuttlefish-goat aliens—the ones called Sinen—pauses to look at the swarm. Adrenaline makes Else's borrowed heart beat faster, but the swarm keeps a steady pace, walking as if it had every right to walk. The Sinen hesitates, steps after it, then turns away. A wide-bodied Carryx lumbers into view at the end of a corridor, its abdomen dancing from side to side like it is impatient and wants to go faster than its thorax. The signal would lead the swarm toward the huge, murdering arms, the wide, black eyes. Instead, it turns away, finds a little chamber with round containers filled with a fluid it doesn't recognize.

Though the risk is immense, it remakes its flesh again, burning energy that would surely shorten the lifespan of the host body, in the unlikely event the swarm were to remain in it into senescence. It finds the frequencies of the cry. It responds.

Where are you?

Don't approach, *its hidden ally says.* We are taken. Don't approach.

What are you?

The pause lasts less than a moment, and then a flood of information, all encrypted in ways that the swarm knows without knowing, like hearing words in a language it had forgotten it could speak. The pilot replays the battle, the trap that was sprung at Ayayeh and the damage that the Carryx sustained. Its capture, and the capture of its cohorts. All that it has learned by being questioned, all the questions that the Carryx interrogator has asked. The swarm swallows the information, folding it into the packet of all that it has learned.

The signal between them stutters, the swarm cuts off its broadcast, turns away, walks as casually as it can down the paths it followed to come here. They were heard, they were noticed. The agents of the Carryx will be hunting them. It can't be caught, not now. Not ever.

Go! *Else urges.* Run. What are you waiting for? Get out of here!

The swarm shifts its flesh back into a more nearly human appearance. It can claim it got lost. It can ask for directions back to its cell.

They'll put us together with the signal, *Ameer thinks.* Two weird things at once makes a connection between them. If they find you, they'll look.

The swarm agrees with the dead girl. It retraces its steps, pulling itself back inside its own skin. If the distress call is still out there, it chooses not to hear it. If there is more information... It wants the information badly, but has drunk too deep already.

The swarm drops down the stony ladder, turns to the ramps leading down, descends to lower levels of the vast prison palace. As it does, it reviews all that it has just learned and is intoxicated by the information. It plays the damage estimates again and again like a favorite song. The Carryx dying by hundreds on the surface of Ayayeh, the ships being pummeled in the dark void.

For a moment, it forgets the Night Drinkers and Dafyd and Tonner. It forgets Irinna's death and the abasement of Jessyn. The fall of Anjiin. The great war has touched the swarm. It wants desperately to reach back.

"What was the signal?" Ekur-Tkalal asked.

The white-eyed Sinen shifted, uncomfortable. "The half-mind suggests it was a report of the events in Ayayeh. We didn't get the full message, but there was enough to make context from."

The interrogator-librarian lifted one fighting arm off the floor, and the Sinen flinched back. It didn't make sense. It needed to start, or Ekur's patience with animal incompetence would end. "How strong was the signal?"

"Enough to cut through the dampers inside this complex, but not more than that. No one outside would have received it."

There was nothing within the animal holding complex that the captive could have shared information with. Not in any way that mattered.

"It may only be a hiccup," the Sinen said. "A reflex that the captive triggered inappropriately because of their physical distress."

"Perhaps," Ekur-Tkalal said. "That's something we'll ask them."

Twenty-Five

Now that he'd been accepted back into the fold, there were times when Rickar missed being an exile. The long, empty days sitting with Synnia and looking out the window, talking about nothing in particular. The two of them mourning quietly together while Tonner whipped the others into becoming a human clockwork. As though he believed that, under his magisterial direction, he could make everything right again through the sheer force of intellect. Being on the outside had seemed unpleasant at the time, but he wondered now if it hadn't also given him the chance to heal in a way the others hadn't.

The impulse to carry their history with them, to be the same research group they'd been at Irvian, to will some kind of familiar order into their daily lives… It had been hard to resist. It had also been an illusion. The truth was that they'd had their lives cut in two. Before and after. Everything they'd known and thought and believed and hoped, and then… And then, the Carryx.

Tonner had given him time for his soul to grow still again after that. To find a kind of peace in being burned to nothing and starting over. Maybe he should have been grateful.

"Do you need anything?" Jessyn asked.

He chuckled, and it was a rueful thing. Anything? Yes, anything. A book. A film. A guitar. An afternoon walking in the gardens outside Dyan Academy with the trees turning red for the autumn. Dance with me. Come to bed with me. Anything to fill his hours besides prison and Carryx and how to turn the little organisms they called berries into something more useful to them. "No," he said. "I'm fine."

She nodded, headed back toward the kitchen and whatever it was she was getting for herself. Rickar was going to have to start going on the walks with Else and Synnia. He wouldn't enjoy it. The awe that came from passing by a dozen different creatures from as many unknown worlds was fun for about the first fifteen minutes, and then he could feel himself shutting down. There was a constant sense of overwhelm that haunted him. Haunted all of them, except maybe Dafyd Alkhor. Rickar had thought very little of Dafyd, before. The nephew of a powerful woman, a middling scientist, a half-assed lab drone. He'd always seemed like he was moving through life on autopilot.

Now, though, Rickar thought he'd underestimated the young man. Now he seemed like he was only moving slow while he put all the pieces together in his head, readying his game-winning move. Rickar thought maybe constantly being underestimated was just part of the strategy.

As if the thought had summoned him, Dafyd's door opened and he came into the corridor, toweling his hair dry. Rickar didn't know if Dafyd had always been the youngest in the workgroup, but with Irinna gone he surely was now.

"Dafyd," he said. "Do you think we could talk the librarian into giving us some paint?"

Dafyd looked confused. "Paint?"

"It's a good idea," Jessyn said. "This place could use some sprucing up."

"I was thinking of the outside of the door, actually," Rickar said. "Something that would tell the others we were here if they saw it."

Campar leaned back on his stool, his eyes flashing with a little merriment. "Beware of dog? No trespassing?"

"Student financial aid," Rickar said. He didn't know why that was funny to him, but he started laughing, and the others joined in.

The scratching at the door stopped them. For a second, Rickar thought he'd imagined it, but it came again—claws scraping against the outside of the door like a pet asking to come in. Rickar's heart tapped at his ribs. Dafyd went pale and gray. Tonner rose to his feet, the pen clasped in his fist like a weapon.

"What is it?" Jessyn said from the kitchen, and Rickar didn't know if she hadn't heard the noise, or had but hadn't realized what it was.

Dafyd raised his hand, telling them to keep back. Jessyn grabbed a pry bar. The air felt heavy with threat.

Dafyd shifted the door a crack, just enough to look out of, and then slammed it closed again. When he spoke, he had the matter-of-fact calm of a surgeon whose patient was dying on the table. "It's them. They're back."

"The others," Jessyn said. "Where are the others?"

"Else and Synnia are patrolling," Rickar said.

The scratching came again, fast and insistent. A high chittering followed. The voices of the enemy. Rickar wanted to say something noble and funny. Something like *If this is it, it's been a pleasure working with you*. The only thing in his mind was *shit shit shit*...

Jessyn, Tonner, and Campar lined up facing the door, faces grim. Dafyd passed them knives. Tonner handed his knife off to Rickar and instead grabbed the last two papery bulbs of poison. "It's what we've got," he said.

The scratch came again, louder this time. Longer. More insistent. They shifted into a rough semicircle around the door, millions of generations of evolution expressed as the readiness for violence.

"We could just wait," Campar said. "They might go away."

"Or Else and Synnia might get back, and we can hide in here listening as they're murdered."

"Ah. Well," Campar said. "Dammit."

Dafyd nodded. "I'll open on three."

Rickar's mouth was dry. Tonner was squeezing the bulbs so hard, Rickar worried he'd pop them early and have to run around smearing the goo on the enemy…

Dafyd hauled the door open. A dozen of the murderous little animals stood arrayed in the hallway, chittering and shuffling back and forth. Tonner lifted a bulb, ready to splash the first one that charged in…

The Night Drinkers knelt, lay on the deck, and spread their arms out at their sides. All of them except for one, who moved forward from the back of the group, its head shifting from side to side like it was searching for something. It had an object in each hand. In its left fist, a dull charcoal-colored square that Rickar recognized as a translator, even though it wasn't hung around anything's neck. Its right hand had something black and tarry, a mess that Rickar's mind rebelled at.

The ambassador Night Drinker set the box down at the edge where the door would have been, and the black thing beside it. It stepped back, chittering loudly, gnashing its teeth. It held out its hands, opening and closing its fists like it was squeezing the air.

Rickar recognized the gesture from when they'd made their attack on the Night Drinkers' base. He hadn't known what it meant then. He was starting to guess now. It was a sign of surrender. They'd been trying to surrender.

The voice that came from the box was the eerie, toneless one that had announced the death of Anjiin. It was exactly the same.

"No more war. No more fighting. No more."

Dafyd, the only one of them without a weapon, stepped forward. The Night Drinkers pressed their heads more firmly into the ground, preparing, it seemed, to suffer violence without complaint. Rickar saw the wet, black thing for what it was: a severed head. They'd killed one of their own as a peace offering. The ambassador squeezed the air more frantically as Dafyd stepped toward it.

"What is your name?" Dafyd asked. The little box was silent for a moment, then chittered and squeaked. The Night Drinker that had carried the offerings forward looked up. It was difficult to see it as anything but startled. It bared its teeth and squawked.

"Don't hurt us. We submit."

"We're humans," Dafyd said. "We're from a planet called Anjiin. We didn't want to come here. Was it like that for you too?"

But the little enemies—former enemies, maybe—crawled backward, arms still out at their sides. When they'd gone two body lengths, the ones at the back chirped, got to their feet, and fled. A heartbeat later, the others were up and gone as well. Tonner stepped out into the corridor, the bulbs of murderous goo still in his hands. Rickar realized he'd been gripping his knife so hard that his hand had cramped. He felt shaky.

"Well, that's a surprise," Campar said. "Are we assuming that was sincere? I don't mean to imply the alien monkey is a liar, but..."

Tonner rolled the little blood-soaked head onto its side with the toe of his shoe. "This one seems pretty committed to the gesture."

Dafyd knelt, picking up the translator like it was as fragile as spun glass. It was the same size that all the others had been, even the ones the massive Carryx carried. It only seemed larger compared to the Night Drinkers' slight bodies. "This is amazing. It changes..."

"Changes what?" Tonner asked. It could have been contempt, but there was no heat in the words. It was like he was actually curious.

A brightness was in Dafyd's eyes Rickar hadn't seen there in weeks. Maybe ever. "Come on."

Dafyd stood, striding out and down the corridor like a child who was expecting a present. The rest of them exchanged looks in various shades of uncertainty.

"He seems pretty confident it's not an ambush?" Jessyn said, her inflection making it a question.

Rickar moved toward the doorway, but not to follow him. Just to see where he was headed. Only once he was at the threshold, he kept going. Jessyn trotted to come up beside him.

"Any idea what we're doing?" she asked.

"Following Alkhor."

Dafyd strode to the cathedral, and then through it. At first, Rickar thought they might be going to the Night Drinkers' enclave, but Dafyd didn't stop. He kept the same quick stride, the same excited focus, through the whole space and out through a wide archway. Rickar looked back, but Tonner hadn't come. That was probably wise. Someone should be there when Else and Synnia came back from patrol. Empty rooms would have been ambiguous in unfortunate ways.

Rickar had never been to see the librarian in its den, but he'd heard Tonner talk about it. This seemed like the right path. The broad hallway with its arches that led to other spaces, other microclimates, other sets of alien life laboring under the Carryx yoke.

Dafyd paused before one of these. On the far side of the archway, a short corridor opened into a huge space, as large as their cathedral, but built with what looked like ropes hanging down the walls. A clicking came from everywhere and nowhere, like a swamp at evening when the insects began to stir. Dafyd slowed, his gaze ranging across the space. Rickar and Jessyn caught up to him.

"What are we looking for?" Rickar asked, but Dafyd was already off again. Something had lumbered out from among the vines or ropes or tentacles. It was the size and build of a hairless bear with half a dozen eyes arranged in a brightly colored face.

Dafyd went toward it, and when it deflected its path around him, shifted to block it. He held the little square from the Night Drinkers in his hands.

"Excuse me," he said. "I'm sorry. We need help. Can you understand me?"

It might only have been Rickar's imagination, but the ticking in the room seemed to grow louder for a moment. The bear stopped and the colorful face shifted, looking Dafyd up and down, then Jessyn, then himself. He felt the fear like a hand around his throat.

And then the translator spoke. It said, "I can."

Dafyd's smile was pure joy. "Good. That's good. Have you seen other creatures that look like us?"

Jellit sat down gingerly. The wound on his right leg ached, but not as badly as it had the night before. He resisted the urge to pluck away the bandage. Looking at it wouldn't help.

"You all right there, old man?" Allstin asked. He was at least four decades Jellit's senior, and he called all of them old man or old woman. The joke had never been funny, but had now stopped being annoying and had just become an idiom of their little group.

"Not dead yet," Jellit said. "What about you?"

"Spry as a kitten. Strong as an ox."

"You can do my chores, then."

The routine phrases completed, Allstin let out a little grunt and headed for the ladder up to the sleeping chambers. Dennia and Kell were up there already. Llaren Morse was gone, off to the meeting. It was Jellit's turn to take watch. Not that he could fight, but he could shout. That was going to have to be enough.

Once he was alone, he dimmed the common room lights. The brightly colored walls faded into shadows of themselves. The boxy kitchen off in the rear fell almost to black. The others liked keeping the space bright more than he did. The chance for a little twilight was the advantage that came from standing guard. It wasn't even that he liked the darkness that much. It was just the joy of being able to control something—anything—about his circumstances. And he wasn't going to fall asleep.

He settled in, preparing to sit through the long hours of the night. The gun that Kell had rigged up sat on the table beside him, a little black knot of violence waiting for its moment. They only had three cartridges left. He didn't know if they could make more. The group had made these, but what Jellit knew about weapon crafting could be written on his palm with room to spare. He forced his jaw to relax, kept his back upright and strong, and he waited for Llaren Morse or morning, whichever came first.

Neither came first.

The first sounds were clunks, footsteps or pipes or the vast architecture of the Carryx prison expanding and contracting with the day's temperature shifts. But they got louder. Grew regular. Jellit put his hand on the butt of the gun, not raising it. Not yet.

And then: "Hello?"

He knew the voice, and he didn't. It wasn't Llaren. It wasn't any of the workgroup. But it was human, and it wasn't coming from one of the black translation boxes. He levered himself up, limping toward the door. He was afraid to speak. He was afraid not to.

"Who's there?" he said.

"Hello?" the other one repeated, and the adrenaline hit his system like a hammer. He pulled the door open, and against all probability, against all hope, she was there. Thinner than he remembered. A haunted expression around her eyes, but Jessyn. Unmistakably Jessyn. And behind her, Rickar Daumatin and Dafyd Alkhor.

Tears rose in Jellit's eyes. He felt stunned. Like he'd been struck with a current that left his arms and legs limp and powerless. Jessyn stepped into the room, and even in the dim light, he saw she was weeping too.

"Hi," she said.

PART FIVE

FISSURE

He wasn't unique, or not more than any other individual being would be. He had no insights that changed the way I saw the order of things, he didn't have any particular philosophy that opened the doors of reality. He was one among many, with variations as any of them had. The only thing that I think made him stand out at all was the depth of hatred that the others came to have for him.

—From the final statement of Ekur-Tkalal, keeper-librarian of the human moiety of the Carryx

Twenty-Six

Jessyn was drunk. All they had was water and the slowly degrading mix of simple foods they'd had before. None of the alterations they'd made to the berries produced euphorics or intoxicants, though now that she felt this way, it occurred to her that they could. It would make for a better party.

Still, she was drunk. Inebriated by relief at the presence of her brother, by the novelty of new human faces. The long, leonine jaw and flowing white hair of the man named Allstin. The stark remnant of a man that was still recognizable as Llaren Morse. Their presence—their existence—put a grin on her face that was so wide it ached and so deep she felt it in her chest.

Llaren Morse stood at the window, looking out at the vastness of the sky like he was seeing it for the first time. Jellit was propped between the centrifuge and the kitchen counter with Rickar and Synnia and Tonner, all so tightly packed in that it seemed like they'd crawl into each other's laps. Jellit, with his bandaged leg, was sitting. The others looked like supplicants allowed to stand before the merry, delighted king. Jessyn herself was with Allstin and Else and Dafyd in the hall, pushed out of the main living space by the lab equipment and the press of three new bodies.

"So there I am, yeah?" Allstin said. "Stripped naked and dragged along by the beast's leash like the world's least plausible virgin sacrifice, trotting through the halls with all the demons the Gallantists could dream up looking at my cock like they were wondering if it was removable. I'm sick. I'm dizzy spun up. I don't have any idea what's going to happen t'me. You all had something like it, yeah?"

"We kept our clothes," Jessyn said.

Dafyd laughed. "Speak for yourself. I had clothes, sort of, but they weren't mine."

Allstin wagged a finger between himself and the younger man—*you and me*. "So it was that moment. And the great fucking beast hauls me into this room, four other people in it, and one of 'em is my department chair. Woman I've known for fifteen years. They're all in the local uniform by then, so I'm the only one wearing my Pope's robes, if you see what I mean. And the beast starts making introductions. And this woman—Merrol, her name is. You'll meet her. Merrol starts blushing and she's staring me in the eye so as to not look elsewhere. So I look back. We've locked eyes. And I don't why, but Little Allstin starts taking the moment for something it ain't."

Else buried a little shriek in her hands, shaking her head with hilarity. "You didn't. Oh, God. That's not true."

"You can ask anyone," Allstin said. "They were all there. Not like there was any point trying to hide it. So the great fucking beast cuts me loose and I excuse myself, wash up because I was fair a wild man by then, and when I come back out, clothed now mind you, everyone's formal and dour and pretending like I hadn't just waved at 'em all with my hands tied."

Dafyd choked, his shoulders trembling with mirth.

"Normal biological reaction," Tonner shouted at them from the kitchen. "Humans have been getting horny in the face of death since the beginning of the species."

"Don't you hate it when some killjoy tries to explain away the joke?" Campar shouted back at him.

"So," Allstin continued, as though no one else had spoken, "what could I do to break the ice now that I'd already shown everyone my best material?"

The sly smile after it was funnier than the punchline, and Jessyn had to lean against the wall and catch her breath. She'd known people like Allstin before. Natural performers who made themselves the center of every conversation. Usually, they grated on her nerves, but not now. Not today.

In the space by the kitchen, Jellit was holding the latest bright-colored not-turtle that they were meant to be feeding. The others had been used to make basic protein assays or had starved to death while the group's attention had been elsewhere. This most recent one had a line of crimson along its jaw that might have meant something in a different evolutionary context. Here it was just decoration. Meaningless.

Tonner, to judge from the motions of his hands and the few words that Jessyn caught, was speeding Jellit through months of research and theorizing, and Jellit was doing his best to seem like he followed it all or cared. Very polite of him.

Jessyn felt soft. Relaxed. Like a pain she'd carried so long she'd stopped noticing it until it eased. Llaren turned away from the view, ambling toward the four of them with a vague, stunned expression. The months of their captivity hadn't been kind to him. The last time Jessyn had seen the man, he'd been on a screen on

Anjiin, talking about the objects he'd discovered and their mysterious approach. His skin was grayer now, and he had a patchy beard. He'd shed enough weight that his cheekbones had gone sharp. He looked ill, but maybe they all did. Certainly none of them were the people they had been.

"This place is beautiful," Llaren Morse said. "These are the best quarters I've seen them give any of us."

"It's the window, isn't it?" Else asked, giving Dafyd a conspiratorial wink.

"I don't know how long it's been since I saw an outside," Llaren said. "I've been living in a prison cell."

"We all have," Else said. "Even with the view."

Llaren's smile was real, but thoughtful. There was something behind it that Jessyn couldn't quite fathom.

Dafyd made a small sound and raised a hand like he was a child in a schoolroom. "The Carryx that took you to your workgroup. Do you know if it was the same librarian we have?"

The question was directed at Allstin, but Llaren answered. "How would we know? We didn't spend a lot of time chatting. It hauled us all together, told us to apply the scanning protocols Morse here was using for his heliospheric work to their pet datasets, and vanished."

"Did you ever try to find it again?"

Allstin chuckled and cuffed Dafyd's shoulder. "We'll want to arm up before we do that, yeah?"

In the main room, Tonner said something, and Rickar laughed. It was strange to see them getting along. Jellit scratched his head and asked them something she couldn't quite make out. Tonner launched into an answer, his hands moving in a kind of pantomime that could have been protein structure or evolutionary pairing maps or maybe just Tonner needing to get out more information at once than a single channel of speech could carry.

Llaren Morse cleared his throat, catching the whole room's attention, and said, "I don't think we're going to break Jellit's family reunion up anytime soon, but Allstin and I should be getting back."

"I'll go with you," Tonner said, maybe a little too quickly. "Jellit can take my room." There was a flicker of something in Else's expression—embarrassment or regret or guilt—at Tonner's hunger to be away from her and her new lover.

"I'd like to see your place too," Rickar said. "Can I tag along?"

"Ooh," Campar said. "A sleepover, only without the booze and dancing."

"Might be some dancing," Allstin said. "One can never rule it out. I'll take these three with. We've got room enough for them now."

Llaren's expression sobered, and Jessyn wondered how Jellit's workgroup had come to have the extra space. At a guess, it would be a lot like how they had Irinna's room open. Still, the darkness passed quickly. It wasn't long before Tonner, Campar, and Rickar were heading out the wide door, following Allstin like he was the teacher and they were all heading to their first day at a new school. The night had fallen long before, and the dawn would be a long time coming. They moved the equipment and made a circle on the floor with cushions from the seats and pillows from the beds, sat and lounged and talked like they were all young again. Like the universe still had joy in it. And so, for a while, it did.

Jellit and Llaren Morse told their story. The broad strokes were all familiar, and it made the details matter more. The two of them had shared the passage, and so they took turns telling the stories of it: the man who'd tried to kill one of the other prisoners, the woman who'd started hallucinating spirits from beyond space and time, the group that had started a choir and spent their time in hell singing together. Then their placement in a room, and their version of the alcove, though this one was stocked with visualization arrays and single-photon diffraction slopes and banks of telescopic data that might have been real or simulated.

Dafyd and Synnia told about the attempted coup and the alien that had exploded and made everyone sick as dogs, and how that had led to Dafyd spending days in the ruins of a pink nightgown. If Jellit and Llaren Morse exchanged a glance at that one or seemed to already know the details of it, Jessyn didn't notice at the time.

It should have been terrible, and it was, but telling the stories and singing the songs and laughing about it all let Jessyn feel like they had some power over the horror.

"And how did you wind up tracking us down?" Llaren Morse asked. "I'd given up on finding you."

"I didn't," Jellit said.

"That's true. Jellit would have kept looking until doomsday. He made contact with three other groups all on his own."

"How many of us are there out there?" Jessyn asked.

"We've found a couple dozen groups," Jellit said. "There are more out there. At least, I hope there are."

"But but but," Llaren Morse said with a laugh. "I still want the story. How did *you* find *us*?"

"That was Dafyd," Else said, and touched his arm. The younger man had the good taste to blush. Jessyn retold the war with the Night Drinkers, and the peace offerings they'd made. Her brother and Llaren Morse listened like she was reciting a vast epic, and at the end, Llaren looked puzzled.

"But that wasn't— No offense, but that wasn't Dafyd here, was it?" Jellit said. "That sounds like you if it was anybody."

"My part was after," Dafyd said. "When we got the device, we could talk with the other inmates instead of just gawking at them as they passed."

"Dafyd was the one who started asking them if they'd come across one of us that smelled like Jessyn," Else said.

"Well," the boy said, more defensive than he needed to be, "I figured since they were siblings, and a lot of animals on Anjiin—animals on both trees of life—were better at chemoreception, that it made sense to ask."

"Does make you wonder if that's why the red shower cleanser is changing our smell," Jessyn said. "Maybe there's something in the human odor spectrum that's causing crossed signals with some other chemorecepting species."

"Or the Carryx themselves," Else agreed.

"And the Carryx already had the red goo waiting for us when we arrived, so they already knew what the problem would be," Jessyn continued. "And the solution."

"An interesting idea," Else said.

"Stop sciencing all over my story," Jellit said. "The fact is that it worked."

But Llaren Morse looked grave. "It's just…we're all talking about home in past tense these days. Like it isn't still out there."

All of them grew sober. There were a few tries at getting the euphoria back, but the night had wilted on them, and before long Synnia declared she was going to get ready for sleep. They took Llaren to Tonner's room as they broke up for the night. Else and Dafyd both went to her room, and no one said anything about it. This was how things were now. Things that would have been unthinkable were normal now.

Jessyn and Jellit stayed in the front room with the berries and the not-turtle and the messy dishes from their dinner. For a while, they were quiet, just doing simple domestic chores together. Jessyn ran warm water in the sink, washed the dishes, and handed them to her brother to dry. His eyes kept sliding to the window. The dark had turned it into a kind of half mirror. The two of them in the kitchen and also the distant ziggurats of the Carryx, glowing faintly. The superposition seemed like it meant something, like a dream that carried some significance.

"I was worried about you," Jellit said.

"I was worried about me too," she said. "I was afraid I wouldn't see you again."

"We got lucky."

For a moment, he seemed like he was on the verge of saying something more, but instead he kissed her forehead.

Afterward, she lay in her bed and willed herself to sleep, but her nerves wouldn't let it come. Now that the first bright candy coating of the day had washed off, her mind was taken up by what the joy and surprise had under them. It wasn't as simple as the pleasure had been.

She shifted in the bed that her captors had given her, her pillow bunching at the base of her skull or flattening until it hardly felt like more than a fold of thick cloth. Images floated into her unquiet mind. The café she'd gone to at Dyan Academy. The music that used to filter down through the ceiling of her first rooms at Irvian, their upstairs neighbor's chords resonating with the softly curving coral of the grown walls. The first boy she'd kissed. The first girl who'd kissed her. The taste of a cold beer on a hot summer afternoon.

Seeing Jellit's face, hearing Llaren Morse's voice, even meeting Allstin for the first time, all of it conspired to remind her of the life that was gone. And it made her present circumstances clear.

She remembered one of her therapists saying *Anger is pain in a party mask*. It had seemed wise at the time. She wasn't sure she agreed with it anymore. Maybe anger was a scab over a wound, or maybe it was what happened when the universe spun you so hard that you lost everything. Or maybe it was just a thing that welled up in you when you found yourself lying sleepless in the dark of a prison work camp with no idea what your future might be or if your past mattered.

She didn't remember opening her eyes, but they were open again. The ceiling was a darkness with just the thinnest spill of gray where the crack at the top of the door let the light in. She watched it shift as someone walked past in the hallway. She didn't recognize the footsteps, so Llaren Morse. Everyone else was as familiar as a song heard for the thousandth time.

Jessyn levered herself up. Sleep wasn't happening, and lying in the darkness wouldn't change that. She could check on the latest run of changes to the berries' internal farmland. Or sample the latest not-turtle for more data about what might sustain the one after. Or, if she was lucky, find someone in the main rooms who she could talk to until the version of herself she'd created to survive in prison slipped back into place. Something.

In the hallway, Synnia's door stood open. Llaren Morse leaned against the frame, his head bowed, speaking low. Synnia was before him, her eyes on his mouth like she was reading lips. Jessyn paused when she saw the open hunger in the older woman's eyes, and a little hit of adrenaline eased into her bloodstream.

She heard Synnia say *Yes, tell him I'll help* before she noticed Jessyn watching and the more familiar look returned. Llaren Morse followed her glance, smiled at Jessyn, and gave her a nod before pushing off back down the hallway toward Tonner's empty room.

"Everything all right?" Jessyn asked, feeling how idiotic the question was even as she asked it.

"Fine," Synnia said. Her eyes were bright and hard. "Everything's fine."

Jessyn didn't know then who Llaren Morse and Synnia had been talking about. But she'd have been very damned surprised if it turned out things were really fine.

Twenty-Seven

"How long have we spent looking for other people?" Dafyd asked.

Else shrugged as they turned down the hallway toward the cathedral-wide common room where their alcove once was. "Depends on how you count it," she said, but Dafyd was too much in his own mind to follow her thought.

"And as *soon* as we had the translator, we found them. The same day. I keep wondering, if we'd thought to ask the librarian for one of these of our own, would it have given it to us?"

The square itself was in his hand. Lighter than its size would suggest. There was a loop where a strap or a lanyard could go, but there was nothing there. No place to open it, no way to access its interior, nothing that showed where it took its power from. When it functioned, the whole body of the thing vibrated and grew cool, like its effort drew in more energy than it put out. There were a million mysteries that the object posed, and Dafyd was too excited by the idea of using it to pause at any of them.

"If they were easy to get hold of, it wouldn't have been much of a peace offering," Else said. Her voice was tense in a way he thought he understood.

"Maybe," Dafyd said. "But when the Carryx see us carrying it, they don't seem to care. So either we're not prohibited from having one, or enforcement of the rules is surprisingly lax."

Ahead of them, the flow of traffic thickened, but today the overwhelming strangeness of the bodies that passed was leavened by Dafyd's sense of possibility. Before, they had all been like animals in a pandemonic zoo, inmates in a prison separated by impossible gulfs of language. Now, each one was the chance to know more. To understand more. To get his head around what had happened to him and everyone he'd known.

A broad-shouldered thing with six legs and bright rills down its sides lumbered by, crossing paths with a group of four fast-crawling stilt-legged things with iridescent black shells. A swarm of not-quite-insects rolled past in the high air.

"So," Dafyd said. "Where do we start?"

It is the size of a large horse, covered in chitin the color of bone. Its legs articulate strangely, folding with each step, and then extending until they seem to thin to almost nothing. Its eyes are deeply set, and a bioluminescent glow flickers at its joints like static charges grounding out. When it speaks, it chitters.

We were the Phylarchs of Astrdeim, once. Once, we were, though that was long ago. We hold the memory of those times close, and we share it so that it never fades. A hundred worlds we called our own, though they were shared with the Elmrath and Colei who were found wanting in the eyes of the great ones and thus culled. They are gone now, but we carry their bones in our songs and memories.

We built palace worlds and temples to our own ingenuity with roots that sank to the planetary mantle and rose to the edge of space. They lived, those buildings. They held worlds within them, and we were proud, or that is the history. We were proud, and the proud are brought down, our philosophers warned, though now we call them prophets.

The Carryx came and yoked our young. They bound the architects and stripped the stations of the gods to use for storage sheds. The Elmrath, they drove from their paper hives and drowned in the sea. The Colei, they took as they took all things then, to a white plain above a lavender sea. Under that cold sun the beautiful Colei lost their will to live, withered, and passed to dust. But we, we carried our souls within us. Cut from all we had known, we built.

All of this you see, we built. Not the Carryx. They live well within it. They make use of it. Even then, they see only its use, not its spirit. They have no soul for it. We do not weep for them. One servant sees a slice of the spectrum, hears a fraction of the music, and is content. Why should the masters be different? No, no, we are grateful. The Carryx have given us a wider sky to grow into. A thousand more palace worlds than we had dreamed to construct. We are grateful for the chance to build and pleased with our place within the function of the whole. We remember our childhood playmates. The Elmrath. The Colei. We are grateful, grateful, grateful not to be them. We are not Phylarchs any longer, nor will I see the spires of Astrdeim before my eyes are dust. But what we still are, we still are, and if I were not pleased by that, I would not be anything at all.

Do you see? Do you hear that? We love them, and we live. We eat their leavings and we smile and they give us our draft of pleasure. I would not say this if I were not valued, but you are young. Do as we have done. It is the best life that remains to you.

If they're individuals, then they're the size of horseflies, but fleshy and pink. If the cloud of them is only one animal of many parts, then it's a little smaller than a child's ball. The buzzing it makes varies in timbre and volume, but the change that comes when it speaks is a scent like cabbage and mint.

No. I will not talk with you. I will not tell you my name. Whatever it is you're planning will fail and all of your kind will burn. Go away. We will not burn with you. Go away.

The alcove is structurally similar to the one they had for their research: a little length of hall leading off from the vast main chamber. There, however, the similarity ends. The walls here are crusted with ropy tendrils like finger-thick vines. A soft ticking sound comes from them, and a deep, rich, swampy scent fills the air. Glimmers of golden light flicker on and off again, illuminating pale grubs that cling to the surfaces. When it speaks, nothing in the room seems to change. It isn't clear if the vines are speaking or the grubs. Or the room.

History? I have no history. Maybe I did once, but how would I know? To rise isn't the same as to un-fall. What is lost is lost, and why regret a dream I had when I was young just because the universe woke me from it? I'm here, and I have no ambition to be elsewhere. Other instances are in other places. They do what the great ones need them to do. Scrub air in places where it's tainted. Take in what is polluted and put out what is pure, depending on what the great ones say is tainted and what they want made pure. It doesn't matter to me. My place is here, in this space. I learn how to do what it wants, and then I am harvested, and I learn again, but I never leave. How would I?

Nothing here has a history except for the Carryx. I don't. You don't. None of those things muttering outside do, even the ones who think they do. They can't. Having a past of my own with the

Carryx is like having a shadow in the dark. It might be pleasant or it might not, but since it's impossible, it isn't either one.

My homeworld? I don't understand the question. I don't have a homeworld. I don't have a home. I don't have a world. Wherever I was plucked from, I was plucked from. *From.* I have a task, and I do it. Anything more than that hurts.

Name? I had a name. I don't know what it was.

You should stop. I don't like talking with you anymore.

It is a little over knee high, and twice as broad. The form of its shell suggests that it evolved in liquid. It looks made to slip through something thicker than air. Its three sets of legs are short, wide, and flexible as tentacles, though there are distinct and visible joints. It has strips of cloth and brightly colored stones as clothing or adornment.

If I talk to you, I will be killed.

It is a standing flicker of blue, like a flame without the heat. There are shapes inside the light, generating the glow and shaping it like a swarm of gnats built from crystal. They're hard to see. Hard to look at. When the voice box translates, it doesn't make sounds, but glimmers.

We *are* the Carryx. There is no difference between them and us.

Yes, yes, yes, I know about bodies. They aren't significant. But all nature is porous. Once, there was the Carrying One, but its children are gone. Its harp is broken. The singing of the stones has gone quiet. There is no sorrow in that, but joy. None of those things were the Carryx, and we are. Why would we celebrate the enemies of what we are?

Before, we sang for base reasons. We were in service of nothing, of ourselves. Now we are part of the greatness. We sing the songs of war, and through our singing, spread that which we are.

Yes, I know, but *we are* the Carryx. What ennobles the Carryx, ennobles us. What strengthens the Carryx, strengthens us. This is the beautiful way. Submission to glory is glorification, and we are glorious.

"I have to sit down," Else said. Her face had gone ashen. Dafyd followed her to the edge of the huge chamber. The voices and sounds of a thousand individuals from hundreds of worlds filled the air, and it sounded weirdly like a train station. As if all the hubbub, however exotic the setting and the source, was on some level also all the same.

She sank to the ground, her elbows resting on her knees. Dafyd sat down beside her. After a moment, he put a hand on her shin, comforting her without knowing exactly why she needed comfort.

"Overwhelmed?"

"There's so much," she said. "Half a day. Half a *day*, and look how much more we know. All the things I've seen up to now. All the things I've learned. We know more about the Carryx…And then it turns out we've barely taken a sip."

She gestured out at the passing crowd. Dafyd saw another of the Phylarchs of Astrdeim lumbering gently among the bodies, and it was almost like recognizing a friend. The eeriness wasn't gone, but it was less because he knew something.

"We could find clues about what worlds they all came from," she said. "What they all do for the Carryx. How the Carryx gather them up, domesticate them, use them. We could know so *much*."

"We will, given time," Dafyd said. It didn't seem to reassure her. "But really, who are we going to tell?"

Her gaze shifted, the dark of her eyes fixed on him like she was seeing him there for the first time. The ashen look was fading, and something that was almost a blush was coming in its place. She opened her mouth as if she were going to speak, but then closed it again and shook her head.

"Is something going on?" Dafyd asked. "I mean, you seem...I don't know."

"Like something's going on?" she said, and her voice was low and teasing, like a gently mocking viol.

"Well. Yes?"

Her eyes softened, and a small, rueful smile appeared on her lips. "I would like to be able to tell you everything. Even the parts that are hard."

"That's what I'm here for. That's all I want."

The smile widened, complicated, teased. "That's not all you want."

"It's not. But it is part of it."

Something huge passed between them and the light at the top of the cathedral. The shadow fell over them and passed in a flicker. Else curled her fingers around his.

"I'm not going to be good for you," she said. "I'm not going to make you happy."

"You already do. Look, I understand that we don't have much freedom. We are powerless to choose most of the things that shape our lives. But what we do have? What we *can* have? I want. Does that make sense?"

"Not absolutely," she said, then shook her head. "I mean, we're not absolutely powerless. We're just...mostly powerless."

"A deep and subtle difference." It made her smile. That was a victory.

"I'm not what you think I am, Dafyd."

"I look forward to meeting you. Over and over and over."

She laughed. "Oh, you have no idea what you're saying."

"I'm in love. People in love never know what they're saying."

Her fingers were warm on his cheek, but her smile had gone rueful again. Something in the crowd caught her attention, and the moment was gone. Else sat forward and gestured with her chin, pointing out and to their right. "Is that... our librarian?"

The Carryx moved through the crowd with an escort of Rakhund. Aliens of a dozen species shifted and jumped to clear its way. Dafyd recognized it by the way it moved and the colors of its flesh as clearly as if it had had a human face. The librarian of the human moiety.

He didn't answer Else except by rising to his feet. She followed him as he moved along the cathedral wall past the entrances to half a dozen other alcoves. The librarian moved forward, lumbering with its massive forelegs, its abdomen hurrying to keep up. He couldn't have said why, but he had the sense that the Carryx scholar was pleased. It moved forward for a few minutes, then turned, curving to a place at the wall.

A familiar place, it turned out.

Another of the Carryx was waiting at the mouth of the Night Drinkers' alcove. It was broader than the others Dafyd had seen, and a wide chip was missing from its head, like something had taken a bite out of it when it was young.

The little feather-haired, amber-eyed Night Drinkers were jumping from the holes in the fungal sponge that filled their space, running madly out into the crowd, then fleeing back to disappear into the wall. Dafyd took the translator, pointing it as best he could toward the cacophony of their screeches. It didn't do anything.

As their librarian approached, the notch-headed one lowered

itself, spreading its dark, powerful arms to the side and pressing its body to the ground. The act of obeisance and surrender was strange to see in a Carryx body. Like seeing his father naked or vulnerable. The Night Drinkers scurried over to the debased Carryx, plucking at the air like they were trying to haul it back up through main force of will.

"This can't be good," Else whispered.

Dafyd shook his head, but he wasn't sure if he meant *No it can't* or *I don't know.* He thought he caught the bass chirp and trill of the Carryx native tongue, but it was hard to be sure in the noise, and his translator box was making no attempt to interpret. Other aliens were pausing to watch. A crowd was forming, making the same rough circle that surrounded violence since the first schoolyard. Dafyd took Else's hand and drew her through the press of bodies. The vault above them echoed with inhuman voices. Whatever this was, he needed to see it happen.

The notch-headed Carryx spread out its legs—four from the abdomen, the two thick, dark ones from its thorax. Even the pair of pale feeding arms. Eight limbs spread. The librarian of the human moiety shuffled slowly around its colleague, paused, and then with a crack like a whip, its huge arms snapped out and down onto one of the thin legs of the other Carryx's abdomen. The Night Drinkers shrieked and wailed, but the notch-headed Carryx only hauled itself up to its feet. The one leg hung broken and limp, but the others were enough to support it.

Whatever the ritual meant, it seemed to be over. The two librarians stood face to face, and from closer in, Dafyd was sure he heard their rumbling birdsong. Their demeanor seemed less like attacker and victim than two workers commiserating over a cup of coffee. After a few moments, the humans' librarian shifted its attention to the pale Rak-hund soldiers, and the soldiers swarmed forward.

Knifelike legs shuddered against the spongy wall, ripping it apart. The Night Drinkers poured out in a group with lengths of metal like blunt-headed spears in their small hands and rushed at the minions of the Carryx. When they struck, the spearheads popped like a gun, and pale blood poured out of the Rak-hund's sides. There was no grabbing at the air. No attempt at surrender. This was life or death.

And it wasn't life.

It only took a flicker of one of the Rak-hund's bone legs, and a Night Drinker would fall. Some of them screamed as they went down. Others just folded. Two of the Rak-hund turned their attention from taking down the wall, and put their full efforts into slaughtering the animals that came out of it. At the side of the ongoing extermination, the Carryx chatted. The viewing crowd jostled for a better view, but they seemed to understand that Dafyd and Else had some connection to the abomination playing out before them.

It took more than an hour to slaughter all the Night Drinkers and tear what had been their home out, piling it into a heap of crust, ink-black blood, and weirdly beautiful amber eggs that Dafyd had never seen before. In the end, a handful of the little aliens gave up on protecting their home and tried to flee, clutching armfuls of the eggs as they ran. They were cut down.

Then, as if by common agreement, it was over and the crowd unknotted. The Rak-hund kept hauling bits of dark substances out of the exposed alcove, but with the demeanor of janitors cleaning up a mess. The bodies of humanity's little rivals lay in a heap that rose as high as Dafyd's hips. All dead. Dafyd thought about vengeance for Irinna, and then almost threw up but choked it back. This wasn't anything more than a massacre. He wanted to flee from the scene but couldn't, not certain why he wasn't moving. Else stood beside him, her face calm.

"Was this us?" he asked, and his voice seemed to come from a long distance.

"Was what us?" Else asked.

"When we got them to surrender, did that mean . . . this?" he said.

Else sighed. "What is, is," she said, quoting the oft-repeated Carryx saying, and Dafyd finally vomited.

Twenty-Eight

Jellit had changed. It was more than the thinness in his cheeks, more than the threads of gray that had popped into his hair like the time since the fall of Anjiin could be measured in decades. She couldn't help wondering what changes he saw in her.

Today, he'd taken her to the quarters he shared with his work-group, made a lunch of the salty paste that the Carryx had left them as food and the plain water from the sink tap. Their conversation felt off, though. Like her brother had become shy. Or he was hiding something.

The conversation circled back to the fall of Anjiin, the event having a gravity that bent all meaning back to it.

"How did it happen?" he said, leaning back on the little chair where he or one of his crew kept watch. When he smiled wide enough, the dark gap of a missing tooth peeked out, but just for a moment. She didn't know how he'd lost it. "That was... it feels like that was a long time ago. Let's see. Llaren and Allstin and Dennia were all part of the near-field visualization group. We were letting them use our equipment since they were there for the... ah..."

"End-of-year at the Scholar's Common," Jessyn said.

Jellit pointed at her, meaning *Yeah, that.* It wasn't the first time since they'd found each other again that he'd had trouble coming up with words.

"So when they came, they just got all of us," Jellit said. "We were waiting for a security escort to someplace safe, but it never showed up. The Carryx brought us here and gave us a lab. They wanted us to re-create Llaren's thin-spectrum lensing work. Show them how he'd managed to see them before they wanted to be seen. And..."

And.

There was a lot of room in that *and.* Loss and trauma. She knew it without having to be told. There was evidence everywhere: bedrooms in their little compound that had been used and weren't anymore, names that came up in conversation—Barris, Simien—without a living person to go with them, a sense of the space where people had been. And there were habits like the keeping of the guard that implied violence.

Everything she heard from Jellit was like an echo of what she'd been through. The abduction, the passage, the violence, the loss. Not her way through the mess, but a similar one. And the same mess.

Even the rooms were like a funhouse mirror of each other: different and the same. The architecture here was blocky and rectilinear and enameled in low-saturation primary colors, like a child's playroom with the vibrancy taken out. Color and rhythm in place of her own window on the sky. The kitchen was like the one back at their rooms. They even had the exact same cups and plates. But here, there was only one shower, and each of the bedrooms had a toilet and sink of its own. The bedrooms themselves were up on a second floor, only reachable by ladders. Here, there was a wide door, but it swung out instead of rolling. All the same pieces, arranged in more or less the same way, but with a carelessness. It was like the Carryx had a vague level of accuracy in making space for their pet humans, and close enough was close enough.

They didn't care enough to keep them safe from violence, though. Or from committing it.

"I was worried, you know," he said. "Simien had been taking something for his blood. It was hereditary. Easy to manage. It was supposed to be easy to manage, you know. But they didn't get it for him."

"Did he die of that?"

"No, not of that," he said. And then, "I'm really proud of you. Making it even though . . . you know."

"Even though my brain kept trying to kill me?"

He barked out a little laugh, and for a flicker, she could see the version of him she remembered. Bright, energetic, curious, alive. "Yes," he said. "Even though your brain was trying to kill you."

"It was close, sometimes."

"Close is okay, as long as you made it. Rickar said you led the battle even before the medication came all the way back up. I guess all those coping-skills sessions with the therapists paid off after all." He smiled as he said it, both teasing and not.

For a moment, she was in the house they'd lived in when she was thirteen, the summer her head had first betrayed her, sleeping in the main room with her father on a cot beside her because they weren't going to leave her alone until the medications started working. Her father, or her mother, or Jellit. Barely older than her, he'd still taken a turn making sure his baby sister didn't hurt herself. She didn't know how a memory could seem that immediate and that far away at the same time.

She'd been sure she was going to die back then. She'd known it like she'd known that the sun rose in the morning and set at night. Like she'd known that sugar was sweet and not salty. The only thing that had confused her at all was why her family didn't see it too. When her mind had clicked back into joint, it had been like it made a sound. The soft, wet, low crunch of a dislocated shoulder going back in its socket. She'd been just as sure that the rotten-brain part of her had been wrong, and that this better version of Jessyn was the real one after all. She'd thought her family would see that too. Wasn't that why they'd been standing watch over her? But the watch hadn't stopped so much as relaxed a little. There had never been a time after that when someone hadn't been watching her at least a little.

And that had been good, because her brain was a bastard, and it slipped when she least expected it. Even when she'd grown up and they'd moved away from her parents, Jellit—if no one else, always Jellit—had been there to see when she started to lose her footing and sit with her through the hard nights.

This captivity was the first time in her life she'd actually been able to see whether she could survive a bad stretch on her own. The answer was no, she hadn't been able to. But she had been able to find other help. The insight was critical and deep and monstrously, monstrously unfair.

"If—" she began, then cleared her throat and started over. "If we were back on Anjiin? If we were back home? I'd let you go. I wouldn't let you pass up any more postings because of me."

"If we get home, we'll talk about it," he said.

Their wide door swung open, creaking on a hinge that seemed to be made from some metallic fabric. Jellit sat back in his chair, putting a little space between them like he didn't want his older friends to see him sitting too close to his kid sister. Some things didn't change.

Allstin was the first one in, wagging his eyebrows like he was following up some punchline, making whatever he'd said funnier by insisting that it was. Two women followed him. Dennia, walking with the habitual deference of a research assistant. Merrol, tall and broad-shouldered with a curly mane of black hair and weary confidence. Whatever conversation they'd been having stopped as they entered. Their smiles were warm and welcoming. Even after days of talking and eating together and sharing space, it still gave Jessyn a little rush of joy to see the less familiar faces. The fact that people existed who weren't Tonner's workgroup was an ongoing source of relief and evidence that sometimes the unexpected could be good instead of tragic.

They exchanged pleasantries, and Merrol pulled up one of the blocky, pastel-colored stools, but they didn't close the door. It drifted slowly back toward closed but without latching. It would have been the work of a push to do it, and it seemed odd that none of them did until the door swung open again and Llaren Morse came in with Synnia.

It wasn't odd that one of her group should accompany Llaren and the near-field group. That wasn't what raised the alarm. After all, Jessyn was there herself. Campar and Rickar had come for meals and the diversion of sleeping in a different set of rooms. Tonner stayed there whenever the discomfort of being around Else and Dafyd was worse than the discomfort of being away from his lab. And Dafyd and Else, busy as they were interviewing whatever aliens passed by, still made the occasional appearance.

No, something else raised the small hairs on Jessyn's neck. Something about the brightness of Synnia's eyes and the tautness of her smile. This wasn't the quiet presence by the window, the woman who was slowly working through her grief. This was the

Synnia planning violence in the dark. The thought was deeply unsettling even before the door swung open again and the other man came in.

She didn't recognize him at first. In addition to shaving off his hair and growing a sharp, pale beard, Urrys Ostencour had put on a lot of muscle and lost what little fat he'd had by the end of their passage in the cold, orange-lit cell. His arms and neck were ropy, the musculature so defined it was like the skin had been painted onto a medical model. She thought he was deliberately dehydrating to make himself look like that.

Ostencour, who had organized the failed revolt in the transit cell, smiled almost shyly and put out his hand. Jessyn hesitated. She had seen this man at his most vulnerable, near naked, sick, vomiting and shitting himself and weeping on the alien mat. He'd seen her in intimate moments because everyone had. She'd had lovers when she was younger she'd shared less of herself with than she had with this man she barely knew. She felt exposed just seeing him, reminded of her humiliation, and of his. There was no etiquette for meetings like this.

She stood and shook his hand. His grip was just firm enough to say that it could have hurt if he'd wanted it to.

"Ostencour," she said.

"Jessyn. I'm glad you made it."

"Likewise."

He let her go. Llaren Morse hauled over a stool for Ostencour and then sloped over to lean against the kitchen counter. The others arranged themselves in a rough semicircle, like they were wings and Ostencour was the angel. Jessyn glanced at her brother. His shrug was a confession. This meeting wasn't coincidence. It had been planned.

"I told you we'd found other groups."

"You did," Jessyn said. "You said that."

Ostencour lifted his hands, palms out. It looked more placating than surrender. Jessyn sat back down, not realizing that she'd shifted to put a solid wall at her back until she'd already done it.

"You probably feel a little ambushed," Ostencour said.

"Why would I feel like that?"

"Because I kind of ambushed you." His smile was quicker and easier than she remembered it from the cell. He also had more color in his skin than dull orange and black. She had a powerful memory of the man sitting by Synnia in the near dark, promising her that it wasn't over. "Not ambushed in a bad way, I hope. But I heard about your workgroup and everything you've been through. I think we should talk, and I don't know how much the big guys are listening in on us, but I try to give them as little to go on as I can. It's just good security hygiene."

Behind him and to his left, Synnia nodded like one of the pious hearing a preacher.

"You're in contact with a lot of other human groups?" Jessyn asked.

"It's been my project since I got here. Tracking down as many of us as I could find." He sighed. "I think we know where about three hundred of us are, all told. This complex seems to be a lot of the research and administrative captives. There were artists and writers in the cells too. Either they're in a different complex or a different part of this complex or..."

"Or?"

"There were rumors that the artists got classed as extraneous. That they were executed. I don't know if that's true. There are a lot of rumors that don't seem to come from anywhere. We have

Llaren's visualizations group, your biochemistry folks, a couple labs' worth of energetic physics, some logistics and administration departments. That's less than half of the people we know were taken, but it's what I have to work with."

"It's not my group," Jessyn said. "It's Tonner Freis's group. I just work there."

Ostencour's gaze flickered toward Synnia and away again. "The way I heard it, Tonner's not entirely in control these days."

"I guess you can make the argument that Dafyd Alkhor is setting some of the agenda that—"

"Not him," Ostencour said. "You."

Jessyn laughed. No one else did. "Me? How do you figure that?"

"You're the one who fought off the Night Drinkers," Synnia said. "And you were the one who took the fight back to them. Tonner didn't. Dafyd didn't. Campar still calls you the war leader."

"He's teasing me," Jessyn said.

"He's not."

"I'm not asking you to fight," Ostencour said. "I have other people for that. But I do need a favor that only your group can do for me. Support."

"Support for what?" Jessyn asked. But she already knew. Stress, power, love. They didn't change people, but they revealed people as who they were. Ostencour, on the journey from Anjiin, had been ready to fight and kill. Now that he was here, his defaults were still the same.

"The big guys give us a lot of freedom when it suits them to," Ostencour said. "You've noticed that. Your Night Drinkers were able to make bombs. I've seen other species gutting each other with mechanized drones and knives. We've been able to make these."

The object he took out from under his tunic was black and heavy. The metal shone in the light. If he'd been holding a venomous snake, Jessyn would have felt the same urge to recoil away.

"They're just little slug throwers," Ostencour said. "About half of them are chemical propellant. The other half are magnetic pulse, but those burn out fast. There's no rifling. The accuracy's a joke. But they can still pop a hole in something."

"You made guns."

"And they let us. They don't care. Why do you think that is?"

When Jessyn didn't answer, Merrol did. She had a pleasantly deep, smoky voice. In another context, it would have put Jessyn at ease. "Because they aren't scared of us. The things we can make aren't a threat to them."

"Maybe," Jessyn said. *Or maybe the Carryx that are here are low enough status that the real powers don't care if a few of them die.* She didn't say it aloud. The alarm in the back of her head was still sounding.

Ostencour put the gun on the table in front of her. She thought he was presenting it for her to inspect—like she'd be able to tell from looking that it was the real thing, that he was telling the truth. When he sat back and folded his hands in his lap, she realized she'd just been given it as a gift. She had a gun now, all she had to do was pick it up. She didn't.

"If you're planning to start some kind of prison riot, I'm going to remind you how well the last one went," Jessyn said. "You can't win. Look at everything we've seen. Do you remember stepping out of the transit cell and seeing this place? You could put every human in Irvian in just this one wing of this one building. And the planet is covered with them. An insurrection can't win."

"Depends on what the goal is," Allstin said. "If you're looking to get your old apartments on Anjiin back, yeah. Chances are grim. If winning means something else, though. See?"

"I do not," Jessyn said, but she did. Ostencour meant dying gloriously, striking a blow at their oppressors. Like an ant biting the toe of an elephant that had just crushed its nest. It wouldn't even rise to the level of moral victory.

"You know how this is going to go," Ostencour said, and the warmth was gone from his voice. The coldness in its place wasn't angry or aggressive. He wasn't talking to her anymore, not really. Everything he said, he was saying to himself. "If we're good pets and do all the things we're told, we get the chance to live for another few days. Or months. Or years. If we're young enough, maybe we can have children to hand over to the Carryx for whatever they want to do with them. Is that the future you want?"

"It's that or die."

"It is," Ostencour said. "It's live as long as they let us live, and die how we're told to die. Or..." He shrugged.

Something in the way he looked at her now made Jessyn pick up the gun. She examined the ugly knot of steel in her hands. It was slipshod and awkward, but she believed it would function. She wondered how many nights—just the absolute number of them—she'd have opted to use something like this instead of seeing the dawn. They thought they were suicidal. Allstin and Merrol and Llaren Morse. Even Jellit, who should have known better. They thought their fear and claustrophobia were the same as what she carried.

They were mistaken. Jessyn was a citizen of that darkness. What Ostencour was peddling was a *meaningful* death. A die-on-your-feet-or-live-on-your-knees ending. He had to paint death as noble to get people to go along with it.

He was an amateur.

Jessyn found the gun's chamber. There was a chemical cartridge in it, and a little lump of what might have been steel as the slug. She could imagine how it would feel if she held it out to Ostencour and plucked back the trigger. The surprise in his eyes. She could imagine holding it under her chin and doing the same, except that would upset Jellit.

And, a little to her surprise, because she really didn't want to.

"What are you asking me for?"

"We can make a few tools, but we don't have ways to mass-produce chemicals," Ostencour said. "You do. You've already made biological weapons and used them successfully. Design some for us. Something that can break down these Carryx sons of bitches. Bloody their noses for real, and make them think twice before they mess with human beings again."

His smile was soft and wide. "You make them, and we'll use them."

Twenty-Nine

"Can we do it?"

Tonner opened his mouth, closed it. The only thing in his mind was surprise. The only thing he could think to do was laugh, and it wasn't the funny kind. Jessyn and Synnia sat across from him, the big window at their backs so they were mostly silhouettes. Jessyn looked serious. Synnia looked hungry. The silence was the hum of distant machines carried through the flesh of the prison walls and the breath of thin wind against the glass.

Around them, the others—Campar, Dafyd, Rickar, Else—were sitting on the lab equipment or leaning against walls. None of the new people had come. This was just the family, and Tonner didn't have any clear idea what he could say.

Campar stepped in for him. "It seems to me that's not the first question. I think we should start with why we would even consider it. Don't misunderstand, I appreciate dramatic flair, but we're talking about group suicide."

"We're talking about fighting back," Synnia said.

When he'd first arrived at the prison, Else had told Tonner about Ostencour and the way Synnia's grief had locked her into his plans for insurrection. It hadn't seemed critical at the time. It was a thing that had happened, only here it was, still happening. The past hadn't passed at all.

"A distinction without a difference," Campar said. "If *you* fight back, it's still *my* head on the pike. And I'm not in the market for a death, however noble."

"I agree with Campar," Else said. "This seems like rushing into something we're not ready for."

Rickar shook his head, shifted his weight. "How much prep work can we be expected to do? If we're waiting for a good, safe time to revolt, that's the same as agreeing that this is our life now. We're going to do what the Carryx tell us to do. This isn't temporary. This isn't a rough period we're going to get through." His voice grew tighter with every word. Tonner felt himself tensing up with him. "We can talk about the phrasing and the details," Rickar went on. "Jessyn's asking if we're willing servants."

"If you aren't going to fight back now," Synnia said, "when are you going to start?"

"When there is a faint hope of success?" Campar said. "When it isn't futile? I'll keep looking for synonyms, but the central point I'm reaching for here seems clear to me. Is it not for you?"

"Hey hey hey!" Tonner said, rising to his feet. The sharpness of his voice snapped their attention back to him. He looked over to Dafyd, but the younger man was folded in on himself, thinking and watching and keeping his own counsel. Tonner lifted his eyebrow. *You want to take this?* Dafyd didn't seem to notice him.

This was the man Else had left him for. What a fucking joke.

"I'm not interested in the philosophy of freedom," Tonner said, maybe a little more sharply than he needed to. Or maybe not. Maybe what the group was missing was a smart tap across the cheek. "Jessyn. What exactly is the project Jellit's friends are proposing?"

"They know what we did with the Night Drinkers. It's the same idea, just pointed at—" She paused, carefully avoiding the word *Carryx*. "At a different target."

No, it's not the same idea, Tonner thought. The words were half formed before she finished speaking. The Night Drinkers had made the weapons, and they'd only had to reverse engineer them. They'd even had the jump start that they were beginning with the same basic materials. They'd had a Night Drinker corpse and performed a dissection and basic protein assay. Getting samples of the Carryx or their knife-legged Rak-hund and exploding squat-bodied Soft Lothark wouldn't be possible.

No, they couldn't do it. Except.

What if they could?

"I understand," Else said, "that they want to take a stand, but—"

"This isn't about our emotional health," Synnia broke in. "This is about what we are. As a fucking species."

Dafyd had gone to the librarian's den enough that another visit wouldn't raise suspicion. He wasn't going to get the bastard to lie down for an exam, but he might be able to police up the alien equivalent of skin flakes and hair. The Night Drinkers had been able to make bombs. Jellit's friends had built pistols.

"Tonner?" It was Else. Her gaze was on him, her chin down, her head tilted just a degree. Pulling him out of his head the way she used to back when the universe made sense.

"I'm not saying it's a good idea," he said. "But is it a *possible* one? Maybe."

Campar threw his hands in the air. "Are you serious? These things killed millions on Anjiin in the blink of an eye. And that was when we had warships and missiles and armies. You think a few scientists are going to do them damage with improvised handguns and biochemically active water balloons?"

"I'm not saying that, no. But what's the first step? If. If we did it, the first step would be to figure out what we can about their physiology. Way before we got to application, there's a lot of basic research that's kind of begging to get done. And there's no downside to that. To knowing more. We know some basic things already. We know they need a high-oxygen environment. We know they evolved as an aquatic species."

"We know," Campar said. "We know what now? How do we know that?"

Tonner shot him the look he might have given to a first-year asking the most obviously stupid question in class.

"Look at them. The physiology and size. Classic aquatic markers. But something drove them out of the sea at some point in their past into the high-oxygen atmosphere of this planet. It's the only thing that allows a creature of that size to—"

"Great, all we need is a big fire and some buttery sauce and we can have a beach bake," Campar said.

"Just saying there is research we could do," Tonner replied, sounding more petulant than he wanted to.

Synnia put her hand toward him, palm up, as if she were presenting him to the group. "And since we aren't fighting those others any longer, we can use that part of the schedule for the resistance."

Else looked down and away, her fingers rubbing together unconsciously like she was craving a cigarette. He'd seen her tempted often enough to know what it looked like, and he felt a little thrill—small and petty—knowing that he could still get to her. Maybe it was only on an intellectual level, but really that was where they'd always been the best together.

"Do you really think they're going to give us the resources to construct some kind of Carryx plague?" Campar asked.

"Well, they aren't afraid of bombs and guns," Tonner shot back.

Dafyd spoke for the first time since Jessyn and Synnia had returned with Ostencour's request. He had that same dreamy tone that he got when he'd only half been paying attention. "No, it's us. They're not afraid of *us*. Interested in, maybe. Hoping that they can use us. But they aren't afraid."

"Whatever," Tonner said. "So our answer to Ostencour is not right now. But I don't see any reason we shouldn't start gathering the information and background that might let us—"

The wide door shuddered and rolled open. The librarian of the human moiety stood in the corridor. Tonner's stomach lurched and he took a breath he seemed unable to exhale. The black eyes shifted among them. When it trilled, Tonner thought, *This is it. This is how I'm going to die.* But the voice that came from its translator was the same reedy, pleasant tone that it always had.

"You will all come with me."

Campar glanced a question to Dafyd, and the younger man shook his head. Synnia's breath went ragged and the color had gone from her face, but her chin was high and defiant.

"Is there something wrong?" Dafyd asked.

"There is an alteration. You will come with me."

Rickar shifted, and Tonner saw that he had the crowbar in his hand. The thought passed through the whole group, a shared understanding that had everything to do with living together so intensely and so long. If this was slaughter, they'd go down together, and they'd go swinging.

Dafyd stepped toward the Carryx first, then Else and Rickar. The librarian turned its back and started off, not bothering to see if the others followed. Tonner trotted over to the kitchen and picked up a knife before he followed. It wasn't much, but nothing was going to be enough. His hands shook.

The librarian moved along the path they always took, heading for the vast common area and the laboratory alcove. The traffic of a dozen species parted before it, everything from every planet shifting to avoid its attention. They didn't just go about their business, though. A little crowd was forming even as it kept its distance. Bystanders at the disaster waiting to slake their curiosity.

Jessyn fell into step beside him. Her expression was blank and bland. Tonner knew the fear behind it, but she made it easier for him to pretend calm too.

When she spoke, her voice was steady and soft enough that it only just carried over the ambient hum of the place. "No soldiers."

It was true. Among all the strange bodies and uncanny eyes all around them, there weren't any of the usual enforcers. They passed the empty socket that had been their alcove lab. The holes in the counters where they'd wrenched out the equipment looked like the wreckage of a war. That they'd done the violence themselves didn't make it better. He shifted the knife to his left hand, stretching out his right where it had started to cramp.

He didn't recognize where they had been led at first, but he saw when the others did. Rickar's eyes widened, Jessyn's narrowed, but it meant the same thing. The alcove was brightly lit, and the counters in it were like the ones they'd had in their own lab. There was even the red stripe at the top of the archway. Without the fungal mat filling it, there was no way to identify it as the Night Drinkers' former home and the site of their slaughter. All marks of the little animals who had killed Irinna had been erased.

Inside, the space was similar to the one they'd had, but not identical. In one sample case at the back, a branched stick had a population of the little self-contained farming organisms they called berries. In another, the brightly colored, three-legged thing that wasn't a turtle. The librarian stopped in front of the cases and turned toward them. If it was aware of the weapons and fear that had followed it to this place, it didn't show any sign. The smaller, pale arms next to its mouth gestured at the cases.

"These are from one of our subject worlds. This is of another. You will make these first organisms nourishing for the second."

"The Night Drinkers," Dafyd said. "The ones that were here?"

"You have earned access to their resources. As you prove more useful, you will earn access to more resources."

Tonner heard the unspoken other half of the statement. *Fail to be useful, and someone else will be moving into the space you used to live in.*

When the librarian moved, they all shifted out of its way, just the same as all the other subject races had. At the mouth of the alcove, other things shuffled back and forth and began to disperse. The show was over. If they all seemed a little disappointed that there hadn't been more blood and death, that might only have been Tonner's imagination.

"Oh, look at this," Campar said, running his palm over a cabinet. "This is a dynamic imaging deck. I've always wanted one of these."

Jessyn put her hands on her hips, scowling at the space. "This stuff isn't going to fit in our rooms."

"Maybe it doesn't need to," Rickar said. "If the little shits are all dead, security isn't as big an issue, right?"

"Unless some other set of monsters is out there we don't know about," Jessyn said. "Or unless one shows up from someplace the Carryx ate after they ate Anjiin. We can't pretend we're safe. Not now, not ever."

Synnia's smile was triumphant. Tonner didn't like it. "You know what this is. This is a sign."

"A sign," he said.

"The tools we needed to take on our new project, given to us exactly when we needed them. It's the universe telling us that Ostencour's plan is the right thing to do."

"Or the natural playing out of consequences," Campar said, trying for lightness. "Hard to tell those apart sometimes."

Synnia shook her head. "It's a sign."

"Whatever it is, let's start with inventory," Tonner said. "Did anyone bring a pen?"

In the end, Dafyd and Campar stayed to catalog the new equipment and begin the long process of calibrating everything to match the familiar devices back in their rooms. Jessyn and Rickar stood guard at the mouth of the new alcove, him with the crowbar and her with the knife, talking to each other softly as they swept their gaze across the passing monstrosities. Else and Synnia headed back to the rooms, to guard them and keep the protein assays running and maybe rest or eat or eke some space out of the day for something like a life.

Tonner wanted a book. Or music. An entertainment feed showing bad comedies. He wanted a piece of art to look at and a glass of wine to sip. He wanted a café with a live band and a little bamboo dance floor. He wanted food so spicy it burned the next day when he took a shit. He wanted to meet a stranger in a library and to spend an hour flirting with them. He wanted a life. He wanted a possibility.

Instead he had an imaging deck, a magnetic lensing microscope, a more advanced protein library with self-generating speculative databasing and automated synthesis paths, a soft-tooth separating grinder that would probably be able to take tissues down to their cells without breaking as many cell walls in the process. Wonderful toys for a game he was tired of playing.

Between manufacturing medicines for Jessyn and whoever else wound up needing some in the future, and building the berries into a reliable food source for the turtles, they were already taking on a workload suited for twice as large a team. And then add on becoming a secret bioweapons lab in their spare time...

What he needed was more people.

What he needed was to care less about all of it.

He didn't know what he needed.

Urrys Ostencour, sitting on a stool, looked up as Dafyd stepped into the room. His quarters were four levels down from Tonner's group, and in the opposite direction from Jellit and Merrol and Allstin. The security man had kept his quarters spare and simple. Yellow walls and an off-white floor. The same little kitchen that Jellit's quarters had, and an open room with chairs and stools and a low table of enameled metal. The others in his group were elsewhere or sleeping. Dafyd didn't know which.

"I was wondering which one of you it was going to be," Ostencour said.

"Which one of us?"

"Jessyn's brought you my proposal. Somebody was bound to respond. The obvious choices were you or Freis. Or it could have been Yannin. Sit, please. Tell me what's on your mind."

"I'm not here as a spokesman. I mean, I'm not carrying some official message or anything."

"As a friend and colleague, then. Really. Sit." Dafyd sat, and Ostencour's smile widened a fraction, like he'd won some subtle point. "All right, Alkhor. Tell why you think we shouldn't."

"These projects they're having us do? They're only partly about the tasks."

"I agree," Ostencour said. "And I think we both know what the larger question is. All this? It's about domestication, isn't it."

"Every new species I talk to, they're either in fear or they're resigned to what's happened. Or they're enthusiastically going along with it. The people like you and Jellit and Synnia. You're missing."

"Survivor bias," Ostencour said. "The ones who raised hell are all dead."

"Or who wouldn't engage with it. I think that's what happened to the hallway crows."

"The what?" Ostencour asked.

"And the ones who didn't fit the mandate. Who couldn't make themselves fit in, if they weren't in open revolt. The Night Drinkers weren't trying to burn the librarian down. They were trying to burn *us* down, and they failed. I'm just trying to get my head around the whole thing. What the Carryx really want. Where the line is."

"And you think it matters," Ostencour said. His voice was gentle in a way that made the small hairs on Dafyd's neck stand up. "Look, I agree with you. We're seeing the same things, you and me."

"The Carryx killed an eighth of Anjiin in a blink. We're in their territory. There's no kind of guerilla war against them that we can possibly win."

"That's true."

"Then what are we talking about?"

Ostencour leaned back, the front legs of his stool lifting off the floor. He looked at ease, and at the center of his calm was a cold rage. "I remember you from the trip over, you know. How you tried to protect the jailers instead of fighting alongside Synnia and the others. I want you to know that I don't resent your cowardice. I understand it. What I'm asking you to be part of takes an exceptional courage."

"They can kill us. Not just us. If we convince them that humans can't be domesticated? I think that's everyone back home too. The Carryx see everything that isn't them as a tool, and I think they throw away anything they can't use."

"You think they'd kill Anjiin, if we rebelled here."

"I don't know how to risk that possibility."

"That's already happened, son. That happened the day they took our sky for their own. You know what you're doing? You're thinking that if you just show your belly hard enough, if you just surrender utterly enough, you can control what they do. It's a grief reaction, and it's an error. Don't be ashamed of it. It's natural. But it's wrong."

"But you're comfortable making that choice for everyone? Your noble last stand that gets everyone else killed is clearly right?" Dafyd was almost surprised by the buzz in his own voice.

"I don't think there's any decision to be made. I have worked my whole career at the intersection of humanity and violence. The Carryx are trying to figure out whether we're domesticable, but I already know the answer to that. We aren't. We never have been. Someone is going to fight back. That's just the kind of primate we are. Curling up and being good pets? It isn't going to happen, so we have between right now and whatever day the Carryx figure that out to do some damage."

"We can't win."

"I'm not stupid, Alkhor. I know we're going to lose. We already did. But I'm good at organizing, I'm good at fighting, and I think I can bloody their noses on the way down. If I don't, someone who maybe isn't as good as I am will eventually try. And when they do, the consequences are going to be whatever your friendly librarian and its bosses decide they're going to be. There's not a goddamned thing any of us can do about it."

Thirty

There's not a goddamned thing any of us can do about it.

Dafyd sat in his usual spot watching the play of alien traffic through the cathedral. There had been a joy in it before. He had wanted to share it. Wanted someone to be at his side while they admired the grandeur and strangeness of it all.

He remembered feeling that, but he didn't feel it now.

He knew some of them. The bone horses were Phylarchs. The clicking globes were Oumenti and Soun. The dog-sized crabs wouldn't say their names.

Before, he had been an observer. He'd been an unintentional intruder in the vast organism. Now he knew names and histories, he had glimmers of the competitions and rivalries that shaped the beings there. The intersection between evolution and politics that came when whole species could be put to death.

When his species could be. Would be. And *there was not a goddamned thing any of us could do about it.*

There was a way that the world prison was very much like one of the berries. The way that the berries were really just a balloon skin around a rich pulp of other organisms that it managed and exploited, the Carryx were a boundary civilization that farmed other species, gathered other aliens, managed them. Lifted some up, and edited others out. This was the pulp. They were the farm.

Except that even the berries worked to keep their little farmed organisms alive. The Night Drinkers had possibly been poisoned into madness by too much oxygen in their air. One of Ostencour's group had been dying of a very treatable hereditary disease. Jessyn had nearly become suicidal before they coaxed the berries into making medicine for her. And the food supply was dwindling by the day. At every turn, the system the Carryx had set up said *Be useful to us*. But it seemed part of being useful was solving your own damn problems. Every species moving past him in the cathedral had faced the same challenge: Find a way to stay alive and produce something of value to the Carryx.

And as his sense of the prison as a vast organism, a city, a tissue made from a thousand different kinds of cell grew deeper, the knowledge also intruded on him that there was a black thread in it. Little knots of humanity planning out their revenge like a cancer still too small to detect. He knew it was there, and it laid a sense of dread over everything. He wished that he knew the details of the plan, and he was glad that he didn't.

A Soft Lothark ambled past on its long, furry legs, the same kind that had exploded once and sickened him. The same kind that he'd seen eaten by its fellows. A flock of Jayaster swirled overhead, glittering the yellow and blue of an angry conversation. Dafyd rose and turned toward home, walking slowly, pouring his attention into the slow shift from one foot to the other like he was pouring the weight from one half of an hourglass into the other and then back again. Letting his mind rest on something meaningless, innocuous, simple. The weariness in his body wasn't lack of sleep. Resting wouldn't fix it.

He turned left instead of right, moving deeper into the cathedral-wide common area and toward the new alcove. The new lab. The spoils of war. He didn't particularly want to go there, but he didn't particularly want to go back to the quarters either. If there had been a bar, even if it had been half a day's walk away, he'd have been heading for it.

Jessyn was standing guard alone, and he saw her before she saw him. Captivity had changed her. The short, round-bodied woman that she'd once been had changed to someone thinner and sharper, like someone had put her on a grindstone and turned her into a knife. Her eyes had a darkness they hadn't had on Anjiin, and she held her shoulders back and her chin up in constant, unconscious aggression. He tried to think when it had changed. On the transit, maybe. Or when she'd led the attack on the Night Drinkers. There were so many changes they'd all gone through. Dafyd wondered what she'd see in him, if she thought to look.

She raised a hand as he approached. From the alcove behind her, human voices came. Campar and Tonner, each talking over the other. Dafyd nodded toward them, and she shrugged.

"They have a difference of opinion," she said. "Tonner wants to start feeding things to the not-turtle. Tolerance testing. Campar thinks we should keep mapping the plasticity of the berries' internal farm matrix."

Her smile was thin, and he knew what it meant. *As if any of this matters.* She wasn't ready to say it aloud, but she thought they were all going to die. The conspiracy against the Carryx would come to its climax, make whatever mark they could against their oppressors, and then humanity would follow the Night Drinkers down to slaughter. His sense of weariness redoubled.

In the lab, Tonner snapped *It doesn't make sense.* The expression that flickered in Jessyn's eyes could have been impatience. Or contempt. Whatever, it wasn't how either of them had reacted to the team lead's temper before they'd come here.

Dafyd wanted to ask how Jessyn was, what she thought about Ostencour's proposal. If it made her feel as powerless as it did him. Instead, he nodded and walked away. Jessyn went back to peering at the crowd and waiting for the next unanticipated violence. The mutter of alien voices and footsteps made a gentle roar, like a waterfall. It drowned out the need for thought, and he let himself walk the pattern that habit had made for him.

At the rooms, the wide door was cracked open, but nothing uninvited seemed to have made its way in. The common area was empty, and the handwritten notes that had been tacked on the wall shifted in the faint breeze. The resonance scanner was ticking to itself thoughtfully as it went through its run. Everything was as it was supposed to be, except that no one was there. Outside the window, the local sun beamed down through a brilliant blue-green sky. Dafyd sat alone, looking out, and remembering how it had felt when he was an adolescent and his parents left him alone at home for the first time. The emptiness and the possibility.

That boy was gone now and would never come back. The world he'd known had gone with him.

A soft sound came from the hall, cloth against cloth. When he looked back, Else was standing in the shadows. Her hair was messy from her pillow, and her face was sober and pale. Still, when their eyes met, she managed a little smile.

"Where is everyone?" Dafyd asked.

Else shook her head, as if she were saying she didn't know, but then answered anyway. "Tonner and Campar are working at the new lab. Rickar and Synnia went somewhere with Jellit. Jessyn might be with them."

"She's not. I saw her at the lab."

"She's there, then. I was out... I was out for a while. Exploring."

"You should take someone with you. It's not safe out there."

"I know, but..."

"What are you looking for, anyway? I understood it when you and Synnia were trying to find other people. Or patrolling. But the Night Drinkers are gone and we found the other people, and you're still looking."

She stepped out into the light. He expected her to blink or squint, but the shift didn't seem to bother her at all. Her fingers tapped against her thigh, fast and tight. Her lips moved as if she were speaking, but no sound came out.

"Else?"

"They can't fight back."

"Ostencour and Synnia and all the people with them? They're going to. It's their pathological move. It's reflex. It's the organism we are."

"If they try to kill the librarian or raise some kind of insurrection, we'll die here."

"I know. But... maybe it makes sense to go down fighting."

Her jaw slid forward, and her hands curled into fists. "It doesn't. It makes sense to *win*."

"I don't see how that's an option." He tried to be gentle, but whatever storm was raging in Else's mind, he wasn't able to calm it. She moved sharply, pacing from the kitchen to the window and back again. Her lips twitched into the shape of words. Dread was a stone in Dafyd's chest. If Else was breaking down, it was fair. She was the only one who hadn't, so far. It was her turn. But he wasn't sure he had the reserves to help her. He was too near the edge himself.

She paused at the window, looking out into the vastness. The grid shone in the sky, the ziggurats squatted below them, standing in ranks that passed off to the horizon. They were silent for a moment. She turned, leaned her shoulders against the glass. He had a powerful memory of being in her room on Anjiin, her leaning against a doorframe with the same posture. That had been just before the sirens started shrieking to announce the attack. It felt like an omen.

"I'm going to tell you some things," she said. Her rage had been replaced by an eerie calm. "I need you to promise you'll hear me out before you pass judgment."

"On you?"

"Promise me."

He shifted, leaned forward. "Of course."

Else gathered herself, but only for a moment. The resonance scanner chirped that it had finished its run and went quiet, waiting for new instructions.

"There is a war," she said. "The Carryx are fighting a vast, terrible war. They have been for generations. It's touched hundreds of solar systems. Maybe thousands. You've seen all the species they've put the collar on. For every one of these, there are many they've judged unusable and eradicated. But this great war has another side. There are forces that are pushing back against them."

"How did you find out about—"

She lifted a palm, commanding silence. "They knew. The other side? They knew the Carryx were coming for Anjiin. And they knew how the Carryx treat conquered worlds. Six months before the attack, they snuck a weapon onto Anjiin. It was... I don't know how to describe this. Think of a billion tiny machines that can take over a living host. Hide inside it. The other side, they didn't give it a lot of information in case the Carryx found it. Just enough for it to perform a mission. Connect itself to someone who would be taken back into Carryx territory. Sneak in . . . here. Right here."

Else paused. Distress drew a vertical line between her eyebrows. Her fingers moved like she was looking for a cigarette she'd put down, then brushed her lips. The ghost of an old habit. Dafyd wasn't sure if she was waiting for a response from him or gathering her thoughts. He waited. The silence only stretched a few seconds.

"This spy was supposed to get all the information it could. Intelligence gathering. And then it was supposed to find a way to send that data back out to the other side."

In the sky behind her, something flared a bright yellow and faded just as quickly away. The stone in his chest was still there, but it meant something different.

"And you knew about this . . . this spy thing? It was in touch with you?"

"Yes."

The air seemed to have gone thin. "You knew they were coming. You knew what they were going to do."

The words came out from her, high and fast, slowing as she went, until she stopped like a balloon gently deflating. "I did. In general terms. The workgroup was high status, and that's who the Carryx take. It's who they think they can learn from. Make use of. However you want to phrase it. But I knew it was coming. I knew."

"And you didn't warn anyone?"

"I couldn't. More resistance from Anjiin would have changed nothing. The only result would be the Carryx wondering how the security forces knew. A reason to suspect. Maybe find the spy." She stepped away from the glass, pushing off from it with one shoulder and stepping closer to him. "There's hope. That's the thing. There is hope, but it's a long kind of hope. A slow one. It will take a lot of suffering along the way, but—"

"The spy? Where is it now?"

Else lifted her hand. For a moment, he didn't understand. Then the motes shifting under her skin darkened and grew, flowing like a black snowstorm along the surface of her fingers, the subtle lines of her palm, before fading away again.

"It's in you?"

"It's in me."

"For how long?"

She looked away. It could have been embarrassment. "A long time."

"Is it conscious?"

"Yes."

Dafyd's breath was slow, and it shook. The world had taken on a distance, like this was a dream he was having. He recognized that he was having a reaction, but he couldn't pinpoint the emotion he was feeling, only that he wasn't angry. He was surprised by that. "Is it you? I mean, are you still Else?"

"I'm Else," she said, quickly. Sharply. "I'm just…"

"Cooperating with it?"

"Something like that. It's complicated. I've been looking for a way to send out everything we've learned. There isn't one. The Swarm's creators knew security would be tight. They suspected that it would be difficult to get information out while we were on one of the Carryx homeworlds. If we can get transferred to a conquered system, it should be less rigorous. And they do it all the time. There were probably a dozen different species they brought to settle on Anjiin. We just need to survive long enough that they see a reason to take us along."

"But that's not going to happen."

"Not if Ostencour goes through with his plan. I know this is a lot to take in. You don't have to say anything. Just . . . I know why Ostencour and Jellit and Synnia and all the rest of them want to fight. I want to fight too. And I could. I am the weapon of their greatest enemy. I could kill many Carryx before they destroyed me, if I chose to."

"But that's not why you're here," Dafyd said.

"No. Because then I would be destroyed and everything I've learned would be lost, and all to take lives the Carryx themselves won't care about. They think that if one of them was weak enough to be killed by an animal, then it should have been killed by an animal. *What is, is.*"

"You're saying we beat them all at once, or not at all."

"Yes. The others want to make all this terror and pain right, but they want to do it fast, and if we go fast, we lose."

"So we tell them," Dafyd said.

Else's smile was unmistakably her. He'd been thinking about that smile since he'd first joined the workgroup. He took her hand. It felt the way it always had.

"How would that go?" she asked. "Best-case scenario would be a debate with a lot of people arguing about it. The Carryx might seem like absentee landlords, but don't assume they don't have ears everywhere. I wasn't even going to tell you, except now I need you to know. And . . . I owe it to you."

"Then isn't telling me right now a huge risk?"

"I can make sure no one listens for a while. But it's dangerous to do too often. The absence could become noticeable."

"Does Tonner know about the thing inside you?"

"God, no," she said with a laugh. "Can you imagine? He'd have me listed up there as another project to schedule out."

Dafyd found himself laughing too. His mind clung to the warmth, the normalcy, like he was drowning and it was the only thing afloat. Else tapped his hip, motioned for him to move over. He made room, and she sat beside him. He leaned into her, then remembered the swirl of darkness under her flesh and shifted away. He felt her start to move toward him, to close the distance, and then hold herself back.

After a time, he said, "I don't know how I can stop Ostencour. I don't even know who's working with him, not all of them."

"You can't do it. But you know someone who can." Her expression was an apology. "The librarian."

When he recoiled, she grabbed his arm. She didn't feel machine strong. Was she? If he just got up and walked away, would the thing inside her stop him?

"Wait, Dafyd," she said. "Think it through. If we warn them, then it's not all of Anjiin that can't be domesticated. Just part of it needs to be culled. If I report the insurgents, then the Carryx will look at me more closely, and we can't let them do that. Of all of us, you're the one who assimilated the most. It would make sense coming from you."

"If I warn the Carryx, they'll all be killed."

"They're going to die anyway. And everyone else with them. And more than that, we'll all die for nothing. We sacrificed the lives we knew for a chance at this. Maybe we didn't know it at the time, but it's what we did. If we can keep that chance alive, even just for a little while, we have to. We owe it to everyone who didn't make it. Nöl and Irinna…"

In his mind, he saw Jessyn sitting beside her brother for the first time since the attack. The darkness and pain that she'd carried, and the moment of light that the universe had given her. Dafyd thought about being the man who took that away from her.

"You kissed me just before the attack. Was any of what happened between us real? Or was it just part of your plan. Turn me into a willing tool for your mission. Because the choice you just dumped on me? I wouldn't ask that of my worst enemy."

Else didn't answer. The machine inside her didn't answer. Dafyd wondered if he'd have been able to tell the difference.

"I have to think about all of this," he said when it was clear she wasn't going to speak first.

"I know that I'm asking a lot. And I understand why you'd distrust me. Just while you think it through, don't tell anyone about me. And Dafyd? Don't take too long."

Thirty-One

Rickar shifted onto his side. Dennia's bed was the same size and shape as his own, the mattress the same thickness and texture. It was only that there were two of them that made it feel different. Exotic. Dangerous.

Dennia had been a technical specialist working with the high-precision lasers that the near-field visualization technology used. An engineer, not a researcher, but a critical member of the team all the same. She had a mole on the back of her neck and scars on her legs that she wouldn't talk about. She had a husband and a son back on Anjiin. Maybe she did. She didn't know if they were alive or dead. She didn't know if she would ever see them again.

Rickar ran his thumb over her temple. Her pale brown hair was darkened now with sweat. Her eyes matched the color of her damp hair.

"That was lovely," he said. And when she chuckled, "I mean, I hope it was. Was for me. Is there something I should be doing right now? Because if there's some finish work that needs attention—"

The chuckle turned into a sigh. "That's very thoughtful of you. I'm fine."

It had been a very long time since he'd felt this kind of release. He felt a little intoxicated with it, relaxed and warm and loose in the joints. Dennia stretched, the same slow, easy movement as a cat in sunlight. Rickar reminded himself that this was a bad moment to decide whether he was in love. Better just to enjoy it and let the future take care of itself.

"I do have work," she said. "We should probably..."

He kissed her again, once on the mouth. Once not. Then again. She caught her breath, shuddered, and pushed him gently away.

"That won't help me work."

"True," he said.

They dressed. Rickar felt the lack of an in-room shower. Next time, perhaps, she could make her way to his quarters. They could sit by the window afterward and watch the sky.

Jellit and Merrol were at their kitchen as Rickar saw himself out. They ignored him, but not coldly. In a world without privacy, etiquette had to suffice.

The walk between the two workgroups' quarters was growing as familiar as a commute. The wide, low plaza where groups of vaguely avian aliens gathered in a complex flock. The long, red-lit hallway with galleries leading off that smelled of mushrooms and peat. The well-known ramps. The curling halls that passed around the cathedral and the laboratory alcoves, of which they now owned—or at least had use of—two.

Rickar was astounded, as he walked, by how good he felt. How light the burdens of the world were in that moment. He was hungry. He was pleased. He could imagine himself feeling just the same while sitting in a street café outside Dyan Academy and watching the aurora.

The revelation was so obvious now that he'd had it. Even in prison, people indulged in affairs or fell in love. Even in prison, he could be surprised by moments of unexpected beauty. Life in captivity was still life. Unless and until he was thrown in total isolation, there would be the chance to make a human connection. He had food. He had shelter. He had work. He had a ration of joy and pleasure. There was no reason to think he would keep them, but he had them now.

His life hadn't ended. Yes, he'd been hurt, displaced, traumatized. He wasn't safe, and likely never would be. But he wasn't killed. And life—even the joyful part that he would have thought was the first to wither and the last to return—was still there. People sang songs in death camps, and that wasn't a comfort until you were in a death camp yourself.

As he turned the last corner, he saw Synnia. She was sitting alone, her back against the wall, across from the wide door. He walked toward her, slowing as he came close. Her legs were crossed under her, her hands folded in her lap. The lines in her skin seemed deeper than they had back on Anjiin, or even in those first days after they'd arrived when she'd been his only companion during the exile that Tonner had imposed on him.

She didn't acknowledge him as he sat beside her. He shifted his weight, finding a good position. They'd spent days sitting beside each other before. The silence between them was comfortable and well practiced. He relaxed into it. His mind had wandered onto old memories of a lecturer he'd had early in his career who had broken up his classes with jokes and political commentary, when Synnia spoke. Her voice was calm and matter-of-fact.

"I don't know how old I am. I know how old I was the night they came. I know how old I was when they killed Nöl. But how long ago was that? I must have had a birthday since then. Maybe two. Three? I don't know. I've lost track."

"I think we all have. No watches, no calendars. No days, not the way we're used to them. The time in our spaceship cell coming over. That had to have been weeks, but I don't think it was months." He thought back to the dim half-world. The thinness of the people who had come out of it, himself included. The beards. The rags that had been clothing. Had it only been weeks? He wasn't sure now.

"I tried to move past it."

"It?"

"Nöl. I won't help the Carryx. I won't ever do what they tell me to do, but when we found out Jessyn was in trouble I thought maybe it would be all right. I could stand to help with the work if it was really for her. For one of us. But I hate them. I just hate them so much. I can't get past it. I can't get over it. I'm scared all the time, and I miss Nöl, and I'm only angry now. Everything that isn't fear or anger is gone away." She puffed her cheeks and blew out, like she was scattering dandelion seeds on the wind.

"Is that why you're sitting in the hallway?"

"Tonner was talking with Jessyn about making food for the mock turtle. He's still doing what they want him to, and I couldn't listen to it anymore. Not right now. I didn't want to be in that cell of a bedroom, and I wanted to be alone."

"Ah," Rickar said. "Well, I screwed that up for you."

"It's not the same with you. We were exiles together. You're the one I can be alone with."

He took her hand. For a while, they sat together.

Jellit had just returned from a meeting with Skinnerling and Kos, the two engineers who were in charge of manufacturing more guns. The conversation had to be clandestine because the head of the engineering workgroup had made it very clear that she didn't want anything to do with Ostencour's plan. She'd been in the transit with Ostencour and Jessyn, and a friend of hers had died in Ostencour's first attempt. Her emotions had the best of her, and she wasn't to be trusted. There were a lot of people who weren't to be trusted.

Dafyd Alkhor, for instance.

Jessyn's friend was waiting for him outside the quarters, trying to look casual and failing. In the time since they'd appeared on his doorstep, he'd started wondering if bringing Tonner Freis's workgroup into the plan had been a good idea. Maybe he'd been wrong to vouch for them. It was just that he remembered them fondly from their old lives. And they'd taken care of Jessyn when he couldn't. He'd let his emotions get the best of him too.

"Hey," Jellit said.

"Good to see you," the research assistant said. "I was wondering... This feels weird, but is there someplace we could talk?"

Synnia had warned that this might happen. Dafyd had been opposed to the revolt in transit. Had gone so far as to insert himself in the attack and been made sick for his troubles. The older woman expected that he'd want to put the brakes on the plan now as well. And, unless Jellit missed his guess, here were the brakes.

"Sure," Jellit said. "Come on in."

The truth was, he'd liked Jessyn's workgroup. Been grateful to them, even. The presence of other people in his sister's life, of work that she could feel pride in and be celebrated for... It had been a relief. Dafyd had been in the background: a pleasant, deferential man who'd brought coffee and pastries. The one who stayed behind to make sure the lab equipment was cleaned and dusted. There had been some connection to a rich family in the administration, but Jellit hadn't paid much attention to that.

Abduction and imprisonment had been rough on the assistant. Had been rough on them all, Jellit included.

Merrol was standing guard, and she nodded at Dafyd as they came in.

"I can take over," Jellit said. She knew him well enough to read all the nuances of the words.

"You're up," she said, and he knew her well enough to know that he and Dafyd were welcome to their privacy for the moment, but that she'd want a full report when he was gone.

She left the gun and went to the ladder, hauling herself up to the second level and the bedrooms. Jellit sat where she'd been. "What's on your mind?"

"I just... I've been thinking? About your joint project?"

"I know the one," Jellit said.

"I wanted to ask if, just hypothetically, if you found a good reason not to go through with it... or even just to go slower? Put it off for a while? Would that be possible?"

Jellit crossed his arms and leaned back on the stool. "I don't know what that would be."

Dafyd shifted, something like chagrin passing over him. "Fair point."

"Let's try this again," Jellit said. "What's on your mind?"

The tension in the air changed. "I'm worried about your sister."

Jellit's jaw tightened. Dafyd had no idea how wrong a tack he'd just taken, and Jellit didn't feel any need to lift him out of his hole. "Tell me about that."

"I was with her on the trip over. I saw her here when she was struggling, and when she got hurt in the attack. She didn't talk much about how badly she missed you, how much not having you in her life hurt her, but I think it was hard. I think losing you made everything else she was going through worse. And I don't want her to lose you again."

"Lose me by...?"

"Fine. I'll speak plainly. I don't want her to go through the things she'd feel watching the Carryx kill you. And if that plan goes forward, you and everyone else involved with it being executed is the best case. That's what I'm saying."

"All right," Jellit said.

"All right?"

"I hear you. You're here to see if I'm really committed to the plan. If I'd reconsider. Maybe step back from it for Jessyn's sake."

"Yeah. Yes, that's right."

"I can help you with that," Jellit said. "I'm committed. I'm all the way in. Deep as anyone can get, that's how much I'm part of it. I watched these things kill people I know. My world was taken. My life was broken, and everyone else's too. The plan where I just sit here like a good pet and try to make them happy? I'd rather die. I'd rather have Jessyn die. I'd rather have all of us die than live on our bellies, licking Carryx shit. Does that clear things up for you?"

Jellit hadn't meant to stand up and start shouting, but he also hadn't meant not to. It was done, and he didn't regret it. He sat back down.

"What happened to you?" Dafyd asked, his voice small.

"A lot," Jellit said. "Enough."

"You're making a mistake."

"I'm playing the hand I was dealt. Same as everyone else." *The same as you only you're trying to make nice with the fuckers who put their boots on your neck.* He didn't say the last part, but the implication hung in the air like a bad smell.

"All right," Dafyd said. And then, more to himself, "All right."

He didn't say goodbye, just lifted a hand in a half-hearted wave and made his way out the door. Jellit took a deep, slow breath. Then another. The tightness in his chest, the warmth of the rage. He knew they weren't about the research assistant. Dafyd was just a little, frightened man, scared of rocking the boat because of what it might mean for him. Most people were cowards. Being angry about that was like being angry at time for passing.

Still, he wished Jessyn and Synnia hadn't taken the weapons proposal to their whole group. However loyal they felt to Tonner's team, discretion would have been a better plan. It was maybe an hour before Merrol came back down the ladder. She'd showered, and her hair was a long, damp braid. She didn't speak, only nodded at the door that Dafyd Alkhor had left through. Jellit understood what she meant.

"He may be a problem," he said.

Merrol considered for a moment, then nodded at the gun. Jellit understood that too.

Alarm courses through the swarm's consciousness. It does this constantly now, each worry giving rise to greater worries in a spiral that rises forever. The others that are a part of its mind match the patterns of its distress, making analogies and connections the way that their minds evolved to do. Else recalls a time when she was young and sleeping overnight in the wilderness with her family. She woke in a cold morning, and neglected to check her boot. The animal that had taken shelter there had come boiling out just as she was about to press her sock-covered toes down into that darkness. The sense of discovering a threat at the last moment feels familiar.

As it searched for a transmission route, danger had been growing all around it, unseen. Humans linking to each other like roots of a bad weed, and it hadn't known. If Jessyn had not led the attack on the Night Drinkers, if Dafyd had not used the translation device to find the others, if and if and if. The swarm sees all the ways its mission might have failed. All the ways it still might.

The echo of Ameer Kindred, dead now for so long her body has surely returned to the soil of her distant homeworld, remembers being caught on a malfunctioning transport. The edge of the road speeding by her too fast. Her powerlessness at seeing the drop-off and knowing that her mortal danger was both a fact and utterly beyond her control. They are all hostages to chance and the will of others now. The parts of the swarm that benefit from sleep cannot rest, and fatigue toxins exacerbate the host's endless swirling anxiety.

If it fails, much more than Anjiin will be lost, but all its memories are of that world. Of that sacrifice. Else Yannin remembers the playground where she used to swing with her cousins. Ameer Kindred thinks of the scent of her mother's lentil soup on a cold winter evening. The swarm has nothing of its own to call back. It takes these small pleasures and it mourns their passing. These are the things that are burned on the altar of war in the hope that prayer will bring peace.

Not peace. Victory.

The swarm is in its room, its door closed, but its skin is taut with sensor arrays, its eyes are altered to take in backscatter too subtle for the human tools to match. The walls, the floor, the ceiling—all of them are translucent to the spectrums and wavelengths where it keeps its attention. In the next room over, Campar is sleeping, a large hot lump in the center of the room's cool space. Across the hallway, Tonner Freis, who was once its lover, paces, his muscles and mind a storm of impulses and energy. The fingers of his right hand flutter the way they sometimes do when he is lost in thought. It doesn't know why he is agitated. Jessyn and Synnia in the main room are bare outlines, almost lost in the fog of solid matter. And Dafyd...

He should have been back by now, *Else thinks. Ameer doesn't disagree. The swarm feels her fear and the fears that fear inspires.*

The wide door rolls to the side, and it rises from its bed, walks out into the hallway. Dafyd is exchanging pleasantries with Jessyn, but the swarm can smell the distress in his sweat.

Else, *Synnia says.* Are you all right?

Yes, fine.

Your eyes... Is there something...?

The swarm puts a hand to its face, rubs at the eyelids while it changes the sclera back to a more human whiteness, returns the irises to the color that Else's had been. It is a stupid mistake. It shouldn't have made it. And if it can make that mistake, what other mistakes is it making?

Ooh, *it says.* I guess I did have something in them. That feels weird. Dafyd, do you have a minute?

Sure, *he says. They turn back. It hears the subvocal click of Synnia, but doesn't know if the reaction is amusement or disapproval.*

When they are alone, Dafyd sits on the edge of the bed, his hands in his lap. The distress is a shudder of static coming from his brain, a fast tapping like Tonner's fingertips, an echo of the swarm's own unease.

I don't think I can do this, *he says.*

The swarm presses its fingers to its lips. It is a very human gesture.

Dafyd looks up into its eyes. His heart is beating fast. The anxiety in his expression is as painful as the fear has been. It hates that it is hurting him. It hates that it has to continue hurting him. This is so fucking wrong, *the ghost of Ameer says.* And I thought it was gross when you were just screwing him. *The swarm ignores Ameer, and sits beside Dafyd on the bed. When he starts to move away, it takes his hand. He hesitates.*

What happened, *it asks.*

I have to tell Jellit about the spy. He's not going to let go of the plan unless he knows.

If we do, he'll go to the librarian with you? He'll keep it secret?

I don't know. *The swarm moves chemoreceptors to the edge of its skin, tasting the air between them. Dafyd's uncertainty is like the flavor of tin.*

What if he just sees it as another alien? *the swarm asks.* You're not comfortable with it, and we're us.

Dafyd starts to object. It can actually see his tongue move as the words form and then fail him. It sees the storm of activity across his brain as he struggles with his choice. The swarm sees him more deeply than Ameer or Else have ever seen their lovers, and it makes them both look. It forces them to understand him. When it kisses him this time, there is no conflict within it. No shame. No judgment. Even Ameer, who is not attracted to him, now feels the affection and the sorrow.

We can't tell him, *Dafyd says.* We have to, and we can't.

There are other problems, and he would know that if he stopped and considered. But all his feelings have become knotted around this one idea: that Jessyn will be crushed by her brother's death, and Dafyd will be responsible. It's not a rational position, and a rational argument cannot dislodge it. Not without time, and they have no time.

Is that the price? *the swarm asks.*

What?

If I promise you that Jellit will play along, will you go to the librarian? Say that Jellit came to you because he was afraid the others would know if he went himself. Say that he'll share everything he knows, only he wants to be spared.

He won't.

If I promise he will, will you go? Would that be enough?

Dafyd struggles. I know it's the right thing to do. I know, but it's so hard.

We can't save everyone, *it says.* That was never an option. But we can save the people it is possible to save. We can do the best that we can do.

He is silent. Still. It can feel the turmoil in his brain and his body like it is sitting beside a fire. The sorrow like acid in his soul. Else's heart aches for him. Even Ameer loves him a little in that moment.

All right, *he says, and relief washes through the swarm. Relief and anticipation and grief. Dafyd kisses the back of its hand. Not a sexual gesture, but an intimate one.* Would you lie to me about it?

Do you want me to?

No, I mean…The spy, it already stood by while millions of people died on Anjiin. We're talking about feeding dozens more to the Carryx. Telling me a lie to make it happen…It's not the worst thing you'll have done, is it? Would you lie to me about this, if that's what it took to convince me to do it?

Else Annalise Yannin's heart breaks. Ameer feels her new affection for Dafyd growing a little. The swarm wonders if it may have misjudged how clearly he can see past the storms in his own heart. Dafyd Alkhor is an easy man to underestimate. That is part of why it loves him. Oh, you love him now? *Ameer's contempt is visceral.* We do love him, *Else answers for them both, sadly. Dafyd is staring into their eyes.*

Would you lie to me?

If the swarm says no, he will recognize the falsehood.

Yes. I would, *the swarm answers,* but I won't.

Dafyd thought there should have been a limit. The universe could only change so many times, could only reveal so many unexpected, inconceivable aspects of itself before he got used to it. It could only ask so much of him before he became strong enough to do what was required of him.

Outside the window, dawn threatened. It was one of the odd days that his physical schedule and the astronomic realities of the Carryx homeworld fell into sync. Soon, the librarian would be active and in its office. It wasn't a long walk. He'd made it any number of times before this. It only felt like an overwhelming journey because of the context. Because of the conversation waiting for him at the end.

The grid that surrounded the world prison like a net holding a marble caught the light first. Then high clouds brightened, going from gray to pink and gold to a blinding white. Something dark moved in the sky. If they'd had a telescope, he'd have been able to see what it was. A ship or an animal or some alien artifact that didn't fit his understanding of how things worked.

There is a plan among some of the humans to kill the Carryx. To kill you. Jellit asked me to come and warn you about a plan among the humans to kill you. Jellit wanted me to ask for your help.

A door opened in the hall. One of the bedrooms. Campar strolled out. He was wearing the same pants that the Carryx had given them since they'd come, but instead of a shirt, he had a towel slung across his shoulders.

"Good morning, young master Alkhor," he said. "I don't suppose the spirit has moved you to start brewing the sad pisswater that passes for tea these days?"

"What? Oh. No, sorry."

"The burdens we suffer," Campar said lightly as he found a pan and poured water into it. "A senior researcher such as myself forced to boil my own water. The indignity of it."

A spike of rage flowed up through Dafyd, starting in his gut and rising up, thickening his chest and neck, clamping down his jaw. It was gone as quickly as it came.

In the kitchen, Campar made a small, interrogative grunt. Then, a moment later, "Is something the matter?"

"Every day I wake up knowing I might be killed and probably won't even know why. And you're always making a joke."

Campar put a mug on the counter, then took another and lifted it toward Dafyd. *Do you want some?* Dafyd nodded as he stood.

"This is what I do instead of curl up on the floor weeping. I mean, except for the times when I curl up on the floor weeping. I think we all remember that. When I can't make fun of it, I can't do anything at all," Campar said. "If you'd rather I didn't talk right now..."

"Your constant joking is annoying and exhausting and I don't want you to ever stop."

"Mixing the message a bit."

"I don't want to lose you people," Dafyd said. He hadn't put the words to the feeling until he'd already spoken them. "You and Rickar. Jessyn. Synnia. Even Tonner. I don't want to lose anything that I haven't lost already."

The water in the pan muttered. Campar took a tin of wilted greens from the cabinet. It clanked when he opened it.

"Well, that's the thing, isn't it," he said. The humor was gone from his voice. "The first thing our captors took from us was all of our choices."

Except that I still have one, Dafyd thought, and then felt the answering realization like a weight being placed on his back. *Except that I really don't.*

Another door slammed open. Footsteps pounded down the hallway. Tonner Freis stormed into the main room. His hair was a gray halo, defying gravity in its wildness.

"Pen," he said. His clothes looked like they'd been slept in. His eyes were bloodshot and angry. He snapped his fingers with impatience. "Pen. *Pen!*"

Dafyd scooped one of the metal styluses off the centrifuge along with a nub of gummy ink in a waxy wrapper. Tonner was at the little dining table, throwing paper aside. When Dafyd got close enough, Tonner snatched the pen and ink out of his hands and began scratching what looked like a molecular diagram onto a blank page. Campar met Dafyd's eyes, and shrugged as he dropped half a tin of minty-smelling leaves into the boiling water.

"Do you need anything else?" Dafyd asked.

He might as well have been in another room. Tonner ripped the page aside, took a fresh sheet, and started drawing on it. Half a minute later, one diagram in either hand, Tonner marched to the window. He put one page over the other, pressing them against the glass so that the light of the rising sun shone through them, superimposing his diagrams over each other.

He let out a low, growling obscenity. When he turned to Dafyd and Campar, his face was a mixture of rage and triumph.

"I know how to feed the fucking turtle."

PART SIX

SMALL BATTLES IN THE GREAT WAR

The genius of the Carryx is that we brought the peculiar and often idiosyncratic brilliance of a thousand different species into a central system of control. We conquered asymmetric space by harnessing the birth shrieks of the Temperantiae of Au. We built machines of loyalty by harvesting the poem-patterns of Janantie moss gardens. We built world-palaces designed by the Phylarchs of Astrdeim, communication networks woven from the bodies of the Void Dragons that eat the foam at the edge of black holes, battleships strengthened by the living shells that choked the oceans of Sinyas and Vau.

What would these have been without our guidance? Glories, but lost glories. Feral glories. The Carryx are the bones and nerve fibers of the unconscious universe. We are the scaffold and mind that shapes the nature and extent of its deterministic will.

Humans are structureless. They live in conflict with themselves and each other. Their great genius is rationalization: lying into mirrors until they bully and seduce themselves into things they would never otherwise do. They are creatures of self-delusion, regret, and desire. That is their way, and for a time we harnessed it as we did everything.

For a time.

—From the final statement of Ekur-Tkalal, keeper-librarian of the human moiety of the Carryx

Thirty-Two

Though Dafyd had lost consciousness a few times during the night, it would be a stretch to say he'd slept. The knowledge of the task that was coming with morning was like a constant angry buzz that kept him awake. The others were in the main room, babbling about Tonner's new insight. Functional enantiomers, analogous regulatory sites, the structural bottlenecks of carbohydrate variety. All the same conversation that they'd had back at Irvian. It felt like a dream that meant something. Like an omen.

Else the spy sat with him most of the time. She left before he rose to make himself a breakfast of protein paste and salt tabs that he was too tense to eat. He didn't know where she'd gone, but it didn't matter. Nothing changed the burden of the day.

Now, standing in the librarian's office with his hands behind his back, fingers wrapping wrist to keep them both from shaking, he felt lightheaded. The physical details of the room stood out like he was seeing them for the first time. The subtle pattern on the floor where the dust gathered along the lines of some magnetic field. The dark ring on the librarian's pale foreleg, like an old scar. The smell of musk and salt, imperceptible until fear and guilt and the stress of standing at the hinge of history rubbed his senses raw.

He wanted to vomit. He wanted to lie down someplace dark and warm and sleep forever. He wanted to be someone else, someplace else.

You're saving lives, he told himself. *This is your fight. This is how you save the ones who can be saved.*

When he imagined the words in Else's voice, they carried more weight.

He laid out the whole conspiracy, but as soon as he had reached the part about building biological weapons to harm the Carryx themselves, the librarian's demeanor had changed. The legs on its abdomen had gone still. The fighting arms of its thorax shifted forward a few degrees. Even with the time he'd spent learning about the librarian and its habits and gestures, all he could tell now was that it was listening, and his words were having some effect.

"And the one who asked you to carry this message?" it asked through its translator.

"Jellit. His name is Jellit. He and I knew each other before. His sibling is part of my team, and so he'd spent time with us. He trusted me, and he knew I had been working more closely with you than the others have."

The librarian trilled, cooed. The voice box said, "Yes, yes. I know the one you mean."

And what will you think when he comes here and denies all of this? Dafyd thought. He was fairly certain that the Carryx would be able to torture the information from him, or if not from him from one of the other names Dafyd could give them. But if the librarian doubted him, he could be punished as well. And Dafyd knew about Else and the spy.

The moment was a hinge. It could swing either way.

The librarian was still for longer than he liked. Dafyd made himself remain still as well. If he didn't know what the Carryx was thinking, what it was likely to do, the best hope he had was to mirror it, only calmer.

It whistled again, the fluting bass carrying through the room. The translation didn't come. Whatever the librarian had been calling for, it wasn't meant for human ears. It only took a few seconds for it to be answered. A Rak-hund slithered into the room behind him, its bone-knife feet hushing against the floor. A shiver went up Dafyd's spine. *I won't tell them about the spy. Even if they hurt me, I won't tell them that.* He tried to believe it.

But the librarian only sang to the Rak-hund, and the Rak-hund's reply, if there was one, wasn't in a register human senses could detect. The beast turned with the same undulating shiver and sped out of the room. Dafyd's relief felt almost like nausea.

"He will come to us. I will explain that his safety is unimportant. He will be made to understand."

"Yes," Dafyd said. "Thank you."

The librarian shifted its weight, its dark eyes clicked from one position to another like it was watching half a dozen things at once, and Dafyd couldn't see any of them. It shifted its abdomen, folding in its legs, and tilted forward. He couldn't help but think of it as leaning in to whisper.

"The task you were given. You say that has gone well?" The reedy, calm voice seemed eager.

"Um. Yes. Tonner thinks he's found a way to make the berries a reliable food source for the other animal."

The librarian let out a series of sharp ticks and its thin, pale feeding arms plucked at each other like it was grooming itself. Or fidgeting. It was the most recognizably insectile thing Dafyd had seen the Carryx do.

"Tell me what you know of this," it said.

He tried to remember what he'd heard Tonner saying, what Campar and Rickar and Jessyn had said in return. As he stumbled over the half-understood ideas and concepts, his mind was racing ahead. He'd put his faith in Else and the spy that she'd made common cause with. He'd put his life in her hands because she was Else and the story she'd told him had seemed plausible in the moment. Now that it was too late, his certainty eroded.

What had he really seen? A few dark motes moving under her skin. It was strange, but so many things were. Why couldn't it have been a plot by some other rival species? Why couldn't it have been some experiment of her own that had gone bad? What did he actually know?

That if he'd done nothing, they would all have died. Not just the people here in the prison, but everyone back on Anjiin too. He did know that, regardless of anything else. Panic could wash at the back of his mind, convinced that Jellit would come in and deny everything. A calmer, darker part of his mind knew that at worst, it would mean his death coming just a little sooner. At best, a longshot chance at a kind of vengeance. There were worse things to die for.

He couldn't imagine what Else would say to Jellit that would change his mind. She'd asked Dafyd for his trust, and he'd given it. Once he'd jumped off the cliff, it was too late to try going back…

"Could this work with other organisms?"

He'd been talking. He wasn't sure what he'd said.

"It's possible," he answered, reaching back to his time in research and the careful phrases his aunt had mocked as empty, meaningless, careful. "With more time and resources, we might be able to generalize strategies. My guess is it would take more research and a deeper field of data. But yes. It's based on the same body of work that reconciled the two trees of life on Anjiin. And it seems to have worked again here."

"How tragic," it said.

"Tragic?"

"To have come so close and not see the end. But at least it progresses."

Not to see the end of what? Dafyd thought, but before he said it, a Rak-hund appeared in the doorway. It undulated and ticked its way into the room. Jellit followed it.

Even if he hadn't known the context, Dafyd would have seen that something was wrong with the man. His skin had a grayish cast and his eyes were bloodshot. He held his arms stiffly at his sides, not swinging at the shoulder or elbow at all. His steps were careful and unsteady in a way that reminded Dafyd of animals suffering the last stages of brain disease. More disturbing than any of that was his expression.

In the thousands of times Dafyd had imagined this moment, he'd prepared himself for cold rage or blank denial. He'd pictured Jessyn's brother lunging for him, trying to kill him for his betrayal, or else breaking down in tears of despair. The blankness was unexpected. Jellit's gaze moved over the room, only pausing for a moment on Dafyd, and then without any sense of recognition. His first thought was that Else had poisoned him. Slipped enough narcotic into his food that he'd lost himself, in hopes that he would agree to any question that was put to him.

The librarian moved forward, and Jellit's attention, such as it was, shifted to the Carryx. His hands trembled violently once, then went still. Dafyd's heart tapped against his chest. He didn't know what would happen if Jellit lied and said there was no conspiracy. He didn't know what would happen if he told the truth and said that he was committed to the plan. A partisan, and not the ally to the Carryx that Dafyd had made him out to be.

For a moment, Dafyd saw Jessyn the way she'd been the day that Irinna died: bloodied and empty-eyed. Drowning in an ocean that none of them could see. Finding her brother had carried her up from that almost more than her medication had. He didn't want to be the one who kicked her back down into darkness.

I opened a door for you, he thought, willing Jellit to understand him. *You can live. But you have to step through it. Please.*

"You know this one?" the librarian said, gesturing a pale claw toward Dafyd.

"Yes," Jellit said without turning to look at him. "His name is Dafyd. He's an assistant to my sister's workgroup."

"Did you offer him a message to bring to me?"

Jellit was silent. His mouth opened, gaping like a fish hauled out of the sea, closed again. Blood darkened his face and throat like he was being strangled. If the Carryx recognized the struggle, it didn't comment.

"I...did."

Dafyd sank into himself, his joints loosening with relief. Tears were streaming down Jellit's cheeks, but his voice only grew stronger.

"The near-field workgroup that I'm part of is involved in a wide conspiracy that is planning direct and violent action against the Carryx. The local leader is Urrys Ostencour, but there are two others working at his level. One of them is Ferre Luminan who is with the energy physics group. I don't know the other one. We have weapons and two strike teams of twenty people."

"You will give me all the details you know," the librarian said.

"Yes," Jellit said. "I will."

Dafyd let his chin fall to his chest as Jellit spoke. Names he didn't know, plans he hadn't heard of. Whenever Jellit reached the edge of his knowledge, he said as much and gave the name of someone who would be likely to know better than he did. The extent of the resistance was much wider than Dafyd had guessed, and Jellit exposed it carefully, thoughtfully, and completely. When he was done, the librarian stood silent for a long moment.

It sank down, its legs folding under it, then lifted its two thin feeding arms like it was about to pluck some invisible fruit from the empty air. Its trill was higher than Dafyd had heard before, almost in the range of human speech. Or human song. When the voice came from its translator, he imagined it sounded rueful, but that might only have been his imagination.

"You would have failed, not only in our intentions but in your own. Instead, you have found success beyond your understanding. You are too small to see the pathos, and I am too impure to escape it. What is, is."

Jellit swallowed. His hands were fists at his side. "I apologize for my part in this. I beg you to let me live and serve the Carryx."

"If you are strong, you will serve in your life. If not, you will serve in your death. All serve." The librarian rose. "You will both remain here. If you have physical distresses, speak."

The librarian whistled and chirped to the Rak-hund. The snake-thing undulated, shifting into a living barrier that separated Dafyd and Jellit from the exit. It wasn't clear if that was to keep them from leaving to raise an alarm, or to protect them from whatever "physical distresses" they might have. The librarian summoned an array of shapes made from light, floating in the air, shifted them in ways that seemed meaningful to it, then erased them and left the room.

Jellit stood motionless, his eyes fixed on the place where the librarian had been. His tears had dried, though there were tracks of salt on his cheeks and his eyes were even more bloodshot than when he'd come in. The walls creaked, and in the distance something made a wide, angry buzzing, like a hornet's nest that had just been kicked.

Dafyd sat, crossing his legs under him. It didn't occur to him until he'd done it how it echoed the librarian. Jellit's breath was ragged. He seemed as likely to explode into violence as to collapse in tears. Dafyd waited, the silence pressing him to speak. He didn't know what to say. There was nothing to be said. The consequences of what he'd just done—what they'd both just done—were out of their hands now. The bullet fired, and nothing would call it back into the gun.

When Jellit finally moved, he turned and walked to the wall. He leaned his back against the dark surface, then let himself slide down. The tunic rode up as he slid, bunching at his armpits and exposing his belly and ribs. The intimacy of seeing his skin struck Dafyd as subtly obscene. Jellit began to shake, the movement small at first, then larger, more violent. Sobbing or laughing or both.

"Oh my God," he said, and his voice sounded strange. Higher, and almost unfamiliar. "Everything about this is so unethical."

"I'm sorry," Dafyd said. "I know it isn't worth much, but I'm sorry about everything."

Jellit's smile didn't look like the man he'd spoken to back in his rooms. The rage was gone. He seemed only exhausted or wistful. He held out his hand, and Dafyd, uncertain, took it. His skin was hot to the touch and dry.

"We did what we had to do, that's all," Jellit said. "You were very brave. I know how hard this was for you, but it was the right thing. In the years that come after this, you're going to wonder if it was. When you do, remember this moment. Right here. Remember me telling you it was the right thing."

Dafyd's throat thickened. The fear was gone, or at least the occasion for fear. The relief felt like sorrow. Like horror. He wished Else was with him, or that he was wherever she was. Someplace that they could talk, that she could hold him and be held by him. Someplace that they could make all this violence and terror seem balanced by something kind.

Jellit made a hushing sound and squeezed Dafyd's knuckles gently, bringing him back to the moment. Dafyd took a long, shuddering breath and nodded his thanks before letting go of Jellit's hand.

"She told you? She explained it?"

Jellit shot an arch look at the Rak-hund. It didn't have a voice box around its neck, but Dafyd didn't know if it needed one. Or if all things in the librarian's office were listened to, or by whom. Jellit lifted an eyebrow.

"She gave me a deeper understanding of the situation," he said. Then a moment later, "She did what she had to do."

"She's an amazing woman."

"Don't... don't idealize her, Dafyd. No one falls in love with the right person. We all just follow the paths we're on and do the best we can."

"I know. I hear what you're saying. But she was with me on the transit. Me and Jessyn and Synnia and Campar. We all went through that together. And... you understand. It makes a bond. I don't know how I would have survived without her. Not just her. Them. All of them. I had to go through with this. It was the only chance I have to save them. Even if it's only some of them."

Jellit was quiet. He rubbed a palm across his cheeks, wiping away the tracks and tearstains. "Would you have done it without her... argument?" He meant the spy.

"I don't know. Maybe. If I hadn't done it—"

"I know, I know. We can't be domesticated and everybody dies." He looked down. "You still feel like you're collaborating with them, though. Don't you."

"Yeah. You too?"

"Me too," Jellit said. A flash of something passed over him. Rage, grief, madness. It was gone as soon as it came. "I think I'm about to lose a lot of people who matter to me."

"Not your sister, though. And she's not going to lose you. Not again."

"True enough. For now."

A rumbling came like the padding of hundreds of bare feet, then it faded away just as quickly. Something inhuman shrieked and was cut off. Dafyd pulled himself over to sit at Jellit's side. He hadn't thought the man would come around, even if Else told him about the spy. He was more than glad. He was grateful. He'd feared death—his own and the others'—but not far after that, he'd been afraid of being hated. If Jellit could see that he'd done what he had to—if he could forgive him—it couldn't be too hard for the others.

The others that were left.

Jellit leaned against Dafyd's shoulder, exhausted. He smelled odd. Like a skillet left too long on a stovetop. Overheated metal. Dafyd had worked in a lab early in his career where they'd concentrated hemoglobin in a crucible. It had smelled the same. "What do you think is going on out there?"

"Nothing good," Jellit said.

They waited for the librarian to return. Or the others to find them. They waited to know the consequences of what they'd done, and they waited a very long time.

Thirty-Three

Jessyn liked the new alcove for several reasons, not the least of them being that it gave her a chance to get away from the rooms for a while. Moving the equipment from the first lab to the common area at home had been a good idea for defense, and it had made things possible at the time that wouldn't have been with the Night Drinkers still mounting their attacks. But the enemy was gone, and the new alcove felt like opening up. More space, more safety, less of the claustrophobic pressure that came with being under siege. It was a small pleasure, and it was in the shadow of a lot of bad things. But that made the small pleasures matter more.

Added to that, it was a nice space with good equipment. The lab equipment was better, not just in quality, but as a mutually reinforcing set of tools. There was just more that they could do with these. Even the quality of the lights seemed more pleasant, like their spectrum had been tuned to match an early spring afternoon. And, of course, there was the constant, mostly subliminal knowledge that this space had belonged to the fuckers who had killed Irinna. And that she'd seen them all dead.

The murmur of the cathedral reached back into the alcove, but it was almost soothing. The sounds of aliens and animals going about their business had become like the sound of traffic in a dense city. Background noise, less a sensation than an environment. True, they were never there without a guard. Synnia was sitting at the mouth of the alcove now, watching for anything suspicious and visiting with Dennia, who always seemed to be somewhere in Rickar's vicinity these days. Despite that, Jessyn was able to forget that she was a prisoner, forget the grinding sense of loss and displacement, Ostencour's simmering rebellion, Irinna's death, the abasement of Anjiin. Sometimes, for a little while, she could live in the moment.

It was as close as she could get to freedom.

"All right," Rickar said. "I think we are ready for the next phase."

"Meal prep?"

"Meal prep."

The container was the size of her two cupped hands. Enough to hold a generation of berries that crept and shifted, as sleepy as starfish in a tide pool. Tonner's breakthrough didn't require raising dedicated animals for sacrifice. All the alterations he wanted could be done with a few catalysts and a mild acid bath. Rickar plucked one of the berries out from among the crowd and tossed it to her. She caught it out of the air and stepped to the little trough.

"How many of these little guys do you think we've gone through?" she asked as she slit the berry's skin and squeezed the pulp into a dish.

"Thousands, I imagine," Rickar answered. "The harvesting part always reminds me of eating clams. I used to spend summers at Causon Bay with my uncle's family. We'd dig up dinner and cook it on the beach. Cracking open the clams and pulling out the meat was... I don't know. It seemed like a chore at the time, but it's the part I miss."

"Funny how that goes." She discarded the skin and held her hands up to catch the next one. At the back of the alcove, in the sample case, the little animal that wasn't quite a turtle scratched at the wall of its cage like it knew that something important was happening. The scraping of its claws sounded like anticipation. "Did you ever wonder what you'd have done if you hadn't gone in for research?"

"I apprenticed in industrial coral," Rickar replied. "Three years. If I hadn't done this, I would have been growing houses in Dunstenai. Freezing through the winter at four times base pay and vacationing all summer someplace green and calm."

She caught a third berry, slit it open, squeezed out the pulp. "Why do research, then?"

"Honestly? There was a girl. By the time it didn't work out, I had a career path. What about you?"

"I was always going to be this." She held up the dish. "I think this is about enough?"

"Wouldn't want to overfeed him," Rickar agreed. "Let's cook."

The process was brief, and less complex than making a slightly fancy dinner. The pulp was a warm off-white to start. When Jessyn poured in the acid, there was a smell like yeast and lemon. Five minutes later, they added the catalytic compounds, and the pulp began off-gassing, bubbling, and turning dark like a casserole just taken from the heat. Rickar spooned up a lump of the sample and fed it into a set of five microsampling slides. Fifteen minutes later, the pulp had turned a uniform toast-brown, and the data reports were all in the expected ranges.

"Is it ridiculous that I'm actually excited about this?" Rickar asked. "I mean, this has got to be the worst set of conditions anyone's ever done serious research under. And at the same time, we're about to reconcile two trees of life that we didn't even know existed before we got the assignment. It's amazing."

"It hasn't happened yet," Jessyn said. "Even if we have the nutrition right, it may taste rotten."

"But you know what I mean, yeah?"

"Yeah," she said. "Curiosity dies last, I guess."

"I was thinking less curiosity and more the unending drive to feel competent at something. But maybe that's two ways of making the same point. D'you want to see if our shelled friend thinks this smells edible?"

"I do."

When she looked at it more closely, it didn't really look that much like a turtle. It was wide and flat, but its shell didn't seem to be joined to its body in quite the same way. The colors shifted in the light in a way that had nothing to do with dyes and everything to do with diffraction, like a butterfly's wing. And Jessyn had never seen evolution favor a three-legged design before. She wondered what kind of environment it had risen up in—mud or water or land. Its face was roughly like a turtle's, though, and its jaw gaped in a toothless ridge. Rickar put it on the countertop, placing it gently on its belly, and put down a plate of the pale brown mash that was biochemically almost identical to its own flesh.

The not-turtle lifted its head and opened its mouth like it was trying to bite the air. Jessyn had seen snakes and dogs do something very similar when they were trying to catch a scent. The not-turtle turned its head to the left and then the right, and then, like it was flipping a switch, began a mad scrabble across the countertop, racing toward the food. When it reached the dish, it threw its head into the pulp, scooping jawfuls and swallowing them with an enthusiasm that bordered on lust.

Rickar laughed. Jessyn felt the smile pulling at her lips. The turtle gulped down more.

"Well, I don't know for certain that it'll be nutritionally complete, but he seems to like the taste."

"Not even any extra salt," Jessyn said. "Synnia! Hey, come look at this. Synnia?"

"Huh," Rickar said. "That's..."

He was looking out toward the mouth of the alcove. Concern had furrowed his brow. And then fear. For a moment, Jessyn was back in the first lab, the smell of explosives in her nostrils and Irinna bleeding in her lap. The memory was so vivid, so transporting, that all she could look for were the small, feather-haired enemy, returned from their deaths. It took her the span of an extra breath to see what was actually there.

Synnia was where she'd been before, arms crossed and looking out at the pandemonium. But instead of leaning or sitting, she'd stood up. The thing approaching her was familiar, in a terrible way. One of the Rak-hund, pale and snakelike, stood before their guards. The bent-knife legs rippled without moving them, like a man flexing his hands before a fight.

Synnia looked back over her shoulder. For a moment, her eyes met Jessyn's. It was a look that she would remember for years. For the rest of her life. The peaceable old woman who had worked, her lover at her side, in Tonner Freis's labs on Anjiin was gone. The angry, grief-stung woman was absent as well. In that moment—that fraction of a second—Synnia had become something regal. Something more than human, or else what humans can become when they face the universe and refuse to look away. There was no fear and no pleasure and no hope. Maybe serenity, if serenity could sometimes be terrible.

Dennia shouted *Run!* and pulled something out from under her tunic and pressed it to the Rak-hund's head. The report of the gun was a violence in itself. Synnia spun, put her head down, ran. The Rak-hund reared back, pale blood pouring from a gash where something like an eye had just been.

It pushed Dennia. It didn't seem like more than that. Like a bully on a playground, fighting over a toy. Dennia cried out once and folded to the ground. The Rak-hund snapped down on top of her, stabbing her with a dozen of its legs all at once.

Rickar grabbed Jessyn by the shoulder, hauling her back into the alcove. He stepped in front of her, the scalpel they used for shucking the berries wrapped in his fist. He was chanting obscenities like he was trying to remember them. Jessyn felt herself come unstuck, the freezing horror letting go of her with a click. She needed a weapon too. She needed something to fight with. She had a gun back in her room. Why had she left it in her room? The only thing at hand was the empty flask that the acid solution had been in, so she picked it up like it was a grenade and turned to face the enemy.

The Rak-hund shivered forward, leaving a trail of blood. Pale blood from its wound, crimson from its feet. It chittered to itself. The seconds lasted lifetimes.

It turned back, curving to press against the back half of its own body as it departed, undulating away into the crowd that had paused to watch the mayhem.

Rickar walked to the mouth of the alcove, and she followed, the empty flask still in her fist. Her mind was cold. He knelt at Dennia's side. Her death was unmistakable. Her eyes were open, but sightless. Her face was slack and calm. One of the wounds had taken her in the throat, and from the angle of it, Jessyn guessed it had severed her spine. If so, it had been a mercy. The blood was only seeping from her wounds. There was no heartbeat to push it out from severed arteries.

"Shit," Rickar said softly, but she didn't have the sense he knew he was speaking. It was a reflex. "Shit shit shit."

Jessyn stayed cold. Detached. Dissociated.

"Her. Not us," Jessyn said. "They came for her and Synnia. They checked to see who we were, and they let us live. Because they wanted to."

"I don't understand," Rickar said. "I don't understand."

Jessyn did. "We haven't said yes."

"What?"

"Ostencour's group. The bioweapons against the Carryx. Synnia was part of his group since the transport. The whole near-field team was all in. But us? We hadn't said yes. And they knew it."

Rickar's face was gray except for two bright, unhealthy splotches of red on his cheeks. "Someone talked."

"Or no one needed to, because they're listening to everything we say all the time. How the fuck would we know?"

"Right."

Jessyn dropped her flask. It was a pathetic weapon, anyway. "I have to go. You stay here with her. And the work. Take care of it."

"No, I'm coming with you."

"Rickar, you have to stay. You have to be with her."

He looked down at the woman he'd been sleeping with. The lover he'd taken in hell.

"She's not here anymore," he said. "She won't mind."

For a moment, the monstrosity of leaving the corpse unattended seemed vast, impossible to overcome. And then, a heartbeat later, it seemed trivial.

* * *

Synnia ran, moving faster than she had in years. If she had been hoping to save herself, she would have gone someplace new. Someplace they didn't know to look for her. She headed for the near-field quarters instead. If there was a chance she could warn them...

Her side hurt. The same sharp ache that she'd suffered as a girl running too long and too fast in the play yards at school. Synnia gritted her teeth and pushed through the pain.

The path to the near-field workgroup's quarters had become as familiar as the much shorter one to her own rooms. It was only fear that made it seem strange. The alien bodies she passed felt like trees in a vast and unsafe forest. Everything was infused with menace and the threat of violence. Everything could kill.

When she got close, the sounds of violence came to meet her. Human voices raised in alarm, the growls and shouts of alien throats. The deafening explosion of cartridges and the dry crack of electromagnets. As she pulled herself around the last corner, a Rak-hund's body lay splayed on the deck. Allstin, a gun in one hand, was helping Merrol over the corpse with the other. Llaren Morse stood at the open door, gesturing like he could pull the pair of them toward him by grabbing at the air.

"Wait!" Synnia tried to shout, but it came out barely more than a whisper. "*Wait for me.*"

Allstin saw her, pushed Merrol toward the door, and waited, God bless him. His mouth was all white teeth and rage. Synnia clambered over the dead Rak-hund. Its legs shifted and clattered under her. And then Allstin had her by the hand, leading her into the quarters. Merrol and Llaren Morse hauled the door closed, creaking on its fabric hinge, and barred it with a crowbar.

"Ostencour," Synnia said. "We have to warn the others."

"I was with Ferre," Merrol said, her low, vibrant voice reduced to a croak. "She got away. I think she got away. Vivan didn't."

"What we need," Allstin said, "is weapons and a place to make a stand."

"The energy physics group," Llaren Morse said. "If we can get—"

The door boomed. In the silence that came after, the four of them looked at each other. Synnia watched the others as they all came to the same understanding. The door boomed again, and shook against its frame.

"No back way out, then?" Synnia said.

"There is not," Allstin said. He looked at the gun in his hand, opened its magazine, then tossed it aside. The door boomed a third time, and a crack appeared shaped like a lightning bolt, only dark, running through its center. Merrol shrieked, not in fear. Or not only fear. Frustration, rage, sorrow. Llaren Morse ran to their little kitchen, the mirror of her own, and took a knife in either hand.

Synnia had imagined how she would face death. She supposed everyone thought about it sometimes. In some scenarios, she was brave and stoic. In some she was lost and fearful. Now, at the end of all things, she found herself just standing, like she was waiting for a train. Waiting for Nöl to come from the garden and join her.

The door split open, and two Rak-hund boiled through the shards. At the last moment, she charged toward them, her hands in fists. Something punched her just under her rib cage, and she lost her breath.

Somewhere very far away, Allstin was screaming.

The wide door of the near-field group's quarters stood in ruins. A smear of blood marked the side of it. The smell from inside was like a lab that had spent the day in sacrifice. Blood and fear. The body of a Rak-hund lay in the corridor, its knife legs splayed like the petals of some terrible orchid.

"Look," Rickar said, pointing at the ground. The same dots of red that the Rak-hund had left walking away from Dennia. Jessyn put her hand on the remains of the swinging door and pulled it open.

Allstin sat where they'd kept their guard post. Blood had soaked his tunic and pants, turning the pale fabric a deep purple-red. His eyes were open like he was still watching the door. Still guarding, even now that all reason for the watch was gone. Synnia lay on the floor, face down. The pool of blood around her was small. She hadn't lived long enough to bleed out.

Rickar, in the kitchen area, made a small, despairing sigh. Merrol and Llaren Morse lay side by side on the floor, both face down and motionless. Rickar didn't look angry or frightened. He looked old. He looked weary.

"We have to check upstairs," Jessyn said. For a moment, she thought he hadn't heard her. Then he nodded.

The ladder leading to the bedrooms and the shower had streaks of blood on the rungs and bright new scratches in the metal. Jessyn lifted herself up, trying to imagine how the Rak-hund would have swarmed up the ladder. She dismissed the trembling in her hands and legs. She had work to do. Weakness could come later.

She paused in front of Jellit's room, too aware that the next few seconds might divide her life into before and after. There was no lock. All she had to do was pull on the little handle. She didn't want to.

Something touched her hand. Rickar. He wrapped his fingers around her palm. She took his hand. She had to do this. She was grateful she didn't have to do it alone.

She took the little handle and pulled. The door swung open silently on papery hinges. It took her almost two long, unsteady breaths to understand that the body on the floor wasn't her brother.

Else Yannin lay on her back, one arm folded across her belly. Her chest was still, her face pallid in death. Her copper-colored hair spread around her head was the only red in the room. There were no wounds, no blood. They knelt beside her corpse, still hand in hand.

"This isn't like the others," Rickar said.

"All right," Jessyn said. The emptiness of her voice said the rest for her. It didn't matter. Something inexplicable had happened. Someone they knew and cared about, maybe even loved in their way, was dead. She didn't have the resources to care about the details.

She squeezed Rickar's hand and let it go. There were more rooms to search. More opportunities for destruction. But all the other bedrooms were empty. Jellit wasn't there. It didn't mean he was alive. He could have been visiting one of the other workgroups or off on some errand for Merrol or Ostencour. The Carryx could have slaughtered him someplace she didn't know to look.

When they were done, the rooms all searched, they walked out to the corridor together. Rickar swung the shards of the wide door closed and leaned against the wall beside them. One of the tall, bone-carapaced aliens lumbered by. A Phylarch. A group of things that looked like jeweled crabs. Four of the squat-bodied, long-limbed Soft Lothark, moving together and making soft screeching noises at each other that were probably words, gathered around the body of the Rak-hund, gesturing at one another and at it.

"We should..." Rickar began, and then seemed to lose his train of thought. He seemed distracted or sick. In shock. Of course he did.

"We'll go home," Jessyn said. "They'll need to know about Synnia and Else. There might be news about the others."

"Yes. I hope the others are all right. I can't believe that Dennia... I mean, I can, but... I don't know what I mean." He took a deep breath and blew it out. "It's all happening again. Just like on Anjiin. It's all happening again."

"Not again. Still. It's *still* happening, we just lost sight of it for a little while."

"Yes. Yes, that's right," Rickar said. Then, a moment later, "I think I'm going to scream now." He said it like a sick child announcing he was about to vomit. Equal parts dread and apology.

"Go ahead," Jessyn said. "It's all right."

Rickar blinked, nodded, then took another deep breath. The first howl was weak and tentative. The second, deeper and more authentic. All the ones after that were raw and ripping, the kind of grief and horror that tore the throat and darkened the face with blood and loss. His jaw didn't close between them, just gaped. He leaked spit and tears and snot as he screamed and screamed and screamed. After a while, he sank to his knees and Jessyn sat beside him. The aliens walking past didn't pause or stare. Why would they? For all they knew, this was normal. Just something primates did.

Thirty-Four

The last of the fivefold captives of Ayayeh system died reciting a series of concepts in a loop, and Ekur of the cohort Tkalal debated with itself whether the repetition was a symptom of mental collapse or a chosen death ritual. Reflex or prayer. Either way, its five limbs spasmed, curled upward, shivered, and ended their biological activity. What had been the physical manifestation of a mind became an inanimate object. That was what death meant.

The interrogator-librarian settled in its niche isolated from the animals, distilled its conclusions, and prepared to pass a report up to its superior. The things it had learned would inform the superior's report to the tier above it, and so on until it reached the regulator-librarian and, through it, the Sovran herself. *The organism claimed to be artificial: a half-mind built from living tissue. The truth of the claim is ambiguous as evidence exists to both support and refute it.*

The summons came before it had a chance to finish its final composition. The chamber it was called to wasn't in the same part of the world-palace, but it wasn't a long journey either. Ekur-Tkalal put away its tools, rose up on its legs, and went to the transport queue at the top of the great arch. It had no subordinates to inform of its actions, and the summons had come from above it in the order of things. The only ones that might be concerned with this unexpected meeting were the animals it passed along the way, and the interrogator-librarian had no interest in them.

The ship that waited for it was small, but well-appointed. The pilot wasn't an animal, but a Carryx artificer successful enough that it was still male. Ekur-Tkalal was prepared to be ignored, but the pilot was welcoming and deferential despite its higher status. When they lifted off, they continued straight up into the higher atmosphere.

The ship they landed in was the color of bone, wider than a level of the great arch, and buoyed up by thousands of gold and silver drones. The transport landed in a dock of polished stone, and the guards that waited to escort the interrogator-librarian were as tall as soldiers, but gendered. These male guards were red and gold, the scents from their bodies acrid and floral and full of threat. The strangeness of it all made the librarian's head swim. That, or the cocktail of pheromones in the air.

The dock was like well-turned ground and rain-slaked stone. It was rich and biologically active. Organs in Ekur's abdomen, long ago shriveled to vestigial nubs, filled with blood for the first time in decades. The escorts exchanged looks as they helped guide it down a wide, bright hallway, amused, the librarian thought, by the ways its steps weaved and stumbled. Its body was changing in answer to chemical signals it didn't consciously understand, and the sensation was eerie and intoxicating.

When the two guards ushered it into the meeting chamber, its legs gave out at the joints. It sank to the deck, overwhelmed. Its fighting arms spread against the cool stone and it pressed its face to the floor.

The Sovran sat, her vast legs tucked beneath an abdomen sheathed in filigree and pulsing with light. Her hundred eyes shifted with a glorious independence, and her feeding arms—each as thick as the librarian's fighting limbs—were tucked elegantly against her thorax. If she had commanded it to die, the librarian would have ceased to be without a second thought.

At her side, the regulator-librarian was less overwhelming only by comparison. Ekur-Tkalal felt the organs of its body softening, beginning to liquefy, preparing to remake itself in whatever form was required of it. Even without direction, the metamorphosis was underway.

"We have news," the regulator-librarian said. "The battle at Ayayeh is ended. The dactyl you served is gone."

"Yes," Ekur-Tkalal said.

"Your place within the moieties has altered. Your duties and responsibilities will alter as well."

"I submit."

"There is a subject species that appears to be related biochemically to the pilot captives you brought. We have come to honor its keeper-librarian and address an incident. Your service to the Carryx will involve these."

"It will," Ekur-Tkalal said, and its flesh shifted and lurched as its body hurried to accept the changes, becoming again what it was told to become. "I will. I will."

When the slaughter was over and the keeper-librarian of the human moiety returned, it had two Soft Lothark escort Dafyd back to his rooms. He didn't know where they took Jellit. Someplace else. Walking home, he kept imagining the moment when he told Jessyn that her brother was all right, picturing her relief. It was the only good thing in a world full of bleakness and guilt. He clung to it.

Two Rak-hund were shifting restlessly in the hallway outside their quarters. The wide door was rolled open. Jessyn, Rickar, and Campar were sitting by the window, as silent as people at a funeral. Tonner, in the kitchen, was taking plates and cups one by one and smashing them on the floor. Else and Synnia were missing. *She's dead. Else is dead.* Tonner had said it. *They're all dead.* It had been like a brick thrown at Dafyd's forehead. The sense of impact first, and then a slow bloom of pain that overwhelmed everything.

After that, even the news that they'd traded Jellit's life for Ostencour's conspiracy seemed small. Now that the other deaths had come, they were all Dafyd could think about.

The Carryx came for them on the morning of the next day. The sun had come up long enough ago that the rose and gold had vanished from the high clouds. A glimmer of lights that Dafyd thought of as ships or transports or some technology he hadn't yet imagined passed across the brightness of the sky. The wide door slid open, and two of the Carryx were in the hall, half a dozen Rak-hund behind them. One of the Carryx was the librarian. The other, Dafyd hadn't seen before. It was a little larger, its flesh was darker and more purple, and it had streaks of bright red along its massive forelegs.

"Come with us now," the new Carryx said. Its voice box rendered it in lower tones than the librarian's, and with a flatness of affect that felt like a threat.

"All of us?" Campar asked.

"All of you," the new Carryx said.

"Can you give me a moment to pack?" Campar said, his tone light and breezy the way it got when he was angry or stressed. "I'm sure I have my overnight bag here somewhere."

The new Carryx raised up a bit, one of its heavy fighting arms coming up off the floor. Campar immediately bowed and said, "I will come with you," all the mocking humor gone from his voice. The arm lowered.

The five survivors of Tonner Freis's celebrated workgroup lined up like schoolchildren under the eyes of a strict teacher. The Rak-hund pulled the door closed behind them and then walked at their sides as they went. The hallway they took led up along wide, metallic ramps. Dafyd noticed the aliens around them shifting to make way or to join their formation. More Rak-hund and Sinen and Soft Lothark. The war dogs of the Carryx. More of the Carryx themselves, and more of those with the carapace and larger build of soldiers. Fewer of the bound species that served in the wide cathedral and alcove laboratories.

The Carryx turned at a huge archway, leading them out onto an open-air platform. The air smelled rich, like the end of a rainstorm, and the wind was cool against his cheek. The transport they were led to looked too thin and delicate to hold them all, but the Carryx and their guard didn't pause, so Dafyd didn't either. When it rose, humming, into the wide air, Jessyn caught her breath. It was the first time they'd been outside a building since they'd arrived.

The transport swung out wide around the massive structures. Huge bulwarks with tens of thousands of windows like the one they'd lived behind flashing in the light like sightless eyes. The ziggurats shifting with the parallax of flight, showing just how massive they really were. The planet below was so far down, it seemed impossible that there was atmosphere enough for them to breathe. The Carryx whistled and trilled to each other, but no translation came. Whatever they were saying, the little box around Dafyd's neck didn't think it was meant for human ears.

When it approached a different building, or maybe a different arm of the same vast world-palace, Dafyd had to fight the sense that they were being swallowed. The entrance they passed into was more vast than any cavern. The pillars that rose through it were larger and taller than the Scholar's Common back on Anjiin, and they seemed tiny and thin in the space. The transport's hum grew deeper, and it began to descend. The space below them was like an arena or a theater without quite being either one. A rough semicircle centered on a dais, and kneeling in rows like the pious on their pews were more human beings than Dafyd had seen in one place since the fall of the Irvian Research Complex. There had to be thousands of them. A sea of grim, terrified faces.

At the center of the dais, with a dozen Carryx soldiers on either side, was the largest Carryx that Dafyd had ever seen. Twice the size easily of the bone-pale one they'd been presented to when they'd first arrived. It wore a mesh of silver and emerald, and its abdomen was encrusted with a complex of fine wire that seemed to pulse with a life of its own. Its massive forelegs were as thick around as the librarian's chest, and the thinner, mantis-like arms were folded together before it as if in prayer.

Two only slightly less massive Carryx stood at its sides in carapaces of crimson and gold, radiating a sense of menace and barely restrained violence. Guards, or executioners.

The transport landed just before the dais, and the Rak-hund guided the five of them out to a bare place on the floor where, from context, it seemed they were meant to sit.

"Does anyone know what's going on?" Tonner asked. His voice was peevish. "We did what they wanted. We made the thing work. We saved them from Ostencour, even when it meant losing our own people. You'd think that half a minute's orientation wouldn't be too much to ask."

Rickar cleared his throat. "Tonner, this isn't the time for complaints to the management."

Tonner bristled, but he sat. Dafyd knelt down too, and the others followed. Across the way, also in the front row, Jellit was sitting, legs tucked under him. His face looked thin and pale, but his eyes were as wide and amazed as a child at his first circus. Dafyd could tell from the relaxation in Jessyn's shoulders the moment she saw him, and he felt a little relief too. Whatever he'd done, he'd kept Jellit alive. Or Else had, whatever she'd said to him. Or shown him. With a little shock, he remembered again that Else was dead, and the memory was like a vast hollow opening just behind his breastbone.

Another transport arrived, floating down from the wide air like a basket being lowered on invisible strings. Another dozen people spilled out and were taken to their places at the back of the grouping. The best of the best of Anjiin, if Else's spy was to be believed, all humbled and humiliated together. A few were looking around the way he was, faces turning one way and another, searching for someone or something familiar. Many more stared straight ahead, their eyes emptied by all that they'd been through.

At the dais, the huge Carryx stepped forward, and a procession of smaller animals or machines that Dafyd hadn't seen before appeared, trundling out to surround the dais. They were the size of large dogs, but where the heads would have been, they opened up like gigantic lilies. When they'd taken their places, a roll of sound began—chirping and trilling and humming like deep birdsong. The voices of a hundred Carryx lifted together. The chorus reached some deep part of his brain that said *predator*, and made him want to stay very still.

When the chorus ended, the huge Carryx trilled and muttered, its forearms tapping together in a complex pattern that might or might not have meant anything. Its vast abdomen swayed like a boat on gentle waves. Tonner, beside him, leaned forward.

"What are they saying?"

"I don't know."

"You didn't bring the... thing? The translator?"

Dafyd pointed at it. The silence coming out of the box was self-explanatory.

Tonner let out an exasperated sigh. Deep in his memory, Else said *When he's overstressed, Tonner can get petty. It's his pathology.*

"Given context, I assume this is about the resistance," Campar said.

"Could be about our finishing the project the way they wanted," Tonner said. "I think you're all underestimating how important our work is. Look at all the different species they have under one umbrella. If we can make it so they don't have to have a separate agricultural source for every one of them, we're made from gold."

"Keep your voice down," Jessyn said.

"We stopped the conspiracy too," Tonner said, and Dafyd winced. "They wouldn't have known a damned thing without us. We paid a lot. A fucking *lot*. Be nice to see that recognized."

On the dais, the Carryx with black-and-red arms stepped up in front of the larger one, tucked its legs under it, and lowered its head like it was praying. Dafyd could hear its voice—what he assumed was its voice—but not coming from the dais. The flower-headed dogs were relaying the sound like speakers.

He let his gaze wander, following the arc of soldier Carryx arrayed behind the huge one. An honor guard, maybe. As if this particular individual was too important for any mere alien to serve. One of the soldiers caught his attention, and for a moment, he didn't know why. It was large, but no larger than the other soldiers. Its shell was a vivid green. It was larger than the librarian—than any of the librarians—and still dwarfed by the grand Carryx on the dais. Its head was odd, though. Like something had taken a bite out of it when it was young…

And he understood. Between one moment and the next, it came into place like something he'd known before and was only remembering. The librarian of the hallway crows with its three scars, and the soldier with the matching marks. The Night Drinkers' librarian with its broken leg transformed now into a green soldier on the dais. The translator's hiccup when he'd upset the librarian. The difficulty that the system had suffered trying to change a single, unified Carryx idea into something a human could understand: *essential nature and place in society.* An animal doesn't choose that. And neither did the Carryx. Carryx changed with their social status. Their place in society literally determining the form of the bodies.

The ones who were victorious were better suited. The ones that failed were inferior because they had failed. Possibility was an illusion. That was what the librarian had said, but what it meant was choice. What happened, happened. What didn't, didn't. A species was useful to the Carryx, or it was not. They ruled their universe because they did. The other species didn't because they didn't.

For a moment, Dafyd Alkhor saw the universe the way a Carryx would, and it was beautifully simple and utterly horrific.

The huge Carryx intoned something in reply loud enough that it wasn't repeated by the dogs. The new red-armed one shuddered in a way that Dafyd thought of as a bow, and it started moving off to the side. The humans' keeper-librarian marched forward, solemnly taking the place where the other one had been. Tonner made an impatient sound.

Then he stood up.

"Excuse me," Tonner said, raising his hand. "Hey, *hey*. Excuse me? Could we have a translator here at least? We are part of this, you know."

Jessyn's face went pale. Rickar and Campar exchanged a look of confusion and alarm. Tonner took a few steps toward the curve of flower-dogs, his arm still raised in what he didn't know or didn't remember was a gesture of challenge. An invitation to violence. The librarian and the huge Carryx both turned toward him. The librarian leaned back into the four legs of its abdomen, lifted its massive forelegs like it was getting ready to embrace the universe.

Dafyd didn't choose to move. If he'd thought about it at all, he wouldn't have. The time it took to think would have been longer than Tonner Freis's life. He was already up and running, fully committed, by the time he knew he was going to. He barreled into the backs of Tonner's knees. Tonner yelped as he fell, but he hit the ground. The assembled mass of humans gasped and murmured as Dafyd grabbed Tonner and rolled him onto his belly.

"Put your arms out at your side," Dafyd said as he took the position himself.

"What are you talking about?" Tonner spat. "I'm not going to—"

"Lie face down. Put your arms out. They are about to kill you. You are seconds away from being dead."

Tonner scowled and lifted his head. The librarian had its forearms out at its sides. The crushing blow would have taken less than a heartbeat.

"He is young," Dafyd shouted into the ground, hoping that he would be heard, and that there were translators somewhere that would pass the message on. "We are both young. He didn't know better. He meant no disrespect. He's young!"

Tonner looked back. The universal fear on the sea of faces seemed to snap him back to reality, and he let his head drop to the floor. A moment later, he pushed his arms out to the side.

"I am young," he said, his voice hardly more than a breath. "I didn't mean anything. I'm young."

The librarian didn't move, but the two massive red-and-gold Carryx surged forward. Dafyd didn't think about it. As if by instinct, he stood, lifted his knee, and stomped down on Tonner's elbow with his full weight. The snap of bone and Tonner's pained shriek filled the air. The Carryx paused.

"I take responsibility for his correction," Dafyd said. "He is humbled."

Dafyd lay back down on the floor at Tonner's side and waited to see if it had been enough.

For what felt like hours but was a minute at most, they were still before their captors. The huge Carryx sang something, and the clicking of sharp, knifelike feet announced a Rak-hund coming close. Dafyd closed his eyes, waiting for the attack, but instead something grabbed his ankle and hauled him backward, scraping along the floor. His tunic rode up to his armpits. The Rak-hund released him back beside Jessyn and Rickar. Another dropped Tonner beside them before returning to their place among the guard. Tonner sat up, his face pale except for a long, bright scratch along one cheek.

On the dais, the librarian turned back to the huge Carryx.

"I just wanted to make sure we got credit," Tonner said, weeping and cradling a rapidly swelling arm. "We did all the work. We should get—"

Campar put a wide, comforting hand on Tonner's shoulder. "Be quiet, love, or I'll snap the other one for you."

Their librarian was chirping and trilling its deep bass. It planted its dark forelegs and leaned forward until the pale arms reached down to touch the floor, the back of its neck exposed to the one in silver and emerald. The soldiers shifted from side to side in excitement or anticipation. The flower-dogs murmured a wild chorus of trills and chirps: the voices of a thousand Carryx who were there but not physically present. The large Carryx let out a deep, fluting moan unlike anything Dafyd had ever heard.

Then the two guards stepped forward and placed their heavy fighting arms on the librarian's back. The huge Carryx in silver and emerald gently placed one of its massive arms on the librarian's head. The crack when its head was crushed reverberated like a gunshot across the dais.

Afterward, they were taken back to their rooms. For a long while, no one spoke. Campar sat on one of the sofas, leaning forward with his elbows on his knees. Rickar and Jessyn constructed an ice pack and splint for Tonner's broken arm.

Campar broke the silence. "What just happened?"

"Dafyd broke my fucking arm," Tonner said.

"He saved your fucking life," Jessyn said. "What were you thinking?"

"I wasn't," Tonner said. And then, a moment later, and with an exhausted kind of sorrow, "I'm not really myself right now."

Rickar lay down on the floor, and raised one arm in a gesture that was at the same time open and despairing. Dafyd wondered if, in another time, they would have been as sapped by the violence. There were only so many horrors they could witness, only so much outrage and fear they could hold in their hearts, before they were just exhausted by it. The weight that bent Campar's shoulders and pressed Rickar to the ground wasn't the execution of the librarian. Or not just that. It was Synnia and Else. Nöl and Irinna. It was the destruction of Anjiin and the Night Drinkers and the execution of the near-field group. Even the moments of success were drowning in darkness.

Dafyd tried to imagine what Else would have said, where she would have sat, how she and the secret spy would have made sense of it all. He couldn't.

Heavy footsteps sounded from the hallway. Rickar sat up. The Carryx that opened the door and came in was the same black-and-red one that had escorted the librarian to its death. The one that had spoken on the dais and survived. It moved with a calm grace, its steps so smooth it seemed like it was gliding. It had one of the translators around its neck, but its muttering and chirring weren't being passed on.

Tonner walked toward it, then hesitated and stepped back like he was trying to judge its reach. Campar watched it like he was watching a lion in a menagerie, like there was some invisible cage that kept him safe from it. The new Carryx shifted its eyes from one to the other of them. Dafyd couldn't tell if it was identifying each of them or watching for signs of an attack or lost entirely in its own thoughts. He'd only ever spoken to the librarian. He didn't know what gestures and habits were common to all the Carryx and which had been idiosyncrasies of the one individual. He'd find out, though.

Something moved behind the Carryx. A more familiar form, walking just behind it. Jellit limped into the room. Jessyn let out a cry and ran to her brother. For a moment, they held each other.

Dafyd watched the embrace and tried to take comfort in it himself. Whatever else he'd done, he'd also done this.

The Carryx planted its massive black-and-red forelegs, leaning its weight onto them. Its abdomen shifted gently from side to side on smaller, graceful, uneasy legs. It seemed to consider them all, and then turned to Dafyd, focusing its attention on him as if by breaking Tonner's arm he'd identified himself as the leader in the Carryx's eyes.

When it spoke, the voice box translated it with a different voice. Not the genderless matter-of-fact of the soldiers or the reedy calm of the librarian, but something more fundamentally threatening.

"I am Ekur of the cohort Tkalal, and I have been made the new keeper-librarian of the human moiety. Your place within the moieties has altered. Your duties and responsibilities will alter as well."

It shifted its weight. It waited, as if it anticipated some response. None of them spoke. After a moment, its pale feeding arms unfolded, its clawed hands interleaving in something like prayer.

"First," it said, "as your librarian, I congratulate you all on your success..."

Thirty-Five

First, as your librarian, I congratulate you all on your success, not only for your kind, but in the project you were given. Your species possesses qualities, perspectives, and particular utilities that place you high among the ranks of beings useful to the Carryx. And you as individuals have gained specific attention. As your people are redistributed and reassigned within the moieties, your positions will be noted and your usefulness recorded.

In the time between now and the commencement of your new duties, you will remain in these quarters. When your duties change, you will be found here and the details of your new responsibilities will be presented to you. The duties you are given will be assigned by me and guided by those who direct me. My duty will be to lower myself by interacting with animals for the greater advantage of the Carryx. In this, I will give you advice and equipment as required for you to succeed and survive in your work.

Your assignments will not be uniform. You will not have a voice in what your place within the moieties will be. The stability and advancement of the Carryx is your only path to a pleasant day-to-day life. If, as a subject species, your use to the Carryx changes, your place within the moieties will also change. With greater usefulness, your access to resources will increase. With less, it will decrease. As your keeper-librarian, my position will vary with your own. In this way, we remain certain that your interests and mine are aligned.

Some of you will be put in danger. The danger that you face will be balanced against the utility that your duties provide. Other subject species have proven unwilling or unable to address their duties, and their places have been altered to better fit their essential natures. This will also be true for you. Some of you will remain here, others will travel to places within Carryx control. Regardless of your location, you will answer to me as your librarian, and I will stand in aid of you to the degree that is appropriate.

You will not approach or make requests of other members of the Carryx. Outside of your assigned duties, you are permitted other activity to the extent that it does not interfere with your work. You are permitted to reproduce and breed. If your circumstances allow you to do so, you will be informed.

It will be your responsibility to identify and maintain an optimal level of personal function. If you have requirements that you do not identify, this failing will affect your function and lead to a change in your position within the moieties. If you suffer developmental changes that affect your function, these changes will lead to a change in your position. If circumstances outside your function change the context and needs of the Carryx, these changes will lead to a change in your position.

I understand that it is comforting to you to believe your efforts have meaning, and that comfort improves your function. In that spirit, know that through your efforts, we have determined that the world from which you were taken is better preserved than unmade.

The cities your kind built stand for the time being. The lineages that produced you continue to exist. The artifacts of your culture are permitted and will be incorporated into the moieties as they are found useful. In this way, you have achieved the possibility that your species will spread to thousands of worlds you would otherwise never have known and can flourish under the protection of the Carryx. Your people will be granted space to be fruitful and fecund as servants of the Carryx beyond anything they could have managed on their own. They will be given guidance and structure that will keep them safe from dangers that would have erased them from the universe had they stumbled into them.

The moieties of the Carryx are, among other things, a great protection. You have won your species a place of calm and safety in a malefic universe. In this, you are your people's saviors. Continue.

What is, is.

"In this," the new librarian said, "you are your people's saviors. Continue."

Its feeding arms plucked at each other, and its eyes moved from one to the other of them where they sat in the common room, among the cables and equipment and old, worn chairs and couches that had been new when they arrived. Outside, one thin layer of clouds passed among the ziggurats and another softened the sky above them. Dafyd waited. He didn't have the energy for more than that.

"What is, is," the translator box said.

It felt like a promise and a threat.

"You will be taken from here when your places are ready," the librarian said, with a kind of finality.

"Will we stay together?" Jessyn asked.

The librarian paused, said, "That is unlikely," then turned to Dafyd in particular. "The development of the human moiety is to change now. Your people were permitted to access their librarian before. That will end. You have presented yourself as the apt tool, and so you will be used according to your ability."

"All right," Dafyd said. And then, a moment later, "I don't know what that means."

"Beginning now, all communication from your moiety will reach me through you as your connection to the Carryx moves through me. Their needs are your charge, and their discipline is your duty. They will speak to you, and you will speak to me. In this way, my exposure to animals will be minimized. Those whose duties take them to the lesser worlds will also report to you, though their duties will require them to have other animals to whom they answer. Any humans who approach me without you will be killed."

"I'll be sure to pass that along," Dafyd said, and was interrupted by his own small, choking laugh. In the deep sludge of his mind, objections and concerns began to bubble. It felt at the time like the first stirrings of wakefulness after a troubled and unrestful sleep. "I'll need to know who they are. I don't know where people are, or what their workgroups are. I don't know anything."

"That will be provided."

"And what you expect of us."

The librarian paused, as if this were a new thought for it. Dafyd didn't understand what the hesitation meant.

"I will give directions to you," it said. "You will arrange for them to be carried out."

If Dafyd had had this position before, he could have stopped Ostencour's rebellion without losing anyone. He could have found an argument for something besides open rebellion or total obedience. Fewer of his friends would be dead. Else would be alive. It was too late for her, for Synnia. It wasn't too late for the rest of them. His mind began tripping forward, moving in subtle ways, like the sound of water under snow. If he did this, he was going to need to be very careful how it got presented to people. Everyone was raw, traumatized, as emptied as he was. If he could be the one who made all this make a little bit of sense…

"Can I ask…? The old librarian. The one who was killed. Why did that happen?"

"You," the Carryx said.

"The rebellion? Ostencour's plan to kill the Carryx got too far, and that was the punishment?"

"There was no punishment. There is no punishment. That one was given great honor, being touched by the Sovran. But it was saved by an animal. There is no place in the moieties for a Carryx that was saved by an animal. Do you understand?"

"I'm starting to," he said.

"Good," it said, then lumbered out of the room on its massive red-and-black forearms, its abdomen gliding along behind like a servant struggling to keep up. The wide door closed, and they were alone in what had been their home for a time. Their shared prison.

As the librarian had delivered its speech, they'd fallen almost unconsciously into a rough circle, like children at story time. Dafyd looked at them now as they sat in silence. Campar, with his broad shoulders and wide hands, always ready with jokes and laughter, and hollowed out now. Tonner Freis, who had been so arrogant and whose arrogance had been so justified. Humiliated now, and still brilliant. Still the one whose mind had completed the Carryx puzzle. Jessyn with her newfound violence, and Jellit at her side. Rickar and his rage. And Dafyd himself. What a strange, broken group they were.

And then there were the ghosts. Else and her spy. Irinna. Nöl and Synnia. The gaps in the line.

"The team scattered to the winds is a strange look for victory," Campar said.

Dafyd sat forward, lacing his fingers together. The building around them ticked, and a thin wind muttered at the window. In the distance, something wide and dark rose from the top of a ziggurat. A Carryx warship stretching its wings, preparing for another battle, another Anjiin, another wave in the permanent war that had eaten them. A moment later, another rose. And then another one after that.

The endless violence of subjugation and conflict unfurled before Dafyd's eyes. The resistance. The purge that followed. The death after death after death. It was a strange moment to discover peace, but there peace was. And more than peace, a clarity that seemed to reach deep into his mind and reorder him. The feeling that flowed through him was what he imagined the release was in the last breath of life. The moment when the end was obviously inevitable. How odd that it should come at the beginning of something too.

"There's a war, you know," he said.

"There is," Jellit agreed.

"And if there's a war, there's an enemy. Something out there that wants the Carryx dead."

"Excellent taste on their part," Campar said. "If they have a charity, I'll give them a percentage of my salary."

"I'm starting to understand the Carryx," Dafyd said. "To understand how they think. Not all of it, but some. Enough."

Rickar snorted. "Not sure that's something to brag about. They seem like a bunch of bloodthirsty monsters to me."

"They aren't, though. They're something else. They have different assumptions and axioms. Different ways of understanding things like free will and what it means to be a person. Different blind spots. But some of it, I get. I'm like they are in some ways. Or I can be."

"Again," Rickar said. "Not something to brag on."

Jellit leaned forward and touched his arm gently. Tonner chuckled, and then Jessyn. Dafyd felt the anger and the pain in the laughter, and also the warmth. They'd become like siblings who knew each other too well for terms like love and hate to apply anymore. They had become complicated. He felt Else's presence as if she were still in the room and not only a memory.

"So," Campar said. "Now we wait and see what they require us to do next?"

"No. I don't know," Dafyd said. "If we're part of this grand mechanism of theirs, then maybe we can be the grit in its gears too."

"You're starting to sound like Ostencour," Jellit said.

"More patient. I'm more patient. Ostencour wasn't wrong, he was just too fast about it all. He wanted a final battle when it was still something he'd lose," Dafyd said, thinking it through as he spoke. Finding words for the shape of his revelation.

"So we all get sent off to who knows where while you fight your patient war?" Rickar said. "Now you're the high priest of the human race?"

Everyone was staring at him. Rickar was right. The Carryx had made him their high priest, the only voice between them and a vicious, capricious god. So, he needed a prophecy, then.

"I don't know what's going to happen to us all," Dafyd said.

"But I just want to say while we're still in the same place, while we're here together, that I'm going to find a way to kill them."

The faces in the circle were sober, filled with doubt, but yearning to believe.

"I'm going to learn everything about them. I'm going to figure out how to get in their heads. And I'm going to kill them all and burn their fucking towers to the ground. It's my war now."

Thirty-Six

The swarm is in chaos.

Part of this is the nature of its new flesh. For the first time, it feels the cognitive deformation of a high-testosterone environment, and even with shutting off the hormone as soon as it had taken control, the brain and body have been formed in ways that are subtly different. The new host fights more violently against his death, the rage and despair taste different. There are moments when the swarm feels like it could almost lose control. Not in the way its hosts have lost control, of course. It cannot die or be displaced. It is as if Jellit has been reduced to a series of habits and tics that the swarm will revert to if it isn't careful.

It looks out the window at the wide, blocky structures of the Carryx using new eyes. For all the changes and alterations that it worked on Else Yannin's flesh, there had been some underlying commonality. Jellit sees things differently. The swarm shifts through the spectrum, remaking its sensorium. It finds the lines of force that arc through the high air, the flickers of heat on the distant ground, the shimmer at the edge of ultraviolet frequencies. Jellit's body experiences all of them a bit differently. Like two different dancers performing the same choreography.

Are you all right? *Jessyn asks.*

The remnants of the man scream and push and flail, but these are only metaphors, because he has no body to scream or push or flail with. The others—the two dead women—watch and sympathize.

Just thinking, *the swarm says.*

If we go... If we go, maybe they'll send us to the same place.

The swarm smiles and takes her hand. Jellit's conflict shifts through it. The heartbreaking love of the brother for his sister, the resentment of yet another scenario where he is called upon to support her, the rage and horror at experiencing her fingers lacing around the swarm's.

Maybe, *it says.* Maybe.

And its heart aches.

The right thing to do is leave. The right thing to want is to leave. If it can find its way to a colony world, a captured planet with less vicious security than the world-palace, it will transmit all it's learned. It will whisper the secrets that might give its side an edge into vast radio ears that are waiting for it. That is the reason for its presence. That is what all the people it has been died for. What all the dead that they loved took to the Carryx's altar with them.

It doesn't want to go.

The swarm is in love.

That's bullshit, *the remnant of Ameer says.* Else loves him. You're just in the habit of feeling what she felt.

I loved him but I was already dead, *Else says.* I was never with Dafyd before I died. I was dead before we even kissed. *She means* It's not my fault. *As though originating intention could be separated out in the soup that was becoming their shared minds. The swarm tries not to pay attention to the distracting chaos of their echoes. The mind that once was Jellit screams. It chooses not to attend to that either.*

There is another way, it formulates. It can create a data packet, carve a part of itself away, insert the military intelligence into the body of one of the others. They can carry it to the far stars without knowing that it is there. And when it is safe, the packet will bloom. It won't be pleasant for the carrier, but it will let the swarm remain.

Won't be pleasant, *Ameer says.* It'll kill them. But what's one more corpse?

It lets Jessyn's hand go without meaning to. Or perhaps Jellit—the echo of Jellit—releases her in hopes that she will move away. Instead, she leans her head against the swarm's shoulder. It smells her hair, experiences Jellit's flashbulb memory of holding her when she was in the hospital. When she was sick. It puts its arm around her and hopes that she will not have to die.

Its mind turns to Dafyd. The thrill in its new blood is different, but familiar. The guilt and shame are bound up with the remembered warmth of his body, the taste of his mouth. The comfort that it has taken in him, that it still longs for. Dafyd is in his own room now, and when it reaches out its senses, it can hear the peculiar harmony of his breath. The rhythm of his heart, just a little different from all the others, like the timbre of his voice.

It remembers him, full of focus and purpose and a steely cold swearing himself against the Carryx, and it lets itself dream. The minds of the two women it has lived as have taught it to do that. To imagine fictions, and place itself in them as an escape, as a comfort. It imagines the two of them, spies in the world-palace, working together. The burden of its mission shared at last, with someone who could know it completely. It imagines finding some secret path to the heart of the Carryx, of detonating a bomb at the root of the world. Of holding hands while they watch the towers fall. Of making love on the corpse of a civilization. And why not? Even if they fail, why shouldn't they try?

What will it be like to kiss him with these lips?

He's not going to want you, *Ameer says.*

He was in love with me, *Else says.* He thinks it was me. And you killed me. Twice over, you killed me. He'll hate you for that. He's going to hate you.

Far out, beyond the atmosphere, something bloomed in a geometry of radiation and magnetic force. Circles define hexagons, hexagons define intersecting planes, all of it opening and then falling away, like the ideal of an orchid playing out on five-dimensional space. The swarm records the phenomenon, tucks the data in with all the rest. It doesn't know what made the effect, but it isn't called to. It is only meant to look, listen, record, and transmit. It is made to deceive and go unnoticed.

The longing that pulls at it, the despair and the hope. It was not designed for them. It feels them all the same. Dafyd, my love, it is not just your war. You and I. We will burn this world down together.

Acknowledgments

As always, this book would not exist without the hard work and dedication of Danny and Heather Baror, Bradley Englert, Tim Holman, Anne Clarke, Ellen Wright, Alex Lencicki, and the whole brilliant crew at Orbit. Special thanks are also due Carrie Vaughn for her services as a beta reader. And we're grateful to Naren Shankar and Breck Eisner, who were always understanding when we blew off the other work we were supposed to be doing to finish this book.

And, as always, none of this would have happened without the support and company of Jayné, Kat, and Scarlet.